Malignant Invasion

Malignant Invasion

§

Raphael Hirsch

For Bella

A man said to the universe: "Sir, I exist!"
"However," replied the universe, "the fact has not created in me a sense of obligation."

STEPHEN CRANE

PROLOGUE

Dr. Alex Becker swung open the double doors to the autopsy suite in the basement of Chicago University hospital. It was ten at night and he had expected the room to be empty. But one of the large operating lamps was burning over a stainless-steel table in the center of the room. A body lay on the table, naked except for a yellow tag on the left, great toe. A tall young man was leaning over the table, dressed in an apron and rubber gloves, a scalpel in his hand. He had just made a long incision down the entire length of the body's abdomen.

Becker gasped. "What the hell are you doing!"

Jim Hunter, first year resident, jumped at the interruption and the scalpel clattered to the floor. He looked up and recognized the chief of Pathology. Becker looked more a mouse than a man, really. The sallow skin of his face was pulled taut across his facial bones. His eyes were recessed deep into the sockets of his skull. A long piece of greasy, black hair was pasted down across the top of his otherwise bald head.

"I thought I'd get a head start on tomorrow's schedule, Dr. Becker."

Becker's eyes threatened to pop out of his head. He rushed to the table. "Can't you read, you idiot!"

The frightened resident took a step back. "Sir?"

Becker grabbed the tag on the body's foot and ripped it off. He thrust it into Jim's flustered face. "What does this say!"

Jim looked at the piece of paper dangling in front of his eyes.

"Well, what does it say?"

"It says, 'For Becker', he whispered.

"That's right. Are you Becker?"

Jim coughed. "Sorry, sir. I didn't notice."

"Obviously," Becker snapped. "Next time, read the damn tag."

"Yes sir."

"I think you should go home now."

"Yes, sir." Jim began pulling off his gloves. He untied the apron and tossed it over the hook on the wall. It missed and fell to the floor. He glanced at Becker, who was glaring at him. He picked up the apron, carefully set it on the hook, and hurried towards the door.

"Well, goodnight, sir."

"Goodnight. . ." Becker grumbled.

He listened to the young man's fading footsteps. When he was sure he was alone, he took the portable lamp and rolled it to the head of the table on which the body lay. Then he went to the door and bolted it. Finally, he shut off the main lights. He stepped towards the middle of the room. A circle of light highlighted the corpse's head. The face was that of a man in his thirties.

Becker put on gloves and approached the table. He grabbed an arm and a leg and, despite his small frame, easily flipped the corpse onto its abdomen. He picked up a scalpel and, in a bold stroke, sliced completely through the back of the scalp. Then he pulled the skin back, revealing the white occipital bone. He grabbed the bone saw off the shelf, laid it across the skull, and flipped the switch, creating a high-pitched whine of metal against bone. When he had cut entirely through, he removed the top of the skull and looked inside.

Becker grabbed the side of the table to steady himself. He had seen this hideous sight twice before, but it still made him queasy. He took a deep breath and stuck his hand into the open skull. A shudder went through his body as the grotesque tissue touched his glove. Grimacing, he pulled the brain forward and, with his other hand, cut through it at its base. He lifted the mass out of the skull, his head turned away so that he would not be forced to look at it.

With hands outstretched, he rushed to the incinerator and, with a yell, threw it in. He caught a brief sight of the grisly tissue before the flames rose up and consumed it. Steadying himself against the wall, he took a few deep breaths to calm himself.

When he felt his knees could support him, he returned to the autopsy table, pressed down on the foot pedal, and began speaking into the microphone hanging from the ceiling.

"This is Alex Becker. Tuesday, November eighth. . . Autopsy on Michael Stuart. . . The body is that of a young male. Period. . . External anatomy appears normal Period. . . The cranial case was opened posteriorly through the occiput. Period. . . Brain anatomy is entirely normal. Period. . ."

PART I

ONCOGENESIS

He who is set upon by the Sartan in a hidden place, better that he should not recover. For if he recovers, he will surely die.

HIPPOCRATES

1

David Blaire sat in the waiting room of Dr. Robin Jones, Chief of Dermatology at the Chicago University Medical School. He uncrossed his legs, put down the two-month-old issue of PEOPLE magazine he had been pretending to read, and glanced again around the room. There were three others waiting. To his right sat a scrawny, pimply-faced kid of about sixteen. On his left were two women in their sixties here for God knew what.

A plump, mildly attractive nurse appeared at the door to his left. She looked around the room at each of them before her eyes settled on him.

"Mr. Blaire?" she guessed.

David nodded.

"Please follow me."

David followed the nurse into an exam room. She placed a paper gown on the exam table.

"Please undress down to your underwear," she said with a sterile smile. "The doctor will see you in a moment."

The nurse closed the door behind her. David unbuttoned his shirt as he looked around. There were two chairs and a small desk against the near wall. Above the desk, a glass cabinet held a series of bottles and some stainless-steel instruments. David smelled the nauseating antiseptic odor that permeated every doctor's office. He finished undressing, slipped on the short-sleeved gown, which reached to his mid-thighs, and sat down on the exam table.

There was a knock at the door and, before he could answer, Dr. Jones entered. David had his first surprise of the day. Dr. Robin Jones was a woman, a very attractive woman. She was in her early forties and wore a white coat over a gray sweater and skirt. Her long auburn hair was tied in a bun held in place by a black pin, and David wondered how she would look with her hair down. He felt self-conscious in the revealing gown.

"Hello, Mr. Blaire, I'm Dr. Jones." She held out a hand. David shook it. It was cool.

She sat down and opened her clip board.

"Your doctor has informed me of the mole on your thigh that he wants evaluated."

Dr. Jones removed a pen from her pocket and crossed her legs. "When did you first notice it?"

"About two weeks ago."

She began to take notes. "I see. And what change occurred in the mole that concerned you enough to see your doctor?"

"That's just it," David responded. "I never had a mole there before. It just came up all of a sudden. When I first noticed it, it was about the size of a nail head, but it's been growing like crazy."

Dr. Jones smiled. "That's not an uncommon misconception, Mr. Blaire. Patients often fail to notice moles, especially when they're on a part of the body hidden from view. But I can assure you that they don't grow so quickly. You've probably had it for years."

David shook his head. "No way. I tell you, it came up over two weeks."

Dr. Jones frowned. She usually saw half a dozen malignant melanomas a year. This *month* she had diagnosed twenty-seven cases, and each and every one of them had sworn that the nevus had appeared over a period of a few weeks. That was not the natural history of this cancer. While it was extremely aggressive once it metastasized, it took years to reach that stage. Unless, as she was beginning to suspect, these lesions represented some new, more virulent form of melanoma.

"Have you noticed any bleeding from the lesion?"

"It started bleeding yesterday when I got out of the shower. It's been kind of oozing since then."

She raised an eyebrow and made a note in the chart. Bleeding was a worrisome sign.

"Is it painful?"

"No. I don't feel a thing."

"Are you otherwise healthy?"

"Yes."

"Have you ever had any serious medical illness?" she asked the questions automatically, in rapid succession as she recorded the Review Of Systems in the chart.

"No."

"Have you had any other symptoms?"

He was about to mention the severe headaches he had been having, but he was sick and tired of all the questions and he wanted her to get to the damn point, his mole.

"No, none."

"Are you taking any medications?"

"No."

She looked up at him. "Is there any history of skin cancer in your family?"

David felt a twinge of anxiety. "Not that I know of."

"How about other types of cancer?"

"My grandfather died of colon cancer. And I had an uncle who had some kind of cancer, I'm not sure what type."

"Do you have any brothers or sisters?"

"I'm an only child."

"And your parents?"

"My father has high blood pressure. That's all."

She stood up. "Very well. I'd like to examine you now."

David sat on the edge of the exam table, his legs dangling over the side.

"That white mark on your cheek, how long have you had it?"

"It's a birthmark."

"I see. Could you slip your arms out of the gown please."

She scrutinized his chest and stomach and David wished he had been exercising more. She had him bend at the waist and she ran her fingers lightly across his back.

"You have a number of nevi, or what you call moles, on your skin," she said as she looked him over, "but they look completely normal and are not excessive in number. Most people have an average of twenty nevi on their body, mostly on the back and chest."

David nodded hopefully.

"Now Mr. Blaire, could you lie down please so I can have a look at the lesion on your thigh."

She lifted the gown up to his crotch. She touched his legs, pushing his thighs apart.

"I put a Band-Aid over it because it was oozing."

"Yes, I see."

The Band-Aid only covered the center of the lesion. She pulled it off and could not help gasping. The lesion was large, almost three centimeters in diameter, coal-black, with an ulcerated center which was oozing a bloody pus. A putrid odor emanated from it. She was certain at once of the diagnosis-- malignant melanoma, the worst case she had ever seen. Her medical experience rejected the possibility that this lesion had appeared over a two-week period. Melanoma could grow quickly, but not that quickly. It must have been present for a year before it reached this stage. She wondered how he could have possibly ignored it for so long. In its early stages, melanoma was curable by simple excision. The prognosis at this advanced stage was dismal. The only question remaining was how far it had metastasized. If it had already spread beyond the regional lymph nodes, the mortality rate was close to a hundred percent.

"Mr. Blaire, could you please remove your underwear so that I can get a better look at the skin in your genital area and feel your lymph nodes."

He raised his buttocks off the table and pulled down his underwear to his mid thighs.

Dr. Jones stepped away from the table and opened the desk drawer. She snapped on a pair of latex gloves. She returned to the exam table and began to examine his genital area, gingerly pinching a piece of his scrotum and raising it so she could look underneath.

"Mr. Blaire, I have a high level of concern over this lesion. It needs to be biopsied. I can do that now in the office. I'll rush the specimen so we should have the results by tomorrow afternoon. In the meantime, I'd like you to have some blood tests and X-rays. If the biopsy shows malignancy, you'll need to come into the hospital for some more tests."

She walked over to the intercom. "Nancy could you come in here with a biopsy tray?"

The plump nurse appeared carrying a stainless-steel tray on which rested two small glass jars and a pile of blue cotton towels. The nurse lifted the gown up over his waist, exposing him completely. He felt a nauseating lightheadedness.

"Mr. Blaire," said the nurse. "Could you bend your left knee and spread your legs apart so that the lesion will be easily visible to Dr. Jones."

"Oh, my!" she exclaimed when she saw the black, oozing mass.

She picked up a gauze pad and soaked it in a dark-brown solution. "Mr. Blaire, you're going to feel something cold. It's simply the cleaning solution to sterilize your skin."

He forced himself not to withdraw his leg. He could feel the nurse rubbing the skin of his upper left thigh in a circular motion. When she was done, she laid the towels across his thigh, leaving only a small triangle of skin visible.

"He's prepped, Doctor."

Dr. Jones approached him, holding a syringe.

"I'm going to inject the anesthetic now. You'll feel a little stinging as it goes in."

David gritted his teeth. He felt a lot of stinging. Tears came to his eyes.

"Do you feel me touching you, Mr. Blaire?"

"No."

"How about here?"

"No."

"Okay. Please hold still now. This will only take a few moments."

She took a scalpel and forceps from the tray. He felt a tugging sensation on the skin of his thigh. Then he heard the sound of snipping and felt his flesh being tugged at again. It felt like the doctor was cutting out half his leg, but he forced himself to hold still.

"Nancy, could you open the specimen bottle?"

The nurse held out a glass jar and a bloody object dropped into it. It formed swirling red clouds as it settled into the clear liquid.

"Could I have the suture please?"

He felt some more tugging. Then some cold fluid again as Dr. Jones cleaned the area. Then she dried it and bandaged the leg.

"Okay Mr. Blaire, you can sit up. It's all done."

The nurse helped him up.

"I want you to be very careful how you walk so that you don't rip the sutures open. And please don't let it get wet for twenty-four hours."

"What do you think it is?"

Dr. Jones pressed her lips together. "I don't want to say anything for certain until I see the biopsy results, but I do have a high level of concern for malignancy."

"What if it is malignant?" David asked nervously.

"Let's discuss that when we have the biopsy report and the results of the blood and X-ray studies. The secretary will give you the forms and you can have the tests done tomorrow morning."

"All right."

"I'll call you as soon as I have the results. Call me if you don't hear from me by tomorrow afternoon." She smiled at him and gave him a nod before leaving the room.

"You can get dressed, Mr. Blaire," said the nurse. "I'll meet you at the front desk and give you the necessary forms."

David dressed and left the office, limping and anxious. The sutures pulled at his skin with every step and he wondered if he had already ripped them open. By the time he reached the parking lot, he had developed another one of his splitting headaches.

Dr. Jones watched through her office window as David left the building. She picked up the telephone and dialed a number.

"Dr. Ferguson, please. Tell him it's Dr. Jones. . .Hello Barry?. . .I've got another one for you. I'm sending you the specimen right away . . .Do you have any idea what we're dealing with? . . .Is the meeting still on for tomorrow afternoon? . . . Good, I'll see you there."

She hung up the phone, took a deep breath, and exhaled slowly through her nostrils.

2

Ellen Rhodes shivered as an icy gust whipped open her coat hem and bit into her exposed legs. A quickly extended hand shot down to restrain the garment, which continued to flap rebelliously against her thighs. She hurried across the courtyard, marveling at the chill in the air. The weather on campus appeared to have changed overnight. The grass had turned the color of straw and the trees were naked, save for a few wrinkled, dead leaves which stubbornly clung to their branches, resisting the inevitable.

Ellen was a fourth-year medical student, bright and ambitious. At that moment her ambition was to get out of the cold. She reached the building at the far end of the courtyard, its gray stone walls covered with the lifeless stems of vines which had recently supported a blanket of green. She ran up the stone steps, pulled on the massive wooden door, and opened it just wide enough to slip inside before the wind slammed it shut again. A sudden, delicious warmth enveloped her. She tilted her head back, ran the fingers of both hands through her hair, and shook her head briskly. Her hair was naturally straight, too straight as far as she was concerned. She looked at her reflection in the window by the door. If not for her mouth, which was too large for her face, she felt she would be quite pretty. She ruffled her hair with her fingers, pouted when it fell flat again, then laughed out loud at the funny expression on the face in the window.

Ellen headed up the bare concrete steps towards the second floor. Jackson Hall had originally been built to house the Anthropology Department. That had been some sixty years ago. It was now home to the Genetics Department of the Medical School. A large painting of a Neanderthal clan, huddled around a fire, covered the massive wall opposite the entrance, a relic from the old days which for some reason had never been removed. Ellen loved that painting. It gave character to the building. She had requested the rotation in the lab of the chief of Genetics, Dr. Joe Malcolm, as one of her six-week electives. Most of her fellow students had chosen clinical rotations, but Ellen wanted a lab experience since she was planning an academic career. Six weeks was not enough time to do any meaningful research, but it was giving her a flavor of it. She was a quick learner and had already figured out that the work could be tedious. But there was something intensely seductive about this place. Here scientists were dissecting apart genes, rearranging them, and splicing them back together like a reel of film to create new forms of life. She knew of no place else where could she find that kind of excitement in medicine.

She reached the second floor and hastened down the narrow corridor to the main office. Lois, the department's secretary of twenty years, looked up from behind her desk. Her light brown hair was streaked with gray, and she had a few crows' feet around her glass-rimmed eyes. Ellen had grown very fond of her in the two weeks she had been rotating in Genetics. Since her husband had died of a heart attack eight years ago, Lois had devoted her time and energy to running the office. She treated the doctors all like school children. And they let her get away with it because without her the place would collapse in anarchy.

"Morning, Ellen. How are you?"

"Freezing," she replied as she peeled off her coat and hung it behind the door.

"Coffee's on. Help yourself."

"Thanks. Can you believe the temperature outside?" She poured herself a cup. A pleasant shiver ran down her spine as her hands enveloped the simmering mug. She headed for the door.

"See ya, Lois. I'm gonna check on the result of my first cloning experiment. Wish me luck."

"Honey," Lois said, "could you drop off a cup with Bob on the way to your lab? He's been hiding in his lab since before I got here, and I'll bet my behind he's been there all night again. He needs to take a break from killing himself for just a few minutes."

"I'd have to spike his coffee with Valium," Ellen replied with a laugh.

She walked out of the office, a coffee cup in each hand. She stopped in front of Room 213, placed her own cup on a table in the hall, and open the door. Black slate counters lined the walls, cluttered with loose papers, plastic Petri dishes, microscopes, and a myriad of different sizes and shapes of glassware. The lab looked pretty much like the one two doors down where she was rotating, except for the row of animal cages on the back shelf.

Newman was crouched over a laboratory counter, a tuft of black hair escaping from behind the collar of his white coat. Even in his bent over position, the broadness of his shoulders was evident. She watched his body move as he toyed with something on the table. Probably playing with one of his blessed rats again. Ellen generally loved animals, especially little furry animals. But nothing made her hair stand on end like the sight of a rat.

She watched him for a few moments, taking pleasure from observing him without his knowledge. Robert Newman. What a mild name for so intense a man. His whole person seemed to radiate heat. What a contradiction, since he was just about the coldest son-of-a-bitch she had ever met. The students all steered clear of him, forewarned about his temper. She had been introduced to him by Malcolm on the first day of her rotation and he hadn't said a word to her since, other than a grudging hello in the hallway. He was obsessively dedicated to his research and yet, she had never seen him display a trace of human emotion, other than hostility. Correction. She *had* caught him staring at her legs during research seminar a few days ago, which proved he was human. An asshole, but a human asshole.

"Bob?"

Calling him by his first name made her flush, but she wasn't going to make an exception for him just because he was so intimidating. *Especially* not because of that. She had decided on her first day of med school that the faculty would be her colleagues soon enough, so it was best that they treated each other that way from the get-go.

She pursed her lips and tried again. "Bob. . ." What could he possibly be so absorbed with? She stood at the door, cup of coffee in hand, watching the white coat. She took a step towards him. Was it her imagination or was the room noticeably warmer as she approached his figure? She suddenly realized that the cold had left her body.

She touched his broad shoulder hesitantly. "Cup of coffee, courtesy of Lois."

Newman straightened up from the table. His sharp-angled face filled her field of vision. His eyes grabbed hers. She had never before seen dark, almost black, hair accompanied by such steel-blue eyes. She blinked.

When her eyes opened, she saw the large, white rat that he held, its beady red eyes squinting at her. Its pink nostrils were in constant motion at the end of its long, narrow snout. The creature squirmed in his hands, and she took an involuntary step backwards.

"I don't believe it!" he muttered. Then loudly, "Son-of-a-bitch! It's un-fucking believable!"

He lifted the cover of the cage, tossed the rat in, to her relief, and turned towards her, grinning from ear to ear.

"Ellen, did anyone ever tell you that you're an absolutely stunning woman?"

He grabbed her face in his hands and kissed her hard on the lips. Then he pulled off his lab coat, exchanging it for his medical coat hanging on the door.

"Do me a favor and lock up, would you? I've got to run."

"I don't believe it!" he said again as he rushed out the door. Then he was gone, leaving her standing in the middle of the room, cup of coffee still in her hand. She stood there for a moment, too stunned to move. Her favorite blouse was probably permanently coffee stained. Her face smelled of rat. And her lips hurt. She drew them into her mouth and massaged them slowly with the tip of her tongue.

3

Bob Newman stood in front of the elevator door. He jabbed at the 'up' button again, but the lighted numbers above the door displayed no urgency in moving from the eleventh floor. *The hell with the damn elevator.* He headed to the stairwell and climbed the three flights to the skyway connecting Jackson Hall with University Hospital, taking the stairs two at a time.

The experts be damned. He had finally done it! He had cured a genetically inherited disease, not just treated it, cured it by replacing the faulty gene of each and every cell in the body of a rat with a normal one. No surgery, no bone-marrow transplant, no manipulation of cells in a test tube. He had done it with a simple, one-shot vaccine containing a tiny virus. The implications were colossal.

When he reached the third floor, he left the stairwell and turned into the familiar, glass-walled skyway. He stopped at the entrance and stared down the long corridor. The hospital entrance was thirty yards away. Down that corridor his patients lay waiting. The skyway was bright with the natural light from outside that enveloped it on both sides, but to Bob it was filled with dark shadows. How many times had he marched down this corridor? A thousand? Ten thousand? And always, as if he was walking down a gangplank with a guilty verdict awaiting him at the other end. He always hesitated at this spot, taking a last deep breath of fresh air before forcing himself to take the first step. As he would near the other side, the air would grow heavy and a weariness would settle on his body. And always, as he stepped out of the corridor and into the hospital, he would whisper to himself, *I'm getting closer.* But closer was not good enough.

For five years he had struggled for this day, setting all else aside, ignoring all other needs and desires, the whole of his being subservient to one need. Images flashed through his mind, memories of long nights bent over the computer, forcing eyes that wanted to close to focus on the screen for just one more minute, forcing a mind that begged for rest to concentrate on just one more formula. How his body had rebelled against sleepless nights piled on top of sleepless weeks, against the overdose of cold, greasy pizza and bitter, black coffee. He remembered the moments of frustration when he realized he had spent another month going up yet another blind alley. And through it all, his guilt drove him recklessly onward.

'There's nothing you could have done for her,' they had comforted him when Diane died. But it *was* no comfort, because there must have been *something* he could have done. Now, finally, he had that something. He squeezed his hand into a fist. Her sister had a chance now, a slim chance, but at least there was a weapon to fight with.

He breathed deeply and commanded his legs to move forward. When he reached the end of the skyway and entered the hospital something felt wrong. He had expected this moment to be absolving, triumphant. Yet nothing was different. He was greeted with the same sterile walls, the same bright lights, the same polished floor.

"I've done it!" he whispered through clenched teeth. But everywhere there was silence.

He headed to ward 5-East. A group of residents in white coats stood in front of a patient's room, making rounds. Further down the hall, a phlebotomist carried a plastic basket of syringes and blood-filled test tubes. Bob reached the nurses' station, mired in its usual bustle of activity, and approached a buxom blonde.

"Hi, Debbie."

Debbie was the charge nurse, the cerebral cortex in the brain of that creature known as the hospital ward. Her external softness masked a tough interior. She was, as the title implied, in charge, uniquely capable of creating order out of the chaos of neuronal impulses racing through the ward.

Debbie looked up. A warm smile formed on her face.

"I didn't expect to see you again until evening rounds. Couldn't stay away from me, huh?" She leaned her firm figure forward slightly and her fingers toyed with the ends of her thick, blond hair.

Bob looked at her, stone-faced. "You are difficult to ignore, Debbie."

"Dinner tonight?" she teased.

"You never give up, do you?"

The nurse rolled her eyes. "The only reason I put up with your attitude is because you're the best damned doctor in the unit and I know what you used to be like before you turned into such a bear."

"That's two reasons."

"Well then, there's a third. You've got a great ass." She waited for a response that did not come.

"Come on, it's about time you stopped wearing black," Debbie cajoled.

The left side of Bob's mouth curled up into the first hint of a smile since the conversation had begun. "Thanks for the advice."

"I see a crack in that shell you've built, Robert Newman. One of these days, I'm going to break it right open."

"Don't break your head in the process. How's Janie?"

Debbie's smile faded as she returned to business. "Her respiratory rate rose to thirty-five last night. I got PT up here to start pounding on her chest." She reached over to the chart rack at the edge of the counter. "I need you to write the order."

Debbie was the best nurse in the hospital, as far as Bob was concerned, and the only one not intimidated by him. He found her sass refreshing. "I see. Would 'q six hours' be appropriate, Doctor?"

"If you doctors would answer your damned pages, we nurses wouldn't have to do your work for you," Debbie growled. "We've been doing them every four."

Bob raised his eyebrows. That was a lot of pounding for such a frail body. "Do you really think that's necessary?"

A stubborn look flashed across Debbie's face. "If I didn't think it was necessary, I wouldn't have threatened the physical therapist with bodily injury if he didn't get his ass up here at two in the morning. She's had two treatments already and her rate's down to twenty-five."

"Very well, every four it is." He wrote the order. "Anything else I can do for you?"

The nurse smiled coyly. "Is that an offer?"

Bob smirked.

"She seems a bit better this morning, Bob," Debbie volunteered. "She still isn't eating, but she got out of bed for an hour."

Someone was always begging him to perform an act of God and pronounce the girl recovered. If only he could.

"I'm glad to hear it. Unfortunately, she can't be getting better. She has a terminal disease. I'm going to drop in on her." He started down the hall.

"Oh, Bob. By the way. . ."

He turned. "Yeah?"

Debbie frowned and waved him back. She lowered her voice. "Simpson just got back from his CAT scan. His liver lit up and he's got mets to his lungs and brain."

"Shit! Does he know yet?"

"No. I figured you'd want to tell him."

Bob tilted his head towards the ceiling and squeezed his eyes shut. Damn. Damn. . . damn! A wife and three kids. *Three kids*!

He felt a hand on his shoulder and opened his eyes. Debbie was looking up into his face. "I'm sorry."

"What's happening to me? This is the third patient of mine who's been diagnosed with cancer this month."

"It's not *you*," Debbie scolded, shaking her head. "We've got a dozen cases on the ward."

Bob ran his hand through his hair. "A dozen cases? A dozen cases of cancer on a genetics ward?"

Debbie shushed him. "Pipe down, please. You want to alarm the patients? The epidemiologists have been sniffing around here for the past few days."

The phlebotomist approached the desk and handed a batch of papers to the ward secretary. Bob lowered his voice.

"Someone ought to be alarmed. We could have a carcinogenic contamination on the floor."

"It's not just our floor. The oncology ward is bursting at the seams. They've been turfing patients to wherever there are empty beds. We've got a half a dozen of them up here."

"How long has this been going on?"

Debbie narrowed her eyebrows. "Don't you read the newspaper?"

He gave her a blank stare.

"You don't, do you?"

Bob shrugged. "I don't have time."

Debbie shook her finger at him. "You should lift your head from your laboratory bench for a breath of fresh air once in a while. The papers have been filled with it all week. Medical centers around the country are reporting an increase in the incidence of malignancies."

The residents appeared at the nurses' station. Rounds over, they began grabbing charts to write their morning notes. Bob took Debbie's arm and drew her away from the desk.

"How high an incidence?"

She shrugged. "A hundred times normal, according to the news reports. But I know it's much higher. The nurses have been screaming about this for the past few weeks. Nobody paid us any attention."

"I've got to run, Debbie. Thanks for the information." He headed down the hall, making a mental note to talk to Joe Malcolm about this news as soon as possible.

Bob poked his head into Janie's room. It held two beds. The farther one, which had been empty, was now occupied. The figure in it was partially obscured by the drape running down the center of the room. He turned his attention to the nearer bed, where Janie lay. She looked younger than her fifteen years. She was pale, but her black, shoulder-length hair stood out against the bleached, white bed sheets. A plastic tubing ran from her left hand to an i.v. pole at the head of the bed. Her eyes were closed and Bob could tell by the pattern of her breathing that she was asleep. He walked over to her and brushed the bangs off her forehead. He decided not to wake her.

He glanced over at the far bed holding the new patient. An elderly woman lay under a crisp white bed sheet. Her skin was so pale that her face appeared camouflaged by the white pillow on which her head lay. Her emaciated limbs barely disrupted the smoothness of the sheets. A casual glance would miss her presence entirely, so few were the lines of contrast.

His curiosity aroused, he walked over and pulled the clipboard off the lower edge of her bed. The purple stamp on the upper right-hand corner identified her as Mildred Stone, admitted to the Oncology service. He glanced at the birth date and tried to guess her diagnosis. A seventy-eight-year-old comatose, white female with a malignancy. No respirator, so metastases to the lungs were unlikely. That ruled out colon cancer, which made breast carcinoma the most likely diagnosis, with coma secondary to brain mets. He flipped the page and read the diagnosis: 'Lymphoma, metastatic'.

How strange. He looked at the old lady, watching the sheets rise and fall in the regular pattern of her shallow breaths. He frowned. Something wasn't right here. He walked to the head of her bed and bent closer. He touched her pasty cheek. It was cool. Her mouth was open and her lower lip sucked up against her teeth with each raspy breath. Something about this woman did not fit, but he could not put his finger on it. The answer began to nibble at him. Something about her breathing. . .

Her eyelids popped open and she gaped at him. He yelped and jumped back, startled. After a moment, her eyes shut again. He forced himself to laugh. Comatose people could have reflexive muscle movements, including the eyelids. But what was it about this old lady that bothered him? He watched her breathing for a while longer, then shook his head, perplexed.

He returned to Janie's bed and sat beside her, watching her sleep. He lay his large hand on hers. "Janie," he said softly, "I've got a big surprise for you when you wake up. Those rats I told you about, they're cured, and I can cure *you*. You're going to make it, Janie. I promise."

He watched the girl sleep a while longer, then leaned over and touched his lips to her forehead. As he got up to leave, he glanced back and a chill went down his spine. Across the room, the comatose lady's eyes were wide open and they stared unblinkingly at him.

4

The setting sun illuminated the eastern bank of the Potomac River near M Street where a tall, white-haired man stood waiting. It was cold in Washington for this time of year and the man dug his hands into the pockets of his overcoat. He began pacing up and down the embankment on the waterfront, his gaze alternating between the river and the deserted street under Whitehurst Freeway behind him. The street along the river was lined with old warehouses which cast long, dark shadows onto the pavement. As the sun set on the opposite side of the river, he stopped for a moment, as if listening for something, then glanced at his watch and continued walking. Suddenly he stopped again and peered into the darkness in front of the building to his left.

"You're late," he said.

"I know. It could not be helped," came the response from the shadows.

"You've requested contact in person," the white-haired man said. "This is unusual."

"The orders I have for you, Senator, could not be trusted to the normal communication channels."

"Oh?" Since his transformation had begun, carrying out his orders was increasingly pleasurable. He waited, silent but eager, for his companion to continue.

"Have you heard of Doctor Robert Newman, Senator?"

The white-haired man thought for a moment. "No. Should I have?"

"The matter has not been under your jurisdiction. Doctor Newman is a geneticist at Chicago University who has been attempting to remove defective genes from human cells in order to cure his sister-in-law of a lethal genetic disease. We have an agent planted in her hospital room and have just learned that he may have succeeded in his goal."

The white-haired man thought for a moment. "I fail to see how this affects anything."

The man in the shadows moved a step closer. "Did you hear what I said? He can splice genes out of the human gene pool. *Any* genes."

The white-haired man nodded his head slowly. "This could complicate matters."

"It could do much worse than that.   Newman has, unwittingly, placed our plans at great risk. He could ruin us. His technique must not be allowed to leave his laboratory."

The white-haired man noted the hatred in his companion's voice. He himself did not feel that intensity of emotion. Perhaps he would, in time.

"How do you propose to accomplish that?"

"We're not ready for an open confrontation. We don't have the strength in numbers and we want to maintain the element of surprise. You must stall this at the political level."

The white-haired man nodded and smiled. "Don't worry, I can keep this in committee for months."

"Precisely our hope, given your influence on the Hill." He paused for a moment and added, "Of course, we do have contingency plans."

"What type of contingency plans?"

From out of the shadows a heavyset figure appeared, a head shorter than his partner, dressed in a black overcoat. His face could not be seen in the darkness. He moved towards the white-haired man, who laid his hands on the shorter man's shoulders and bent his head forward until the two were so close to each other that it appeared their foreheads were touching. They stood frozen in this position for close to an hour. The frigid wind blew onto the motionless figures from across the river. When the moon began to rise over the horizon, the two men suddenly stood upright, turned in separate directions, and departed without a word.

5

O'Donnell's Bar and Grill was permeated with the faintly sour smell of stale beer. The old, wooden tables were polished to a fine hue with forty years of grease and dried Budweiser. The aroma of fried burgers wafted in from the kitchen.

A waitress carrying two oversized mugs of hot cider with rum approached Lois's and Ellen's table in the back of the dimly lit room. She slung down the drinks and headed back to the bar.

"He kissed you?" Lois exclaimed.

Ellen nodded and took a sip from her mug. The hot fluid felt good on the back of her throat.

"So, what did you do?"

"Do? Nothing. I was absolutely in shock."

"You're the first woman Bob Newman has even looked at in five years."

Ellen felt a warmth in the pit of her stomach. Was it the rum or the mention of his name?

"I just happened to walk in on him. Otherwise, I think he'd just as soon have kissed his rat."

Lois twirled a cinnamon stick in her mug, causing steam to rise up around her face.

"That bad, huh?"

Ellen shook her head. "No, not at all. I think the rat would have liked it."

Lois laughed and Ellen joined in.

"You know, you're different than the other students. Most of them don't know anything they haven't read in a textbook."

"Well, between you and me, I wasn't too big on books before I got here. I'm just a small-town girl from Pine Island. Girls don't go to med school where I come from. Hell, *guys* don't go to med school. I was supposed to marry my high-school sweetheart and have three kids by now."

"So, what happened to spoil that wonderful plan?"

Ellen took another sip from her mug. "I dumped the high-school sweetheart after he knocked up my friend, Betsy, and decided to become a nurse. After a year of nursing school, I realized the nurses were the ones working their asses off while the doctors were getting the respect. I came home during summer break and told my parents I was switching to premed. They figured I must have gotten into some heavy drugs on campus. They told me if I really wanted to be a doctor, fine by them, but they couldn't help with tuition. That kind of money wasn't in their game plan. So I spent most of my nights in premed working in places like this while hitting the books during the day. Since I started med school, I've had to give up the night jobs if I'm going to have a chance in hell of passing my courses."

"How are you paying tuition?"

"Let's just say I have a long-term relationship with Bank of Chicago for the next fifty years, to the tune of two hundred thousand dollars at seven percent interest."

Lois laughed. "At least you know they'll be faithful."

"Oh, yes."

"Speaking of relationships, it sounds like our Bob has the hots for you."

Ellen thought for a moment. "I wouldn't read too much into it. He seemed crazy at the time."

Lois nodded. "He is a little crazy. Ever since his wife died."

His wife? Ellen felt as though a mystery was about to come to light. She wanted to know more about this man who could be a robot one moment, then so passionate in another. "Tell me about her."

"It's still difficult to talk about. Everyone had such high hopes for them."

The lines around Lois's eyes grew deeper as she remembered . . .

* * *

The Department of Internal Medicine held its annual party in the grand ballroom of the Drake Hotel. Lois munched on a carrot stick near the hors d'oevre table. Her friend, Nina, Joe Malcolm's wife, stood beside her, sipping a glass of white wine.

"These functions are so boring," Nina whispered.

Lois observed the hundred and fifty faculty and their spouses milling about and nodded. "Why do you come year after year?"

"Joe feels obligated. You?"

"Beats me. Each year I swear it will be my last. The food's not worth thirty bucks a plate, and neither is the entertainment. Hey, look who just came in?"

They both saw the tall, young man with the dark hair enter the room. "Isn't he gorgeous!" Nina said.

Lois smiled. "A bit young for you, Nina."

"You're never too old to look. Joe is absolutely ecstatic about the recruitment. He says Bob Newman is one of the most brilliant young scientists in the field."

She raised her hand and waved. Bob saw her, smiled, and crossed the room.

"Good evening, ladies. You both look ravishing."

Nina took Bob's arm and invited him to join them at their table. As the dinner began, Newman leaned over and whispered into Nina's ear, "Who's the girl over there sitting next to the bald guy?" He nodded in the direction of a group two tables away.

Nina smiled. The young man had taste. "That's the bald guy's daughter. He's the biggest donor to the medical center in the city."

"Does the daughter have a name?"

"Diane. Would you care to meet her?"

"Yes, please."

After dinner, Nina introduced Bob to Diane Kelly. She was petite, with brown hair cut short in back and bangs over her forehead. Her eyes were large and almost black. She wore a blue, low-cut dress which hung loosely, but which could not hide a shapely figure underneath.

They shook hands. "Would you care for an after-dinner drink?" he asked.

She took her hand away from his. "No thank you, but it was nice to meet you."

"Perhaps another time, then."

Diane smiled coolly. "Perhaps."

"So?" Lois asked when Nina returned to the table.

"I can't believe it, but he struck out."

Ten minutes later, Lois leaned over and whispered to Nina, "The second inning is about to begin." She nodded towards the bar. Bob was heading towards the far end of the room, a glass of wine in each hand.

He approached Diane, who was admiring a painting. "Would now be a better time?"

Diane turned, startled, then an angry look appeared on her face. "Dr. Newman, I was trying to be polite, but I thought I made my intentions clear."

"Do you find me that unbearable to look at?"

"Don't take it personally. There's a whole harem over there licking their chops for a piece of you."

A hint of a smile flashed across his face. "I thought an artist would be more sensitive than that. You disappoint me."

She looked at him suspiciously. "Who told you I'm an artist?"

"You did."

"I don't recall having mentioned it."

"You didn't. But in your grudging handshake I could feel the wrinkles in your fingers. You're either doing a lot of dishes or you spend most of the day with your hands in clay. You don't strike me as the type who spends her time at the kitchen sink."

She stared at him for a moment with her dark-brown eyes, then looked down at her fingers. She ran her thumb over the tips of the other four digits. She looked at his face and explored it again, this time with her artist's eye. Her eyes settled on his. "I *will* have that drink now."

They were married three months later and moved into a house in Irving Park, one of the fashionable suburbs of Chicago and a convenient twenty-minute drive to the University. Diane set up her studio in the basement. Their passion for each other never dwindled as the months rolled into a year and then two.

Then the fairytale romance ended. Diane developed increasing difficulty pressing the hard clay she worked with every day. When the symptoms worsened, a sinking feeling entered Bob's chest. He was sure now that she had a neuromuscular disease. Joe Malcolm confirmed the diagnosis. Pompe's disease. There was no cure. Within months she could not work at all and required a cane to walk. Shortly after that she became bedridden. Bob was frantic. He approached Joe daily with a new suggestion, another therapy to try. Sometimes he called in the middle of the night. Joe was the only person who could keep Bob from becoming completely irrational.

A few days after Diane was admitted to the hospital, Lois heard a conversation in Joe's office through the partially open door.

"There's got to be something else we can try, Joe."

"Bob, I know how hard this is. You've got to be realistic."

"I'm not going to let her die, Joe. I'm *not* going to let her die."

She heard a muffled sob.

"I wish there was something else I could do for Diane. We have no treatment for her."

"How about another injection of gamma-globulin?"

There was a moment of silence. "Bob, I'll do it if you insist, but I don't think her lungs can handle the fluid load."

"Then what are you recommending, Joe? As her doctor."

"As her doctor, and as your friend, I'm recommending that we stop torturing her and let her die in peace."

"Oh God, Joe . . ." Bob croaked. "Oh God. . ."

On an afternoon Lois would never forget, she and Joe visited Diane's hospital room. Bob sat on the bed, caressing her hair. Diane had deteriorated so markedly in the last two days that Lois could barely recognize her. The color had left her face, and her body had withered away to almost nothing. A dull film covered her once sparkling eyes. Diane tried to speak to them but could not find the strength. She raised her hand and laid it on her husband's arm.

"What is it, sweetheart?" he asked, bending his head down towards her face.

She opened her mouth. "I love you, Bobby," she managed to whisper. She tried to lift her head off the pillow.

Bob smiled at her. "Shhh. I love you too, baby."

"I think it's time."

Bob shook his head, his face twisted in an anguish so intense that Lois began to weep. He put his arms under his wife's shoulders and lifted her torso towards him. Tears streamed down his cheeks. "Please, sweetheart . . . don't strain yourself."

"Promise me one thing, Bobby," she whispered.

"Anything."

He began to sob uncontrollably. Diane made an effort to speak, but no sound came from her mouth. She coughed in uncontrollable spasms. Bob held her tightly. "It's okay, baby. You don't have to talk now. Just rest."

Diane shook her head. She reached up, with a trembling hand, and wiped the tears from her husband's face. "Bobby," she whispered, her voice barely audible. "I'm not afraid to die. You need to go on with your life. Promise you won't cry for me when I'm gone."

"I promise, sweetheart, I won't cry," he croaked, drawing her frail body against his.

He held her in that position for a long time. Eventually he seemed to sense that she was no longer breathing, and he lay Diane gently down. A muffled noise escaped from his chest. He stiffened, his eyes closed and his jaw clenched. When he opened his eyes, they were dry. His face went chalky-white and Lois feared he was about to faint. She rose out of her chair, reaching out towards him. Bob drew away and rushed out of the room . . .

* * *

"How horrible. . ." Ellen whispered. Her eyes were wide and moist, and the tip of her nose was red. "He still hasn't gotten over her?"

Lois opened her purse and fumbled for a tissue. "Joe and I spent that evening looking for him, but he didn't return to his home. The next morning, I found him in his lab, and he's practically lived there ever since. He never spoke about Diane again. He has one obsession now, to find a cure for genetic diseases."

She handed Ellen a tissue and wiped the tears from her own eyes. "Bob was a brilliant scientist, but for the past five years he's shunned the entire world, including the medical community."

"But it wasn't his fault," Ellen said. "He can't possibly blame himself."

Lois shook her head. "But he does, as irrational as it seems. He has become totally obsessed, almost to the point off madness."

"Why doesn't he ask for help?"

Lois laughed. "Bob doesn't ask for anything."

Ellen dabbed her eyes and blew her nose. He ought to get some professional help. There's a time for mourning and a time to go on living."

"Honey, I haven't told you the end of the story. Diane had a little sister, Janie. Well, after Diane died, the whole family was screened. Janie came up positive. About a year ago, she started to suffer the same symptoms. She's in the hospital now, one of Bob's patients. He's watching his wife die all over again."

Ellen was stunned. The story sounded like a Greek tragedy. "Do you think he found what he was looking for today? He ran out of the room like a maniac."

"I wouldn't be surprised. He's very driven and extraordinarily talented. I have no doubt that his name will go down in the history books."

"You think it's that revolutionary?"

"Hell, yes. He's trying to remove from human cells the genes that cause disease and replace them with normal genes. If he can do that, do you realize where it could lead? Not only will doctors be able to cure practically every disease, but they'll be able to literally alter the human body at will. You want to fly? Just add the bird gene that grows wings."

The magnitude of the possibilities began to dawn on Ellen. Such a technology would be both fascinating and terrifying. It would not be the first time that the course of history was changed by the obsessions of a single man. And this man had a pathologic obsession. She had sensed it before she had heard his incredible story.

Lois blew over the rim of her mug. "By the way, you're wrong about him kissing you just because you happened to be there. I've seen the way he looks at your butt."

Ellen wrapped her hands around her mug. Was she falling for Robert Newman after a single kiss? There was something frightening about the thought, and she had never before been frightened by any man. It was her own vulnerability that scared her. She had always been a sucker for a bird with a broken wing, but now she realized that Newman was a vulture.

"I'll tell you what. If Bob Newman wants to look at my ass, I'll take a photo and drop it in his mailbox. But no more touching without permission. Now let's have another drink."

6

A tall, lanky man stood across the street from O'Donnell's, dressed in a gray overcoat. He had followed the two women from Jackson Hall and had been waiting for the past two hours. They would have to come out eventually. He was in no rush. He found the chilly air stimulating.

The door to O'Donnell's opened again and he raised his chin. There they were, bundling themselves against the cold. He waited for the distance to be right, then crossed the street and began to follow them. After two blocks he slowed. The women had stopped and were exchanging farewells. One headed to the left, the other continued on ahead. He hurried forward to identify the designated target. She was walking more briskly now and he picked up his pace.

The woman turned left onto a narrow street lined with large maples and three-story brick apartment houses. At the fourth house, she hurried up a set of stairs, fumbled in her purse for the key, and unlocked the front door. She disappeared inside and the man rushed up the stairs and managed to get the toe of his shoe in the doorway before it latched shut. A bit of good luck, as picking the lock on the street would have been risky this early in the evening.

Lois stopped half-way up the second flight of stairs. She had not heard the familiar click of the front door shutting below. The spring must be busted again. She made a mental note to call the super in the morning.

There were two doors on the third level and she stopped in front of the one on the left and opened the door to her apartment. She locked the door behind her, hung up her coat, and slipped out of her shoes. In the darkness, she walked to the bedroom and flipped on the light switch. The room was cold. She twisted the knob of the ancient radiator standing against the wall and heard the reassuring hiss of steam. Then she headed for the bathroom. As she switched on the light she heard a click. It was a foreign noise. She hesitated, waiting for the sound to repeat itself. After a moment, she decided it must have come from the radiator's metal fins expanding in the cold air.

She reached behind her back and unbuttoned her skirt. She stood over the toilet, pulled down her panties and sat herself gingerly onto the toilet seat, bracing for the feeling of cold plastic against her skin. A creaking noise stopped the flow of urine midstream. She held her breath for a moment, but the noise did not recur. It did not sound like the radiator, but she was tired and the three drinks at O'Donnell's had dulled her senses.

The flush of the toilet echoed through the room. She finished undressing and tossed her clothes in the laundry bin. Naked now and shivering, she flipped off the bathroom light and rushed on tip toes to the bedroom. The hardwood floor was ice-cold and it creaked with each step. She grabbed the nightgown on her pillow and slipped it on over her head, then slid under the covers and wiggled around in the cold sheets until her body began to warm them.

Lois was beginning to doze off when something caused her to awaken and open her eyes. A streetlamp outside the window cast a soft light through the closed curtains. In the near darkness, she saw the tall figure of a man standing over her. A scream began in her throat, but at the same moment a hand was thrust over her mouth and nose. She struggled against the hand, but it held her face firmly down against the pillow. In the next moment, he was sitting across her chest, pinning her arms against her body. She was suffocating and her bulging eyes stared in terror at her assailant. She could see the shape of his face, but the features were hidden in shadows. A syringe with a long needle glittered above her momentarily as its surface caught the faint light coming through the window curtains. The hand left her face and grabbed her right arm below the elbow. She gasped, filling her aching lungs with air. She felt a sharp prick at her elbow, then a burning sensation traveling up into her shoulder. She managed a weak cry, which was no more than a loud sigh, and then she lost consciousness.

7

Bob sat in the darkness on his sofa, his legs sprawled across the coffee table. The room was dark except for a soft, red glow from the stereo system. Tchaikovsky's Violin Concerto in D had concluded hours earlier. The vivid image of Diane filling his mind, her long dark hair, her warm smooth skin, her penetrating eyes. The pain of her terrible death burned deep in his chest. He became aware of a damp sensation on his leg and looked down. The glass he had been resting against his thigh was covered with beads of moisture which were soaking into his pants. He lifted the glass and took a sip. The drink was warm and watery and he could not remember what he had poured. A martini maybe? He glanced at the digital clock on the video recorder. It read 1:52 a.m.

He knew, from a very young age, that he was different from everyone else he knew. He wondered at the uncertainty he noticed in others, and the lack of it in himself. His was not an arrogant overconfidence, but rather, the quiet self-assurance of someone who made decisions that were almost always right. People wondered whether he had extra sensory perception or the ability to read minds, but he had none of those supernatural talents. What he did have was an uncanny ability to rapidly integrate the sensory information entering his mind. The process was not a conscious one. The result was an almost casual ability to read people and situations in a fraction of a moment and respond appropriately.

When he was called stat to the emergency room for the first time as a medical intern, he had rushed to the bed of an elderly man surrounded by frantic doctors and nurses. At a glance, his eyes noted the white hands, the blue lips, and the tremor around the neck. His nostrils smelled the faintly sweet odor on the man's breath. His fingers felt the cold, clammy skin. He did not need to see the EKG strip or the results of the blood tests his senior residents were waiting for. He knew at once that the man had suffered a myocardial infarction and was acidotic. He did not need to put his stethoscope to the man's chest to know, with certainty, that his heart was beating irregularly, and that he needed CPR. He knew how much epinephrine the body could handle, how much bicarbonate to give to correct the acidosis. His colleagues never understood how he arrived at correct decisions so rapidly, nor for that matter could he himself explain it. But it was quickly accepted by both. His opinions were always sought, his orders never questioned.

Within five minutes of meeting Diane, he had captured enough of her essence to know, with certainty, that he was in love with her and that they were meant for each other. Their two years together had been the happiest of his life. And then, when she fell ill, he had experienced a completely new sensation. *Helplessness.* He could not save her, could not even ease her pain. It had been death, not he, that had finally brought her suffering to an end.

Rather than admit his helplessness, he had resolved, with a vengeance, to defeat it. He had walked into the lab one morning five years ago, sat down at his computer, and begun to systematically search for a cure for Diane's disease. This morning he had claimed victory, cure in hand. And yet, his victory was bitter-sweet, because the moment of his greatest triumph had also been the first moment in his life that he fully realized his limitations. He could not, after all, bring Diane back.

He suddenly felt overcome with fatigue, too tired to even drag himself upstairs to the bedroom. He shoved one of the couch pillows under his head and stretched out. Within a few minutes he was in a deep slumber.

8

Ellen stepped into the tube-shaped entrance to the darkroom and swiveled the door one hundred and eighty degrees. She was plunged into utter darkness. She reached over her head and pulled on the string controlling the red lamp. The table on the back wall appeared dimly, not two steps in front of her. The dark room was the size of a very small closet.

She slid the agarose gel, which had the consistency of Jello, off the electrophoresis tray and onto the UV box, careful not to break the fragile material. She donned protective glasses and put her finger on the light switch attached to the UV box. "Third time's a charm," she whispered. She hesitated a moment, then flipped the switch. The light flickered, then a purple band appeared half-way down the gel.

"YES!" she exclaimed.

She smiled with excitement. She had finally cloned a gene. This all but assured her a grade of outstanding for the rotation. She punched the print button, tore off the three-inch square photo of the gel, and pulled again on the string over her head. Feeling behind her in the darkness, she stepped into the swivel door and turned the handle a hundred and eighty degrees, back into the brightly-lit lab room.

"There you are," said a skinny, blonde woman in a white lab coat. "You've got a call. I was just about to take a message."

"Thanks, Monica." Ellen dropped the photo on her desk and picked up the phone.

"Hello?"

"Hi, Ellen."

She caught her breath.

"It's me. David."

"I know who it is."

"I hope it's okay that I called. I miss you."

She was angry, despite herself. "David, we've been through this."

"Please, Ellen. You may have no feelings for me anymore, but I need to talk to you. If you don't see me now you may never have another chance."

She heard the panic in his voice. "What's wrong, David?"

"I don't want to talk about it over the phone."

She had been manipulated by him too often to be that naive. She had met David Blaire in her first year of medical school while he was a graduate student in political science. It wasn't love. Ellen had never really been in love, not like in the movies. She doubted that was in her cards. When she was in high-school she thought she was in love with her boyfriend, but that was just her romantic side wishing for something that wasn't there. She had seen the crazy things her friends had done for love and she wasn't about to sacrifice her career for such foolishness. Not after how hard she'd worked.

But she did enjoy David and he seemed intelligent, mature, and self-confident. By the end of the semester Ellen was living in his apartment. Gradually, she realized that his uninhibited behavior was not liberated, but irresponsible and childish. The self-confident attitude that had so attracted her was a front. He needed constant pampering. When she fulfilled those needs, he could be a surprisingly loving and sensitive person. When she had her own needs, he was insensitive and selfish. When she had finally gotten out of the relationship, it had felt like a thick, suffocating cloud had lifted from around her head.

"David, tell me what this is about."

There was a moment of silence, then, "Ellen, I'm dying."

She hesitated. "What do you mean, you're dying?"

"I have cancer,"

He knees felt suddenly weak and she sat down on her desk.

"Ellen, I really want to see you.   Do you think you could spare just an hour or so?"

She felt guilty for her earlier abruptness.   "Of course I can."

"Can you get away now?"

"Now?" She hesitated.   This was her last week in the lab before she began her cardiology rotation and she needed to prepare a presentation for her supervisor, Dr. Malcolm.   But Malcolm would not be in the lab until the afternoon.   The gel result could wait a couple of hours.

"I could get away for a short time."

"Good.   Can you meet me at Cafe Americana in twenty minutes?"

"Okay, David.   Twenty minutes."

"Thanks."

The phone went dead and Ellen replaced the receiver.   She grabbed her coat from the office and left the building.   David had been healthy and vigorous the last time she had seen him, almost six months ago.   She had talked to him on the phone a number of times since, but finally she had asked him not to call her anymore.   One thing about David was that he kept his word.   But this was different.

She walked into Cafe Americana and unbuttoned her coat.   This was where she and David had met in the early days of their romance.   She no longer felt that sense of eager anticipation as she looked around the mostly-empty establishment for him.   What she felt was dread.   She did not want to be here.   She did not want to face him.   Not like this.

David was sitting at their table near the back.   She forced a smile as she approached.   He rose to meet her.

"Hi."

"Hi, David." They looked awkwardly at each other.   David's face was thinner and his eyes were surrounded by dark circles, accentuating the white birthmark on his left cheek.   There were streaks of gray in his rich, brown hair.   Oh David, you have your faults, but you don't deserve this.

"Sit down, Ellen."

Instead, she put her arms around him and hugged him. "David. I'm so sorry. I don't know what to say."

She held onto him for another moment, then let go and smiled. They sat down opposite each other.

"You look good," he said.

"Thank you. You, too."

"What have you been up to?"

"David, you first. What have the doctors told you?"

"I have malignant melanoma."

Ellen breathed deeply. Melanoma was the deadliest form of skin cancer.

"When did you find out?"

"Yesterday. I'd been losing weight for a few weeks." He laughed. "At first I was happy about it because I wanted to drop a few pounds. But I had no appetite. And then this mole appeared on my thigh and it kept growing larger. They removed it, but they're worried that the cancer has already metastasized. I'm going into the hospital today for some more tests."

"And the treatment options?"

"You should know, Dr. Rhodes."

"Medical student," she corrected. "And I haven't done my oncology rotation yet."

"Well, then I'll save you the trouble of going to your books. The chances of a cure are only ten percent, once it's metastasized. I wanted you to know. I don't know why, but I needed to tell you. You still mean a lot to me, Ellen. I don't want to die without saying goodbye."

She rolled her head back and shut her eyes, then looked at him through a film of tears. "David, you mean a lot to me, too. Is there anything I can do?"

"You can pray for me."

She shook her head forcefully. "Don't talk like that. You can't just give up. I'll speak to someone in Oncology. There have got to be new treatments for melanoma."

He smiled. "Thanks."

They looked at each other in silence.

"How's second year?"

She found it difficult to talk about herself now. "Good. I'm leaning towards an academic track. I'm just finishing up a lab rotation in Genetics."

"So you're going to be a scientist, huh? You've come a long way from Pine Island, baby."

Ellen laughed. "I know. It surprises me, too. But I love it. I just cloned my first gene this morning. By the way, how'd you know where to reach me?"

David's face went blank for a moment. "I can't remember. My mind's been playing tricks on me lately. Doesn't matter."

She looked at him anxiously. David had a photographic memory.

The blank look returned. "Do you ever see Robert Newman?"

"Do you know him?" she asked casually, trying to keep the tension out of her voice.

"No. Funny, his name just kind of popped into my head. Heard of him from somewhere."

"I don't really have much to do with him. His lab's down the hall from me, but he keeps to himself, mostly." She wanted to change the subject. "I don't want you to give up, David. Things aren't as gloomy as you think. You have to fight this."

David said nothing. The sense of apprehension he had been feeling for the past week returned. He winced at a sudden pain in his temple. Another of the terrible visions sprang into his head. He saw Ellen standing in front of him, naked and smiling. In his mind, he grabbed her by her long, silky hair and plunged a needle into her neck.

He began to tremble. Ellen leaned forward across the table. "David?"

He stared past her, trying to relax, but the image returned. She stood before him again and his arm rose up to strike her. The needle became a sharp rock which he sunk over and over into her soft neck as her body writhed under the blows. The thought began to please him. Again, again, again, as Ellen shrieked . . .

"David, are you okay?"

Ellen stared at him anxiously, her hand squeezing his arm.

"I'm fine," he said weakly.

"You're awfully pale."

"No really, I'm fine." He stood up. "I'm sure you've got to get back to work. And I've got to get to the hospital. Thanks for seeing me, Ellen."

Ellen got up and followed him out of the cafe.

"Keep your chin up. You'll beat this yet," she reassured him.

"Thanks."

"Take care of yourself, David." She hugged him briefly, and he departed down the street.

Ellen stood at the corner and watched him leave. She thought about the mole on David's thigh. It could not have been there earlier. She knew every inch of David's body. It must have appeared very quickly. But why? And why now? She had read somewhere that depression could cause cancer. She had been more patient, more understanding, with David than any reasonable person could expect. Why then, did she feel so guilty?

9

"He's expecting you."

"I know."

Bob headed for the far door and opened it without knocking. The dean's office was large by University standards. Diplomas, awards, and a framed photograph of the dean shaking hands with the Mayor covered the wall opposite the door, carefully situated so as to be plainly visible upon entering the room.   The wall on the left held a large picture window with a view of the quadrangle. To the right, the room was dominated by an oak desk, four leather chairs, and a coffee table.   Two of the chairs were occupied.

"Bob, come in, come in."

Dean Wright was not a particularly attractive man. He had squinty eyes, a round face, and was fifty pounds overweight. His soft-spoken manner and frequent smile were a calculated deception.   In the world of academic medicine, ego replaced money as the measure of success, and Sam Wright was loaded with it.

"Joe's been filling me in on some potentially interesting data."

Bob looked at the other chair, which was filled with the generous figure of Doctor Joseph Malcolm. His round head was completely smooth, save for some white hair around the temples. His three chins, together with the twinkle in his eyes, explained perhaps why children and puppies invariably bounded onto his lap the first time they met him.

"We've been discussing our division's budget for next year," Joe said.   "I've been explaining why we need new resources to expand the division, and our conversation from this morning came up. I figured you'd better come up here in person, since I don't want to give Sam the wrong information."

Bob's guard was up as he took a seat.   He had already concluded that Joe was in the midst of his annual meeting with the dean, in which he had to justify his existence, as well as that of his division. Joe must have let slip the results of Bob's gene therapy experiments.   He had told Joe about the results that morning, but had asked him to keep it quiet. There was too much at stake, both for Janie and for his own career.

Wright looked at Bob disarmingly.   "So, I u-understand you think you've made some interesting observations."

Bob always thought it odd that Wright stuttered.   It was surprising for a man whose ego was bigger than his vast rear-end. "The data's preliminary," Bob replied, not wanting to volunteer any information that Wright did not yet have.   He glanced at Joe sternly, both to admonish him as well as to signal him to avoid further disclosures.   Joe looked back sheepishly, communicating that he understood at least the first part of the message.

It was difficult to be angry with Joe.   He was a truly nice guy in a sea of sharks.   The annual competition among the divisions for university funding was always difficult for Joe.   While he was a brilliant and respected physician and scientist, genetics was not a medical specialty in which high-paying procedures were performed.   Translated into financial terms, this meant that divisions such as genetics operated off the profits of the procedure-driven specialties, such as surgery, cardiology, and the intensive care units.   The major academic centers supported the non-profitable divisions for political reasons, since the absence of a subspecialty would diminish the stature of the institution. However, these divisions were kept on a tight budget which was never adequate.

"I-I take it you think you've found a new method to perform gene therapy in vivo," Wright persisted when Bob remained silent.   That was the second time Wright had used the word 'think'.   As far as Wright was concerned, practically every scientist, excluding of course himself, constantly misinterpreted the data from his experiments.   And Wright loved to point out to his colleagues where they had erred.

"I detect a note of skepticism," Bob replied calmly, hands folded across his lap.

Wright's eyes narrowed into tiny slits when he smiled.   "I'm always skeptical until I've seen the data.   But Joe is impressed enough to think it merits a big increase in funds for next year."

"I didn't say that," Joe interrupted.   "I said Bob had informed me of some exciting results.   I haven't seen the data either, but I have complete confidence in his scientific judgment."

Wright had never been fond of Bob's work. As far as he was concerned, a true scientist studied basic principles. Applications should be left to the pharmaceutical industry.

"What Joe has told me is that you've succeeded in performing gene therapy in vivo. I'm not sure what the big deal is. It's been done already, but if Joe's excited, I'd like to hear more."

Much as Bob despised the thought, he knew he needed Wright. The dean's support was crucial if he was to get expedited approval for human trials through the FDA. The question was, what price would he have to pay?

"In a nutshell, I've designed a new viral vector to infect cells in vivo. The contents of the viral capsule have been altered to contain both a restriction enzyme and a normal gene. The restriction enzyme has been specifically designed to splice the DNA open at the two ends of the mutated gene, which allows the normal gene to be integrated in its usual location downstream of its natural promoter. This ensures normal expression of the gene product."

Wright was not ready to believe any of this. He leaned back in his chair. "And which tissues express the gene product?"

"As I just explained," Bob replied with a hint of impatience, "the fact that the gene is integrated at its natural site insures that the gene is expressed by those tissues that normally express it, and only those tissues."

Wright studied Bob, who sat comfortably in the chair with his arms folded across his chest. His blue eyes stared straight into Wright's without blinking. He certainly was a self-confident bastard. And bright, too. In fact in some ways he reminded him of himself. If there really was something to Newman's assertions, the possibilities were mind-boggling. Wright's smile faded ever so slightly from his lips.

"I'm well aware of what you explained. But that's impossible. People have been trying to do it for twenty years with absolutely no success."

Bob did not reply, but a thin smile appeared on his face. He enjoyed the uncertainty in Wright's eyes.

"Have you determined what percentage of cells contain the gene?"

"Approximately ninety-eight percent."

Wright shifted his ample body. Under the best of circumstances, in vivo gene therapy resulted in correction of one cell in a million. He leaned forward and whispered, "You can't possibly have infected every cell in the body. There would be too strong of an immune response."

"I block the immune response with immunosuppressive therapy."

"The gametes are infected, too?"

Bob raised his eyebrows and nodded. Wright grasped the implications immediately. If the gametes contained the normal gene, the offspring would also be normal. Taken one step further, it meant that genes could be inserted and removed from the human genome at will. This was the stuff of science-fiction!

"Now let me make sure I understand this. You're telling me that with this technique you could replace any gene in the human genome?"

Bob nodded. "If one knew the exact sequence of the gene and its promoter, then yes." He crossed his legs. "Look, I see what you're getting at, but you're way ahead of things. It would take twenty years before we could even begin to attempt to improve on the human genome. I'd rather not discuss it in those terms because that opens up all sorts of ethical dilemmas which are entirely theoretical at this time. What we are talking about is very straightforward, the removal and replacement of disease-causing genes, that's all. Let's leave it at that."

"The news media won't," Wright responded.

"Exactly. Which is why I don't want this publicized until I have a paper in press. Otherwise people are going to blow this out of all proportion."

"Of course. I understand."

Bob unfolded his arms and stared straight at Wright. "There's one other thing."

Wright noticed the change in tone.   He raised his chin expectantly. "Yes?"

"I've written an application to the FDA to permit a clinical trial on a small number of patients with Pompe's disease, on a compassionate needs basis.   That's another reason I don't want any publicity.   I want this approved without a public debate."

"How many patients?"

"Five."   He was not about to single out Janie.

"Can you justify it?"

"They'll be dead within two months," Bob said simply.

Wright's eyes became tiny slits. This was too easy. "Let me think about it for a few days. You do realize that we'll need to show the FDA all the data, before they'll even consider it."

Bob caught the meaning of Wright's smile, and the use of the word 'we'. The bidding had begun. "Of course," Bob replied. "But I don't have a few days. I need to send out the request today."

"Impossible. After all, I am familiar with this field. I was the first to show that restriction enzymes could be used not only to remove gene segments, but also to insert them. That's the whole basis of your discovery."

At one time, Wright had once been among the most brilliant molecular geneticists in the world.   But he had not published anything truly novel in ten years.   It was a steep price, but Bob had no choice, and the bastard knew it. "Your name will be on the paper if you sign the FDA forms today."

Wright squirmed.   Why was he being so blunt about it? There were rules to the game, after all. Newman was always a challenge to handle.

"Well, I appreciate your desire to acknowledge my contribution, but I can't agree to my name being on a paper until I've seen all the data. It's not only my own reputation that's at stake, but the institution's as well."

Joe spoke up. "I have a suggestion. Why don't the three of us meet in an hour in my office. Bob, you can show us the data in detail. Do you have the FDA forms prepared?"

Bob nodded.

Joe continued, "We can take care of that afterwards."

"Agreed," Bob replied.

Wright nodded. "Let's meet in an hour."

Bob got up to leave.

"Oh, and by the way," Wright called after him. "I want you to stop by the legal office today and speak to o our patent attorney. We must have a patent filed before the FDA gets hold of this. Don't forget that the review committees are open to the public."

10

"I'm Roy. I'll be performing your CAT scan. Come with me, please."

David followed the technician through a door and into a room nearly-filled with a glistening, white scanner, the central part of which was shaped like a huge doughnut. Through the 'doughnut hole', and extending in front of it about eight feet, lay a narrow, concave table.

"Have you ever had a CAT scan before?"

"No," David answered, looking at the scanner with mild apprehension.

"Well, there's nothing to be concerned about. There's not much more radiation than a normal X-ray, and it's completely painless. Your doctor requested a total body scan. That will take about an hour and a half. In a moment, I'm going to have you lie down on that table and you just need to relax and hold still for about forty minutes. The table will move your body slowly through that doughnut hole where the pictures are taken, and they'll be displayed on the computer in the room over there." He pointed to a glass wall, behind which David saw a panel of lights and some computer monitors. "Then I'll inject a contrast dye into your hand and repeat the procedure. That's all there is to it. Okay?"

David nodded.

"I'd like you to go through that door there and put on one of the gowns you'll find. Then we'll get started."

When he had the gown on, David returned to the scanner room.

"Ready?" the technician asked.

"I guess."

Roy led David over to the CAT scanner and helped him lie down on the concave table. He put a small pillow under his head and tightened a strap across his forehead. "Sir, I want you to lie perfectly still for the next forty minutes. You won't feel any pain. Just relax. Take a nap if you wish."

David nodded and the technician left the room. He heard a voice. "Mr. Blaire, I'm speaking to you through an intercom system. Can you hear me?"

"Yes."

"Good. Now if there's any problem, just holler. Please keep your arms by your sides and remain completely still."

The table under him moved. David watched the doughnut getting closer. When his head was in the hole, the table stopped. After a few minutes, he felt a rumbling under him as the bed moved a centimeter forward to image another slice of his brain. He closed his eyes, trying to relax. He'd probably feel better after all these tests were over.

The radiation to David's skull was minimal, but it was enough to accelerate a process that had already begun in the cells of his brain's frontal lobe. As his body entered further into the scanner he became increasingly uneasy. He had the sensation that someone or something was standing behind him. *Just anxiety.* But the feeling grew stronger. It took all his will power not to turn his head and look back. His skin began to tingle and his hair stood on end. A prickle of fear nibbled at his consciousness. He heard voices coming from behind him.

"Did you say something?" David called out.

"No, sir," the technician responded from behind the glass wall.

The table began to rumble and David was withdrawn from the doughnut. The technician's face appeared in front of him.

"Jeez, look at you! You're sweating like a pig!" He wiped David's brow. "You okay?"

"Is it over?"

"The first half."

"I must have fallen asleep. I think I had a nightmare."

"Well, if you feel up to it, we're going to do the contrast scan now." He wrapped a flat rubber tourniquet around David's arm, pinching his skin and causing the veins in his hand to bulge. "You're going to feel a poke," he said as he plunged a needle into his hand. He injected the dye into David's vein.

"Just relax for another forty-minutes," he said as he left the room.

David breathed deeply. The table began to move and his head entered the doughnut hole. The feeling of apprehension returned and, with it, the agitation. An ominous sense of trepidation overcame him.

"Please hold still, Mr. Blaire, so we don't need to re-shoot the slices."

Slices. An image appeared in his mind of a gigantic knife slicing through his brain as though it were a hunk of salami. As each slice fell off the knife, it melted into hundreds of small worms that wriggled onto the floor.

He screamed and tried to rise up, straining against the belt tied across his torso.

The technician ran into the room. He looked at David's bulging, crazed eyes and yelled behind him, "Larry, call a code! I think this guy's having a dye reaction!"

He ran to the table and tried to hold David down.

"I've got to get out of here!" David screamed.

"It's okay, sir!" the technician reassured, trying to restrain him. "The doctors are coming. It's okay!"

Within moments, the room was filled with white coats. David was still struggling to get off the bed, against the weight of four people.

"Give him an amp of Demerol!"

The drug flowed up his arm vein and reached his heart. Within moments, it had been ejected into his carotid arteries and was bathing the cells of his cerebral cortex. The voices faded into the distance as David lost consciousness.

A half-hour later, Roy walked into the viewing room and fell into his chair.

"Whew, that was scary," he said to his associate, Larry.

"That guy went bezerko," Larry replied.

Roy glanced over at the monitor, which still held the image of the last slice of David's brain. He squinted.

"Hey Larry. Take a look at this, would you?" He pointed to the image of the frontal lobe, in the forward part of the skull. "What's this high-intensity pattern?"

Larry looked for a few moments. The front of the cranium was filled by a star-shaped mass, with tentacle-like projections reaching back towards the cerebellum.

He exhaled slowly. "Beats me. I've never seen anything like *that* before. I'm surprised this guy can walk and talk. Circle it and let's see what Dr. Glass says."

11

The nitrites from the coal plant in Gary, just across the state line, reached Chicago in the westward-moving upper air currents of the fall. The heavy air above the city brought them down into the lower atmosphere and into a courtyard outside the Chicago University Hospital, where George Peterson rested on a bench. The air was chilly, but Peterson wanted to get as much fresh air as he could. Peterson was a thirty year old black male with sickle cell anemia, a genetic disease that was slowly destroying his tissues. Next week, Dr. Newman would give him his bone marrow transplant, which would cure him. If he survived. He would be locked up in an isolation room for at least four weeks. Who knew when he would be able to breathe fresh air again?

As he inhaled the crisp, early morning air, a minute quantity of nitrites entered into his lungs, and from there made their way into his bloodstream. They reached the liver, penetrated through the cell membranes, and were swept by the eddies and currents of the intracellular cytoplasm through the pores in the nuclear membrane and into the nucleus itself. There they were drawn by a natural affinity to an odd sequence of nucleic acids on chromosome nine. That sequence was a promoter, a segment of DNA controlling expression of genes downstream of it on the DNA chain. As they bound tightly to their target, the DNA double helix began to unravel at that point, exposing a set of genes which had lain dormant for millennia.

Since the industrial revolution, the concentrations of nitrites in the atmosphere had been gradually rising, but the levels had never been high enough to activate that specific promoter of more than a few cells in a given body. Now, a process began which had not occurred for eons, as an unusual group of dormant genes became activated, transforming one cell after another of Peterson's liver.

Peterson felt nothing unusual. But over the next few days, the cancer would begin to grow. The malignant cells would soon compress the normal surrounding tissue, distorting the liver's architecture and infiltrating it with tentacle-like projections. Even then, Peterson would be oblivious to the process underway in his body. He would remain happily naive until it tentatively caressed his brain tissue. Then he would sense a subtle change, a prickle of fear. As the gentle touch tightened into a crushing grip, he would know a nightmare too hideous too imagine. But that would be days from now. Today, Peterson could still enjoy a crisp November morning.

12

Bob burst through the door of the dean's office and slammed a newspaper onto the desk.

"What the hell is the meaning of this?"

Sam Wright looked up, startled.

"So you've seen the morning paper."

"You're damn right I have. I thought we had an agreement, no publicity until the results are published in *Science*. Isn't that what you, Joe and I agreed to yesterday?"

Wright leaned back in his chair, looking at the hardness in Newman's eyes. There was something deadly about that man.

"Now don't go off half-cocked, Bob. I agreed that we would avoid any sensationalism. This article is not sensationalist. Besides, this is too big to sit on for six months. We're talking big bucks here."

Bob worked his jaw muscles. "I could have had it in press in six weeks. The religious right's gonna turn this into a political battle. Do you want demonstrations in front of the medical center?"

"A few demonstrations might not be so bad at all," Wright responded, a smile on his face. "You're not looking at the public relations angle of this, which is completely understandable. You're a scientist. Leave the public relations to me."

"You double-crossing son-of-a-bitch," Bob said evenly. "We had an agreement."

"Listen Bob, this was meant for consumption by our financial donors. It gives me something to show them while I'm sticking it to them for money, see? And you'll get a piece of it, too. A big piece, I promise you. Most people won't even notice the article. This is all going to blow over. Trust me on this one. It's what I do for a living. I suggest you get back to your lab and keep doing what it is you do so well. Oh, and by the way, I asked you yesterday, would you please stop by the legal department?"

Bob's eyes narrowed. "Go screw yourself!" he barked and stomped out of the office.

Wright shook his head as Newman disappeared from view. The man was brilliant, but so damned difficult!

"Trust me," he called after him. "By Monday morning nobody will even remember the damn article!"

*   *   *

"Dr. Newman! Dr. Newman, could we have a few words! Dr. Newman, over HERE!"

The yelling came from all directions at once as Bob stepped out of Jackson Hall. He squinted his eyes against the sun. Jackson Hall was a building under siege. Dozens of cars were parked in front of the building, on the sidewalk, even on the grass. Reporters from all the major news organizations were camped in front of the building with cameras and electronic equipment. On the grass, a group of about a hundred demonstrators carried signs reading, KEEP YOUR HANDS OUT OF MY GENES, and chanting "No gene vaccine! No gene vaccine!" Campus police mingled through the crowd, trying, with little success, to restore some semblance of order. Where had all these people come from?

Someone shoved a microphone in his face. "Dr. Newman, do you have any comments on the Senate subcommittee hearings?"

Bob glanced around. He was completely surrounded, with no escape possible.

"I think the Senate subcommittee should leave this in the hands of the FDA. This is a medical issue, not a political one."

"What do you think of the statement from Senator Delany's office?"

"I'm not aware of Senator Delany's statement."

"Delany's office released a statement this morning that your gene vaccine raised serious ethical issues that must be addressed. Do you have any reply?"

As Bob was about to respond, a man standing among the group of demonstrators yelled, "You Nazi pig! We won't allow genetic experimentation on human beings!" The crowd roared its approval.

"I've got patients to see," Bob said, shoving the microphones away from his face. He forced his way through the crowd of reporters and found himself face to face with a uniformed police officer. "Do these people have a permit to demonstrate?" he yelled, pointing at the crowd opposite him.

"I don't know, sir."

"Well find out, and if they don't, get them the hell off this campus!"

He slipped back in through a side door and headed towards the hospital. For the past twenty-four hours, he had been besieged with interview requests and obscene phone calls. He had stopped answering the phone, but it was still damned near impossible to get any work done. All this publicity was exactly what he had wanted to avoid. It now seemed probable that the FDA would withhold compassionate approval until the Senate subcommittee had finished its investigation. That could take months and Janie had only four to six weeks to live. If she was going to have any chance, he would have to treat her within the next two. The way things were developing, that meant breaking the law. It was not a trivial offense. He could lose his medical license and ruin his career. If she died under his treatment, he could be charged with manslaughter.

He reached the genetics ward and approached Debbie at the nurse's desk.

"Good morning, Professor. How does it feel to be world famous?"

"Don't ask. How were things here last night?"

"Rough, but it's quieted down."

"Anything I need to know?"

Debbie hesitated. "Janie had another difficult night. Lots of pain. We used some morphine like you ordered, but she didn't sleep much. Didn't complain, though."

"She never does. Peterson okay?"

Debbie gave a thumbs-up. "He's sailing. He's down for his first dose of radiation as we speak."

"Great. I'm gonna drop in on Janie."

"Sure. Let me know if you need anything."

He poked his head into Janie's room. The girl's eyes were closed. He glanced across at the comatose old lady still lying in the far bed. She was in the same position he had always seen her in, lying on her back, her head resting on a pillow. She looked even paler than usual. Her watched her shallow breathing and wondered again at the tenacity of the human body.

Then it hit him. Her breathing! That's what had bothered him the other day. She was not Kussmaul breathing. A person in a deep coma had a very characteristic breathing pattern which began with short, shallow breaths that became progressively longer and deeper until the breathing stopped completely for a time, only to resume the cycle again. He walked over to the old lady's bed and observed her chest rise and fall in a regular pattern. He leaned over her face and lifted one eyelid with his thumb. Her pupil constricted slightly. He tried the other pupil and got the same response. This lady was not in a coma, at least not anymore. He lifted the sheet off her legs and pinched her thigh. There was no response. He frowned. She should have felt that. He tried her reflexes. They were normal. There was something very peculiar about this lady. He picked up her bed chart, noted her doctor's name, and decided to give him a call later.

He walked back to Janie's bed.

"Morning, Janie."

Janie opened her eyes and managed a weak smile. "Hi, Bobby."

She was very pale and her eyes were glassy and slightly unfocused. He sat at the edge of the bed, smiled at her, and brushed her bangs with the backs of his fingers, casually touching her forehead. She was febrile.

"How did you sleep last night?"

"Fine."

"The nurses told me you were up all night."

Janie's face brightened with a familiar, devilish expression. "They just don't want you to think they get paid for nothing. Who you gonna believe, them or me?"

Bob grinned. "We've already established that you are a pathological liar."

"I've reformed."

Bob laughed. "Never. Anyway, how you feeling now?"

The listlessness returned to her face. "About the same. Other than my tummy, the pain's not bad."

"I'm going to order you some more morphine. Use it. If you don't ask for it, I'm going to order the nurses to give it to you round the clock."

A desperate expression appeared on her face. "Bobby, please don't do that."

"Listen, there's no need to be stoic."

"It's not that. The morphine makes me groggy and I want to be awake and aware of being alive every moment that I've got left."

He held his breath.

"I know I'm dying."

His eyes softened and he took her hand in his. Tears welled up in her eyes. "Every time you leave my room I wonder if I'll ever see you again." She began to sob.

He put his arms around her and she hugged him tightly. "I never tell you how much I love you," she sobbed, "because I don't want to make things harder on you."

Her warm tears soaked through his shirt. He rocked her gently and whispered, "Janie, I love you, too."

"I know . . . "

They held each other until Janie finally let go and looked up into his face.

"How much longer do I have, Bobby?"

He hesitated, searching for the right words. "Janie, I'm not going to lie to you. I couldn't if I wanted to. You saw what happened to Diane."

Janie nodded slowly. "It was terrible, those last few days."

He turned away so that she would not see his face.

"Oh God, I'm sorry, Bobby!" She squeezed his hand. "Don't blame yourself. You did everything you could for her. I know you're doing the same for me, too. . . Bobby?"

He opened his eyes and stared at the wall. He remembered it as yesterday. There had been nothing he could do but watch her suffer. This time he had a cure. He could not afford to wait any longer. In a very short time, Janie would be too weak to survive the treatment. How would he react if he were sitting on the edge of another patient's bed? That was the measure by which he always judged the objectivity of his reactions to Janie's illness. What would he do now? God damn it, what would he do now?

There was an axiom in the medical profession that one should not treat a member of one's own family. It was impossible to maintain objectivity under such circumstances. He had decided to become Janie's doctor only because he knew of no one more qualified to treat her particular disease. And she was his responsibility. Her parents had both passed away within a year of Diane's death, after which she had been cared for by an uncle who had trouble taking care of himself. Being conscious of the risks, he could try to be objective. And he did try. He bent over backwards to treat her the way he would treat any other patient. And he was successful, as long as he was not standing in front of her. The murmurs of the nursing staff and his physician colleagues had died down. The murmurs in his heart had not. They gripped him each time he entered her room. Was he being objective now? How would he react if he was sitting on the edge of another patient's bed?

In that moment, he made up his mind. He would not watch helplessly while anyone was dying, not if he had a cure in his hands. He gazed at her. The fire had returned to his eyes.

"Janie, the virus is almost ready. I'm going to give it to you next week."

Her eyes widened. "The FDA gave approval?"

He lowered his voice. "I've been given permission to try it on one patient while they're debating it," he lied. "I've picked you."

"Really? This isn't a trick to get my spirits up?"

"You know I wouldn't joke about this."

"I'm scared, Bobby."

His eyes melted. "I'll be with you, Janie. You don't need to worry."

"It's going to make me real sick, isn't it?"

He nodded.

"Do you think I can survive it?"

"I'll be here to make sure you do. Now listen to me, I don't want you talking to anyone about this, not even to the nurses and doctors. Understand?"

She hesitated. "This is legal isn't it? I mean, you're not doing something that could get you in trouble, are you?"

"Of course not," he reassured her. But like I said, it's highly sensitive. The government doesn't want any publicity for now. But I trust you to keep it secret."

"My lips are sealed." She made a motion across her mouth.

"Good." Bob stood up. "I've got to go now, Janie. Try to get some rest."

She did not answer him. She stared past him, wide-eyed, her mouth open, a look of terror on her face.

"Janie, what's wrong?" He took a step towards her. She screamed. He heard a scratching noise behind him, whirled around, and let out a gasp. The old lady was shuffling towards him from across the room. Her eyes stared wildly at him. Tubes dangled from her arms and nose. Her scraggly hair stood on end. Her mouth was moving and thick beads of saliva ran down her chin.

"Sartaaaan," she hissed. The sound sent a shiver down his spine.

"What did you say?" Bob asked incredulously.

"Sartaaaan. . .Sartaaan. . ." she repeated it over and over, louder and louder until she was shrieking. "SARTAN. . .SARTAN! . . SARTAN!"

She reached Bob and her right arm went up over her head. Bob's eyes caught a flash of light. Then he saw the syringe in her fist, the dripping needle pointed at him. He grabbed her wrist with his left hand. She kneed him in the groin. He groaned and shoved her onto the floor, holding her down by his sheer weight, while she attempted to stick the needle into his face. He was amazed at her strength.

"Debbie!" he yelled.

Janie had already summoned the nurse with the call button. She entered the room. "What the devil's going on here?"

"A hundred milligrams of Thorazine!" he yelled.

"Right!"

The old lady was still writhing under him, cackling, when Debbie returned, a syringe in her hand.

"Give it to her!"

The nurse gave her the shot in the arm. The old lady stopped struggling and went limp. Bob lay on her until he was sure she was not going to jump him again. He pulled the syringe from her old, gnarled fingers and drew himself up. He stared at the limp body lying on the floor, then bent down and felt her neck for a pulse. He found it, weak and irregular.

"Debbie, call intensive care and get someone down here with a transport bed! We've got to get her upstairs."

The nurse complied. Bob knelt by the body until the orderly came with the bed. He noted, to his amazement, that the pulse was already growing stronger and she was beginning to stir. He had given her enough sedative to stop an elephant in heat. This was one hell of a seventy-eight year-old lady!

The orderly arrived and, while helping to lift the body onto the cart, he realized that he still held the old woman's syringe in his hand. It was a 50 cc hospital-issue Fisher brand, filled with an orange fluid. He brought the needle near his nose and sniffed carefully. The odor was vaguely familiar. He motioned to Debbie.

"Do you know what this is?"

The nurse looked down at the syringe. "Strange color. Digoxin looks kind of like this, but it's more yellow."

"Do me a favor and send it down to the lab for analysis."

"Sure Bob." She took the syringe carefully from his hand, avoiding touching the long needle.

"Debbie, call her doctor and tell him to meet me in the ICU. I'll go up with her."

He helped the orderly wheel the cart to the door, then turned to Janie. "You gonna be all right?"

The young girl had quickly recovered from her initial terror. "I'm fine, Bobby. But I think I'll go look for some excitement. This hospital is a drag."

"You step foot out of your room, young lady, and I'll personally handcuff you to your bed rail. I'll stop by to see you later."

He could not have explained what made him turn around and motion to Debbie again after he had left the room. It was a subtle sense that Janie was at risk. When the nurse joined him, he placed a hand on her shoulder, leaned towards her ear, and whispered, "Debbie put a security guard on the ward. I want Janie's room watched twenty four hours a day. No one is to go in there without one of the nurses or guards."

"Sure Bob," the nurse replied, puzzled. "What are you worried about?"

"I don't know, Debbie. Just humor me for a few days."

"I'd love to," she murmured as she watched his departing figure.

13

Ellen left her apartment Monday morning and headed for Jackson Hall. It was the last day of her rotation and she needed to sign out with Malcolm and collect her papers. She was unprepared for the mayhem that greeted her upon her arrival. She looked around in fascination at the pandemonium of news reporters, demonstrators, and police.

The reaction to Friday's announcement of Bob's discovery had, at first, been underwhelming. The report had drawn no response from most of the public, and little more than a raised eyebrow from a few, who wondered about the implications. One raised eyebrow belonged to a moderator for National Public Radio, who decided to mention it on his Friday afternoon program. According to the story Ellen had heard, a certain reporter for CNN, in the midst of humping a woman whose name had escaped him, just happened to find the story coming from the radio by the bed hotter than the girl coming on top of him. And so, like the pebble that starts an avalanche, the news tumbled down onto the consciousness of humanity and an apathetic world was aroused. It reminded Ellen of the white-water rafting trip she had taken last year. Occasionally, an event disrupted the flow of human experience like a pile of stones, lodged in a river bed, transforming a timid stream into a suddenly bubbling torrent. As a person in a canoe knew that the current had shifted, so a person living through a vital moment of history could feel the jar. Yet it was not until he looked back over his shoulder that he realized he had just passed through the rapids.

She made her way passed the crowd and hurried up the stone steps to Jackson Hall. A uniformed police officer stood at the entrance to the building.

"I'm sorry, Miss," he addressed her, barring her progress. "This building is closed to the public. Employees only."

"I'm a med student here," Ellen protested.

The officer looked her over with interest. "I'll have to see some identification."

That's not all you want to see, I bet. She searched through her purse and handed over her student ID. The officer looked at the photo carefully.

"Is there a problem?"

He looked down at her and smiled. "Are you a real brunette?"

She snatched the card from his hand. "Are you gonna let me in or am I gonna have to file a complaint with your superior officer?"

The officer opened the door, still grinning. She brushed past him and hurried up to the second floor. As she turned the corner she ran smack into Bob, who was heading in the opposite direction. He caught her by the upper arms and dropped a folder full of papers in the process.

"Excuse me," she said, flustered, stooping down to gather up the papers. Her face was flushed as she handed them back to him.

"That's quite all right," he responded.

There was an awkward moment of silence while they gazed at each other. The sharp lines of his face appeared less angry and there was an anguish in his eyes which she had never noticed before.

"I heard the news," she said. "Congratulations on your discovery."

"Thank you. I hope you don't think I'm being rude, but I'm late."

Great, Ellen, she thought. Couldn't you have thought of anything more stupid to say than, "Congratulations on your discovery"? She wasn't sure she'd have an opportunity to see him again, now that her rotation was ending. And she wanted to see him again. She wondered what he'd do if she grabbed him right there in the hall and congratulated him with her tongue.

"Oh. Sure, I understand." She stepped aside to let him pass. "See ya," she called as he departed down the hall.

14

Bob headed for the hospital cafeteria, his mind occupied with the old lady's attack that morning. Mildred Stone was a widow dying of end-stage lymphoma. According to her doctor, Ed

Sigland, the cancer had spread throughout her body in the last few weeks, despite chemotherapy. He had given up any hope for her. She had metastases in her brain and had been comatose for almost a month. She had had two EEG's, both of which were uninterpretable because of high background interference. He did not recall anything unusual about her CAT scan, other than the obvious metastases in her frontal and occipital lobes. Sigland could not recall if he had ever observed her Kussmauling. Since she recovered consciousness in Janie's room that morning, her condition had worsened. When Bob left the unit, her vital signs were deteriorating. It was as if her amazing physical feat that morning had drained whatever life was left in her shriveled body.

As for her attack on him, Sigland could only suggest that she had been in some sort of delirium. It was the most reasonable explanation, but Bob was not buying it. He had heard of ninety pound ladies lifting cars off of their children in a sudden, concentrated focusing of will and muscle, and he believed such things were possible under the right circumstances. But no such stimulus had occurred this morning. One minute he had been talking quietly to Janie, while a patient lay unconscious and unresponsive to deep pain at the other end of the room. The next moment, the old lady had been fully conscious and on him like a wild boar. It just did not make sense. But he was certain of one thing, that was not a delirious patient. Her eyes had communicated intelligence, and something else--hatred. And eyes never lie, Bob mused. Mouths, yes, but never eyes.

He wondered what the strange word, 'Sartan', meant. She had uttered it so emphatically. The only thing that kept coming to his mind was 'Satan'. Was she calling to the devil for help? Or did she think she was the devil? Not for a moment was he going to consider that her incredible strength had come from some demonic force. Besides, he was sure she had said 'Sartan', not 'Satan'.

His train of thought was broken by a deep, bellowing voice. "What took you so long, Bobby boy? What you do for so many hours all alone in your lab with those rats of yours."

Bob looked up to see Joe Malcolm's generous figure standing at the entrance to the cafeteria. He wore a white coat, unbuttoned because it did not reach even halfway around his substantial torso.

"Funny you should mention it," Bob responded, stopping in front of Joe. "Actually, I was collecting some of my rats' more delicate parts for you to start your diet with." He patted Joe's gut.

"Thanks, but diets are for the meek at heart, slimness for the malcontented. You may think I'm fat, but I see myself as a man who proudly carries his own weight."

"You ought to be proud. That's some load you got there."

Joe chuckled as he handed Bob a tray and they started moving through the lunch line. There were three cash registers at the other end of the long counter. One was abandoned by a cashier who had decided to take a coffee break. A second register had an OUT OF ORDER sign on it. The single remaining cash register was being used to train a new employee, who had not quite caught on to the subtleties of addition and subtraction. The line crawled.

"Seriously," Joe said as they placed their trays on the metal bars in front of the counter. "How are you holding up under the spotlight?"

"I'm managing. But I'd just love to grab Wright by his lying throat and break his neck."

Joe glanced over both shoulders before responding in a lowered voice, "He is a son-of-a-bitch, isn't he? But there's no way you could have kept this quiet once the FDA request was submitted."

Bob sighed. "Maybe you're right. I was hoping to keep it quiet at least until they responded to my request for compassionate treatment for Janie."

"There's still a chance for that," said Joe as he placed a bowl of wilted salad onto his tray. "Any progress in the lab?"

"Didn't even get to the lab this morning. I had a problem while making rounds."

Joe glanced at him. "Oh? Anything serious?"

Bob passed up the salad counter. "Serious? Oh no, nothing serious. Just some old witch who tried to pin my ass to the wall with a hypodermic needle."

They reached the entrees and Joe pressed his lips together and frowned as he studied his options. "What in the devil's name are you talking about?"

"You mean what in Sartan's name am I talking about?"

Joe raised an eyebrow. He was used to Bob's manner of leading into a topic he wished to discuss by dropping subtle hints. He decided to take the bait.

"You developing a Swedish accent? I believe the word is pronounced, Satan."

"So you've never heard of the word, Sartan, either?"

Joe shook his head and decided on the meatloaf.

Bob grabbed a plate of meatloaf, too. It was the only thing on the counter that looked even vaguely edible. "Are you sure?"

"I'm Sartan," Joe answered, laughing at his own pun.

Bob gave him a look of reproach, then proceeded to relate the morning's events.

"Wow," Joe sighed when Bob had finished. "That's a pretty wild story. Could have been a delirium, though."

"Maybe, but I'd bet my medical degree that the woman was fully conscious when she came at me."

Joe shrugged. They reached the dessert counter. He hesitated for a moment, then reached out and grabbed a bowl containing a square of red Jello. "You could be right. I was just reading this week's New England Journal. There's a letter from Wash U reporting, along with the increased incidence of malignancies, an increase in bizarre, psychotic-like behavior in some cancer patients."

"What's causing it?"

"Don't know. The authors suggest that metastases to the brain may be causing personality disorders."

"Doesn't sound convincing. But that reminds me. I've been meaning to ask you, what do you know about the incidence of malignancies here? Are we part of the national trend?"

Joe replaced the Jello and decided on a brownie instead. "There's a meeting of the division chairmen at two this afternoon to discuss the situation."

"What's our incidence?"

Joe shook his head. "Don't know. I assume we'll hear at the meeting. It must be high, because the letter I got from the hospital administration sounded pretty panicky."

"If the problem is really national, the Surgeon General ought to be involved."

"I agree. Circumstantial evidence points against an infectious etiology. This has got to be some kind of environmental contamination. That's the only reasonable explanation. The government better start searching for that contamination."

Bob nodded. "I bet they are already. The elections are only a year away. The President won't let the Democrats make a campaign issue out of this."

They reached the cashier, and Joe pulled a dollar bill out of his pocket. He held it close to his chest with both hands and glanced down at the serial number.

"Shoot," he said, glancing at Bob.

"Seven," Bob replied without hesitation.

Joe scanned the serial number on the bill. The third digit was a seven. He looked at Bob, then back at the bill. "Damn! You win again. How'd you know I was holding a seven?"

Bob smiled.

"My luck will change next week," Joe said with little conviction, as he pulled some bills out of his wallet to pay for their lunches.

"That's what you've been saying for the past year. I tell you, I've got a system."

"Yeah, you cheat," Joe said. "I just haven't figured out how. But I will."

"Who me?" Bob laughed. He picked up his tray and went to find an empty table, while Joe paid for the food. The cafeteria was crowded, but he found a table in the back and sat down to wait for Joe. Barring an emergency, the two men ate lunch together every Monday. By unspoken consent, they both zealously guarded that hour in the week, since it ensured them some time together in two otherwise impossibly busy schedules. Besides being Bob's boss, Joe was his closest friend. They found in each other an intellect equal to their own.

Malcolm was acknowledged as one of the world's experts in molecular biology. But his knowledge was not limited to that field. He was the only person Bob had ever met who seemed to always know more than himself about everything. He was a constant source of information and ideas.

"I see you've lost your appetite," Joe said as he sat down.

Bob poked at a mound of mashed potatoes with his fork. "Ahh. I'm too upset to eat this crap."

"If you ever do feel like eating this crap, that's when I'll start worrying about you," Joe said, his mouth full. "That episode this morning got you that upset?"

"No, it's not that."

"Washington, then?"

"That son-of-a-bitch Wright. I can't believe they're going to set up a god-damned Senate subcommittee to investigate this thing. It should have gone straight to the FDA."

Joe stuffed some moist lettuce into his mouth. "I don't think the FDA would have approved this in any case without a long debate."

"Wright had the gall to call me this morning to tell me that he's heard my statements to the press and he wants me to stop denying that this discovery is going to be the miracle cure for cancer."

Joe put down his fork. "Look Bob, I've known Wright for years. He's always been a son-of-a-bitch, which is probably why he became dean. But he also happens to be brilliant."

"I know that."

"In this case," Joe continued, as he lifted a forkful of meatloaf, "the dean is right about the need for publicity that will get you the funding you need to do the research you want to do. You're interested in genetic diseases, but the money's not in rare genetic diseases right now. The money's in cancer. If you want funding, you have to submit grants on cancer therapy."

Bob stared at his plate. "This is not a therapy for cancer," he said emphatically. "It has nothing to do with cancer. To claim otherwise is a lie, and I'm not going to lie, even to get research funds."

Joe downed the last bite of his meatloaf and followed it with a gulp of water. "Bob, you're onto something big here, something really big. Don't blow everything you've worked so hard for."

Bob looked at him silently.

"There are two things you have to consider," Joe continued. "The first is funding. The second is politics. Let's start with funding. So what if your work is not directly applicable to cancer therapy today? Someday it certainly could be. You know as well as anyone else that cancers have a genetic basis. If one could discover genes that induce cancers, it might be possible to use your technique to remove them. So write that into your grant and use the money to study both genetic diseases and cancer."

Bob had hoped that by limiting the scope of the therapy to genetic diseases he would avoid all the publicity that would delay approval. He realized now that he had badly miscalculated. "You're talking about things that will take twenty years, Joe. I'm talking about patients who are dying today."

"So what if it will take twenty years, or even fifty years?" Joe insisted as he took a bite out of his brownie. "That doesn't invalidate the research.   Now the second issue you raise is political.   You want the government to approve your therapy? Right now it's impossible to overpower the religious right's position on genetic diseases.   On the other hand, the country is becoming panicky about the rate of malignancies.   I'm not asking you to lie, but find a reason why your technique might have applicability for cancer and I guarantee you you'll win your battle for approval."

"It's going to take forever now," Bob protested.

"Bob, I know you're impatient, but all new drugs have to be approved.   It takes time, you know that."

Bob shoved his uneaten plate away in disgust and looked up. "I realize that, Joe.   I'm not an idiot."

"So?   What's got your balls in an uproar?"

"What's bothering me is that these religious moralists think they have the God-given right to stick their organs into every orifice they can find, whether they know anything about it or not. They're not scientists.   They don't understand the technology. They should stick to protesting over women in the ministry."

"It's true that they're not scientists, but they are voicing legitimate concerns that a lot of people share."

"Such as?"

"People are frightened by what they don't understand, and that means any change.   They feel more and more vulnerable because of the pace of technological advancement.   The average person can't keep up with it.   People like stability, and there's precious little of it around anymore.   Now you're about to take away what they thought could never change, the human body. Can you imagine how terrified that makes them?"

"Joe, I'm just interested in relieving some suffering and helping people.   That's all.   I like the human race the way it is.   If it's going to evolve, let it do so on its own, at its own pace.   I'm not interested in trying to play God."

"But theoretically your technique could be used by some nut to create all sorts of biologic mutants.   What if people start inserting the genes for blonde hair and blue eyes? Or what if the religious right passes a law that everyone should be reconstructed in their image?"

"Joe, if you swallow a bottle of aspirins they'll kill you, but a lot of people still think they're the best damn thing for a headache."

"I get the point," Joe replied. "And I agree with you. All I'm saying is that your invention scares people who don't understand it and who fear that it will be an evolutionary short cut to who knows where. People are expressing their concerns and Congress has the responsibility to address them."

Bob looked at Joe, his eyes blazing with fury. "Does Congress have the right to fart around on Capital Hill, discussing the evils of science over a three-martini lunch, while people who are dying could be saved?"

Joe put down the uneaten part of his brownie.

"It's Janie, isn't it?" he said. "I take it the gamma globulin transfusion didn't help."

"No," Bob said, his voice suddenly barely audible. "I've tried everything. She's getting very weak. She'll be dead in four weeks--if she's lucky.."

Joe watched Bob closely. "You want to blow off the FDA." It was a statement, not a question.

Bob looked up. He had an expression on his face Joe had seen only once, five years ago.

"I stood by and watched Diane die," Bob said. "There was nothing I could do for her. I won't let it happen to Janie. Not when I can help her."

"How sure are you that it's going to work on a human being? That's an awesome responsibility to place on yourself."

"All I know for sure is that she'll die without it."

"Do you think she's strong enough to handle the treatment?"

"I don't know. I'm using the T-six virus because it has a big enough capsule to carry both the glucosidase gene and the restriction enzyme.   But it's virulent as hell, and she might not survive the infection. That's why I can't wait much longer."

Joe shoved the last bit of brownie into his mouth and rubbed his fingers, dropping a few crumbs onto the tray. "When will the virus be ready?"

"It can be ready in a week."

"And if the FDA hasn't given the go ahead by then?"

Bob knew Joe would disapprove of his decision. He also knew that he would not try to stop him, even though it could conceivably cost him the division chairmanship.

"I know that you're responsible for what happens in your division.   That's why whatever I do, I do on my own, with nobody's knowledge, so no one else gets hurt."

The two friends stared at each other in silence.

"I won't let her die, Joe," Bob whispered. "I couldn't save Diane, but I *will* save her sister."

15

It was a sunny, breezy morning in Washington and warm for November. Senator Herman R. Delany stood in front of the Jefferson Memorial, gazing out across the Tidal Basin. His thick, white hair blew across his high forehead. Each day, as his transformation progressed towards completion, he felt more distant from his old self. He had been a sentimental fool, merciful, self-reflective and weak. Now he felt a growing, exhilarating confidence that Sartan was about to assert its rightful place in human affairs.

He turned to the shorter, heavy-set man standing beside him. "When will Dr. Newman complete his transformation?"

"The attack on Newman failed," his companion replied, "and we've lost our agent watching him and his young sister-in-law. But his secretary was injected successfully. If she survives, we'll be able to keep close tabs on Newman while we make another attempt."

Delany stared at the tiny ripples disturbing the tranquil, blue water of the river. "This complication troubles me."

"That's the remnants of your old self speaking to you. Don't worry, we'll know the moment he attempts his therapy on the girl. We won't allow it, of course."

Delany thought for a moment. "Yes, I sense that. He'll treat the girl. But he doesn't plan to apply his vaccine to the cancer epidemic. I don't see a threat."

"We're waging a war," the shorter man insisted. "A small threat will be dealt with before it becomes a big threat. There's already been talk about using his gene vaccine to cure cancer."

Delany felt a growing, disquieting anxiety. Something wasn't right. . . something. . . He reached back into his memories to an earlier time, a time before Sartan had made its presence felt.

"There's a risk to overplaying our hand. Newman himself has insisted that his technique has no applicability to cancer."

"If only he knew how wrong he was," his companion hissed.

Delany looked out across the horizon. He could see Georgetown on the other side of the river. Tiny human figures moved across the river front, darting in and out of the restaurants and coffee houses. Unlike his companion, who was fully-transformed, Delany still understood people like Newman. Give him a reason to be suspicious and he might discover the truth.

"Why do you insist on helping him realize his error? He's interested in Pompe's disease. Let him perform his gene therapy. Don't distract him from that and he'll be little threat."

"Sartan doesn't leave even a small threat unanswered, not after we've been so patient for so long. It's our time now, time for action. He'll be injected in the next forty-eight hours. If he continues to raise difficulties, he'll be eliminated. It won't be difficult."

"It may be more difficult than you think," Delany countered. "You've failed once already."

"We failed in transforming him," the heavy-set man replied. "You know the odds against a successful transformation. Killing him will be easy."

Delany shut his eyes. The fool. Everything was at stake now.

16

Bob opened the incubator door and removed the flask of monkey cells in which the virus for Janie's vaccine was growing. He slid it under the microscope and smiled upon seeing the dark blotches in the cell cytoplasm representing thousands of individual viral particles.

The phone rang. "Bob, it's Debbie. I just got the lab analysis of the contents of that syringe."

He had forgotten about that. "Let's hear it."

"Vinyl chloride, fifty milligrams per ml, and midazolam, two hundred milligrams per ml."

Bob furrowed his brow. "That dose of midazolam would not only have knocked me unconscious, but I wouldn't have remembered a god-damned thing. It's the most powerful amnesiac in clinical use."

"Sure. We use it for sedation procedures. But what's vinyl chloride?"

"It's an industrial solvent, one of the most, if not *the* most, carcinogenic agent known to man." He wondered where the hell the old lady would have gotten her hands on vinyl chloride, and why did she want to inject him with it. "What about the old lady?"

"Far as I know, she's still in the ICU," Debbie responded.

"Listen, Deb, thanks for the info."

He hung up the phone and went back to work, isolating a sample of DNA from the cells in order to determine the concentration of virus. The procedure was cookbook, and as he washed the DNA in preparation for digestion, his thoughts returned to the old lady and the syringe of vinyl chloride. He was not sure how long it would take to develop a malignancy following such an injection. Probably years. If you were looking an efficient way to kill somebody, this would not be it.

By eight in the evening, the DNA was washed, digested, and running through a polyacrylamide gel to separate out the various strands by size. He had an hour to wait now. He could not get the old lady and the syringe of vinyl chloride out of his mind. He wondered if there was any relationship with the epidemic of cancers. He picked up the phone and dialed Joe's home number.

"Bob, where are you? I just tried you at home."

"In the lab."

"Figured. I should have tried that first."

"Listen Joe, I've been meaning to ask you, how'd your meeting go yesterday with the division chiefs?"

"That's what I was calling to talk to you about, Bob. Do we have ESP, or have we just been spending too much time together? The figures are alarming."

Joe generally did not get alarmed about anything. "What do you mean, 'alarming'? How alarming are they?"

"Ten percent of the population of Chicago is likely harboring a malignancy. And that's probably an underestimate."

Bob's face paled. "Christ! That's one out of every ten people!"

"I see you can still do arithmetic."

"What the hell's being done about it, Joe?"

"The Surgeon General is organizing a meeting in Washington of key scientists. I've been volunteered by our friendly dean. There's going to be an announcement from Washington tomorrow mandating cancer screening for every person in the country, starting next week."

Bob rolled his eyes. "Cancer screening? Are you fucking kidding me? That's a government response if I ever heard one. They should be going after the etiology."

"They are, but they haven't come up with anything yet."

Bob ran his fingers through his hair. Any angle was probably worth pursuing at this point. "Joe, do you know any place in town that produces vinyl chloride?"

"Vinyl chloride?"

"I know it's a strange question, but I figured if anybody would know, you would."

"There was a place on Diversey, on the south side, about ten years ago. I think it was called Alterman, or something like that. I don't remember the street address. Why?"

"Remember that old lady who attacked me with the syringe?"

"Yeah."

"I got the lab analysis today."

"Vinyl chloride?"

"And a whopping dose of midazolam. I've been sitting here wondering whether there's any relationship with this cancer epidemic."

"The government is testing the levels of carcinogens in the air and water," Joe replied. "If vinyl chloride is the culprit, it will be easy to detect. But you don't think the epidemic is being caused by a bunch of old ladies running around injecting people with vinyl chloride, do you?"

No, he didn't. And yet, he sensed that somehow the two were connected. "Listen, I'm just saying there may be some relationship, that's all. It's a very unusual substance to have in a syringe. It certainly didn't come from the hospital."

"Well, if you find out anything, let me know. When are you flying to Washington?"

Bob had been asked to testify at the Senate subcommittee hearings on the gene vaccine. "I'm catching a Monday evening flight. I'm scheduled to testify on Tuesday morning.

"Fine.   Let's sit down before then and thrash this out. Maybe, between the two of us, we'll come up with something."

"Sure. Say hello to Nina. I'll see you tomorrow."

"Goodnight."

Bob hung up the phone and returned to the gel. It was almost dawn when he finally locked his laboratory door. The virus was growing right on schedule. One more week and everything would be ready. One more week.

* * *

Two street lamps threw a dim light over the asphalt surface of the parking lot by Jackson Hall. The lot was deserted, except for a few scattered cars belonging to the nurses and residents on the night shift. Bob approached his Honda Accord and reached into his pocket for his keys. He heard footsteps behind him and he turned to see a tall, thin figure, wearing a dark overcoat, silhouetted between himself and the street lamp. As he approached Bob, the features of his face became evident. His eyes were recessed into his skull and the skin was taut against his protruding cheek bones.

"Doctor Newman," he said in a raspy voice.

"Can I help you?" Bob asked.

"You are Doctor Newman."

"Yes, I am. Who are you?"

"Sartan!" the man yelled and lunged at him.

The blow struck Bob on the left temple and might have killed him, had he not partially deflected it with his forearm. He fell to the ground, dazed. A body landed on top of him and a large, powerful hand gripped his throat. He struggled to free himself, but he could not loosen the fingers squeezing down on his trachea.

A syringe appeared in the stranger's other hand, its needle pointed at his face. Bob grabbed at the forearm holding the syringe, managing to keep the point of the needle from piercing the skin of his neck. The grip on his throat tightened. He began to feel lightheaded, as the oxygen concentration in his bloodstream dropped precipitously.

Focusing his strength, he rolled his body to the right, slamming the stranger's head into the side of his car. The grip on his throat loosened for a moment, but it was enough for Bob to slide his knee up between the stranger's body and his own. With a desperate effort, he straightened his knee against the stranger's solar plexus until the man's fingers slipped off his neck. Still grasping the arm holding the syringe, he rammed it into the side of the car. The needle snapped off and the syringe rolled under the vehicle. He let go of the man's forearm and, with both hands clasped together, struck a blow into the stranger's face. He felt bone give way. The stranger rolled off of him, then got up and ran off into the darkness.

Bob lay on his side for ten minutes, semiconscious and spitting blood. When his strength returned, he raised himself to a sitting position. He sat for a while with his head on his knees, then saw the syringe resting against one of the rear tires. He reached for it and struggled to his feet. He limped to one of the lamps and held the syringe up to the light. It was filled with an orange-colored fluid. He was sure it was vinyl chloride, but he decided to drop it off at the lab for analysis anyway.

It was nearly six a.m. when he finally got into his car and drove off. This had been one hell of a week. He had discovered a cure for genetic diseases. The next thing he knew, two crazed people had tried to inject him with a carcinogen. Or maybe kill him. The first time he had been willing to write it off as the ravings of a delirious woman. But now it was clear that he was a target. But whose? His intuition told him that whoever was after him wanted to prevent his gene vaccine from being put to use. He had been lucky tonight and would have to be on guard from now on.

He reached his home and pulled into the driveway. It was a modern two-story home that he and Diane had bought in a renovated section of Irving Park, about a twenty minute drive from the University. Every nook and cranny, every bit of wall, held Diane's sculptures and paintings. Each one reminded him of a different moment with her. His favorite sculpture, a two foot tall figure of a young girl holding a bouquet of flowers, stood on the table by the entrance. Diane had presented it to him, wrapped in a ribbon, on their first wedding anniversary. The sweet, innocent expression on the little girl's face never failed to move him. He touched one of the iris petals gently, caressed its long stem, then let his hand drop.

He threw his coat on the couch, noticed that it was ripped at the right shoulder, and headed for the kitchen, where he washed his blood-stained face. The left side of his jaw and head were beginning to throb. He removed the ice cube tray from the freezer, dumped its contents onto a hand towel.

He left the kitchen, towel pressed against his head, and walked across the hall to his study. He pulled out Webster's dictionary. "Now let's get to the bottom of this Sartan business," he muttered.

He tried all the spellings he could think of, but the word was not in the book. Figured. He flipped to the front cover and found the pronunciation definitions. A with two dots over it was the sound he had heard, the long 'ah' sound. The symbol was called 'umlaut'.

He turned on the computer at his desk and logged onto the internet. He entered the Google search engine web page and typed, SARTAN. No dice. He was similarly unsuccessful searching for proper names. Maybe it really had been the rambling of a delirious woman. But she had pronounced it so clearly, so purposefully, almost the way someone speaks when

learning a new language. That gave him a thought. He entered
the Library of Congress database and tried a combination search,
SARTAN and LANGUAGE.

After a moment, lines of text began appearing on the screen.
SEARCH RESULT FOR 'SARTAN' AND
'LANGUAGES'.

There was another pause. Then,
'SARTAN'--PRONOUNCED SA¨R-TA¨N, ACCENT
SECOND SYLLABLE.

ANCIENT HEBREW WORD. DEFINITION, CRAB.

HEBREW SPELLING: SAMECH REYSH TAF NUN.

FOURTH SIGN OF THE ZODIAC.

MODERN DEFINITION, CRAB, CANCER.

RELEVANT DATA-- EPIDEMIOLOGY OF CANCER,
HISTORY OF CANCER,

PATHOGENESIS OF CANCER, PREVENTION AND
TREATMENT OF CANCER,

ADRENAL CARCINOMA, BLADDER CANCER, LUNG
CANCER, PANCREATIC

CANCER RENAL CANC

Bob pressed a key to terminate the program. Okay, Sartan
meant cancer. The old lady had cancer, the country was in an
epidemic of cancer, and the syringe had been filled with a
carcinogen. What the fuck was going on?

He returned to the kitchen, dropped the towel of ice in the
sink, made himself a vodka tonic, and carried it upstairs to the
bedroom. Two people, yelling an ancient Hebrew word for
cancer had tried to inject him with vinyl chloride. But why, and
how did it fit with the cancer epidemic and his gene vaccine? His
head still throbbed and he was too exhausted to make further
sense of it. He undressed, letting his clothes fall to the floor, and
slid under the bed covers. He reached out to the night stand,
turned off the telephone's ringer, and shut his eyes. But sleep
would not come.

He clicked the TV remote control and sipped on his drink in the darkness while he stared at the screen. A nature show was on. A brown mouse was sitting beside a rock and a man was speaking.

". . . In contrast, certain kinds of parasites do not live in a symbiotic relationship with their host, but instead feed on the host continuously, until they literally destroy it. This is a wild field mouse that has recently been infected by the larva of the Anopheles Beetle. The larva localizes in the muscle of the mouse and grows there. Here is the same mouse six weeks later."

The scene changed and Bob's eyes narrowed. The mouse was lying on the ground, legs jerking. Most of the little body was devoid of fur and there were large, red, draining ulcers, crawling with white worms.

"These parasites are feeding on the body of their host. This mouse will soon be dead, but by that time, the larvae will have matured into adult beetles and will no longer need their host for survival."

The scene shifted again to show the adult beetles feeding on the remains of the dead mouse. They were big, black and ugly.

"The adult form will devour the host, even though it is already dead, and will then abandon the skeleton and scourge the ground for other dead and decaying matter."

Bob shut off the TV in disgust. He downed the rest of his drink, lay back on his pillow, and closed his eyes. He did finally fall into a restless slumber, but his sleep was disturbed by shifting nightmares. . . of giant black beetles devouring human flesh while old gray ladies stood by salivating in anticipation. . . of viruses swimming in large, cancerous growths. . . of Ellen Rhodes wearing horns and cackling hysterically. . .

17

Lois lay her aching head down on the pillow. The aspirins were not helping at all. She closed her eyes and tried to concentrate on something else besides the pounding in her head and the strange thoughts and voices dancing through her mind. Again she felt the unexplained restlessness, the prickle of fear nibbling at her consciousness.

She jerked herself into a sitting position, her eyes darting frightfully around the empty bedroom. A twitch appeared in the left side of her neck, growing in intensity until her entire head was beating rhythmically. She pounded her fists against her feverish skull. "GET OUT OF MY HEAD!" she shrieked, her eyes bulging from their sockets.

The twitch abated and she struggled to control her rapid breaths. She rubbed her right elbow and arm. The bruise had not yet completely faded. Funny, she did not remember bumping herself. In fact her mind had been playing tricks on her all week. She touched her neck where she had felt the lump a few days ago. It was definitely larger.

The feeling of dread that had been plaguing her returned. She peered anxiously around the room, looking for movement in the dark shadows. There was no one there but herself. And yet, she sensed its horrid presence.

A long, anguished cry escaped from her lips and she began to sob. She felt suddenly warm, and pushed the bed covers off her body so that she was covered from the thighs up only by a thin, yellow night gown. An ominous sense of trepidation overcame her. She pressed her hands against her temples. Suddenly, she froze, her eyes wide with terror, as a deeply-buried, terrifying memory invaded her consciousness. Beads of perspiration appeared on her forehead and her body began to shake violently.

"GET OUT OF HERE!" she shrieked, shielding her face with her hands. Her heart pounded in her chest, pumping a deafening roar of blood through her ears. She opened her eyes and saw her hands in front of her face. In the darkness, she could just make out her fingers. As she stared at them they seemed to change shape. She saw ten wriggling tendrils in front of her eyes. The vision disappeared, but for an awful moment everything was clear in her mind.

"Oh my God!" she whispered, her eyes wide with terror. "Oh my GOD!"

Her crazed eyes darted frantically around the room, seeking help. She had to get out of there! She had to warn Bob! In a panic, she tried to rise from the bed, but her limbs had become numb to her commands. With a desperate effort, she managed to slide her torso to the edge of the bed. She tried to throw her legs to the floor, but they became entangled in the bed sheets and she fell with a thud onto the hardwood floor.

There was no time left! She was rapidly losing control of her body. She tried to stand, but her legs would not support her. She forced herself up on all fours and crawled to the nightstand. Her hands thrashed around on the table top until the telephone and the address book crashed to the floor. She managed to grab the receiver. Frantically, she flipped through her address book for Bob's home number. Her fingers were numb and she had difficulty turning the pages. She tore them out in her frenzy. There it was! Robert Newman. She dialed the number.

"Pick up the phone!. . ." The phone rang ten times before she hung it up.

She put her hands to her head. "Aaaagh . . ." It was coming. It was too late! She grabbed the receiver again. He must be in the lab. What the hell was the number? She had dialed it a thousand times. Somehow, it came to her. Two two eight seven six four six. She dialed three times before her fingers hit the correct sequence of buttons. The phone rang.

"Pick it up! Pick it up, quick!"

There was no answer. She held the phone in her hand and looked frantically around the room. There was no escape. The moment had arrived.

"Oh God. . . NO!" She stared with utter horror across the dark room. She drew back until she was curled up against the foot of the bed and could not withdraw any further.

"NO! NO! NO! Somebody help me!"

She held her hands to her head and shrieked. Then, she lost control of her muscles and her body slid back from the bed onto the floor. She lay there on her back, her night gown pulled up around her waist. Her sweaty buttocks were pressed against the cold floor and she could no longer move.

Lois was a strong-willed woman, and she struggled for control of her mind. Her breathing was rapid and uncontrolled, her body tense, her back arched. Her bulging eyes appeared ready to pop out of their sockets. She shook her head and silently scream the word 'NO'. But she was helpless from preventing her memories from being violently wrenched from her.

Finally, like a gently rolling wave, her mind became clouded with a fog and the terror faded. She no longer had to resist. She no longer could resist. Her muscles relaxed, and the heat from her sweat-soaked body seeped into the cold floor under her. The memories drained out of her mind as if a stopper had been pulled. And at the final moment, she saw it clearly, the unbelievable horror whose existence she had never imagined, and had always known.

18

Ellen peeked her head into room 213. For a moment, she thought the room was empty and felt a surge of disappointment. Then she saw him, sitting at the computer station in the back of the room. He apparently hadn't heard the door open. She wondered how his instant rise to fame had affected him. In the past week, Robert Newman had become a household name, and his 'gene vaccine', as it had been labeled by some anonymous person, had become the main topic of debate around the civilized world. Everyone had an opinion which they are quick to share with friends, relatives and strangers. The gene vaccine would destroy humanity. The gene vaccine was the salvation of mankind. Whatever one's point of view, there was an unconscious recognition, a feeling under the skin, that something in the nature of human existence had changed forever. The human race, after millennia of remaking the world to suit itself, had finally developed the capacity to remake itself to suit the world. And the world, along with its maker, would never again be the same.

"Excuse me. I hope I'm not interrupting."

Bob turned his head towards Ellen and immediately felt his heart rate rise. She wore a soft, low-cut, pearl-white sweater, and a laced bra peeked out along the cleavage of her breasts. He had been wonderfully aware of her from the first day she had appeared in the Division. He drummed his fingers on the desk to hide his feelings.

"Pretty sweater."

She smiled. "Thank you. Have you ever worn cashmere?"

"No."

She rubbed her arms. "I love the way it feels. You ought to buy yourself one." She noticed the gash on his forehead. "What happened to you?"

"It's nothing."

"I really think you ought to have that looked at," she said, approaching him. "You could use a few stitches."

She reached out to touch his forehead.

She smelled good and he was wonderfully aware of her. He pulled his head away. "Ms. Rhodes, I'm really very busy. Is there something in particular you want?"

She withdrew her hand, awkwardly. "Yes. I want to extend my genetics rotation for another month. I'd like to work with you on your gene vaccine."

"I don't take students."

"Really. Isn't teaching part of every faculty member's obligation?"

"Yes, you are correct. But it's up to each individual faculty to decide when they can accommodate a student. I'm too busy."

"You'll find that I'm a very independent person. I don't need to have my hand held every moment."

"I really don't think that you would enjoy it."

"Why not?"

"I work twenty hours a day. You could forget about going home for Christmas vacation."

Ellen puckered her lips. "My mother overdosed on a bottle of sleeping pills two years ago. She left no note, she just checked out. My father died of a heart attack a month later. I don't think he could tie his shoes without her. So, I've got nowhere to go for Christmas. It won't be a problem."

When Bob responded, his voice had lost its acid edge. "I'm sorry to hear about your loss. I didn't know."

"No sympathy required. Do I get the rotation?"

Bob shook his head. "I'm sorry, maybe next semester. My life is just too complicated right now."

"I think that life is always too complicated, and if you wait for the right moment, it may never come."

He opened his mouth as if to answer, then tightened his jaw.

"Do you want to tell me about it?" she asked. "I'm a good listener."

"I don't want to confuse you with all the complicated things I am, Ms. Rhodes. I'm asking you. Leave me alone. I have work to do."

He turned back to his computer monitor, conversation over. Ellen stood there, stunned by the hostility in his voice, and too insulted to respond. She had never been dismissed so callously by anyone. The hell with the bastard.

19

The sun poked through a gray sky onto a snow-covered street. It was seven in the morning and scattered flurries dropped onto the windshield. Bob drove south down Diversey street in an area of Chicago he had never been before, past empty lots and boarded-up buildings. He drove slowly, not wanting to miss the warehouse. He had been unable to find a distributor for vinyl chloride in any of his chemical supply catalogues and Joe's memory of a place called Alterman was the only lead he had. From the looks of this neighborhood, it seemed unlikely that the place still existed.

A large rat darted in front of the car and Bob hit the brakes. The car swerved on the snow. A moment later, he regained control and saw the creature dash across the street and disappear behind a pile of cardboard boxes. He decided to drive another two blocks before giving up.

A warehouse appeared on the right which looked to be in business. At least the windows were not broken. The sign over the building read, ALTMANN CHEMICALS. Close enough. Bob pulled up the snow-covered driveway, which was peppered with potholes, stepped out of his car, and approached the front entrance. It was locked. He peered through a dirty window pane, but could not see a thing. He walked around to the back and saw two trucks parked in front of a loading dock.

He stepped up onto the dock and looked around. A few large, metal barrels and some cardboard boxes were piled under a corrugated roof. The place had the appearance of being used in the recent past. He tried the rear door, but it was also locked. He tried the window, which was jammed shut.

He picked up a piece of discarded pipe, glanced in both directions, and rammed it through the window. The glass shattered. He reached his hand between the jagged shards and opened the door. The room was dark. There were half a dozen large, steel barrels inside, painted black and unmarked. Each was sealed with a heavy, metal lid. He went up to one, tapped on it, and heard a dull thud which told him it was full.

A little further in the room he found an old, wooden desk scattered with papers. A mug of half-finished coffee rested on top of a stack of pink sheets. He lifted the mug and began to shuffle through the papers, trying to make out the writing in the dim light. About a third of the way through the stack he found a sheet with the letters *VC* in the upper right hand corner. In the box marked QUANTITY was written *200 ml*, under PURCHASER the letter *B* followed by *CUMC*. The date was *11/18*, last Friday.

CUMC was the acronym for the Chicago University Medical Center. Someone from the hospital had purchased vinyl chloride last Friday. Who was B? He returned to the barrels and began prying open the lid of one of them, using the piece of pipe still in his hand.

"Hey asshole!"

Bob swung around. A big, burly man stood facing him, a pistol in his hand pointed at Bob's chest. He wore jeans, a flannel shirt, and a worn, leather jacket. The shirt hung out from his pants. A two day stubble covered his face.

"Drop the pipe, asshole!"

Bob opened his hand and the pipe clattered to the floor.

"Very good. I see you've got half a brain. Now, you wanna tell me what the fuck you're doing here?"

"The door was locked," Bob said, taking a step forward. "I was trying to find out if anyone was here."

"One more step and I'll blow your fuckin head off."

Bob stopped in his tracks.

"You're trespassing on private property," the man growled. "You want some of that stuff in the barrel? Here." He threw a crowbar in Bob's direction. It came to rest at his feet.

"Go ahead, open it."

Bob hesitated. The man cocked his pistol. "I said, open it!"

Bob reached down and grabbed the crowbar. He placed the tip under the rim of the barrel lid and yanked. The lid popped off and clattered onto the floor. Bob was overwhelmed by a noxious odor which he recognized immediately. Hydrochloric acid.

"Looking for some of that stuff? Go ahead, put your hand in there and take what you want."

Bob hesitated. "I *said*, put your hand in the barrel." He pointed the gun at Bob's head.

Bob surveyed the room with his peripheral vision. There was only one exit, and the man was blocking it. He was going to have to bluff his way out of here. "That's hydrochloric acid," he said as calmly as he could.

The big man's eyes narrowed. "How'd you know that?"

"Ten-normal," Bob added. "If I touch that it'll burn right through me." He was guessing at the concentration, but he knew of only two strengths sold commercially, one and ten-normal, and the strength of the odor suggested ten-normal.

The man spoke again, less threateningly. "Right. Who the hell are you?"

Bob took a wild chance. "I'm here for the vinyl chloride."

"You think I'm a fuckin idiot? It's illegal to buy or sell vinyl chloride in the state of Illinois."

He was sure now that this place was the source of the vinyl chloride which had found its way into the hospital. He guessed again. "I'm here for the university shipment."

The man's eyes widened. "The professor sent you?"

Bob relaxed slightly and nodded.

The man was still suspicious. "The professor always comes himself, and he's not due till next Thursday."

"He needs some more urgently. In fact, he wants to purchase a batch weekly."

"That'll cost."

"He's prepared to pay."

The man smiled. Bob noticed two missing teeth. The others were yellow and tobacco-stained. "Tell the professor I can increase production even more, if he wants." He slipped the barrel of the gun into the waist of his jeans. "Come on, I've got the stuff out back." He led Bob into another room and lifted a plastic canister, about the size of a milk carton, off the back shelf. Inside the canister was an orange-colored liquid.

"I'll help you load it."

They walked to the front of the building. Bob opened the car's trunk and the man placed the canister inside.

"Thanks," Bob said and turned to go.

"Hey, wait a minute. What about my payment?"

Bob had no idea what the payment was. "The professor will pay you on his next visit."

The man shook his head. "I always get payment at pickup."

"You want to screw up a sweet deal? You know how temperamental the professor can be. He handles all payments personally."

The man hesitated. "Okay, but tell him I expect payment on Thursday."

Bob nodded, got into his car, backed out of the driveway, and drove off. He took a deep breath to calm himself. He had been lucky to get out of there alive. Butt the mystery was only deepening. Who was the professor and what was he doing with the vinyl chloride?

* * *

The telephone rang in Dr. Alex Becker's office.

"Hello, professor."

Becker hesitated, then spoke in a harsh whisper, "I told you never to call me!"

"Sorry. I wanted to tell you I'm not going to be able to get the extra shipment ready by Thursday."

"I don't want an extra shipment!" Becker barked.

"What? A guy came by this morning, said he works for you and you wanted to double the purchase."

Becker stood up from his desk chair. His hands tightened into fists. "What *guy*?"

"Didn't you send anyone?"

"No! Did you get his name?"

"I knew there was something fishy about that asshole."

"His name. Did you get his name?" Becker repeated.

"No. But I got his license plate number. He didn't pay, and like I told you, I got suspicious."

Becker grabbed a pencil. "Give me the number!"

"Sure, it's NNL 249. Illinois plates."

The pencil tip broke on the pad of paper. "Shit! Hold on a second!" He grabbed a pen. "Okay give me the number again."

He scribbled it down. "Are you sure he said he was from the university?"

"Positive. I take it you don't want any increase in purchases?"

"No! The usual shipment! Goodbye." He slammed down the phone. His palm was sweaty and he was breathing rapidly. He stared down at the pad in front of him. NNL 249. Whoever owned that car was a dead man, only he didn't know it. . . yet.

20

Bruce Nevins leaned forward expectantly, watching Thomas Green's scrawny neck stretch in the direction of the mahogany platform in front of him.

"Uh, could you repeat the question, Senator?"

Bruce smirked and settled back into his chair. How predictable. Green, who represented the most holier-than-thou segment of the conservative right, had been squirming around the subcommittee's questions for the past twenty minutes. Bruce was pleased with the nickname he had given Green a moment ago-- Escargot. It suited him perfectly. He was slimy, hard to swallow, smelled bad, and left a bitter taste in the mouth. Escargot because of his pompousness. Otherwise he was just a snail.

"Is something wrong with this microphone?" Les Brown bellowed. He leaned forward on his meaty elbows, his large figure casting an imposing presence from behind the massive mahogany desk where the members of the Senate subcommittee sat. There were seven of them, five men and two women. Senator Delany sat in the center, his straight frame placing him a head taller than anyone on either side.

Brown's burly face glared down at Green. There was a snicker in the audience. "I've been told, Mr. Green, that when I talk on the Senate floor, I can be heard in Georgetown."

The audience roared, and Bruce could not suppress a grin. Actually, Senator Brown was known for being heard on the Senate floor when he was drinking in Georgetown.

Bruce loosened his tie enough to allow some air to reach down around his shirt collar onto his sweating neck. The ventilation system was losing its struggle to handle the heat from the mass of bodies packed into the Senate committee chambers in what was fast becoming the most sensational hearings in recent memory. Bruce felt certain that the ventilation system would regain control of the room in a few days, as the public's attention inevitably turned to a new, preferably scandalous, story.

"I'll repeat the question for you, then. You've just stated that Doctor Newman's invention poses a threat to the safety of American citizens. Yet, we heard testimony this morning that this same invention would lead to cures for all sorts of genetic diseases. The question is, which one is it, a cure or a menace? How does curing sickle cell anemia pose a threat to the citizens of this country?"

Green slid his dark-rimmed glasses back up his beak of a nose. "There is nothing wrong with curing sickle cell anemia or other genetic diseases. But cutting genes out of chromosomes is tampering with something that should be left in the Lord's hands."

Bruce groaned. Why did these people always have to inject God into their arguments?

"And you feel that passing on a different set of genes than an individual is born with, even if they are healthier ones, is wrong?"

"The gene causing sickle cell anemia also protects against malaria, which is endemic in Africa," Green responded. "It's presumptuous to think that we humans know the long-term effects of deleting from the human race those genes which we consider today to be defective. God has given us those genes for a purpose which we may not understand at the moment. Who's to say for what purpose a gene was created and when it will be useful? We are not so wise, gentlemen. The gene vaccine threatens the future of the human race. We call on Congress to ban its use until we have a better understanding of the long-term risks."

Delany, who was sitting to Brown's right, cleared his throat. He wore a dark blue suit and the bow tie which had become the symbol of this Washington maverick. He looked uncharacteristically tired and the furrows deepened in his forehead as he took his pipe into his mouth. He never lit it while he was in the Senate chambers, but for those who knew him the action meant that he was losing patience with the discussion. Delany never actually lost his temper. Now in his fifth term at the age of sixty-eight, he dealt graciously with friend and adversary alike. He could be biting in his criticism, but he was always the gentleman.

"Of course, the real question," Delany interrupted, "is whether this would work in humans. What are your thoughts about that, Mr. Green?"

Bruce sat up straight. Delany had just let the squirming worm off the hook.

Green appeared momentarily taken aback, then accepted the opening. "As any reputable scientist will tell you, human beings are much more complicated than rats, and there is an immense gap between what can be done in rodents and what is possible in humans. Besides, how could we stop scientists from performing gene surgery on people for questionable, or even sinister, motives?"

"That's why we have medical regulatory commissions," Les Brown responded. "You and I and the other people in this room are not medical experts and we can't judge the feasibility, or lack thereof, of this technology. We are here to decide on its appropriateness. If we need to enact legislation to limit use of this technology for approved purposes, we can certainly do so."

"Senator, I urge you all to think very carefully before committing a grievous error. I pray that common sense will prevail."

Delany removed the pipe from his mouth. "Gentlemen, we will adjourn for lunch. These hearings will resume at two-o'clock."

The room emptied and Bruce gathered his papers together. He had heard the description of Newman's invention countless times over the past few days and each time he was fascinated anew. Obviously, it required the proper controls, but this could be the start of a new era in human health. Unfortunately, if the hearings continued like this, Newman's invention didn't stand a chance in hell of ever getting out of his laboratory. The press reports suggested that Newman was a charismatic man, but he would have to be extremely persuasive to convince the public after three days of the likes of Green and his gang.

He answered some questions from a reporter and then walked down the hall to Delany's office. He was surprised to see Green in the doorway.

"Bruce, come in," Delany motioned to him. "You know Thomas Green. This is Bruce Nevins, my assistant."

Bruce shook Escargot's hand. It was clammy, as expected. "Pleasure," he said, making no attempt to conceal his displeasure. What the hell was this snail doing here, and why did Delany always have to be so damned gracious?

Green turned towards Delany. "As I was saying, Senator, I'm sure you can appreciate our concerns in this matter. We are mobilizing the citizens of the country to our cause. I don't need to remind you of the considerable influence we exert, both here in Washington, and in the country as a whole. Including, I might add," and he paused for emphasis, "your own state of Arizona."

Bruce had heard enough. "Are you threatening the Senator, sir? Need I remind *you* that you're addressing one of the most respected individuals in this government? You can't coerce him on an issue of principle!"

"Please, Bruce," Delany said. "Let's not get hot tempered. I agree with you, Mr. Green, that this technology poses a significant risk to the public. You have my full support and my guarantee that I will do everything in my power to prevent its use."

Bruce stared at Delany, incredulous. It was Green who recovered first.

"Uh, well Senator, I'm pleased that we see, uh, eye to eye on this one. I think that with your support we have an excellent chance of passing legislation to outlaw this type of research. I'm glad that you see the gravity of the matter. After all, if this Newman were let loose on the population, once he removed some genes, they would be gone forever. There would be no correcting the mistakes."

Bruce saw the Senator's face turn pale at Green's last remark. His illness must be having more of an effect on him than Bruce had realized. He was certainly not himself. The thick white hair was thinning, the strong lines of his face had turned to wrinkles, and the proud shoulders were drooping. Most of all, the fire was gone from the man's eyes. He thought back to the days when he had first started working for Delany. Only three years back, but what a change three years had made on this man. He had been the conscience of Washington, the upholder of decency, morality and principle. But time could dull even the sharpest edge. He was looking at a man he did not know.

"Well," Green finished, "Thank you for your time, Senator." He turned and left, nodding to Bruce on his way out.

Bruce dropped into a leather chair by the desk. "Senator, what's gotten into you?"

"Now Bruce, nothing's gotten into me." Delany lit his pipe and took a long drag.

"Sir, you have nothing in common with that extremist. You don't want to be associated with him or his kind."

Delany gazed out the window for a while, then sat down at his desk. "Bruce, just because you may not agree with their philosophy doesn't mean that you must always be on the opposite side of the fence. This is a worthy cause."

Bruce was incredulous. "You don't really believe that, do you?"

Delany slammed his fist on his desk and shouted, "That man, Newman, must be stopped! He's a menace!"

Bruce jerked from the sudden fury of Delany's response.

"Sir, the technology is already here. We can ensure that it's used properly and with appropriate safeguards. If you try to block Newman's virus, someone else will develop it."

"Not if I can help it," Delany said firmly. "Now I want you to do a background investigation on Newman. I want to know everything about him, professional and personal problems, who he associates with, any information that might be useful."

"You mean useful for blackballing the guy? I didn't think that kind of activity had any place in the office of the distinguished Senator from Arizona."

"Listen, young man," Delany said, his voice rising again, "instead of second guessing your boss, I think you should concern yourself with doing your job. Unless you want to be looking for a new one."

Bruce stared at Delany in disbelief. The Senator had never talked to him in that way.

"Do you understand me?"

Maybe it would be prudent to check out Newman's background. After all, it would be helpful to know what aims Newman had for the vaccine. It was certainly not worth losing his job over.

"Yes, sir," he said. "I'll get on it."

"Good, Bruce. I didn't mean to raise my voice. I am just a little tired."

"I know, sir. You should go home and get some rest. Are you sure you're feeling all right?"

"My stomach's been bothering me again. I'll be fine."

"Maybe you should reconsider surgery, sir. You were all set to have it done last month."

"It's stomach cancer, Bruce," the Senator answered. "Surgery would only buy a few months.   Thanks for your concern, though.   You're a good man."

"Well, good night, then," Bruce said and walked to the door. He stepped into the hall, then glanced back.   Delany was staring at the wall, stiff as a stone statue.   There was no expression at all on his face.   Then his lips began to move, and as the door shut, Bruce heard a deep, rumbling sound and what he thought were the words, "That man can destroy us," coming from the room. Or perhaps it was just the groaning of the door as it creaked on its hinges.

21

Bob stared at the canister of vinyl chloride on the lab counter.   It was outrageous to think that a professor at the university was conspiring to spread cancer around the country. Besides, what would be the point?   Scientific dogma had it that cancers developed years after exposure to a carcinogenic agent. On the other hand, the history of science was littered with discarded dogmas and the experiment would be easy to set up. Still, he hesitated to do anything that would distract him from Janie's vaccine.

He decided to drop the whole thing.   He returned to his desk and began analyzing the latest data from the gel he had run the day before.   Everything was on schedule.   The vaccine would be ready in five days.

He glanced across the room and again saw the canister sitting on the counter.   What the hell, it would only take a few minutes.   He put on latex gloves, opened the canister, and poured a small amount of the orange substance into a glass beaker.   He removed two flasks from the incubator, one containing human cells and the other E. Coli bacteria. He added a few drops of the vinyl chloride to each and returned them to the incubator.

Twelve hours later, Bob removed the flasks and noticed immediately that the human culture was cloudy. He cursed under his breath. Cloudy fluid meant bacterial overgrowth. He took the flasks to the microscope and placed the human cells under the lens. Maybe he would still be able to see something.

What he saw made him catch his breath. "Jesus Christ!" he whispered.   The   cloudiness   was   not   due   to   bacterial contamination. It was the human cells that had overgrown, faster than he had ever imagined was possible! The flask was full of mitotic figures in the process of dividing.   They all had the unmistakable look of malignant cells.   It had only been twelve hours! He grabbed the bacterial flask. The bacteria had not divided at all. In fact, most of them were dead.

He pulled his head away from the microscope, took a deep breath, and exhaled loudly. How could he have transformed normal cells into malignant ones in the space of twelve hours? It was impossible. And yet, he had witnessed it with his own eyes. The human cells were exquisitely susceptible to malignant transformation, as if they were on the verge of becoming cancerous and just needed a mild stimulus. But they had been normal human lymphocytes! He knew now the explanation for the cancer epidemic sweeping the country. Somehow, human, but not bacterial, cells had been primed for malignant transformation. But how? Perhaps the levels of carcinogens in the environment had reached the critical point where any additional stimulus would tip the scales. Or perhaps the vinyl chloride triggered some master gene controlling the malignant process. Suddenly, the old woman's attack did not seem so inexplicable. If he was correct, she would have killed him had the vinyl chloride-contaminated needle punctured his skin!

Forgetting his other work, he took the flask of transformed cells and began purifying out the RNA, the long chains representing the active genes. By isolating the RNA, he would be able to tell which genes had been activated by the vinyl chloride. If the vinyl chloride induced the activation of a single master gene controlling transformation, then it might be possible to remove that gene. Maybe, just maybe, Joe's offhanded remark that his gene vaccine might be used in the cancer epidemic was not so far-fetched.

The first thing he discovered was that the malignant cells were stuffed full of RNA. The quantity was so large that he was forced to divide it into another tube. He poured a large polyacrylamide gradient gel so that he could separate out the different strands of RNA. While he waited for the gel to run, he sat down at his computer and began reviewing the medical literature on carcinogens.

Four hours later, he had not found a single piece of data showing that cells could be transformed so quickly. Itching to see the results of the RNA analysis, he stopped the gel electrophoresis early and transferred the RNA onto a nitrocellulose filter. He would have to be patient. It would be morning before he could attempt to visualize anything.

The door to the lab opened and Ellen entered, carrying a department store box under one arm.

"Hi," she said cheerfully. "I hope I'm not disturbing you. I was on my way home, and I thought I'd stop by. It looks like you're hard at work, as usual."

He was distracted by her presence. "Yes, the work never ends," he muttered.

"It's a beautiful day. You should try to get out."

"I doubt I'll have time."

An awkward silence developed. Ellen knew she was behaving like a fool. He seemed the complete opposite of her and she was scared to death of being snubbed again. But in the past week, she had moved to that helpless sense of infatuation she had never before experienced.

"Here, I brought something for you."

She placed the box on his desk when he made no move to take it. He glanced at it, then at her. She seemed even more enticing than the first time he had met her and he wanted to take her in his arms, but he could allow no distractions from his goal.

"Ms. Rhodes, I can't accept this."

"You make me feel like an old lady. Please call me Ellen."

"All right, Ellen. I can't accept your gift."

"You don't even know what it is. Open it."

He hesitated, then untied the ribbon and removed the cover. He looked into the box, but did not remove its contents.

"It's cashmere," she said.

"I can see that."

"I thought, with winter coming, you'd need something to keep you warm, and you probably don't have time to shop. You're going to love how it feels on you."

He clenched his jaw. "It's very nice. You'll have to take it back."

She looked at him curiously. "I just meant it as a friendly gesture. It seemed to me that you don't have a lot of people you're close to, and I just thought you might want some--"

"Some what?" he blurted out. "Sympathy? I don't want sympathy. I have everything I need in life, thank you!"

He shoved the box away.

"Don't be so touchy. I'm trying to be friendly."

Bob stood up and paced the room. "Look, don't take this personally. I have a mission to accomplish. That's what I've dedicated my life to."

Ellen walked to the back of the lab and braced herself against the counter. "I've heard about your sister-in-law and I find your dedication inspiring. But you can't stop living."

Bob's patience snapped. "What do you know about life? Since you know about my sister-in-law, then it should be clear to you that I have other priorities."

"Why does it mean we can't be friends?"

Bob stepped towards her. "What do you want from me? What happened last week. . . don't read anything into it. I'm not interested in a romance."

"Really . . ."

"Stop it. I'm sure you won't have trouble finding some stud to satisfy you. There must be plenty out there on campus who'd love to accommodate your needs."

Ellen's face reddened. "I've never let a man treat me like this. I don't know what's happened to me since I met you. And I do feel sorry for you, because as far as you're concerned, everyone's the enemy. You're just a cold, bitter, man pitying yourself because you think the world has screwed you."

Bob's hands tightened and for a moment she was afraid he was going to strike her. "Who the hell do you think you are, telling me what I feel? Who the hell do you think you are?"

She stared at him, awed by the sudden hostility flowing from him. Her voice trembled. "I'm just an observer, looking at a man with no emotion left inside him but bitterness and resentment. You're incapable of any other feelings, aren't you?"

He tried to control himself, but the words gushed out.

"If you mean love, I loved my wife and she's dead. I love my sister-in-law and she's on death's door. Does that answer your question?"

She stared defiantly back at him as if about to say something, then changed her mind. She blinked to fight back the tears, but they flowed down her cheeks and she hated herself for letting him see her cry.

"Yes, completely," she replied. She turned and ran from the room.

Bob pawed helplessly around the desk. At last, he slammed both fists onto it as her footsteps faded down the hall.

22

Alex Becker sat in the front seat of a red Ford Taurus station wagon. It had taken him almost an hour to locate the Honda Accord with the license plate number NNL 249, parked towards the back of the lot. He had been waiting for two hours. The parking lot had slowly emptied, but no one had come to claim the car. Becker was in no hurry.

At nine-thirty in the evening, he saw a tall man walk out onto the pavement. Becker could not make out his face in the darkness, but the man's strut was familiar. He waited until the figure passed in front of his car, then turned on his headlights. For a brief moment, as the figure passed through the beam, his features were lit up. He reached the Honda, unlocked the door, and drove off.

Becker smiled. Robert Newman. Mister gene vaccine. He had not suspected him, but he was not at all surprised. Newman would never be satisfied with his own fame and fortune. Now he was getting his grubby hands on Becker's turf. Well, Newman had gotten just a little too greedy for his own good.

Becker knew someone who would be very interested in this information, someone who would pay a handsome fee, indeed. It would be a pleasure to personally perform the autopsy on Newman. He snickered at the thought, then laughed, a long, high-pitched laugh.

* * *

Bob pulled into his driveway and glanced in all directions before getting out of the car. Satisfying himself that there was no one lurking near the house, he hurried up to the door, carrying a brown paper bag. He glanced both ways again, then slipped inside and bolted the door. He opened the bag and pulled out the pistol he had purchased on the way home. He ran his hand over the cold steel, then, in a deliberate motion, pointed it at the door and pulled the trigger. He heard a soft click. He dropped the gun onto the sofa and turned the bag upside down. A dozen bullets bounced onto the cushion. Leaving the deadly objects on the couch, he walked up the stairs to the second level, peeled off his clothes, and stared for a moment at the lean, hard figure in the bathroom mirror.

He turned on the shower and stepped under the spray, letting the pounding, hot water relaxed his muscles. He thought about his encounter with Ellen that afternoon. Was his bitterness so obvious that a stranger could see it? He hated self-pity more than anything. Yet wasn't Ellen right? Wasn't that just what he was doing with his aloofness, pitying himself? He felt himself tensing up again. No one had ever gotten under his skin like that girl. She was distracting as hell. He knew he was falling for her and he needed to keep her at a distance. He was too close to his goal to be tripped up now.

He got out of the shower, dried himself, threw on a robe, and went downstairs. He poured himself a glass of vodka and sat down on the couch. He took a swig, placed the glass on the coffee table, and began loading the bullets into the gun. Despite the two previous attacks, he felt reasonably safe at the hospital, now that his guard was up. He had no intention of being jumped from behind again. But he did not want to be surprised in his sleep. He had always been a light sleeper, but he would feel a lot better with a gun at his bedside.

He loaded three bullets, took another swig of vodka, and filled the rest of the chambers. He seemed to need a drink every night lately. He was overworked. He had not taken a day off for years. Maybe, after Janie was cured and the vaccine had been approved, he would take a vacation. Yes, that would be nice. Or maybe not so nice. He would have hours on end with nothing to do but to think about his life and his future. He might not like what he saw.

* * *

When Bob reached his lab in the morning, there was a newspaper clipping taped to his door. Scrawled across it in big, red letters were the words, READ THIS AND BE FOREWARNED!! He tore it off the door.

POPE RAPS GENE EXPERIMENTS

VATICAN CITY [AP]--The Pope, in a major speech on medical ethics, this morning attacked genetic experimentation and Robert Newman's gene vaccine as "irresponsible" medical research.

"Science is not the highest value to which all the others must be subordinated," he said. "Higher is the right of individuals to their physical and spiritual life and to their psychic and functional integrity."

The pope called on him to "cease his experimentation at once."

The Pope said that even though scientific knowledge has its "proper laws to follow, it must recognize above all an insurmountable limit in the respect of person and in the protection of his right to live in a worthy way as a human being."

> "The   truth   is   that   this
> technological development suffers
> from a deep ambivalence," he said.
> "While it allows man to take
> control of his destiny, it exposes
> him to the temptation of going
> beyond the limits of a reasonable
> control of nature, risking the
> survival and integrity of the human
> person."

Bob crumpled the paper in his fist and threw it into the wastebasket. Wearing thick, thermal gloves, he opened the freezer door and removed the film cartridge he had placed there the night before. He took it down the hall to the darkroom and fed the film into the developer. When it dropped into the bin at the other end, he grabbed it eagerly and held it up to the ceiling light. Hundreds of dark bands were visible, corresponding to individual segments of RNA of different lengths. He returned with the film to his lab. The telephone was ringing and he picked up the receiver.

"Dr. Newman, this is toxicology. We have the analysis on the sample you gave us."

"Great. Let's hear it."

"Vinyl chloride and midazolam."

"Thanks."

Perfect timing. He was about to find out what vinyl chloride did to gene expression in human cells. He flipped on the view box, and snapped the film onto it. Now he could see the bands clearly. He ran his finger slowly down the film, his eyes moving back and forth, comparing each lane. "Unbelievable!" he whispered. None of the bands in the lane from the malignant cells lined up with any of the bands from the normal cells. Not a single one. What were all these other genes coding for? One band was especially heavy, indicating that it was present in large quantities. Could it be an oncogene, the master gene regulating the expression of all the other cancer genes?

The only way to answer these questions was to isolate the proteins in the cells. The proteins were the final products encoded by the genes. They were transcribed from the RNA templates. If he knew the proteins, he might understand what was inducing expression of the cancer genes.

He incubated a fresh group of human cells with vinyl chloride. Then he had another thought. He went to his chemical shelf and began pulling down all the jars, separating out the chemicals known to be carcinogenic. These he also incubated with human cells.

He looked at his watch. He could extract the proteins and set up the gel tonight. By Monday morning he would have the answer.

23

The Outpatient Clinic Building was the newest part of the medical center complex. Ellen entered through the main entrance and followed a hand-painted sign reading, CANCER SCREENING, up the escalator to the second level. The hospital had been designated as one of twelve locations in the city where the screenings were being performed. She had received her notice in the mail two days ago. She had also received an email from the medical school dean's office that students were being drafted into the screening program to take medical histories.

Another sign directed her down a hallway to the cafeteria. A security guard let her pass after glancing at the ID badge clipped to the pocket of her white coat. She was grateful not to have to stand in the long line winding to the end of the hallway, but felt sorry for the hundreds of miserable-looking people who did.

The cafeteria tables had been removed and a row of curtained booths, resembling voting booths, were set up along the back wall. A few hundred men, women, and children stood in a dozen lines. Additional security guards were stationed at the exits. She stepped up to the front desk and handed her notice to the middle-aged woman seated behind it.

"I'm Ellen Rhodes, a med student. I was told to report this morning."

The woman took Ellen's notice and entered something into a computer terminal. "Your driver's license, please."

Ellen fumbled in her purse and handed over the license. The woman typed something else into the computer and handed back the license along with a yellow plastic card imprinted with her name, date of birth, and social security number.

"Take these to the booth with the first letter of your last name. Remember to carry your yellow ID card with you at all times from now on. It's very important, should you need medical care at some point in the future."

Ellen stepped around the desk. She approached the Q-R-S desk where Lisa, a young nurse she recognized from the endocrine ward, was speaking to a muscled, middle-aged man in a pale-blue tee shirt and jeans. He held the hand of a pretty, dark-haired girl of about seven, with a lump on her neck the size of an egg. The girl looked up at her, wide-eyed. Ellen smiled and the child averted her gaze and snuggled up against the man's leg.

"Sir, I told you, you'll see a doctor just as soon as you've given a history."

"I'm tired of being treated like cattle! I want to see a doctor NOW! "

A guard appeared. "Sir, please control yourself."

The man glared at him. "This is bullshit! I've been told my daughter might have lymphoma and I haven't seen a god-damned doctor. What kind of way is this to treat people?"

"Sir, everyone's doing their best. If you'll please step this way, your daughter will be taken care of."

The man's eyes bulged and his face turned purple. Ellen was sure he was going to punch the guard. She stepped forward and placed a gentle hand on his arm. "I know how frustrating this is," she said in a soft voice. "Come with me, I'll take your daughter to the doctor."

He jerked his arm away, then recognized that the hand that had touched him belonged to a petite, young woman, not a big burly guard. A confused expression played across his face, then he suddenly began to sob uncontrollably. Ellen draped her slender arms around him. His head drooped down against her shoulder, his body shaking against hers in spasms of grief.

"It's all right," she whispered. "It's all right. . . Let's see what the doctor has to say."

Though he was three times her size, she supported him as they stumbled towards the booth behind the desk, the little girl clutching Ellen's free hand. She parted the curtain and they stepped into a small enclosure. Laura Ablin, one of her classmates, was seated inside.

"Laura, this little girl needs to see a doctor," Ellen said.

"I need to get a history first," Laura replied.

Ellen shook her head. "She needs to see a doctor now."

Laura nodded and led them into an examination room. Ellen almost cried with relief when she saw Joe Malcolm inside.

"Dr. Malcolm, this father has been waiting a long time for his daughter to be examined. Can you help him?"

Malcolm seemed to grasp the situation at a glance. He nodded and knelt down in front of the girl.

"What's your name, sweetie?"

"Dawn. . ." she whispered.

"That's a beautiful name, Dawn."

Ellen glanced at the girl's father, who had regained his composure. She touched his arm, smiled, and whispered, "Good luck." She left them in Malcolm's care and returned to the triage desk.

"Thank you so much!" Lisa exhaled as Ellen approached. "I don't know what would have happened if you hadn't shown up."

"The poor man," Ellen replied. "I don't blame him for losing it."

"You have a way with people. You're going to make a great doctor."

Ellen tightened her lips. "If we don't get to the bottom of this epidemic I may never get to finish med school. Listen, I need to be screened so that I can get my shift."

Lisa ran her card through a reader and returned it to her along with a printout.

"Take this to the next open booth behind us. You get a history, then a physical, then blood tests, each in a different room. Takes about an hour."

"It all seems so organized."

"It's like an assembly line here, but it seems to be working. We've processed over two thousand people since yesterday."

Ellen headed for the booth through which she had just taken the man and his daughter, parted the curtain, and stepped inside. Her classmate, Laura, gave her a questioning smile.

"Sorry about that," Ellen said. "The poor man was going to kill someone if he didn't see a doctor." She patted her chest a few times. "I can't believe what's going on here."

"I know, I started this morning and I've seen dozens of obvious cancers. It's awfully depressing. You'll see for yourself after they assign you a shift. . . assuming you check out okay."

"God. . ." Ellen dropped into the empty chair.

Laura went through the routine of collecting the medical history and Ellen answered the questions remotely, still feeling as though it was all unreal and she was going to awaken from this nightmare. She couldn't get the little girl's pretty eyes out of her mind.

Laura handed Ellen a hospital gown and parted the curtain to the rear. "Take this with you to exam room two for your physical. You've got to strip, undies too, and wait for the doctor. Come see me afterwards and let me know that everything checked out, okay?"

"I will."

The two women hugged briefly. Ellen stepped through the open door of exam room two, thankful that Joe Malcolm was staffing room three and she would be spared *that* embarrassment. She shut the door, stripped off her clothes and placed them on a chair, then slipped into the gown and tied it behind her neck.

There was a knock. The doctor entered and they stared at each other in awkward silence.

"Ellen. . ."

She folded her arms across her chest, suddenly self-conscious. "What are *you* doing here?"

Bob Newman shut the door. "We're extremely understaffed. All the hospital physicians are taking shifts in the screening clinic. Genetics has the morning."

She nodded. "Yes, I saw Joe a moment ago."

He glanced at the laced panties lying on top of her clothes and cleared his throat. "I can get another doctor to examine you, if you wish."

Hell, yes, she wanted another doctor, but she was determined not to let him know how embarrassed she was. "That depends. Are you still board certified?"

He smirked at her. "What do you think?"

"Yes or no?"

"Of course."

"Then I suppose you'll do."

"You sure?"

"Hey, it's only a physical exam. You've no doubt seen hundreds of female bodies as exquisite as mine."

Well! does she know it.

"You're right, I have. Hop onto the table."

She stepped over to the exam table and sat on the edge. Bob looked her over, uncharacteristically unsure of where to begin. It was hard to avoid the fact that she was nearly naked. He chose the safest course of action.

"Think you can open your mouth without yapping?"

She opened wide, resisting the impulse to stick her tongue out at him, and he shined a light into her oral cavity.

"Look straight at the wall over there." He focused the ophthalmoscope through her pupil onto her retina. He had to get close, his face a mere inch from hers. He was acutely aware of how good she smelled.

He placed his hands on her neck and felt for nodes.

"How many malignancies have you been finding?" Ellen asked.

Bob was grateful for the distraction. "That information is supposed to be confidential, but it's already been leaked. One in every five people we've screened has cancer, mostly melanomas and lymphomas."

"That's unbelievable!"

"It's scary as hell."

He removed his stethoscope from around his neck, leaned over her shoulder and placed the diaphragm on her bare back.

"Take some deep breaths."

With her second breath, the gown parted. He followed the curve of her spine as it disappeared into the cleavage of her butt and it was all he could do to keep his hand from wandering south. He struggled to suppress an insistent erection.

"Lie down, please."

She lay back on the table.

"I need to feel for breast masses," he explained.

There were fine beads of perspiration on his forehead and by now she knew he was as uncomfortable as she was. "Sure, go ahead."

He seemed at a loss and it took her a moment to comprehend.

"Oh." She slipped the gown off her shoulders, exposing her breasts. She saw how he hesitated and she felt a violent sensation of desire cascade through her. As his hands began to move over her body, an ache reached far down into her and a soft hum escaped her lips. She closed her eyes, giving herself up to it.

Bob slipped her arms back into the gown, turned his back to her and laid his hand on a pile of white sheets. This was the most unprofessional exam he had ever performed. He blew a deep breath, removed the top sheet, and covered Ellen's torso.

"I have to examine your abdomen."

She pulled the gown up, exposing her belly. Bob listened with the stethoscope, then felt her abdomen for masses. He slid a trembling hand under the sheet, feeling for nodes in her inguinal area. His fingers brushed her soft pubic hair.

"Could you stand up?"

She stood, facing him. Bob wavered. As a physician, he owed it to her to complete the exam. He swallowed audibly.

"Please turn around and remove the gown."

She stared at him blankly for a moment, then turned her back to him, reached over her head, and loosened the gown where it was tied around her neck. She let go and it fell to the floor.

She was right, her body *was* exquisite. He reached out his hand and, in the guise of the exam, thirstily touched her skin. He traced her shoulders and spine, finding a few normal-appearing moles and a healed scar on her left thigh. He let his fingers linger on the small of her back, wanting much more.

He swallowed again and cleared his throat. "Turn around, please."

Red-faced, she presented herself to him.

"Lift your arms over your head."

He scanned her skin from a distance, certain that if he touched her now he would be unable to control himself. He found no pigmented lesions of concern. He turned his back to her. "I'm done."

When she was covered she said, "You can turn around now."

He avoided her eyes. "Everything checks out perfectly. The gynecologist will perform a pelvic exam in the next room. Then you'll have your blood drawn and you'll be done."

All she could think of to say was, "Thanks." She scooped up her clothes and stepped through the door. Bob leaned his hands on the exam table for support as he watched her depart.

24

It was after midnight when Bruce Nevins left his office. It was going to be a busy weekend. Robert Newman was testifying before the subcommittee on Tuesday, and Delany wanted the background report on his desk Monday morning. So far, Newman smelled like a rose. He had graduated at the top of his class from medical school. At thirty-four, his accomplishments as a scientist were brilliant. About the closest Bruce had come to anything steamy was the discovery that he apparently had an unusual propensity to attract members of the opposite sex. But there was no evidence that he had ever been unfaithful to his late wife or had in any other way compromised himself ethically. In fact, the more Bruce dug into Newman's background, the more he decided he liked the guy. Delany might be disappointed, but Doctor Robert Newman had the makings of an American hero and the press was eating it up.

Bruce locked his office door and headed down the hallway towards the elevator. As he turned the corner, he saw Delany's tall, unmistakable silhouette up ahead. Bruce wondered what Delany was doing in the building at this ungodly hour. On an impulse, he decided to follow him. It was not an act born of suspicion, but of curiosity.

He lingered back until the elevator door closed, then watched the numbers above the door until they stopped at the garage level. He summoned the elevator and followed Delany to the basement. As he stepped into the garage, Delany's car pulled out of its parking spot with Delany at the wheel. Strange, the Senator never drove anywhere without his driver. Bruce waited until the car left the lot and then hurried to his own car. He rushed up the exit ramp and turned onto Pennsylvania Avenue. The traffic was light and Bruce had no difficulty following from a distance.

Delany turned left onto M street, and Bruce swore as the light turned red before he could follow. This was the exact opposite direction Delany would have taken were he heading home. Bruce was increasingly curious. He looked up and down the street, saw neither traffic nor police, and turned left through the red light. Good, he had not lost Delany. His car was two blocks up, heading west. As they reached the heart of Georgetown, the traffic increased and the street became congested with double-parked cars and limousines.

Delany headed down a narrow road towards the river and pulled over near a row of warehouses. He got out of his car and walked up an alley towards the riverfront. Bruce stopped a block behind him and turned off his headlights. What the hell business did he have here? He waited until Delany was well ahead of him, then left his car and followed from a distance, keeping in the dark shadows.

It was a cloudy night and the alley was dark, making it impossible to see more than a few feet ahead. The wet wind coming from the river nipped at his face and neck. Bruce stepped up his pace, not wanting to lose sight of Delany. The Senator stopped and Bruce ducked behind the nearest wall just as a man appeared out of the shadows. He was shorter than Delany, heavyset and bald. He looked vaguely familiar to Bruce, but in the darkness he could not be sure. The two men approached each other. They began to talk, but Bruce could not make out the conversation. He had a sudden impulse to leave the scene, but his curiosity had him hooked. As quietly as possible, he inched his way along the building, clinging to the shadows and stopping after each step to make sure he had not been heard. Finally, he was within ten feet of the two men and could just make out their words. He dared not come any closer.

The stranger was speaking in a hoarse whisper. "We've had a setback in Chicago."

"Oh?"

"Our second attempt to transform Newman was unsuccessful.   And, he's stumbled upon our vinyl chloride operation."

"Vinyl chloride carries a fifty percent mortality rate," Delany replied. "Do we really need it? Chicago's right across the state line from Gary, and the westerly winds have been very favorable. Besides, the sabotage at the Edison power plant next week will spew tons of carcinogens into the atmosphere. The impact will be dramatic, since we're almost at threshold already."

Bruce was not following the conversation. What action next week? What threshold were they talking about? He leaned forward to catch the stranger's whispers.

"We need the vinyl chloride to transform key individuals quickly. And I do have some good news on that front. The secretary has been transformed successfully, and that significantly enhances our ability to keep tabs on Newman's activities. Now we're targeting the young student for transformation."

"I wonder how he figured out about the vinyl chloride," Delany mused. "He's unusually intuitive."

"Newman's become a major irritant," the stranger grumbled. "There's another issue. We're quite certain that his sister-in-law is to be the first human test of his gene splicing virus, in the very near future."

"Trust me, Delany replied, "the subcommittee isn't going to rule on this for months. I'll see to that personally."

"Our information suggests that he isn't going to wait for the subcommittee ruling. The girl's hospital room is under security guard and we don't know what's going on in there. The best way to ensure that no one uses the technology is to eliminate Newman and destroy his virus, which is why we're arranging a little accident on his way to Washington."

Bruce listened in disbelief. He could hear Delany clearly, but he was having difficulty catching the stranger's words. He inched closer to the two men.

"What type of accident?" Delany asked.

"Let's just say there've been a lot of problems with the airlines lately, near misses and the like."

"We can't just kill him," Delany protested. "Somebody might suspect something."

"I'm surprised at the doubt that still exists in you. Who would ever, in his wildest imagination, suspect the truth? And even if they did, no one would believe him until it was too late."

"There's a difference between doubt and strategy," Delany replied. "We don't need to give our enemy a reason to start down that path."

"Newman's the only thing that can upset the schedule now. Once we have him out of the way, it'll be at least two years before anyone can duplicate his work. By then we'll be in full control."

Delany sighed. "It's unfortunate that his discovery occurred so early. The odds against it were overwhelming."

"Yes, but soon none of it will matter."

In the darkness, Bruce saw movement on Delany's forehead. The stranger whispered, "You miss the contact of the flesh. I yearn for it, too."

Bruce stared in disbelief as the two men embraced each other. He had never before entertained the notion that Delany was a homosexual. Yet there he was, standing in front of him, locked in another man's arms. Or was he? As he continued to stare, he realized that the two men were not actually kissing. Their embrace was very odd, indeed. They had their hands on each others shoulders, their foreheads touching.   There was something vaguely familiar about the sight in front of him. Familiar and terrible.   Bruce felt a mounting, unexplained anxiety, but he was frozen.   Then, as the clouds dissipated momentarily and the moon shone through, he saw a sight that horrified him to the bones. A wave of nausea overwhelmed him and it took all his effort not to scream. His clothes were drenched in sweat, despite the cold. Finally, he could not contain himself and he bent over and retched. When the spasms ceased, he glanced in dread at the two men, but they had not heard him. They continued to grip each other in their strange embrace. He backed out of the alley, clinging to the wall, unable to turn his back on the sight in front of him. When he finally reached the street, he turned and tore down the pavement in the grip of a terrifying panic.

25

Ellen placed her hand on the knob, blew a deep breath, and opened the door to Bob's lab. She was not sure why she had come. She only knew that she needed to see him again or she would burst. He was seated on a stool, looking into a microscope.

"Hi."

He gave no indication that he had heard her. Then, still fiddling with the focusing dial, he said, "You should be in your new rotation."

"You're not my father. My rotation's been canceled and I've been assigned to the screening clinic."

"Then what are you doing *here*, Ms. Rhodes?"

She bit her lip. "You know, you've really got a way of pushing my buttons. If you don't stop calling me 'Ms. Rhodes' I swear I'm gonna get violent."

He lifted his eyes from the microscope and studied her for a moment. Then he did something that caught her completely by surprise--he laughed.

"Okay then. Ellen, what are you doing here?"

She lowered her voice. "I don't know, really. I wanted to tell you I'm sorry about our fight the other day."

"Me, too. I was a bit hard on you."

Ellen smiled. "You know, underneath that shell of yours, you're really a very sensitive man." She held out her hand. "Friends?"

Bob hesitated, then took her hand briefly. "Okay, friends. Now I really have to get back to work."

"What are you doing?"

"I'm checking some bone marrow cells for a transplant today."

"Can I see?"

He stood up and opened his palm towards the microscope.

Ellen sat down and turned the knob until the cells came into focus. "Are these normal?"

"They are now. I've just finished fixing them."

She swiveled the stool around so she was facing him. He looked so calm and self-assured. And yet he was talking about human tissue as if it was a transistor radio.

"Excuse my ignorance, but what do you mean?"

"George Peterson has sickle cell anemia," Bob replied. "He has a mutated hemoglobin gene in his cells that causes the disease. I removed some of his bone marrow cells last week and inserted a normal gene to replace the one that isn't functioning."

Ellen looked back through the eyepieces again. "Did you use your gene vaccine?"

Bob shook his head. "With the gene vaccine I wouldn't need to grow the cells in the incubator. The vaccine would do the work in his body."

He took two large syringes from the incubator and put them into the pocket of his white coat. "You're welcome to stay here and look as long as you want. I've got to get to the ward."

This was the longest conversation she'd had with him that had not ended in a bitter argument. She took a chance. "Sometime, can I see how the gene vaccine works?"

Bob looked at his watch. "Come on."

"Now?"

"Yes, now. Come on." He started out of the room.

Ellen hurried to keep up with his flying, white coattails. He led her down the hall to the animal room, which was about ten feet square and filled with large metal racks on wheels, each with five shelves. The shelves held clear, plastic cages, each large enough to house a single rat. The odor of rodent urine permeated the room. There were no windows, the room being lit by three incandescent bulbs hanging from the ceiling. She heard scratching noises coming from all directions and had to fight the impulse to turn and run.

Bob sensed her discomfort. "Are you all right?"

"I'm petrified of these creatures."

"Don't worry, they're quite tame."

"I can't help it. I grew up on a farm. One day, when I was five, we were playing hide and seek and I was hiding under the hay in the barn. Something latched onto my leg and I started to scream. My brother yanked me out and this rat as big as me had its jaws clamped on my thigh. My dad came running and literally cut the rat in two with an axe. They had to pry the jaws off my leg with a pair of pliers."

"Yes, I saw the scar the other day."

Ellen shot a glance at him and her face flushed.

"I promise they won't hurt you." Bob removed a cage and laid it on a small table by the wall. "Want to have a look?"

She approached the table, but stood a few feet behind him. She was horrified to see that the cover was made of thin metal bars and merely rested on top of the cage without being fastened in any way.

"Can't it get out?"

Bob smiled. "It's perfectly happy to stay where there's food and water."

He lifted the cover and the rat rose up on its hind legs and peered over the edge, poking its long snout out and sniffing. It raised its forelimbs onto the top of the cage and Ellen shrunk back.

"Don't be afraid. It won't hurt you." Bob took the rat by the torso and held it up. "See? This is RN 149, the most famous rat in the world."

Ellen struggled to stay calm. "That's the one?"

Bob nodded.

"It looks just like the others."

"Not at all. Don't you see how pompous it's become? It's now a world-famous celebrity, which is almost certainly a fate worse than death for an unpretentious rat."

The rat sniffed the air in front of Bob's face.

"More people have called requesting to see this rat than have called to interview me. In fact, I've given some thought to buying it a suit and tie and making it my press agent so I can get back to work. But I'm against cruelty to animals."

Ellen smiled. She was seeing a side of Bob Newman she had not known existed. He actually had a sense of humor.

Bob put the rat back, returned to the rack, and removed another cage which he set down next to the first one.

"Now look at this," he said, removing the cover. "This is RN 149's sister."

Ellen's eyes widened. The rat did not look at all like the big fat one in the first cage. Its coat was ruffled and dirty, its bones clearly visible through its skin.

"It looks awful."

"This is one of the control cages," Bob explained. "This rat didn't receive the vaccine."

The rat attempted to stand up, wobbling on its skinny legs. It did not appear such a hideous creature. "Why can't you give it the vaccine?"

"If I gave all the rats the vaccine, I wouldn't know if it worked. Every experiment needs a control group that doesn't get treated."

"Yes, but it's cruel."

Bob studied her. "If you want to be a scientist, you'd better get used to it. It is cruel. But we have to be sure we can interpret the results of the experiments before we try it on humans. It's a choice of whether we prefer to be cruel to rats or to people."

"I understand that. It just seems to me that there ought to be another way to get the information, other than by torturing these poor creatures. Can you really justify it?"

She had not meant it as an accusation, but something snapped in Bob's head. His eyes narrowed and she drew away, frightened. He grabbed her by the arm. "Can I justify it? Come with me, I'll show you how I justify it!"

He half-dragged her out of the room, his iron grip on her arm. She tried to wrestle free, but to no avail.

"Get your hands off of me!" she yelled, clawing at his fingers with her free hand. "Where are you taking me?"

He did not answer, but continued jerking her down the hall. Ellen screamed at the top of her lungs. Bob let go and looked down at her with an expression of such pain that she was stunned into silence.

She glared at him, teary-eyed and furious. "Don't you ever handle me like that again!" she whispered.

"I was about to show you how I justify what I do to those rats. Forget it." He turned to leave.

"No!"

This time it was she that grabbed his arm. "I don't care if you're angry! I don't care if you're hurting inside! I don't care if the world has screwed you! You don't treat people like that!"

She blinked to fight back the tears, then turned her back to him and dabbed at her eyes with the back of her hand.

"I want to be alone now, and don't you *ever* come near me again!"

She felt his hand on her shoulder, and it was gentle.

"Ellen. . . I'm sorry. . . Ellen, please don't be angry. Come, let me show you."

She turned, defiance in her tear-filled eyes. "I'll see what you want to show me--because *I* want to see it."

He nodded. "Come on," he whispered.

"Where to?"

"Genetics rounds."

They walked to the ward in silence. Bob punched a square, metal button on the wall and the double doors to the bone marrow transplant unit swung open towards them. Ellen had never been in the unit before. Bright fluorescent lights bathed the hallway. The walls were clean and sparkling white. Polished wooden hand rails ran along each wall. Large glass windows allowed a full view of the insides of the patient rooms. Each had a single bed in it. Through the windows she caught glimpses of individuals lying in their beds, plastic tubing attached to various parts of their bodies. Each and every patient was completely bald.

Bob stopped half-way down the hall in front of a sink, removed his white coat, and hung it on a hook. He scrubbed his hands and motioned to Ellen to do the same. She stood in front of the sink trying to figure out how to turn on the water. There were no knobs.

"Your feet," Bob said, motioning to the floor.

She found the foot pedals and pressed. After she had washed her hands, he handed her a gown from the adjacent cabinet. He had already donned one. She put it on and then he handed her a mask, which she placed across her mouth and nose. Finally he handed her a pair of latex gloves. He reached into the pocket of his coat hanging on the hook and removed the two large syringes filled with the bone marrow cells.

She followed him into a patient's room where she saw an emaciated, ill-appearing black man lying on the bed, a clear, plastic mask over his face. A nurse stood at his side, adjusting something on the i.v. pole that stood at the side of the bed. She was dressed in a similar manner to Ellen and Bob. Ellen's eyes traced the plastic tubing from the pole until it disappeared under some bandages on the man's chest. The mask was connected to another tube that led to the wall behind the bed.

"Hi, Mr. Peterson," Bob said. "Sorry about this outfit, but those two doses of radiation have knocked out your immune system. We don't want you to pick up any bugs from us that will give you any trouble."

Peterson grinned widely. "Doc! I didn't recognize you under that space suit. Look, still got my hair." He patted the top of his head.

"I hate to tell you this, but it's going to fall out in the next few days," Bob said. "Rapidly growing cells like your hair cells don't like radiation. But it'll grow back."

"It's okay, I don't care if it never grows back, as long as I'm cured." His voice was muffled by the mask, which clouded up momentarily every time he exhaled.

"Let's keep our fingers crossed. Let me have a look at your mouth."

He helped Peterson remove the mask and shined a light into his oral cavity. The oral mucosa was covered with ulcerated, bleeding sores. Bob grimaced. "Looks pretty nasty in there."

"Doc, I tell you, I can't eat a thing. It hurts like a son-of-a-bitch."

Bob turned to the nurse. "Is he getting topical care?"

The nurse nodded.

"This will get better in about a week, Mr. Peterson. It's the same as your hair. You've got a lot of rapidly-growing cells in your mucous membranes. In the meantime, you've got to try to eat, even though it hurts."

Peterson nodded.

"I want you to meet one of my associates. This is Ellen Rhodes." Bob pushed Ellen gently forward.

"Pleased to make your acquaintance," Peterson said.

"It's nice to meet you, Mr. Peterson," Ellen replied.

"Mr. Peterson," Bob said. "Could you tell Ellen a little bit about yourself?"

"Sure. Mind if I take off this mask? I feel like I'm talking through a tin can."

Bob shook his head. "Sorry, but you need the oxygen. We can't take a chance on your red cells sickling until the new marrow takes."

"Whatever you say, Doc. You're the boss. Ellen, I'm thirty-three years old and I've got sickle cell. Born with it. It's been killing me off one piece at a time and, as you can see, there's not much left to kill. I'm hoping that the Doc here can cure me." He turned towards Bob, momentarily. "I know there ain't no guarantees. You see Ellen, Dr. Newman here is the only chance I got. Everybody else wanted to give up on me. I know it's only a small chance, but hey, everybody wants to live, right?"

Ellen managed a smile. "Right, Mr. Peterson. Don't worry, you're in good hands."

"The best," Peterson agreed.

"Shall we get started?" Bob asked.

"Ready when you are, doc."

Bob looked at the nurse who nodded.

"Great. Let's do it." He handed the nurse the two syringes. She injected their contents into a plastic i.v. bag, mixed the bag a few times and then opened the stopcock. The red fluid, containing the bone marrow cells, mixed with the clear i.v. fluid and made its way through the plastic tubing and under Peterson's bandage.

"Q five minute vitals until it's in," Bob said.

The nurse nodded. "Mr. Peterson, you're going to feel this blood pressure cuff on your arm expanding every five minutes. It's all automatic, so don't be alarmed."

Peterson nodded. "I can't believe it. I'm getting a transplant and I'm wide awake and don't feel a thing."

The bag emptied in fifteen minutes. "How do you feel, Mr. Peterson?" Bob asked.

"Great, doc."

"Good. I want you to get some rest now. Remember to keep that mask on, okay?"

"Absolutely. When will we know if the marrow took?"

"We'll start checking your blood in a week, but it'll probably be ten or twelve days before we know anything. In the meantime, your job is to eat, even though you're not going to want to."

Peterson nodded. "I'll do my best, doc."

They left the room, removed their gowns, gloves and masks, and discarded them in a bin. Bob led Ellen out of the bone marrow transplant unit and to the intensive care unit. The unit was a single, large room. The nurses desk stood in the middle, with beds spaced along the walls. Above each bed was a monitor on which tracings of pulse, blood pressure and respiratory rates were displayed. The wall behind each bed was covered with various pipes, tubes and equipment.

"The next patient has Gaucher's disease," Bob whispered. "He has a single gene defect that prevents his liver from metabolizing a protein called glucosamine and it's accumulating in his liver. It's slowly poisoning him."

They walked over to a small bed on which a child lay, clothed only in a diaper. Above the table were two panels of lights and an i.v. tubing which ran into the child's neck. A man and a woman, seated beside the bed, stood up.

"Hi, Dr. Newman," they both said in unison.

"Hello Mr. and Mrs. Kelly. This is an associate of mine, Ellen Rhodes."

They greeted her warmly.

"How's Tommy today?"

The boy appeared about a year and a half old. The first thing Ellen noticed was his abdomen. It was immense, tense as a drum, and had large blue veins traversing across it in a network pattern. The rest of his body looked like that of a stick figure. His head was also covered with tight skin and his ears stood out from his skull. There were prominent veins over his neck and face.

Bob took the chart hanging on the edge of the bed and glanced over it. He looked at the boy's parents. "Please sit down," he said gently. "Tommy had a lot of bleeding last night. He's going to need another exchange transfusion today."

Mrs. Kelly began to cry and her husband put his arm around her. Bob took a box of tissues from the table and offered it to her.

"He's going to bleed to death if we don't get his coags under control."

"I know," she said between sniffles. "He has such terrible blood pressure problems whenever he gets an exchange. Last time, I thought I was going to lose my baby."

Bob squeezed her shoulder. "We'll do the exchange as slowly as possible."

Mrs. Kelly nodded and wiped her eyes.

"Dr. Newman," Mr. Kelly said, "any news about a liver?"

Bob shook his head. "He's on the list, but there hasn't been a matched donor yet."

"I'm almost afraid to ask this, but we were wondering, is there any chance that he might be a candidate for the gene vaccine?"

Both parents stared at him with intense hope on their faces.

Bob took a deep breath before replying. "There's hope, yes. But the alpha one antitrypsin gene hasn't been located yet, and gene therapy can't be performed until it is. I guess what I'm saying is that it is not a viable alternative at this time."

Mr. Kelly nodded his head. Mrs. Kelly simply stared at him.

"How much longer do you think he has?" Mr. Kelly asked.

"That's a difficult question to answer. Tommy is a very sick little boy. You know that. He could die today, or he could survive another six months."

Mrs. Kelly started weeping again.

"My goal is to keep him alive until a liver becomes available. I think we have a shot at that or I wouldn't be putting him, or you, through this."

"We can't tell you how much we appreciate what you've done," Mr. Kelly said.

"Hang in there," Bob replied.

Bob led Ellen off the ward. Ellen was amazed at how gentle Bob had been with his patients. She had not thought him capable of such tenderness. She realized that he wanted her to see this side of him.

"Do you really think the gene vaccine could help him?"

"If we knew the gene's location."

"I still don't exactly understand how it works," Ellen said.

"Each gene in our chromosomes is made up of nucleotides that code for the formation of a specific protein. Inherited diseases are caused by the fact that one nucleotide, in the chain of hundreds that make up the gene, is the wrong nucleotide. That's a mutation."

"I'm a med student. I know what a mutation is. But how does the gene vaccine recognize the defective gene and remove it?"

"That's a bit complicated," Bob replied. "Each gene is separated from the next one on the chromosome by segments of DNA we call junk DNA because they don't seem to code for anything. Actually, eighty percent of the DNA in our chromosomes is junk DNA. Nobody knows the purpose of all that DNA and most scientists think its just filler. But I suspect nature has put it there for a reason that we don't understand. Anyway, we design a restriction enzyme specific for the junk sequence on either side of the target gene and it splices it out. The new piece of DNA goes in its place."

They had reached the basement entrance to Jackson Hall.

"All this pain and suffering must be so difficult to deal with," Ellen said.

He stopped and turned towards her. "That's why I can justify being cruel to rats. Now, I want you to look me in the eye and tell me these people should be allowed to die because of some hypothetical argument about the sanctity of the human genome. I'm showing you reality."

Ellen's eyes were moist. "God, how can you live with this every day?" she whispered.

"I can because I have to."

"Do you get used to it?"

"No."

They gazed into each other's eyes. For the first time since she had met Bob, Ellen realized what he had done to himself. He lived every moment under the unbearable pressure of responsibility for all these patients. He had nailed himself to a cross out of some crazy, stubborn determination to control something no human being had the power to influence. No one could bear such a terrible burden, not even a superhuman Robert Newman. Suddenly, she wanted to hold him and comfort him and tell him to open his heart to her. She wanted to tell him to let go of this burden he was shouldering, that his wife's death was not his fault. She wanted to tell him to stop dying inside every time he stood by helplessly while a patient suffered. She wanted to tell him she was falling in love with him. She wanted to tell him all these things.

"Ellen, I'm working under a tremendous time constraint. I can't afford to let myself be distracted right now. Do you understand what I'm saying?"

She managed a weak smile. He was carrying the world on his shoulders, and a distraction might cause him to drop his terrible burden. But in his own way, he was attempting to reach out to her.

"I understand perfectly."

There was another moment of silence.

"I've got to get back to the lab."

She stared up into his steely eyes, took hold of the corners of his white coat, and tugged them toward her until he was pressed up against her. She laid her head briefly against his chest.

"Go save that little boy," she whispered.

26

Bob arrived in the lab at seven Monday morning, itching to see the protein gel from the malignant cells. He pulled the film out of the cartridge and held it up to the light. An unfamiliar, heavy band was evident immediately, migrating between seventy and ninety kilodaltons. He grabbed his calculator and punched in the numbers to get the slope of the curve and the precise molecular weight of the unknown protein. He looked at the number on the calculator's screen: 78.

"Seventy-eight," he muttered. "Seventy-eight. Why does that sound familiar?" He went to the computer, called up the Genbank protein sequence database, and searched for proteins with a molecular weight of 78. A single annotation appeared on the screen: Gp78.

Gp-78! It was a tumor protein of unknown function, present in practically all malignancies. Could it be the promoter, the trigger gene that activated all the other mysterious genes in the malignant cells? He began to search the computer data banks for everything he could find on Gp-78. He was too absorbed to notice the occasional flickering in the upper right corner of the screen, indicating that his computer was being monitored.

In the office down the hall, Lois stared at her computer monitor and scowled. She still retained the memories of Lois Baines, but there was another presence that dominated her consciousness. Sartan was there, its memories neatly stored in the long stretches of junk DNA between human genes. Over the past several days, its tendrils had invaded deeply, replacing her brain tissue. She rubbed her forehead, feeling the tissue underneath respond to the stimulus. She could access all those memories, the million years of independent existence, the struggle to the death with humanity, The Calamity. Then the millennia of forced hibernation, never total, Sartan's consciousness always burning dimly, subverting, laying the seeds of sabotage in the human soul. Sartan had been patient, very patient, like a hard drive in sleep mode, awakening on occasion to sample the environment. Now, just as the moment to act had arrived, one unexpected obstacle stood in the way. Robert Newman's gene vaccine threatened to rip Sartan out of the genome. But Sartan was awake now, alert within Lois and countless others, watching him and preparing his destruction.

27

Bob was at his lab bench when the telephone rang. He swore, put down the test tube he was holding, and picked up the phone.

"This is Bob Newman."

"I'm calling to warn you," came a hurried whisper, "don't take the seven-thirty flight to Washington tonight."

Bob strained to hear above the hum of his centrifuge. "Could you speak up?"

The whisper became more urgent. "I said, your life's in danger if you come in on the seven-thirty flight."

"Who is this?"

"I work for Senator Delany."

"Is this some kind of a joke?"

"Believe me, it's no joke. Delany doesn't want you to testify. He's going to kill you. They're planning to sabotage the country, blow up the Edison plant, and poison the atmosphere. They must be stopped. I don't know how, but they must be stopped."

Bob had had a number of crank calls in the past two weeks. "I really must be going now," he said, preparing to hang up.

"Wait! I know it sounds nuts, but you've got to believe me. They're going to kill you, do you hear me? It's your vaccine, it's a threat to them."

"Who are 'they'?"

"I'm not sure. The Senator hasn't been well since he developed his cancer, but now it's gotten into his head. It's made him crazy."

The conversation was beginning to spook Bob. "How'd you get this number?"

"I know everything about you, Dr. Newman. I'll prove it. Do you remember-" The line suddenly went silent.

"Hello?"

He heard a male voice, different from the first. "Bruce, who are you talking to?"

"Uh, my aunt Estelle."

"Really? Let me have that phone."

Bob heard a click.

"Hello? Hello!"

A moment later he heard a dial tone. He hung up the receiver, took a deep breath, and rubbed the tension out of his temples. Then he walked down the hall to the main office.

"Lois, I thought you were screening my calls."

"I am. Did one get by me?"

"Some nut who claimed to work for Senator Delany said Delany was going to kill me."

"Did he say who he was?" Lois asked.

"No, but someone came into the room while he was talking and called him Bruce."

Lois shrugged. "I never give out your direct number."

"Forget about it. It's not your fault."

He left the office, then returned a moment later. "Hey, remember the letter explaining the procedures for my testimony tomorrow? Let me see it."

"I don't think I kept that," Lois replied. She began shuffling through the papers on her desk. "It would be in the Washington folder. . . No, I don't see it."

Bob grabbed the folder. "Here," he said, pulling out the letter. "I knew it! Bruce Nevins, assistant to Senator Herman R. Delany."

Lois had a blank expression on her face. She had become difficult to read, of late. She was either angry at him for something or in one of her playful moods.

Bob's eyes narrowed. "What the hell," he said. "Why don't you call the number on this letter and let's talk to Bruce Nevins, just to say hi."

Lois nodded and dialed the number. "Hello, this is Dr. Robert Newman's office for Mr. Bruce Nevins, please." She looked up at Bob. "They're getting him."

After a few moments, she said into the phone, "I see. . . No, that's not necessary. Thank you." She hung up.

"So?" Bob asked.

"He's not in the office today."

Bob shrugged and smiled. "Keep screening those calls, Lois."

He started out of the office, then turned around again. "Look, is this some kind of practical joke?"

"Bob, why would I play a joke like that on you?"

"He told me not to take the seven-thirty flight. You're the only one who knows which flight I'm on."

Lois shrugged. "It doesn't take a genius to figure I'd book you on that flight. It's the last one to National airport and only the most popular flight of the day. If you're really worried, I can change your reservation."

Bob shook his head. "No, forget it. I can't let every quack out there keep me from living my life." He shook his finger at her. "Screen my calls, Ms. Baines."

Lois smiled. "Yes, dear."

28

Some people were anorexic when tense. Ed Lafferty ate. The level of tension in his life correlated directly with his tailor's bill. At least it beat chewing the nails off his fingers. He couldn't stand seeing people do that.

His uniform needed to be let out again he realized, pulling at his collar. Why hadn't he stayed at the university instead of accepting this thankless position as Surgeon General, where he had to wear this damned white uniform every day? He looked like the Pillsbury dough boy.

He grabbed a fistful of peanuts from the bowl on his desk and looked at his chief medical officer. "You mean to tell me you've got nothing at all?"

Dr. David Brown shrugged. "That's about the sum of it."

"I don't get it. You're in charge of compiling the data on this epidemic. Your team has performed dozens of autopsies and you've got access to thousands of others from across the country. How could you have nothing?"

"Nothing may have been a poor choice of words," Brown replied. "We've got notebooks full of data. I can give you statistics on types of malignancies, sites of metastases, patient profiles, et cetera, et cetera. We know that males and females are affected equally, that urban communities are being hit harder than rural ones, that the rates of malignancies are similar across all age groups. But we have absolutely no data on etiology. Unless we can examine recovering patients, we're not going to get an answer. We've got to find out why a certain group is recovering while the rest are succumbing."

Lafferty stuffed the peanuts into his mouth and chewed for a while. "Damn it, can't you tell me anything?"

"I can tell you what it's not," Brown replied. "It's not infectious. That's one thing we feel certain about. There's no evidence for contagious spread of this thing."

"Okay, that's something. We don't have to worry about quarantining affected persons. Let's keep going. What about genetics?"

"There's no specific genetic risk. All ethnic groups have been affected equally."

"Environmental toxins?"

"Either that or our cells are just self-destructing."

"Is that a serious proposal?" Lafferty was willing to entertain anything.

"No. Hell, sure you can hypothesize that we have a built-in ticking bomb in our chromosomes, but you can hypothesize anything you want. There's simply no supportive data for any etiology at the present time."

Lafferty felt his ulcer gnawing at his stomach. He reached into his desk and popped an antacid.

"All right, then give me an unsupported hypothesis."

Brown raised his eyebrows. "Ah, now that's a different question. In my opinion, the most logical explanation is that it's some kind of environmental toxin. The problem with that theory is that it's not localized to any area of the country. There's no history of common exposure among affected individuals."

"You said that people in urban centers are at higher risk," Lafferty reminded him.

"Yes, that's true."

"Well, then it's got to be something present in urban centers. What's present in high concentrations in the cities? Auto exhaust, microwaves, smog, heat, electric currents, what? What's changed in the past twelve months?"

"What's changed is that the incidence of malignancies is off the chart. Maybe we've reached the level of environmental pollution where our bodies can no longer compensate."

"What's the latest estimate on incidence?"

"Twenty percent, based on the data coming in from the voluntary screening program."

Lafferty exhaled loudly. "That's one out of five people!"

"And that's an underestimate because there are certain to be lots of people with cancers as yet too small to detect."

Lafferty tapped his fingers on the desk. "There's got to be something we're missing here. Tell me about the divergent pattern of illness. Anything new to report there?"

"Yes, there are two distinct patterns, and we can't predict who will fall into which. One group of patients follows the typical course we're used to seeing in oncology. Once they develop clinical signs, they progressively deteriorate. Conventional chemotherapy is effective at controlling the spread of metastases, but the majority are not going into remission. It's the second group that's so mysterious. They represent about eighty percent of cases. They recover completely before receiving chemotherapy."

"Have you been able to find any consenting to be examined?"

"Not a god damn one. It's an incredible phenomenon. One day they're deathly sick. The next day you walk into their hospital room and they're sitting up in their chair looking like a rose, before you've had a chance to begin therapy. They refuse all further treatment. If you try to perform any evaluations, they check themselves out of the hospital. Thousands of such cases have been reported to us."

Lafferty fidgeted in his chair. "As we've discussed before, if an individual refuses medical evaluation, we can't coerce him against his will."

"Is this a national emergency or not?" Brown demanded.

Lafferty reached for the peanut bowl, but it was empty. He squeezed his fingers into a fist. "Yes, but we've got a problem of constitutional rights. The President refuses to sanction it. I've talked to him about it repeatedly."

"Screw the President. He's worried about his standing in the polls."

"I didn't vote for him either, but he *is* the commander-in-chief."

"Listen, Ed," Brown persisted, "there's an extremely odd phenomenon here. I can't believe that these people's tumors regress spontaneously with such rapidity. They must still be harboring their malignancies. Somehow, their bodies adapt to them. I want to know why. I'm not sure which is the scarier proposition, people dying of malignancies, or people walking around oblivious to their malignancies."

Lafferty sighed. "I'll speak to the President about it again."

"Why don't you speak to him about it after we have the results? We're losing precious time."

Lafferty frowned. "I'll see what I can do."

"This is your responsibility, Ed. You're the Surgeon General. You're responsible for the nation's health."

Lafferty pulled at his collar again. God, how he hated this damned uniform.

29

Traffic was light as Bob drove south on Cicero Avenue towards Midway Airport. He preferred Midway to O'Hare. It was nearer to downtown and much less crowded. He passed a snow plow clearing the road. Already the white blanket on the sides of the street was stained black. Funny how some things could turn ugly so quickly.

He knew that the public would be watching the hearings, which would be broadcast live. While he had already been interviewed ad nauseam in the past two weeks, this would be his opportunity to state his case fully to the American people. And enough letters from constituents to their congressmen could make a difference.

He turned into the airport access road and parked. He had developed an aversion to dark parking lots and he looked around carefully before getting out of his car. He grabbed his bag from the back seat and hurried into the terminal. When he reached the gate, he handed his ticket to the flight agent. She smiled, and Bob recognized the familiar message in her eyes.

"Excuse me for being nosey, but are you, by any chance, the Doctor Newman who's been in the papers?"

"Guilty, as charged."

Her eyes widened. "Oh, don't worry," she said, dropping her voice. "I won't tell anyone. I'm sure you prefer to travel anonymously."

"Thank you. I appreciate that."

A pained expression appeared on her face. "Doctor Newman, I hate to have to tell you this, but I can't issue you a boarding pass at this moment because the flight's overbooked.

But don't worry," she added quickly, "I promise we'll get you on the flight. In a few minutes we'll be releasing the reserved seats. In the meantime would you mind waiting by the counter over there?" She pointed to her right.

"I don't mind at all," he reassured her.

"I feel terrible about this."

"Don't worry. You're just doing your job."

He walked over to the adjacent counter where a small group of people was standing. Presently a male voice came over the loudspeaker.

"Ladies and gentlemen, could I have your attention please. Northwest flight seventy-one to Washington National Airport is overbooked. We're looking for three volunteers to give up their seats in exchange for a free, round-trip ticket on any of our domestic flights. We can put you on an eight-thirty flight on United Airlines flying into Dulles Airport in Virginia. If you would like to volunteer, please step up to the ticket counter at this time."

There was some grumbling from the group around Bob. A middle-aged man said to his female companion, "What the hell, it's only an hour, and we get a free flight. Sounds like a good deal to me." The woman agreed, and the two of them walked up to the counter.

"I've got to get in on this flight," a middle-aged man said to no one in particular. "My wife's gonna kill me if I'm not home on time."

Bob was thinking about the crank phone call. If Lois found out it had spooked him, he would never hear the end of it. On the other hand, this was a good excuse to avoid the flight.

He walked up to the ticket counter, smiled at the stewardess and said, "I'll take the United flight."

"Oh, no Doctor Newman," she said with distress. "We'll get you on the flight. Don't worry."

"It's fine," Bob said. "I really don't mind. I'm in no rush."

The stewardess looked at him sheepishly. "Well. . . are you sure?"

"Absolutely."

"Okay, then. I really am terribly sorry about this. I'll book you on the United flight right away." She typed into her computer console, frowned, and typed again. After a moment, she smiled with obvious satisfaction and handed him a ticket.

"Here you are, a boarding pass for United Airlines flight twenty-eight to Dulles, departing from gate six at eight-thirty. And here's a voucher for your free flight." She lowered her voice. "I'm not supposed to do this unless the customer asks, but here's a coupon for a meal at any of the restaurants at the airport."

"Thanks."

He had an hour to kill, so he bought a cup of coffee and a copy of Time Magazine. At eight-fifteen, he headed for his gate, where the flight was boarding. He found his seat and peered out the window. The plane taxied to the runway. As it ascended, he could see the lights of downtown Chicago to the north. The John Hancock building rose like a giant, glistening jewel. Streams of car lights moved like living organisms along the Dan Ryan and Eisenhower expressways. The complexity of communications, electrical, water, and transportation networks necessary to allow three million people to live on a twenty square-mile piece of land was mind boggling from this vantage point above the city. Bob felt a shiver go down his spine at the knowledge that he was a part of this wonder.

When his plane landed, he picked up his rental car and headed towards downtown Washington. He turned on the radio just as the midnight news came on the air.

"This is Jean Cotter. Moments ago, a passenger plane with two hundred and seventy people aboard exploded over the skies of Virginia. It is not known if there are any survivors. Northwest flight seventy-one from Chicago was beginning its descent into Washington's National airport when the plane suddenly exploded, lighting up the night skies and scattering debris over a five mile radius--"

Bob slammed on the brakes and pulled the car onto the shoulder, just missing being rear-ended by another vehicle, whose driver blew his horn angrily.

"--of the explosion is not known. No one is thought to have survived the explosion, which occurred at a height of five thousand feet. Amy Fisher has this report from the airport, where families of the passengers are gathered, still in shock."

Bob leaned his forehead against the steering wheel. He should have been on that plane. . . *Your life's in danger if you come in on the seven-thirty flight. . . Delany doesn't want you to testify. . .he's going to kill you.*

His body shook. The plane crash was no coincidence. A hundred and seventy people had just died and he was the target. This was the third threat to his life in two weeks. His intuition told him that these events were connected. But what did Delany have in common with the old lady in the hospital? The beginnings of an answer touched the conscious part of his mind, but then it was gone before he could focus on it. Yet, for a moment the events of the past two weeks had fallen into place clearly. He struggled to bring back the thought, but without success. He knew it was futile to keep trying. The answer would come back to him in its own time.

He sat in the car, wondering what to do. Delany was part of the government. If Delany wanted him dead, other officials might be involved, which meant he couldn't even trust the police. He thought about returning to Chicago, then made a quick decision. If Delany was that afraid of his testimony, then his best defense was to testify. That would negate the reason for killing him in the first place. He could sort the rest of it out later, but he had to give his testimony in the morning. In the meantime, he needed a safe place to spend the night. It wouldn't be long before someone found out he had changed flights and traced him to the United flight, and from there to the rented car.

If someone was looking for him and he did not arrive at the Capital Holiday Inn, where he had a reservation, they'd probably assume he had stopped at a hotel on the way. Instead of heading towards D.C., he turned north towards Gaithersburg, Maryland. He stopped at a small motel on the outskirts of the city. An elderly woman was behind the desk.

"Good evening," she said. "Can I help you?"

"Yes, I'd like a room for the night."

If you could fill this out, please." She passed a sheet of paper to him.

He filled in his name as John Cook, his address as Boston, his company as Johnson and Associates, and his license plate number as RN 149, the first thing that came to mind. The rat wouldn't mind. He took the room key and drove around to the back of the building, parking a few spaces away from his room. He bent over at the sidewalk, grabbed a handful of dirt, and spread it over the numbers on the license plates. Then he walked up to his room door, inserted the key and, after throwing a quick glance over his shoulder, stepped inside.

The room was drab and cold. He tossed his bag onto the bed, turned on the heat, closed the curtains, and locked the door. He wedged a chair up under the door knob and shut off the light. Then he sat in the other chair, facing the door, his feet propped up on the bed.

Something strange and frightening was happening. He did not understand the nature of the danger, except that it was very real and that his life was at stake. Anyone willing to bring down an entire plane of people just to kill him had to be desperate. He sat in the chair, analyzing the possibilities, the various courses of action, the possible reactions, and the least dangerous alternatives. The hours drifted by and the light of dawn was beginning to filter through the window before Bob rose from the chair and stretched his stiffened muscles.

30

Ellen glanced at the clock on her living room wall. It was ten minutes to nine. She flipped her TV to CNN, where the Senate hearings were in progress. Bob was scheduled to testify at nine, and half the country would probably be tuning in. She hoped they were on schedule, as she needed to get to the hospital for her eleven a.m. shift at the cancer screening center.

She poured a cup of coffee and settled onto the couch. The apartment was old and drafty and she drew her legs up to her chest and pulled an afghan around herself. She glanced out the window at the dark sky. The weatherman had predicted more snow.

The scene on the TV abruptly changed to the CNN newsroom. "This is Patrick Leigh. To those of you who have just tuned in to hear Dr. Robert Newman's testimony, his whereabouts remain unknown at this time. Officials at Northwest Airlines have just announced that, contrary to earlier reports, Doctor Newman was definitely not--I repeat, not--on flight seventy one, which crashed last night over the D.C. suburbs with no known survivors."

Ellen bit her tongue so sharply that she tasted blood. Crash? What crash? She had gone to bed early and hadn't heard the news. She grabbed the remote and turned up the volume.

"According to airline officials, he was routed onto a United Airlines flight to Dulles. We are receiving breaking news from Capitol Hill and we go now to Washington correspondent, Wendy Shores."

A reporter appeared on the screen, with the Capitol building behind her.

"This is Wendy Shores reporting from the Capitol where the Senate subcommittee hearings are in progress. Patrick, something is happening below us at this moment. A car has just pulled up at the concrete barriers in front of the Capitol and there's a crowd surrounding it. We're going to try to get down there."

The camera focused on a black Buick Regal, surrounded by reporters. Ellen breathed a sigh of relief upon seeing Bob emerge, wearing a crisp, blue suit. He began making his way up the Capitol steps as reporters shouted questions. He turned just before entering the building and smiled. "I have a testimony to give and I don't want to keep our elected officials waiting. I'll be happy to answer questions afterwards."

Wendy Shores reappeared. "Patrick, as you just saw, Doctor Newman has arrived at the Senate, alive and apparently well. His location for the past twelve hours is still a mystery. We'll hopefully have the opportunity to speak to him after the session ends. Back to you, Pat."

The scene shifted back to the subcommittee chambers. Ellen set the remote on the coffee table and leaned back into the sofa. The committee had just finished with the latest witness. Someone announced Bob's presence.

There was a murmur throughout the chambers. An expression of shock crossed Delany's face and was gone so quickly that Ellen was not sure she had really seen it.

"Doctor Newman is present?"

"He is, sir. He's waiting outside."

Delany hesitated. "We'll take a five minute recess." He rose from his chair and the broadcast went to a commercial break.

Ellen ran her hands through her hair. If Bob had been on that flight, he'd be dead and the gene vaccine with him. Most of the medical community, the pharmaceutical industry, and a cohort of citizens' movements supported approval of the technology. But on the other side, an odd marriage of sorts had developed between environmentalists and the religious right, and those people would be all too happy to see the gene vaccine die.

Happy enough to crash a passenger plane? She wondered. These were the same groups that were bombing abortion clinics.

The senate subcommittee chambers reappeared on the TV and Delany called the hearings into session.

"Doctor Newman, this subcommittee was established in order to evaluate the implications of your discovery for the welfare of our society. Among the various functions of our government are to both protect its citizens from dangerous products and also to encourage the development of beneficial ones. We're attempting to decide into which category your gene vaccine falls. You obviously believe it falls into the latter. Perhaps you could tell us why."

"Yes," Bob answered. "I do believe that the gene vaccine promises to be beneficial for society. In fact, I would go much further. I believe it heralds a third revolution in medicine, the consequences of which are unparalleled in human history."

Bob appeared relaxed and confident. Still, he had the difficult task of explaining a complex science to the non-scientist and convincing the world that his creation was not a thing to be feared, but rather something to be utilized for the good of society. Ellen wasn't sure he could accomplish that task.

"In the entire course of human history there have really been only two medical advances which have had a dramatic impact on human health. Both of these came quite recently, historically speaking. The first, occurring in the last century, was modern sanitation. This one development did more to decrease mortality from infectious diseases than anything ever discovered before or since. The second revolution was the development of antibiotics and vaccines in the early part of this century. This development was truly a revolution, because it turned infectious diseases from the leading cause of death in human societies to minor nuisances. Pneumonia, the Plague, tuberculosis, small pox, the diseases which had ravaged civilization for centuries, were either controlled or eradicated.

"Since these two revolutions, we have spent trillions of dollars, brought advanced technology to medical diagnosis and treatment, and have had very little impact on either the longevity or the quality of life. Until now. For the last thirty years, scientists have been preparing for the third medical revolution. One step at a time, they have been unraveling the secrets of life itself. Why is this a revolution? Because we're no longer attempting to understand life just from the point of view of muscles and organs and nerves and blood vessels. We're now beginning to understand how living things function on a molecular level. Trying to practice medicine without an understanding of molecular biology is like trying to understand how a computer functions without understanding electricity. We have begun to understand how atoms interact with each other in a living cell. And what this means, ladies and gentlemen, is that we are beginning, for the first time since the dawn of man, to really understand life. Medicine, as it's practiced today, is primitive compared to what will be achievable even a generation from now, using the techniques of molecular biology being developed in the laboratories."

Bob spoke with a calm, confident voice. He had no notes, and his eyes made contact with each member of the subcommittee in turn.

"You've been hearing for the past week about all the wonderful and all the god-awful consequences that might occur as a result of this invention. Let's concern ourselves with a realistic discussion of what this technology will provide, and leave the fantasies to the horror movies. These are the facts. Gene therapy will allow patients born with debilitating genetic diseases to lead normal lives and to have normal children. That after all, is the ultimate goal of medicine, to cure. If we deny the medical profession the ability to cure because of the fear of interfering with the natural course of events, then we might just as well shut down all our hospitals and medical schools. We intervene in the natural course of events every day. What makes us human is our ability to manipulate and exploit our environment. After all, treating pneumonia with antibiotics is interfering with the natural course by killing the bacteria that would otherwise kill the patient.

"Now I'm aware that some people think that we shouldn't tamper with genes because they consider it interfering with nature. Some of those people have spoken before you from this chair in which I presently sit. I submit to you that tampering and tinkering is our nature. Everything we humans do is, in effect, tampering with nature. The use of penicillin affects the environmental balance by unnaturally killing bacteria in order to prevent the death of a human being. And there are people who claim that the use of penicillin is immoral for that very reason. Yet human beings from the dawn of history have attempted--and succeeded--in manipulating the environment in order to improve their lives. This is nothing new. It explains why we've transformed this world to suit us instead of becoming extinct after wandering naked for a few million years on the African plains.

"Nature is neither more nor less perfect than we humans. Nature seeks a balance. Nature improves the species at the expense of its individuals. Genetic diseases are not natural events that benefit the species. No, they are the mistakes that nature has allowed in order for the species to evolve. Nature is willing to accept the occasional creation of a few defective genes, mistakes if you will, in order to allow the gene pool of the species to be pliable enough to adapt to changing environments. Natural mutations in our genes usually benefit us, allowing us to adapt when the environment changes. That's why nature has made our DNA so pliable. Occasionally, that very pliability results in the production of a defective gene. Over the course of thousands of years of evolution, it matters little, since these defects will eventually be weeded out. But an individual unfortunate enough to be born with a defective gene endures suffering and misery. Nature doesn't care. Nature has no sympathy. But human beings do.

"We must respect nature, but we have never been helpless before it. When our ancestors suffered because the weather got cold, they didn't say, 'We must not interfere with Nature.' No, they created fire. When the natural order did not suit them, they were not passive. They built unnatural structures to live in so as to keep out the natural elements. They changed the paths of rivers, they built boats to travel on the water, planes to fly in the air. They domesticated animals and plants. They developed medicines to treat their illness. They cut open mothers' wombs to save babies who could not be delivered as nature had intended. Nature would have let both mother and infant die.

"Ladies and gentlemen, genetic engineering and the gene vaccine are simply a continuation of that human history, of our desire to improve the lives of the members of our society when nature has been unkind to them. It is only a continuation of our attempts to control our destiny and our future. It's not a thing to be feared. It will improve our lives, relieve the suffering of our loved ones, and bring an end to diseases for which there has, until now, been no cure.

"We are the only species on the planet with the ability to take our destiny into our own hands, to alter our future, to better ourselves. That is the great gift that nature has given us."

Bob finished and for a long moment no one spoke. The effect of his words hovered over the subcommittee chambers and in the homes of the millions of viewers who were listening in. Ellen knew at that moment that he had won. There would still be argument, the debate might continue for a while longer, but the final outcome was clear. The vaccine would be approved.

Delany broke the silence. "You've answered my question quite eloquently, Doctor. But we must deal in specifics. Would you like to comment on the controversy over the implications of your treatment and the potential for its misuse?"

"To what type of misuse are you referring?"

"Well, one misuse that comes to mind is for people to use this technique to splice out normal genes that they found undesirable, or to splice in genes that emphasized a certain trait of which they approved. For instance, is it true that this procedure could be used to make a person grow wings?"

"That sounds like a flighty idea to me, sir."

The room broke up in laughter. Bob continued, "In all seriousness, while what you ask might, in theory, be possible, we're not even close to understanding enough to be able to accomplish such a thing. People have gotten carried away with all sorts of science fiction ideas. This is a tool to treat medical problems, not to make monsters. Now, one can think of all kinds of crazy uses for which someone could exploit this technology. And as you all know, a lot of crazy ideas have been suggested. There will be more crazy ideas to come. But this technology is sophisticated. It can only be performed in a laboratory with the proper expertise. That's not to say that some day it won't be possible for a kid to perform gene therapy in his basement. But the same can be said for making nuclear bombs. This technology is here. It will be developed, if not by us in the United States, then by the Japanese or the Europeans or someone else. Its potential, both economic and social, is too great to be ignored. So it's up to you, as our legislative representatives, to decide whether the United States is going to lead in this adventure, or follow."

Ellen smiled. That was hitting them where they could feel it.

"Why are you so vehement in your desire to begin human trials at once? Why not give us time to reach a consensus and institute appropriate safeguards?"

Even in Ellen's TV screen, she could see the fire in Bob's eyes. "I have no objections to instituting safeguards. But I have patients who are dying while this debate is going on. Those patients can't afford to wait. I'm suggesting a limited number of human trials for patients who have only weeks to live."

"Some people say that you are obsessed with--"

"You're correct," Bob interrupted. "I am obsessed. I'm obsessed with trying to ease the suffering of my patients. This is a medical issue, not a legislative one, and Congress should leave it in the hands of the medical community to responsibly institute the appropriate safeguards. The decision as to whether to treat or how to treat should be made between the physician and the patient and his or her family, not by the legislature. Congress could take a month, two months, a year to debate the issue. In the meantime, people's lives are at stake, people who may not have a month-- or even a week."

"Doctor," Delany said, "it has recently been revealed that your wife died of a genetic illness and that your research began soon after that time."

Ellen straightened up. She couldn't believe he would have the gall to bring that up. That was striking below the belt. She noticed Bob beginning to sweat under the bright lights.

"You do your homework well, Senator," he responded evenly.

"How would you respond to those who claim that this personal tragedy has skewed your perspective on this issue?"

Bob did not answer at once. Ellen could see the tension building up in him and she saw how hard he was working to control his emotions. This session had taken a definite wrong turn.

Bob took a deep breath, and Ellen realized that she had been holding her own. "I would respond, sir that I have witnessed a great deal of tragedy in my profession and all of it has touched me personally. I know that there are those who would like to stop this technology. And I want to assure all who have placed their hopes in the gene vaccine that the technology will survive even if something happens to me, and the truth will be revealed to the public."

Was there a threatening tone to his voice? Ellen could not be sure. Yet somehow Delany seemed to understand. He stared at Bob silently.

One of the subcommittee members asked, "Doctor Newman, can you tell us whether you see a use of your gene vaccine in the cancer epidemic we are facing?"

Bob nodded. "Some cancers are caused by certain genes, called oncogenes. If these genes could be localized and spliced out of the DNA chain, we could potentially eradicate cancer forever. The sooner we can get this technology into use, the sooner we'll find out if it will be helpful in this epidemic."

Delany stared at Bob with a blank expression. Everyone waited for him to conclude the session, but Delany remained silent. Finally, the Senator to his left leaned over and whispered in his ear. Delany jerked, as if awakened from a dream.

"Thank you for your testimony thus far, Doctor Newman. The members of the subcommittee would like you to give us a detailed description of the gene vaccine. In what form would you like to present this information?"

"I've brought some slides with me," Bob answered.

"Very well. we'll recess for ten minutes while you set up your slides."

Ellen shut off the television. Bob had been poised, confident, and above all, human. His self-confidence was infectious. She had taken his side, even though she herself shared some of Delany's doubts. But she was worried that he had made enemies who might take things into their own hands. Bob was so preoccupied with his work that he would probably never notice the danger. She'd warn him as soon as he returned to Chicago.

31

Bob drove north from Midway airport after landing back in Chicago. Someone wanted him dead and the motive was almost certainly to prevent use of the gene vaccine. He might have concluded that it was a plot by the religious right, but given Delany's opposition to their views, that hypothesis was untenable.

He knew, as soon as he had locked eyes with Delany, that the Senator was involved. He had hoped that Bruce Nevins might provide some answers, but when he had sought him out after the hearings, he was told he was out of town. Probably permanently.

The most obvious course of action was to go to the authorities. But that presented two difficulties. First, he didn't know which authorities to trust. The capacity to bring down an airplane suggested a formidable network involving persons in influential positions. Confiding in the wrong person could be deadly. Second, even if he could trust the authorities, revealing the attempt on his life was certain to delay approval of the vaccine, and he was determined to do nothing that might jeopardize a quick, affirmative decision by the subcommittee. Which meant that he had no choice but to keep the threat on his life secret for now. The only ones who knew about it were himself and the plotters. Lois knew about the phone call, but he would make sure she kept that to herself. As soon as he got back to his office, he would see to it that, in the event of his death, a detailed description of the gene vaccine methodology would be published. He was sure that Delany had understood the message and he hoped that, whatever their motives, Delany and his gang would leave him alone.

Bob still had no idea how the old lady was connected, but he had a strong suspicion that deciphering that event was key to the mystery. And so, he decided to take a different route home so he could make a stop on the way. It was just a hunch, but he had little else to grasp at. He pulled into the synagogue parking lot and glanced at his watch. It was five-thirty. Hopefully the rabbi would be there. He entered the building and followed a sign to the rabbi's office. An elderly woman looked up from her desk. She wore a pair of thick glasses which hung off the end of her nose.

"May I help you?" she asked in a nasal voice.

"Yes, I'd like to speak with the rabbi."

"Can I ask what this is in regards to?"

"It's personal," Bob replied.

"I see," the woman responded, miffed. She looked at her appointment book. "How about next Thursday at two o'clock?"

"Would it be possible to see him now?"

She shot him a sharp look. "Now?"

"Yes. I know it's short notice, but it's very important."

"Rabbi Lipsky is a very busy man."

"I know. Please ask him if he'll see me for a few minutes."

The woman was clearly irritated. "May I have your name?"

"Robert Newman."

Her eyes widened. "Doctor Robert Newman?"

"Yes."

She lifted her glasses to her eyes and squinted through them. "I thought you looked familiar. I'll be back in a moment."

As Bob waited he wondered if he was wasting his time. Still, if there was any connection to the various pieces of the puzzle, the answer might be found here.

A middle-aged, bearded man appeared, his balding head covered with a skull cap.

"Hello, Doctor Newman. I'm Rabbi Lipsky." They shook hands. "Please come into my office." He took Bob's arm and escorted him into a room with book-lined walls. A large desk, cluttered with papers and open texts, stood in front of the window.

"Please," Lipsky motioned to a sofa beside the desk. Bob sat down and the rabbi took a seat in the opposite chair.

"What can I do for you, Doctor?"

Bob glanced over at the secretary standing at the door.

"Thank you, Edna," said the rabbi. "Please close the door on your way out."

The secretary frowned and departed.

"Thank you for taking the time to see me, rabbi. I'm sure you're busy."

"Not so busy that I don't have time to find out why a celebrity like yourself would come to speak to a rabbi."

"I'm looking for an answer to a simple question."

"I see." The rabbi nodded his head a few times. "Simple questions are the ones I fear the most."

Bob laughed. "Perhaps there are some similarities in our two professions."

"More than meets the eye, I think. What's the question?"

"I'd like to know the origin of a Hebrew word."

"Really? Are you Jewish?"

Bob shook his head. "I was brought up Lutheran, although I don't consider myself religious."

"What's the word? I'll do my best."

"The word is, Sartan."

Lipsky raised his eyebrows. "This I did not expect. Sartan? It's a very ancient word whose origin is lost in antiquity. Not even Hebrew, actually. It's Aramaic, an earlier language from which Hebrew arose. The modern meaning is cancer."

"I'm aware of its modern meaning. But do you know the etymology of it?"

Lipsky raised his eyebrows again. "The etymology? Would I be prying if I asked why a scientist like yourself is interested in the etymology of an Aramaic word?"

Bob smiled. "I know it sounds unusual. Actually, a patient in the hospital, an elderly lady in a coma, woke up suddenly and started screaming 'Sartan', and she attacked me."

An anxious expression flashed across Lipsky's face. "She attacked you?"

"Yes. And it's been on my mind ever since."

"Did the woman suffer from cancer?"

Bob nodded. "She did, but I suspect it has significance beyond that."

Lipsky stepped over to the window and gazed out it for a long moment. At last, he exhaled loudly and turned towards Bob. "This is a very strange line of questioning from someone such as yourself. I'm no expert on Sartan."

"Please. It's very important."

Lipsky frowned.   "Doctor, you're entering a realm of mysticism that is outside my expertise.   If you wish to know more, you should consult Eben Ezra."

"Who's he?"

"A Talmudic scholar from the thirteenth century."

Lipsky went to his bookcase.   He searched for a moment, pulled down a volume, and flipped through the pages.   "Eben Ezra had access to some very ancient sources.   Here's what he writes about the matter: 'Sartan is a black, festering boil born of the fiery darkness.   There is no age in which man is safe from his evil'."

Bob felt a chill pass over him.   "What do these things mean?"

Lipsky slammed the book shut and returned it to the shelf. "The sources and meanings of these quotes have long ago been lost.   I'm sorry, but this is all I know of the matter."

Bob gazed at him intently.   "Rabbi, I sense that there may be more you aren't telling me."

Lipsky returned to the window.   He rested his hands on the sill and his shoulders sagged.   He looked out onto the parking lot. "There are other sources. . . fragments of legends.   I doubt they're relevant."

"Please, Rabbi, they may be very relevant."

Lipsky did not answer immediately.   He stroked his beard for a full minute, his gaze alternating between the ceiling and the window.   Then he looked at Bob and spoke in a low voice, almost a whisper.

"Doctor, this is not a matter I generally have reason to discuss.   Sartan was an object of great dread in the ancient past. Man has retained fragmentary memories of an encounter with this evil being.   Much of that memory has been lost through the ages.   Only myths and legends remain."

"Is Sartan the devil?"

"No, not the devil.   There is no devil worship in the Jewish faith.   But the myth of the devil, even one of his names, Satan, derived from human memories of an encounter with this entity, Sartan. That encounter left a great impression."

"Tell me about the encounter."

"There's very little I can tell you, only a story from one of the apocryphal texts. When God created the Earth he made, not one rational creature, but two. Man and Sartan. To each He gave different traits. Man He made merciful, gentle, poetic, and good-hearted. Sartan He made aggressive, cunning, angry, and violent. They shared dominion over the Earth for many years, until a struggle ensued. Man would have lost, but God took away Sartan's legs so he could not walk, and his ability to pronounce, R, so he could no longer speak his full name. He could only hiss, like this: sssst . . . sssst . . . from which the name Satan is derived. The devil has been associated with the image of the snake since time immemorial."

"Why did God take away his ability to pronounce, R?"

"The Hebrew letter for R is Resh, from which is derived Resha, which means evil. R is the most evil sound in the universe."

"How could a sound be evil?"

"The ancients believed that certain sounds carried great power. Joshua brought down the walls of Jericho with the sound of trumpets, if you recall. And the name of God could kill if pronounced out loud, and was only spoken once a year by the high priest in the holy of holies."

"What happened to Sartan?"

"Sartan slunk away into hiding."

Bob leaned forward and gazed intently at Lipsky. "Where is he hiding, Rabbi?"

"He sits behind man's own eyes and peers through them, watching the world. It is said that if you stare into a man's pupils intently enough, you'll see Sartan staring back. On the day when Sartan will sense man's moment of weakness, he will reawaken and pronounce his full name. On that day, only prayer and repentance will save man from utter destruction."

Bob shuddered. "You're not seriously suggesting that the woman in the hospital is possessed by this evil entity, are you?"

Lipsky laughed a nervous laugh. "It's only a legend."

"Do you believe the legend?"

"I believe that legends have a kernel of truth. But it can be difficult to know which part is the kernel and which the chaff. Has this been of any help to you, Doctor?"

"I'm not sure. But thank you for your time, Rabbi. I do appreciate it."

"It's no problem at all, Doctor Newman." He led him towards the door. "I wish you best of luck. Excuse me if I give you just one small piece of advice. One of our great rabbis said, 'The whole world is a narrow bridge, but the essence of life is to not be afraid.'"

"Thank you, Rabbi," Bob replied and shook his hand.

"Goodbye, Doctor Newman."

32

Bob was not in his lab the next morning, so Ellen headed for the Genetics office to speak to Lois. She found Bob sitting on Lois's desk, conferring with the older woman.

"Hey, you were great yesterday! I was so relieved to see you on TV after the report of that plane crash."

"We were just discussing that," Bob replied.

Ellen closed the door behind her. "Good. You're gonna think I'm paranoid, but you've got to start taking precautions. There are plenty of crazy people out there who want to stop your gene vaccine from seeing the light of day. I wouldn't put anything past them, including crashing an airplane."

They both stared at her in silence.

"What?" she finally shouted.

Bob stood up. "If you've reached that conclusion on your own, then who else might--" his eyes narrowed and he glanced at Lois-- "did Lois tell you about the phone call?"

"What phone call?"

Bob approached Ellen and lowered his voice. "You need to keep your suspicions to yourself."

"And why is that?"

"I received a call warning me not to take that flight to Washington. The caller claimed to work in Delany's office. Lois, and now you, are the only two that know. It's got to stay that way."

"Are you kidding?" Ellen replied. "We've got to inform the police."

"No. The police will begin an investigation that'll delay approval of the gene vaccine. I can't let anything interfere with that."

"Agreed," Lois said.

Ellen turned to Lois, shocked that she had agreed so quickly when Bob's life might be in danger.

Ellen shook her head. "Wait a second. Someone sabotaged that flight. Over two hundred people were killed. I think we have a responsibility to report it."

"The phone call and the crash could have been an unfortunate coincidence," Bob replied.

"You don't believe that any more than I do."

"Ellen, you're right. I don't think it was a coincidence. Someone was trying to kill me. Trust me, I'm taking precautions. Now as for the crash, I understand your desire to help in the investigation. I want to help, too. I'm just asking for a couple of weeks, until the vaccine is approved. Then you can tell the authorities anything you damn well please."

She wasn't convinced.

"I need a couple of weeks," he pleaded. "George Peterson and little Tommy Kelly, *they* need a couple of weeks."

She looked into his face, wondering if he was frightened or even knew fear. His icy stare chilled her to the bone. His overpowering presence was irresistible.

She blew a deep breath. "Okay. . . a couple of weeks. . ." she whispered.

Standing behind them, Lois grinned. In a couple of weeks they'd both be dead.

* * *

"Is it going to hurt, Bobby?"

"Shouldn't hurt any more than being trampled by a herd of elephants," Bob replied, winking at Janie.

"You don't scare me."

"Good for you. He tore open an alcohol swab and wiped the skin over Janie's forearm. He waited a moment, then frowned and tied the tourniquet tighter. Satisfied, he reached into his coat pocket and pulled out a syringe filled with a blue-green liquid. Janie grimaced when he uncapped the needle.

"Hang in there, sport. It'll only take a second."

He held the needle above her arm and hesitated. Once the contents of the syringe were injected into the girls body, the act would be irrevocable. How confident was he, really? His heart raced as he pierced the vein and withdrew a small amount of blood into the syringe. Satisfied that the needle was in the vein, he released the tourniquet and slowly injected its contents. Then he withdrew the needle and pressed on the vein with a cotton swab. The deed was done. He wiped the sweat from his forehead with his coat sleeve.

"That's it, sweetheart. It wasn't bad, was it?"

"Not as bad as I thought. It felt like being trampled by just one elephant."

"Come on, when I was a medical resident, I had a reputation as the smoothest venipuncturist in the Midwest. In fact, legend had it that I once drew blood out of an orange."

Janie tried unsuccessfully to suppress a grin.

"Blindfolded," Bob added with a twinkle in his eye.

Janie laughed. "Bobby it's been a long time since those days. I think you ought to stick to giving orders and let the nurses give the shots."

"Very funny."

"What do I do now?" she asked.

"You just lie back and rest, and let this stuff do its job. The nurses have orders to check your vital signs every hour, so don't give them any trouble when they wake you up at night."

"Yes, doctor," Janie teased.

"Remember, as far as they're concerned, you've just received another injection of gamma globulin, got it?"

She nodded.

"I'll come see you tonight."

He frowned as he left the room. The vaccine could kill her, but in the final analysis, he really had no choice. He could not withhold from her the chance to live. There were others who deserved the same chance. It was for all of them that he was determined to prevent Delany from destroying the gene vaccine technology.

As he crossed the skyway, he reached down to his side and felt the cold steel of the pistol under his white coat. Since returning from Washington, he had kept it with him at all times, just in case Delany called his bluff. He wanted to be prepared for anything.

"Morning, Lois," he said as he entered the Genetics office.

"Good morning, Bob. My, you look well today."

"What's the catch?"

Lois laughed automatically, although she felt no emotion. "You'll never change, Bob."

He smiled and grabbed his mail. "I'll be in my lab. If anyone calls for me, I'm in Australia for the kangaroo festivals. Got it?"

"Yeah, only there are two stiffs in blue suits waiting for you. They were very persuasive when I told them you were unavailable."

"How persuasive?"

"FBI persuasive."

"Shit. What'd you tell them?"

She had played dumb, but the men had asked a lot of questions about the plane crash and about Bob. They were obviously suspicious of something. She would have to warn her superiors.

"I told them nothing, just like we agreed."

"Good."

Bob braced himself as he headed down the hall. If the investigation of the crash suggested any foul play, especially if Delany was implicated, it would split the debate on the gene vaccine wide open and delay Congressional action for months. He had to avoid that. On the other hand, protecting Delany would only give him further opportunity to target him.

His guard was up as he entered his lab. Two men in crisp blue suits were in the room. One was leaning against the lab counter. He was tall, about Bob's height, with a buzz hair cut. The other sat on a stool. He stood when he saw Bob enter. The man leaning against the counter straightened up and pulled a badge out of his vest.

"Dr. Newman, I'm agent Jenson from the FBI and this is agent Stuart. We'd like to ask you a few questions, if you don't mind."

"It'll have to be a very few," Bob responded. "I have patients to attend to."

Jenson curled his upper lip. "This won't take long, Doctor."

"What's this about?" Bob asked.

"It's about the plane crash Monday night."

"Yes, what about the crash?"

"Could you tell us why you switched to another flight at the last moment?"

"The flight was overbooked. They asked for volunteers. I agreed."

"Do you generally volunteer to be bumped off a flight?"

"I have, on occasion."

"I would have thought," Jenson persisted, "given your testimony the next day, you'd have wanted to get to Washington without any hassles."

Bob shrugged. "I didn't consider it a hassle, especially since the Northwest flight was jam packed."

"So you had no reason to suspect that something was going to happen to the Northwest flight?"

"Of course not. I assume it was just a horrible accident. Do you have any reason to suspect otherwise?"

"The investigation is just beginning," Jenson replied. "We're exploring all possibilities. Did you know anyone who was on that plane?"

"No."

Jenson walked over to Bob's desk and began to casually jab at some papers. "No one?" he asked again, without looking up.

Bob shook his head. "No one."

Jenson stepped away from the desk and looked at Bob. "Did it ever occur to you, after hearing the news about the crash, that you might have been a target?"

"A target? Of who?"

"You've generated a lot of publicity, Doctor. You must realize that some people have strong feelings against your gene vaccine. You were the only celebrity on that flight."

Bob thought for a moment. "I know of no one who would want to do something like that. Anything's possible, but it sounds far-fetched to me."

"Do you have any enemies, Dr. Newman?"

"Not those kind of enemies."

"What's your impression of the cancer epidemic?"

Bob was not expecting that question. "I'm not following you."

"It's curious that the cancer epidemic and the gene vaccine appeared at about the same time, don't you think?"

Bob's eyes widened. He could not believe what he was hearing! They suspected him of involvement in the cancer epidemic and in the downing of the Northwest flight!

"I'm afraid that's just another coincidence," Bob replied.

The agent looked at him coolly. "You explain away a lot by coincidences."

Bob suddenly remembered the gun under his white coat. He could be arrested for carrying a concealed weapon, not to mention the fact that these idiots would slap him with conspiring to bring down an airplane. He hoped the bulge at his side was not too conspicuous.

"Look, if you're here to accuse me of something, then do so. Otherwise, I've got work to do."

The men stood up. "We'll be in touch, Doctor."

Bob watched them leave, thankful that he had not gone to the authorities for protection. They were a bunch of bungling morons. He took it for granted that the FBI would be watching him from now on. On the plus side, that might give him some protection from Delany and his gang.

He picked up the phone and dialed the front office.

"Have they left?"

"Yes," Lois replied. "By the way, Joe called. I didn't want to interrupt you. He said he had something to take care of and would meet you in the cafeteria at noon. That would be five minutes ago."

"I'd better get down to the cafeteria before the old boy faints from hunger."

He grabbed a large manila envelope off his desk and left the lab.

At the cashier, Joe flipped out a dollar.

"Three," Bob said.

Joe looked at the serial number on the bill. "Damn," he said. "I don't know how you do it. Hell, this is your lucky week."

"There's no such thing as luck. You should know that, Joe."

Joe rolled his eyes. They sat down to eat.

"Impressive speech you gave yesterday. You really knocked 'em dead."

"Thanks."

"You gave us quite a scare, though."

Bob leaned forward across the table. "That plane crash was premeditated," he whispered.

Joe looked at him skeptically.

"Delany tried to kill me yesterday. I'm telling you, because you're one of the few people I trust. If something happens to me I want him to pay the price. And I want someone to continue the work."

Joe looked about to make sure no one was listening. "Do you know what you're saying, Bob?" he whispered back. "Delany's one of the most respected Senators on the Hill."

"I know. I'm telling you, he's conspiring to kill me. I saw it in his eyes yesterday at the hearings."

"His eyes? You're going to convict him for looking at you cross-eyed?"

"There's also the phone call from Delany's aide."

"What phone call?"

Bob related the conversation with the mysterious Bruce.

Joe seemed unconvinced. "The call was probably a prank. What motive would Delany have to kill you?"

"He doesn't want the vaccine approved."

"Why not?"

"That I don't know yet."

Joe mulled it over. "Did you tell this to the FBI?"

"Have they interrogated you, too?"

Joe nodded. "This morning."

"I can't tell the FBI," Bob replied. "I don't want to do anything that might hold up approval of the gene vaccine."

"Well, you need police protection. There are a lot of nuts out there, and you're a visible target."

"I can't do that, Joe."

"Why not? Too macho?"

"Police protection will just increase my visibility."

"You're talking nonsense."

"I won't even consider it," Bob replied. He handed Joe the manila envelope. "Here's the manuscript describing the gene insertion methodology. I'm sending it in today so that it's in print and available to the scientific community as soon as possible. I've made a copy for you to keep until it's published. If something happens to me, I want you to promise me you'll take up the project and see it to its conclusion."

"Stop talking like that, damn it. Nothing's going to happen to you."

Bob returned Joe's gaze. "Nevertheless, will you continue the project?"

"If, God forbid, something were to happen to you, of course I'd continue the project. Now are you going to get police protection or not?"

"Not."

Joe glared at him like a school teacher scolding a misbehaving pupil.

Bob put a hand on his shoulder. "Listen, nothing's going to happen to me. I just want to cover all bases. I've taken all the necessary precautions, including a letter that will be sent to the New York Times if I die, accusing Delany. He knows I'm not bluffing. Now cheer up." He patted Joe on the cheek. "Concentrate on happier thoughts, like ice cream sundaes."

"You're a stubborn man."

"And you're my best friend, Joe. I'm depending on you."

33

Ellen tapped on the hospital room door, opened it, and peeked inside. David was seated in a chair, dressed in a brown velour robe. His arms were folded across his chest, and he was staring at the floor. He looked up when she entered.

"Hi Ellen." He motioned her to a chair beside his. "Thanks for coming to see me."

"David, you look wonderful!" He did. The pallor was gone from his face and he had obviously put on weight since she had seen him last week.

"Thanks. I feel wonderful."

She sat down beside him. "See, I told you things weren't as bad as you thought," she said cheerfully. "I take it the treatments are going well?"

"Actually, I haven't started the treatments."

Ellen looked at him quizzically. "I don't understand."

"You know there's no good treatment for metastatic melanoma. The doctors have some kind of experimental protocol involving a new combination of drugs and radiation treatments, but I don't want to be a guinea pig."

Ellen frowned. "David, I'm surprised at your attitude. What's going to happen if you don't get the treatment?"

"Either I'll live or I'll die."

He seemed awfully nonchalant. This was not the same compulsive David she knew. "Well, then are you going home?"

David shook his head. "I'll stay here for now. I could get worse again. By the way, I've got something for you."

He pulled a small, gift-wrapped box out of the night stand and handed it to her. She remembered how he used to do this sort of thing when they were together. She looked at him warily.

He smiled at her. "Open it."

She was about to object, but then she remembered how Bob had refused to accept her sweater. She unwrapped the box and pulled out a gold necklace with a simple pendant. She did not recognize the gray stone.

"David, it's lovely. But why?"

"I just wanted to give you something to remember me by. Could you do me a favor? Wear it as long as I'm alive. Maybe it'll bring me luck."

She put it on. The pendant rested in the depression of her neck. It felt warm as it touched her skin. "Thank you. It's very pretty."

"Will you wear it?"

"Of course I'll wear it. It's very thoughtful of you." She smiled. "And stop talking about dying."

He looked at her, his eyes unfocused, as if they were staring through her. When he spoke, his voice was distant. "I used to love the way you smiled. I can still remember that."

He had a wild look in his eyes which frightened her. The smile faded from her lips.

She stood up. "I have to go, David."

"Of course you do. Thanks for coming by to see me, Ellen. And don't forget to come again."

There was something definitely wrong with David. His affectless voice and manner seemed threatening. She wondered if the melanoma could be affecting his personality in some way. She put her hand to her neck and felt the pendant. She had a sudden impulse to tear the chain off, but then she decided that was stupid. The least she could do was to wear it, as he had requested. If she took it off and he died, she would feel terrible.

She left the hospital and walked across the street to a small park. It felt good to be outside in the brisk air. She glanced back at the hospital entrance. Her eyes settled momentarily on a man in a dark overcoat standing on the steps. He was short, with black hair and a bull nose. She looked away and watched some squirrels darting up and down a nearby tree. After a few minutes she glanced back. The man was still there, leaning against the wall of the hospital and gazing idly down the street.

The cold air had begun to chill her and she buttoned her coat. She headed away from the medical center towards her apartment, glancing back as she turned the corner. The man was coming down the steps in her direction. For a moment, she wondered if he was following her, then decided that she was being paranoid. She turned left at the next intersection. She knew she was being stupid, but she could not help looking back again. The man was on the other side of the street about thirty feet behind her.

Night was approaching as she reached her neighborhood. Ellen saw a figure leaning against a tree a block ahead of her. It was difficult to make out the features in the near dark. She crossed to the other side and quickened her pace. When she glanced across the street, the figure was gone. She reached her building, ran up the steps to her apartment, and bolted the door. Why was she so edgy today? She was getting carried away with her imagination.

Ellen looked out the window, seeing her own reflection in the glass. A nearby street lamp illuminated the opposite side of the street for about ten feet on either side. She saw a figure emerge into the light. It was the same bull-nosed man!

Trying not to panic, she hurried into the living room, picked up the phone, and dialed the police. The woman on the line took her name and address and said a car would be sent out immediately. Ellen hung up the phone and went back to the window. The man was still there under the street lamp, hands in his coat pockets. After a few minutes he walked out of the perimeter of the street light and out of sight.

The police arrived ten minutes later. They took her report and searched the area, but the man had gone. They told her to keep her door locked and they left. Ellen went into the bathroom and started the water in the tub. She looked at her face in the mirror and used her index finger to rub out the crease between her eyebrows. Her nerves were frazzled. The steam from the bathtub began to settle onto the mirror and after a few moments her face disappeared in the condensation. She stripped off all her clothes, shut off the faucet, and stepped into the tub, lowering herself gently into the steaming water. The bath was soothing and she finally began to relax. She pulled a hand towel off the rack, dipped it into the bath, and lay it over her face. She sunk down deeper into the tub. Suddenly, she felt very much alone and very vulnerable. Despite the heat of the water, a shudder of dread shook her body, and she was attacked by a nameless fear.

34

A lone car made its way down Diversey Street at 5 a.m., its headlights off. The car pulled into an alley two blocks from Altmann's Chemicals. After a moment, the engine cut off. Bob Newman stepped out onto the broken pavement and peered down the alley. There were no other vehicles in sight. He smiled, satisfied that he had lost the FBI men who had been parked down the street from his house all night. He made his way around the piles of broken crates until he was thirty feet from the back of the warehouse, where he crouched down behind a pile of cardboard boxes and waited.

An hour later, with dawn braking and still no activity, he approached the building. The window he had broken had not been repaired and his shoes crunched the pieces of glass that lay shattered on the concrete loading platform. He placed his hand on the door knob and turned. The door creaked open.

The warehouse was abandoned. The metal barrels were gone and the papers had been cleared from the desk. The coffee-stained mug still sat where he had last seen it. Something darted past him. He could not tell in the darkness if it was a rat.

Another dead end and he was still no closer to solving the puzzle. He had pieces: a conspiracy to induce cancers, an extraordinary acceleration in malignant transformation of cells exposed to carcinogens, Senator Delany's attempt to block the gene vaccine. But the pieces did not fit. There was still a missing fragment. He one lead left, the old woman. He returned to his car and headed for the hospital.

When he reached the ICU he stopped at the nurse's desk. "You still got a patient named Mildred Stone up here?"

"Bed eight."

He found her exactly as she had appeared the last time, frail and apparently comatose.

"How's she doing?" he asked the nurse at her bedside.

She shrugged. "The same. Non-responsive to deep stimuli. Vitals have been pretty stable."

Bob looked down at the old woman. Wires ran from her chest and arms to the monitor overhead. A Foley catheter ran out from under the sheets to a urine bag hanging on the edge of the bed. An i.v. was inserted into her left hand. He observed her breathing. It was in the Kussmaul pattern. He pinched the skin of her thigh. There was absolutely no response, neither on the woman's body nor on the monitor above.

Bob leaned over, placed his mouth near her ear, and whispered, "Sartan. . ." The old woman's eyelids fluttered. He looked up at the monitor. Her heart rate increased to ninety-five momentarily, then drifted back down. He leaned over again. "Cancer. . ." There was no response. He tried a few other words, "Vinyl chloride . . . Delany . . . gene vaccine . . ." Nothing.

"Sartan . . ." The eyelids fluttered again. Then her eyes popped open and a deep sigh escaped from her lips. A moment later an alarm went off. He looked up at the monitor. Her heart pattern showed ventricular fibrillation.

"Shit," he muttered. He ripped the sheet from the old woman's body and stuck his stethoscope against her chest. "Call a code!"

He laid the heel of his palm on her sternum and started compressions. In moments, the area around the bed filled up with white-coats. "Someone get an E.T. tube down!"

"This lady is DNR!"

Bob turned towards the nurse, his hands still performing chest compressions. "Are you sure?"

"Of course I'm sure. I'm her primary."

Bob did not want to stop the resuscitation. He sensed that she held the key to the entire mystery. Besides, he worried that he may have caused the arrest.

"Let me see the order."

The nurse grabbed the woman's chart, flipped it open, and held it in front of Bob's face. "See? 'Do Not Resuscitate'. The family decided three days ago."

Regretfully, Bob let his hands drop. Mildred Stone's eyes were still open and they stared at him. He glanced up at the monitor. She was in coarse ventricular fibrillation with the heart impulses rapidly weakening. This old woman had been his last lead.

"Time of death eleven-forty-three," someone called out from the bedside.

Bob walked back to the nurse's desk, picked up the phone and dialed Pathology. "Who's on this month for autopsy? . . . Let me speak to him . . . Sandy? Bob Newman. . . . A woman, Mildred Stone, just died up in the ICU. When do you think you'll get to her? . . . It's urgent . . . In the next seventy two hours? . . . Page me. I want to be at the autopsy . . . Thanks Sandy."

Bob closed his eyes and rubbed them wearily.

35

Two days after her injection, Janie's condition began to deteriorate as the virus reproduced in her body and infected her cells. Bob remained at her bedside through the weekend. He was killing Janie and he knew it.   But if he stopped the immunosuppressants she would die anyway and the vision of Diane's suffering gave him the justification he desperately needed to continue.

Janie developed severe diarrhea, spiking fevers, and red, blistered skin. Her breathing was labored and she required an oxygen mask. It was obvious that she had developed an overwhelming infection. Yet he refused, to the consternation of the nurses, to stop the immunosuppressant medication. They accepted his weak explanations for continuing the drugs, albeit with a degree of skepticism they had never before felt for Bob's clinical judgment. Were it not for their high regard for his medical abilities, they would have reported him to the Physician Review Board.

By Monday morning he was exhausted. He had not slept for three days and the strain was becoming apparent to the staff on the ward. Questions were again being raised regarding the appropriateness of his caring for someone so close to him.

He was walking a tightrope. If he stopped the drugs too early, Janie would be back where she had started. All the suffering he had caused would still leave her with a terminal disease. If he waited too long, her condition would be so precarious that her body would not have the resources left to repair the damage caused by the virus, and she would die. The burden was suffocating him and there was no one he could talk to.

Everything had to be kept secret. He had dialed Joe's telephone number half a dozen times, only to hang up before it rang. He couldn't bring himself to get Joe mixed up in this, no matter how desperately he desired his input.

Janie was only intermittently conscious now. She would still open her eyes when he called her name, but she was otherwise unresponsive. He had planned to wait for seven days, but he could not stand it any longer. He had to find out if the virus had done its job and penetrated into the chromosomes of her cells. He drew some blood from her arm, took a small biopsy from her skin, and a scraping from the mucosal tissue inside her mouth. Then he headed for his lab.

He stopped in the Genetics office for a cup of coffee. Ellen was there, talking to Lois.

"You're a wreck!" Lois said.

"You're always there with the compliments," Bob replied. "I've been busy."

"Well, it's time you unbusy yourself, and I mean right now."

"Thanks, but I've got something I need to do in the lab first."

Lois frowned. If only she could keep him out of his laboratory. Whatever he was doing in there could not possibly be in their interest.

"It can wait. I want you to go home, take a long hot bath, have a nice hot meal, and get about thirty hours of sleep. Then maybe, if you look up to it, I'll let you into the lab."

"That sounds wonderful, but I don't have time for all that. When I'm done in the lab, maybe you could talk me into a long hot bath--assuming you're in it." The corner of his lip lifted into his disarming smile.

Ellen was worried about the way he looked. "How's Janie?" she asked.

"Not well. She's deteriorating by the day."

"Is there hope?"

"Maybe. I'll know by the morning."

"You're not planning to be in the lab all night!" Lois exclaimed.

"That's exactly what I'm planning."

Lois wondered if he had secretly treated the girl. If so, she must die. In either case, Newman had to be kept out of his laboratory. "Bob, listen to me, you're going to kill yourself. You may not care, but I do."

He smiled at her, reached over, and patted her on the cheek.

"Thanks for caring, dear," he said and walked out of the office.

"He looks absolutely terrible," Ellen exclaimed after he departed. "I'm really worried. Maybe I should try to talk to him."

Lois gazed at Ellen. Maybe the girl could be useful after all. "Yes. Talk to him, dear. If anyone can sway him, you can."

"Well, I'm at least going to let him know that we're here if he needs somebody to talk to," Ellen said.

She headed down the hall, knocked lightly on the door, and entered the lab. Bob did not seem to have noticed. He was sitting at his bench, pouring some liquid into a glass container.

"Bob?"

He looked up. "What is it, Ellen?"

She wasn't sure what to say. "I just wanted you to know that we--that I--know what you're going through."

"Thank you. I appreciate that."

His responses were distant and he seemed to be in another place.

"If there's anything I can do for you, anything at all, just let me know. I'll be up late tonight studying, and I . . . I know that sometimes it's helpful to talk with someone. So if you want to take a break for a cup of coffee later, call me."

She jotted her phone number on a piece of paper and handed it to him. Bob took it and stuffed it into his shirt pocket.

"Thanks, Ellen. I do appreciate your concern."

She could not think of anything else to say, and yet she hesitated to leave him alone. "You know, I--" she was interrupted by a shrill beeping coming from Bob's pager. The beeps ended, then:

"Doctor Newman to Five East, STAT. Doctor Newman to Five East, STAT."

His face turned pale. He jumped out of his chair and raced from the room.

Bob was out of breath when he rushed into Janie's room. A dozen people were around her bed. Orders for various medications were being yelled out by the medical residents. He forced himself through the crowd and to her bedside.

"What's happening, people?" he shouted. "Talk to me!"

The nurse, Debbie, grabbed his arm. "Her temperature's a hundred and five and her blood pressure's dropping."

"Janie . . ." he patted her face. There was no response.

"Has she gotten Tylenol?"

"About ten minutes ago."

"What's her temperature now?"

"Still one o-five."

"Give her another dose, rectally."

He yanked out his stethoscope and put it to her chest. She was breathing, but shallowly. Her heart rate was close to two hundred. He felt her pulse. It was weak and thready.

"Increase her oxygen to a hundred percent," he ordered.

"Here's the epinephrine!" a nurse said, shoving a syringe towards the bed.

"Hold that order!" Bob shouted. "Epinephrine will kill her. I want a liter of plasmanate i.v. now!"

"How fast?" asked a medical resident as he prepared the bottle.

"As fast as you can push it. Debbie, get some ice water and towels and start sponging her. I want that temperature down!"

"Yes, doctor," Debbie rushed to respond to his order.

Ten minutes later, Janie opened her eyes. Bob leaned over her.

"You're going to be fine now, honey," he whispered.

Her frail body shook like a leaf. "I'm scared, Bobby."

"Don't be. I'm right here beside you. Everything's going to be okay." He brushed the bangs off her forehead. "Just get some rest now."

"All right." She closed her eyes again.

Bob moved away from the bed. He took a deep breath, then turned and left the room. Debbie chased after him.

"What happened?" she asked when she caught up.

"Her temperature rose so high that the blood went to her skin and she became hypotensive. Debbie, I want her temperature kept in the normal range. I don't care if someone has to stand by her twenty four hours a day sponging her."

The nurse nodded. Her doubts had been erased by the events of the last few minutes. This was the Doctor Newman that everyone knew and respected.

"What about the immunosuppressants?"

He hesitated, then said, "I told you, Debbie, she needs the steroids to prevent septic shock. Hopefully we'll be able to stop it tomorrow morning."

Bob headed back towards his lab. Ellen rushed over when she saw him in the hallway outside the office.

"What happened?"

"She's fine. Just a little excitement. Now I really have to get some work done."

He left her standing in the hall and returned to his laboratory where he began to isolate the DNA from the tissue and blood samples he had taken from Janie earlier in the day. He would then need to probe the DNA to see if the glucosidase gene was present. He estimated that, working all night, he might just finish by morning.

Ellen stayed in the office until eight, but Bob never left the lab. She started down the corridor a couple of times, then turned

back for fear of disturbing him. Although she hesitated to leave
him there alone, she did finally go home, casting a final, lingering
glance down the corridor on her way out.

* * *

Ellen stopped by the Genetics department in the morning on
the way to the screening center. She peered down the hallway
and saw that the light was still on in Bob's lab. He must have
been working all night. She knocked and entered. He was at his
desk, flipping through some computer printouts, an empty cup of
coffee beside him.

"Bob, I can't believe you're still here."

Bob rubbed his bleary eyes and looked up at her.

"I finished a couple of hours ago, Ellen. I just wanted to run
the data through one more time to be sure."

"Well, did your experiment work?" She couldn't imagine
any experiment worth this much abuse.

Instead of answering her, he picked up the telephone and
dialed a number.

"This is Newman," he said into the phone. "Let me talk to
Debbie."

"Debbie, it's Bob. . . How's Janie? . . . No more vital sign
instability? . . . Good. Listen, I want you to stop the Imuran. . .
Yes. . . No don't stop the prednisone yet. We'll taper it over the
next few days so that we don't cause too much stress . . . Yeah, I
think we're going to make it . . . Debbie, I'll be on my beeper if
you need me . . . No, I don't make house calls. . . No not even for
nurses . . . Oh, and Debbie? . . . Thanks for everything."

He hung up the phone, and turned to Ellen.

"Ellen, you're looking at a very happy man."

His hair was disheveled, his clothes wrinkled, and he had a
four day stubble on his face. She couldn't help laughing. "If
you're a happy man, I hope I never see you depressed."

He smiled. "Appearances can be misleading, you know. I'm ecstatic, but too exhausted to celebrate. I'm going home for a few hours."

36

Senator Delany leaned his back against the cool, marble stone of the Jefferson Memorial. He gazed up at the large-than-life, bronze figure in the center of the chamber, illuminated against the darkness of the night by powerful floodlights. There was a time when he would come to this, his favorite spot in Washington, for inspiration. The proud features on the statue's face, the powerful words on the walls, would strengthen his sense of purpose. But that seemed so long ago, nothing but a dream now.

He gazed across the river. The memorial was reflected onto the dark waters of the Tidal Basin. From a slightly higher vantage point, he could have seen the White House, the greatest seat of power on the planet. The man in that house slept comfortably at this very moment, oblivious to the foreign presence growing inside his body. Soon, it would awaken and the struggle would begin, a struggle the President would lose because of ignorance of his enemy's purpose. Humanity's fate was sealed. It was only a question of a few months at most. Everything had been set in motion, the momentum building, gathering force like a boulder barreling down the side of a mountain, too powerful to be stopped. Yet doubt had seeped into his mind. Doubt had been with him most of his life, yet it felt so foreign to him now. He closed his eyes, letting the feeling wash over. After a moment, the intoxicating sensation of invincibility returned. He turned towards the heavyset figure standing beside him.

"I underestimated Newman's persuasive powers. The subcommittee insisted on a vote today, and I was unable to prevent approval."

"I'm not laying the blame on you," his companion responded. "But we cannot allow the gene vaccine technique to be used. It's too risky."

Delany nodded. "Yes, Newman has already stumbled onto Gp-78 and he's beginning to suspect its significance. He's a very intuitive man."

"He'll never figure out the truth, if he's dead."

A misty fog enveloped the night. Delany felt the dampness on his exposed face. A sudden panic took hold of him, an excruciating sensation that they were underestimating their adversary. Why did he still harbor these weak thoughts?

"What about his threat to go public if he's harmed?"

His companion smiled. "We've got that covered."

"Newman made it quite clear that his method would be available to the scientific community if he died."

"It's one thing to read a technical manual, and quite another to reproduce the technique. By the time someone else gets that far, it'll be too late for them."

"Yes, you're right," Delany replied, drinking in the power of his companion's words.

"Our Chicago cell will take care of Newman and his gene vaccine, dnce and for all. In the meantime, we're accelerating our game plan. We're moving the Edison mission up to the day after tomorrow."

Delany looked down at his companion. "That's risky."

"Perhaps, but we need to increase our numbers. Events are moving too slowly."

"Yes," Delany agreed, "speed is essential."

He turned and faced the statue under the high, stone canopy, studying the proud, intelligent eyes gazing out towards the horizon. The nagging doubt returned. Vision, he mused, required more than the mere possession of a pair of eyes. And he felt blind.

37

Bob awoke at eight in the evening, feeling drugged from sleep deprivation. He showered to clear his head, then went down to the kitchen, made a cup of coffee, and opened the morning newspaper. He scanned the headlines while he sliced open a cantaloupe and spooned it into his mouth. The two stories dominating the news were the approval of his gene vaccine by Congress and the cancer epidemic. The epidemic had reached alarming proportions and was spreading around the globe. The data was extremely worrisome, with indications that up to thirty percent of the population was affected.

He left the coffee cup in the sink, grabbed his briefcase and jacket, and drove to the hospital. He went directly to Five East and peeked into Janie's room. She was sleeping comfortably, a half-smile on her angelic face. He lifted the bed chart off of the rail and examined the graph of her vital signs and fluid status. She was making a remarkable recovery. Her temperature was 99.6, still a fever, but definitely improving. According to the nurses' notes, the diarrhea was gone and she was much more alert. Most exciting of all, she was, as far as he could tell, cured of Pompe's. She was going to live.

He decided not to wake her. He went to the ward desk and dialed pathology.

"This is Bob Newman. Let me talk to Stan Morransky."

"He's gone home already, Doctor."

Damn. "Well, do you know if he's gotten to the Mildred Stone autopsy?"

"One second. Let me check."

Bob had not heard from Stan. He had been so engrossed with Janie for the past few days that he had forgotten to check on the autopsy. But it should have been completed by now.

"Doctor, that body was autopsied last night by Dr. Becker."

"Becker? It was assigned to Morransky."

"It says Becker here on the report."

"Fine. Let me have Becker."

"I'm sorry, everyone's gone for the night. The resident's here, if you want to speak to him."

"No. I'll call back in the morning."

He crossed the skyway and headed for Genetics, where he met Joe locking the office door.

"You're here late tonight," Bob said.

"Trying to catch up on some paperwork. How's by you? Any more death threats?"

"No. Maybe the threat's over now that the vaccine's been approved."

"Got anyone in mind as a first candidate?"

"I've received hundreds of requests from people asking for treatment. They're calling to find out if I can cure their hemophilia, or Aunt Shirley's arthritis, even their kid's smelly feet. But I think we should start with someone from our clinic who we know well. I've got a list of seven to choose from. How about you and I sit down tomorrow and go through their charts."

"Sounds fine," Joe answered. "Let's also discuss possibilities for using the technology for the cancer epidemic. It's bound to come up at the CDC meeting in Atlanta on Friday. I want you to attend."

"I've got a couple of ideas. If there are oncogenes in our chromosomes that are triggering these malignancies, we might be able to splice them out using the gene vaccine."

"Good. Let's meet first thing in the morning. By the way, how's Janie doing? I hear she came down with a viral infection."

Bob's mouth dropped. Did he know? Even the nurses on the floor didn't suspect.

"How'd you know that?"

"I'm the head of this department. It's my job."

"Yeah, well she picked up some virus in the hospital." So far, no lie. He hoped he wouldn't have to lie to his friend. He wasn't sure he could. "She's much better now."

"Oh? That's good. Did you find out what virus it was?"

He had to know! Bob studied Joe's face, but he couldn't read anything there. "The lab couldn't type it."

"I bet you could have though, huh?"

Bob narrowed his eyebrows. "How the hell did you find out?"

"I told you, I'm the head of this damned department. I make it my business to know what goes on around here."

"Listen, Joe. I know it was illegal. I didn't want to involve you or anyone else. As far as the records are concerned, Janie only received gamma globulin injections and some analgesics."

"Screw the records. I want to know if it worked."

"I ran the DNA samples this morning."

"And?"

"And I probed for the beta-galactosidase gene."

"The results, for Christ's sake!"

Bob hesitated. "Okay, DNA from skin, lymphocytes and mucosal cells all hybridize specifically to the native gene and not to the mutated one."

He looked at Joe, waiting for a response, for some sign of approval or disapproval. Slowly, a grin began to form on his ample face. "Well I'll be a son-of-a-gun," he exclaimed. "You did it, buddy! You actually did it!"

Bob grinned back. Then the two men grabbed each other in a bear hug.

38

After Joe left, Bob returned to his lab and leaned back in his chair, feet on his desk. For the first time in months he had things under control. Janie was well on the road to recovery. The gene vaccine had been approved. Nobody had tried to kill him for a week. Now he could turn his attention to a new challenge, the cancer epidemic. Part of the Gp-78 gene had already been sequenced. It was a highly unusual sequence, not like a gene at all, but similar to the 'junk' stretches of DNA found between genes. If he could complete the sequence, he could start working on a restriction enzyme that would splice it out of the genome. If that was successful, it would be straightforward to produce a gene vaccine for cancer. Of course, the whole thing was a long shot. He had no idea whether the Gp-78 protein was the trigger for the cancer genes or even if it had anything to do with the epidemic. Still, no one had come up with any better ideas.

His beeper went off. It was the Genetics ward.

"Dr. Newman, this is Shirley. I'm glad you're still in the hospital. I've got George Peterson tonight. I'm concerned about his mental status. Do you think you could swing by and have a look at him?"

"I'll be right over."

He hurried to Peterson's room. Peterson was having his blood pressure checked by the nurse. "Hey, doc, how's it going?"

"The question is, how's it going by you?" Bob replied.

"I'm good, doc. Except for my head, I feel super."

"What's wrong with your head?"

"I've just been having weird thoughts, is all. Must be all the excitement, only, man, it's like I black out and these freaky pictures come into my head.   Having headaches, too.   But I figured that's cause I haven't been sleeping too good."

Bob turned to the nurse.   "How have his vital signs been?"

"He's running a low grade fever."

Bob frowned.   Low grade fever and mental status changes could mean an infection in the brain.   With Peterson's non-existent immune system, it could be anything--viral, bacterial, or fungal.

He pulled a pen light out of his pocket.   "Look straight ahead," he said, pointing the light into Peterson's eyes.   The pupils constricted normally.   "Can you follow the pen, Mr. Peterson?" He moved the pen through all the visual fields.

"Does your neck hurt when you look up at the ceiling?"

Peterson looked up.   "No."

No signs of meningitis.   Still, one had to jump on these patients.   An infection could spread like a brushfire.

"Shirley, draw a CBC, three sets of blood cultures, a UA, and urine culture, and send him down for a chest x-ray and head CAT scan."

"Sure, Dr. Newman."

"And make sure the scan is marked stat or they won't do it tonight. I'll take care of the approval from radiology."

The nurse nodded. Bob turned to Peterson. "Don't get too alarmed by all this. You're probably fine. I just want to be doubly careful we don't miss anything."

"I understand, doc. Better safe than sorry."

"Exactly. I'll be by again tomorrow, okay?"

"Sure thing."

Bob took the ancient concrete stairwell down to the basement and stopped at the radiology film desk.

"Who's attending on CT this month?" he asked a female clerk.

"Glass."

"Is he still here?"

The woman nodded.   "He's finishing up an emergency case."

"Tell him Bob Newman needs to speak to him when he has a sec."

The clerk returned after a few moments.   "He'll be with you shortly."

"Good. In the meantime, I'd like to see a film jacket."

"The patient's name?"

"Mildred Stone. I need her CAT scan."

The clerk punched the name into a computer terminal on the desk, picked up a pen and scribbled down a number.   "Hold on."   She disappeared into the rows of cabinets in the back of the room and returned a few moments later carrying a large manila folder.

"Here you are."

"Thanks."   Bob took the folder and searched through it for the CAT jacket. He searched again. Then he dumped all the X-rays on the table and went through them one at a time. No CAT scan. According to the jacket cover, a CAT scan with contrast had been performed on October 3rd. He returned to the film desk.

"The scan's missing."

"Sorry. That's everything I got."

"Maybe it's been checked out," Bob suggested.

The clerk typed into the computer terminal, then said, "The jacket was checked out by pathology two days ago."

"Pathology? Why?"

"They take the X-rays for the autopsy. This patient must have died recently."

"She did. Was the CAT scan in the jacket when pathology checked it out?"

The clerk shrugged. "I have no way to know."

Bob handed the folder back. "Thanks."

"Bob, what can I do for you?"

Bob turned to see a thin, elderly man with wiry hair and stopped shoulders approach.

"Ron, I'm glad I caught you. Listen, I've got a patient upstairs who had a bone marrow transplant three days ago. He's running a fever and is complaining of headaches and visual hallucinations. Can you scan him for me?"

"Sure. You want it done tonight?"

Bob nodded. "The guy worries me."

"I've already called my wife and told her I wasn't going to make it to the theatre anyway. We'll be done with the present case in about an hour."

"Thanks. There's something else I want to ask you. Do you happen to remember a CAT scan performed last month on a Mildred Stone with metastatic lymphoma?"

Glass thought for a moment. "Don't recall offhand. If you pull the jacket I'll take a look at it with you."

Bob shook his head. "That's just it. I pulled the jacket. The scan's missing."

Glass groaned. "God damn it, you'd think people were plastering their walls with the films! Until we start charging a deposit we'll never get this under control. Let me pull up my dictation. That might help you."

He led Bob to his office and sat down in front of a computer terminal. "What's the name again?"

"Mildred Stone."

Glass entered the name. "Ah yes, here it is." Glass read his report out loud. "The frontal lobe is infiltrated by a mass of tissue extending up from the brain stem. Unusual bony structures are noted. Minimal compression of surrounding neural tissues is observed. . . Oh yes, I remember this case now. It was a *very* unusual scan."

"Really. . ."

Glass held his fist out in front of him. "There was a mass of finger-like projections infiltrating the frontal lobe. There was also new bone formation within the tumor mass. In fact, the whole scan was atypical for lymphoma, or for any malignant process I've ever seen.   And the strangest thing was that there was no compression of the surrounding brain tissue."

"What does that mean?"

"When a tumor grows it compresses the normal tissue around it. But this woman had almost no frontal lobe at all. This mass had just about completely replaced her brain.   I recommended a biopsy, but I don't know if it ever got done."

"It didn't. She died a couple of days ago."

"You know, there was another patient I scanned last week, a young man with malignant melanoma. What was his name? . . . Blaire. That's it, David Blaire. Same God-awful picture. His entire frontal lobe had been replaced with a mass." He held out his fist again. "Let me show you his film."

They returned to the film desk and Glass handed the medical record number to the clerk, who disappeared behind the file cabinets.

"This guy Blaire had a dye reaction while on the scanner so the study never got finished. But wait till you see this image. It'll freak you out. I asked to have him sent down for another study, but he refused."

"He refused?"

"Just refused. He's evidently refusing any further therapy. Very strange case."

The clerk returned with the jacket and Bob followed Glass to the viewing screen.

"Wait till you get a load of this, Bob. . . Where the hell's the CAT scan? . . .God damn it, I don't believe it!"

Glass dumped the contents of the folder onto the table and began searching all the films.

"It's gone," Bob said without looking.

"Shit. We can't run a radiology department in this manner."

Bob put his hand on Glass's shoulder. "Thanks Ron. Can you call me after you've seen my patient's scan?"

"Sure. You gonna be at home?"

"I'll be on my beeper."

"You'll hear from me in a couple hours."

Bob left radiology. He was certain that those films had been deliberately removed to cover up the tracks of whoever was inducing these strange malignancies. The mysterious Doctor B was someone from the pathology department. That could only be Alex Becker.

The partial sequence of the Gp-78 gene was still on the computer screen in his lab. He stared absently at it as he tried to make sense of what he had just learned. Alex Becker was a light-weight. There was no way he could be the brain behind a conspiracy of this magnitude. Still, he would pay him a visit in the morning.

He took a sip from his coffee cup and went back to work on the gene sequence. At one-thirty in the morning, he was still bent over his desk, shifting papers and making entries into the computer. He could always sense when he was alone in the long corridor. A heavy silence descended on the place, the silence of the absence of human beings. The only sounds reaching his ears were the soft humming of the refrigerators, incubators, and various other machines in the room and hallway.

A sudden draft of air made him shiver. Then the door creaked open. Bob stared at the figure silhouetted against the door frame. It was Peterson! He wore a blue hospital gown that was too small for his large bulk and he held a cigarette lighter in his hand. He had a pained look on his face.

"George, what are you doing here? Did you have your CAT scan?"

"Doctor Newman. . ."

'What is it, Mr. Peterson?"

Peterson's expression changed from helplessness to fury.

"I have to blow up this lab, Doctor Newman!" His voice was brutal, his eyes crazed.

Bob reached to his side, but the gun was in the pocket of his white coat, which was lying on the counter on the other side of the room.

"Mr. Peterson, you should be in your room."

"Sartan!" Peterson shrieked and lunged at him.

Bob saw the knife coming toward him. He was out of his chair and had landed his fist against Peterson's head in one blurry motion. Peterson fell to the ground. Bob bent over the limp body. Suddenly, Peterson was back on his feet and Bob caught the glitter of a blade in his hand. He slammed his foot into Peterson's groin. Peterson ignored the insult and lunged again. This time Bob's fist landed on his nose. He felt the bones give way and heard the knife fall to the floor. But incredibly, Peterson was still standing. He grabbed Bob by the throat and wrestled him to the floor. Bob felt cold metal under his right shoulder. He knew he had no chance to loosen the man's grip on his neck. He put his arms around Peterson's torso, and rolled with him to the left. With his right hand, he reached for the knife, found it, and sunk the blade into Peterson's neck, severing both carotid arteries. The body on top of him jerked, then went limp. Bob was breathing heavily as he pulled himself out from under Peterson. He turned the body over and examined it. A pool of dark blood was spreading rapidly across the floor.

Again, he had a sensation of an answer in his mind. He suddenly recalled the strange telephone call from Delany's aide. There was something vital in that conversation, something relevant to this body on the floor. What had he said about Delany? The Senator was ill. What were the exact words? Then he remembered. *It's gotten into his head. It's made him crazy.*

A thought appeared in Bob's mind. It so startled him that he drew backwards as if from a sudden blow. This time it did not fade, but grew larger and firmer. Then, like numbers coming up on a slot machine, thoughts clicked into his consciousness. The three crazed people screaming 'Sartan' as they tried to kill him. . . The phone call from Delany's aide. . . The cancer epidemic. . .

The plane crash. . . Gp-78. . . The syringe of vinyl chloride. . . The CAT scans. . . Cancer. . . The gene vaccine. The gene vaccine!

He put his hand to his forehead. It was ice cold. With heavy feet, he walked to the carbon dioxide tanks feeding the incubator and removed the two-foot long, steel wrench from behind them. He returned to the body on the floor and stood over it, legs straddling the head. He clutched the wrench in both hands, his knuckles white. Beads of sweat covered his forehead, and the blood was gone from his face. He hesitated for a long moment, then raised the wrench over his head, shut his eyes tightly and, with a yell, brought it smashing down on the skull. He heard the bones crack and felt something hit his forearms and splatter onto his face. He opened his eyes. Pieces of tissue were scattered on his clothes and hands. It required all his will power to keep from running from the room. Grimacing, he picked up the knife lying beside the body and pried away the pieces of bone from the skull. As he removed the frontal bone off the forehead, he let out a cry and fell backwards.

A wave of nausea swept over him. Where the front of the brain should have been he saw a tangled mass of fleshy, snake-like projections resembling sea anemone.   He forced himself to examine them more closely. They grew out of the brain tissue, but this was not a human brain. He had never seen anything remotely like this. He picked up the frontal bone. Along the inside surface were dozens of small depressions, some with the fleshy projections still hanging from them like spaghetti. He had a vision from childhood of his mother turning the handle of the meat grinder, the raw hamburger dropping through the holes like squirming worms.

Bob knew now what he had to do. Everything was suddenly crystal clear. He ran from counter to counter, turning on all the gas outlets. As the hissing filled the lab, he reached down and picked up Peterson's cigarette lighter.

* * *

Lois stood in the shadows opposite Jackson Hall, wrapped in a wool coat. She looked at her watch. Any moment now, any moment and Robert Newman would be history. She felt no guilt, nor sorrow. She felt only elation that the enemy was about to suffer an insurmountable defeat. With Newman gone, victory was assured. She smiled with anticipation.

After ten minutes, she glanced down at her watch again. Something was wrong. She took a step in the direction of Jackson Hall. Suddenly, she was blinded by a tremendous explosion that lit up the quadrangle. As she shielded her eyes, the ground under her feet shook violently. Glass shattered in all directions. Giant flames of orange and yellow leapt through the windows on the third floor.

She watched as the flames billowed through the window frame, sending black smoke up into the dark sky. Nothing and no one could have survived that explosion. In the morning, after the fire department had done its job, she would come back to survey the destruction. But the outcome was clear. Newman's laboratory, his notes, his virus, were no more. Newman was no more. Lois smiled.

The flames began to blur slightly in her vision, and she blinked her eyes. Something warm fell onto her cheek. She touched it with her gloved hand and noticed a drop of moisture. A tear? Why a tear? This was a moment of great happiness.

She looked back up at the raging inferno. Another warm drop fell on her cheek, then another, and another, as the flames danced in her glistening eyes.

PART II

METASTASIS

Sartan, what wilt thou accomplish in the mind of man? For thou squeezeth through the holes and the cracks.

PESIKTA RABATI
6th century A.D.

And the snake was more subtle than any beast of the field which the Lord God had made.

GENESIS 3:1

39

The telephone rang as Joe sat at the breakfast table, his belly protruding through a blue, terry-cloth bathrobe. One hand held a custard-filled pastry, the other the morning newspaper. He put down the paper and picked up the receiver.

"Joe?"

He had heard the deep, gruff voice before, but he could not place it.

"Speaking."

"Morning. It's Tom O'Malley. Sorry to bother you at this hour."

Joe put down his pastry with a sudden foreboding. Why was the commissioner of police calling him at home at six o'clock in the morning?

"What's happened, Tom?"

"Joe, I'm afraid there's been an explosion at the university. Your section sustained a lot of damage."

"Anybody hurt?"

"Robert Newman's lab was blown to smithereens. Looks like some sort of a gas leak, as far as we can tell."

Joe's heart began thumping in his chest. "Is Bob okay?"

"There was a body found in the room, burnt beyond recognition. Our forensic pathologists are examining it now. The dimensions fit Newman, but it's all preliminary."

Joe considered his response carefully. "Have you called him at home? Sometimes he works late and sleeps in."

"We've called and also sent a squad car out to his house. There are no signs of him."

"What about accidents on the roads last night?"

"We've checked that too. His car's still parked in front of the hospital. Would you mind coming down to headquarters this morning? I'd like to ask you a few questions."

"Of course. I'll be right over."

He hung up and dialed Bob's home number. He let the phone ring a couple of dozen times before finally hanging up.

He threw on his pants, grabbed a shirt and tie, and slammed the door behind him on his way out. In his haste, he had not thought to put on a jacket, and it was cold outside. But he was too pressed to go back for it now. A fine layer of frost covered the old Ford parked in the driveway and the blades of grass in the yard. He scraped the windshield clean, scrambled into the car, and hurried towards the hospital, ignoring the speed limit.

He arrived in seven minutes. As he pulled into the parking lot, he saw two fire engines, some police cars, and a crowd of newsmen gathered at the front entrance. He did not want to talk to the press, so he parked his car at the far end of the lot and walked around to the side entrance of Jackson Hall, which fortunately was deserted.

As he entered the building, everything looked normal. The first sign that something was amiss was that the elevator was not working. He walked up the staircase to the third floor and opened the stairwell door, out of breath and heart pounding. He noticed two things at once--the lack of lights, and the noxious stench of burnt rubber. As his eyes grew accustomed to the darkness, he saw that the door to the main office was open. He heard voices from that direction and headed for the doorway. Lois was standing inside, along with two uniformed police officers. She ran to Joe when he entered.

"Joe, I tried to stop them!" Lois cried. "Look what these brutes have done."

"Sir, this area is off limits," said one of the officers.

Joe looked around. The office had been turned upside down, not by the explosion, but by human hands. The file cabinet drawers were hanging open. Papers were scattered everywhere.

The contents of the desks had been dumped. Computer discs had been removed from their holders and were scattered across the room.

"Joe, have you heard about Bob?" Lois asked.

Joe nodded. He put his arm around her shoulder. "It's okay, dear. I'll handle things from here."

He took a step in the direction of his office door. The officer who had spoken earlier blocked his way.

"Sir," he said with irritation, "I said this is a restricted area. I'm going to have to ask you to leave the premises or you'll be arrested."

"I'm Doctor Joe Malcolm," he said, acknowledging the officer's presence for the first time. I'm in charge of this department. The commissioner of police has authorized my presence here. Could you explain to me what you two are doing?"

The officer backed off a step. "I didn't realize who you were."

Joe brushed past him and peered through his office door, with Lois shadowing him. It was the same picture, papers scattered about, file cabinets pillaged, computer disks strewn across the desk. He turned towards the officer again.

"You haven't answered my question. What are you two doing here?"

"Sir, as you may have heard, there was an explosion here last night which killed Doctor Newman. We're investigating for clues to arson."

"By whose orders?"

The officer hesitated briefly. "Uh, the chief of police."

"The chief of police gave you authority to ransack my office like this?"

"We're under orders to search the premises for any clues to the cause of the explosion."

"What clues do you expect to find in this office?" Joe exclaimed. "The explosion took place down the hall."

Joe was certain the man was lying. They could have been looking for one thing only, Bob's notes on the gene vaccine. Obviously they hadn't found them. Which meant that he was still the only one in possession of the critical documents needed to reproduce Bob's work. The safest thing to do was to get out of there now. But he needed to see Bob's lab with his own eyes. He had to be sure that, this time, the plot on his life had succeeded. He turned to Lois.

"Lois, I want you to go home now. I'll handle things."

Lois hesitated. Joe had never given her a direct order like that in all the years he had been her boss. She knew he wanted her to obey him without argument. If she refused, her behavior would arouse suspicion. But she did not want to leave the site until she was sure Newman hadn't stashed any copies of his notes somewhere without her knowledge.

"I'll call you when it's time to clean this place up," Joe said. "Hopefully tomorrow."

Lois hesitated. "Okay, Joe. I'll come in as soon as you call." She looked carefully at the two officers before departing.

"I want to take a look at the damage done to the lab. May I borrow your flashlight?"

The officer hesitated for a moment, then handed it over.

"I'll accompany you, sir."

"That's not necessary."

"I'm afraid it is. I've been ordered to make sure nothing is touched or moved from the premises."

Joe shot him a sarcastic smile. He headed down the hall, shining the light ahead of him. Footsteps told him that the officers were following. Bob's laboratory door had been blown off its hinges and was lying in two parts on the floor. The lab was unrecognizable. Nothing was intact except the walls, which were blackened. Shattered glassware lay across the floor and counters. The incubator in the corner was knocked over by the force of the explosion, a gaping hole in its side from the impact of some projectile object. He shined the light on the floor. The blackened outline of a large mass could be seen on the tiles.

"That's where the body was," the officer volunteered.

Joe stared at it for a long time. Then he turned and walked out of the room and back down the hall. He could feel the officers' presence behind him, but he forced himself to walk calmly. When he reached the office door, he handed the flashlight back and left the building.

He headed back to his car, a sense of unreality enveloping him. He could not avoid O'Malley's request to come down to the station. He was not aware of the drive to police headquarters, only that he had arrived and was pulling into the parking lot. He walked up the stone stairs and entered the building. A moment after he had announced his presence, a stocky, muscular man in his fifties came up to greet him. He had curly, dark hair and wire-rimmed glasses and wore a tie loosely around his thick neck.

"How are you, Joe? Sorry to have to see you again under such unfortunate circumstances."

Joe shook O'Malley's hand. "I share the same sentiments, Tom."

"Come into my office where we can talk in private. Leroy!" he yelled, "I don't want to be disturbed for half an hour."

O'Malley led Joe through a long, narrow room, past a row of desks occupied by uniformed and non-uniformed personnel, and into the office at the back. The room was nearly bare, the only furniture consisting of a desk and three wooden chairs. One corner of the desk held a plant which needed watering, the other a picture of a woman and three smiling children. O'Malley closed the door, insulating them from the commotion outside.

"It's been a while," O'Malley said as he sat down at his desk.

"Almost a year," Joe answered, seating himself in one of the wooden chairs.

"How's Jerome?" Joe asked. He had treated O'Malley's son a year ago for cystic fibrosis.

"Great. He's back in school driving his teachers batty."

"He certainly was a tough little nut in the hospital."

"He still talks about you, Joe. He remembers the doc who played 'Spit' with him."

Joe smiled. "I'm glad he's doing well."

O'Malley reached into his desk drawer, took out a toothpick, and slid it between his thick lips. "Thanks. Listen, I wanted to talk to you about the explosion in the laboratory."

"Bob was my best friend," Joe replied. "I can't believe he's really dead. What's the evidence?"

O'Malley mashed on the toothpick with his front teeth. "Just the body in the morgue."

"But you're not sure it's him."

"Not yet. We've got to give the pathologist some time. What do you think could have caused that kind of explosion?"

Joe thought for a moment and sighed deeply. "I'm sorry if I'm a little distracted, but I'm overwhelmed by this whole thing. It could have been a gas leak."

O'Malley removed the toothpick from his mouth. It had been flattened into splinters. He tossed it into the waste basket. "A gas leak, huh? Is that likely in your laboratories?"

"Not impossible, but not likely, either."

"Why not?"

"Bob was too careful a scientist to do something as careless as leave a gas outlet on."

"I understand he'd been working long hours."

"It's still out of character," Joe insisted.

"I see. Then what's your guess?"

O'Malley was already suspicious about something. Best to raise the issue himself.

"I don't know, but I get the impression you suspect foul play, Tom."

"What makes you think that?" O'Malley asked, noncommittally. "Did Newman have enemies?"

"Sure. Just about everyone who was against his gene vaccine was a potential enemy. There are a lot of fanatics who could have seen it as their duty to stop him."

"That's a hell of a lot of people. Can you be more specific, Joe?"

"Not really. Finding suspects is your area of expertise, Tom."

"I'm afraid it is. I'd hoped you might be able to shed some light on this. Listen, Joe. I don't know exactly what's going on with this case, but I can tell you one thing, something doesn't smell right. I got a call from the FBI this morning and they've got their noses in this too. You'll probably hear from them."

"Do you have any suspects?"

"We don't even have a lead yet, or any direct evidence that this was something other than an accident. But I'll keep you informed if anything comes up, okay?"

Joe relaxed. "I'd appreciate that, Tom."

O'Malley leaned forward and placed his meaty elbows on the desk. "Listen, one more thing. What happened to Newman's records?"

Joe's guard went up. "There's a good possibility they were destroyed in the explosion."

"Will you be able to duplicate his work?"

"Possibly."

O'Malley hesitated. "This may not be the best time to ask about this, but ever since Newman's discovery was announced, I've been wondering whether it could be used to cure cystic fibrosis."

Joe understood the direction of his questioning. "It's got great potential. But yes, after a lot more testing, I think it's likely."

"Is the knowledge retrievable without Newman?"

"I think we'll be able to continue the work, although how soon I can't say."

"Are you talking months or years?"

"Soon enough to benefit Jerome, I think."

O'Malley smiled weakly. "You knew what I wanted to hear."

"Of course," Joe nodded.

O'Malley stood up. "Thanks for coming by, Joe. I expect to hear from you if anything else comes up."

Joe rose from his chair. "Tom, one thing before I leave."

"Sure, what is it?"

"I'd like to see the body."

"Sorry, I can't do that."

Joe frowned. "Why not? I figure it's the least you could do."

"It's not that I wouldn't like to," O'Malley replied. "But I don't have the body."

"Tom, if you don't have the body, who does?"

"The Feds."

Joe's eyes widened. "The FBI took the body?"

O'Malley nodded. "They came in this morning and snatched it. I raised hell, but it didn't do no good. They just pulled rank on me and that was that."

Joe shook his head. "I want you to find whoever did this, Tom."

"We'll find them, Joe, we'll find them. Come on, I'll walk you out."

40

John Irving, President of the United States, was a square-jawed man in his late-fifties with thick, salt-and-pepper hair and light-blue eyes. His face still retained a youthful appearance, but the skin under his eyes was beginning to sag. He pulled his wire-rimmed glasses off his nose.

"Come in, Ed. We're waiting for your report." He turned to the men and women seated with him around the oval table. "You all know the Surgeon General."

Ed Lafferty entered the White House conference room, a slide carousel under his arm. He had been trying all day to suppress a growing sense of panic. Something decisive had to be done, quickly. Maybe this would scare those self-serving bastards into action.

"We hope you've got some good news for us, Ed."

Lafferty placed his carousel on the projector. Good news would have to wait for Santa Claus. He pursed his lips. "Unfortunately, the situation has deteriorated since last week."

"Well, let's hear it," the President replied.

Lafferty went to the podium and dimmed the lights. He advanced the projector and the first slide fell into the slot. A line graph appeared on the screen behind him.

"This graph is familiar to all of you. The data is updated as of yesterday. The figures show that the incidence of cancers is continuing to increase. One in four men, women, and children in the United States is now harboring a malignancy."

There was a murmur around the table.

"This is extremely disturbing, Ed," the President said. "That's much higher than your previous estimate."

Good. At least these morons could read a line graph. "Now that the data is coming in from the screening centers, we're getting a clearer picture of the epidemic. But it's not just a question of better data collection. The frequency is clearly increasing."

The President frowned. "There are ten of us in the room. Are you suggesting that two of us have cancer?"

"At least two, based on the laws of probability."

Joe Macchio, the Chief-Of-Staff, cleared his throat. "Of those twenty-five percent, how many are going to die, Ed?"

Lafferty pushed the advance button and the next slide appeared. "As I've presented before, there are two distinct groups of patients." He pointed to the lower curve, a red line. "This line represents twenty percent of those with proven malignancies. These patients present with typical medical histories and follow the usual course for their disease. We don't know how many of them will go into remission, but we think it'll follow past trends."

He pointed to the upper, blue line. "Now these patients, the other eighty percent, are the curious ones. They present with extremely aggressive tumors. They should have the highest mortality rate, but most recover with little or no treatment."

Macchio poured himself some water, leaving a puddle around the edge of his glass. "So if I understand you correctly, the mortality rates are actually lower than they were before this epidemic started. That's reassuring in terms of the election campaign."

Lafferty revised his previous assessment. Even a line graph seemed beyond the ability of these idiots to comprehend.

"No, that's not what I'm telling you at all." He clicked back to the first graph. "Look at the incidence, man. Sixty million Americans have cancer. If only twenty percent die, that's still twelve million deaths. Election campaign aside, we're facing a major public health crisis and a population on the verge of panic."

"Then we need to address how we're going to minimize that panic," Macchio asserted.

"The way to minimize the panic," Lafferty replied, "is to find a solution to this epidemic."

He tapped his pointer against the blue line on the screen, causing the image to waver in and out of focus. "It's these patients who hold the key. We simply must know why these people are recovering. I need your permission to study some of them. Even one would be helpful."

"I can't believe no one is willing to volunteer their cooperation," the President said.

Lafferty shut off the projector, and seated himself at the table. "Sir, the cancers are affecting these people's cognitive functions. That much we know. They're completely uncooperative and we've had a number of reports of very unusual CAT scan images of their brains. We've got to examine these individuals, even if it means violating their civil rights."

Macchio took a sip from his glass. A bead of water dripped off the bottom onto his tie. "We've already had this discussion. Look, Ed, you're not at the university any more. You're in the President's cabinet now. You have to consider the politics. Isn't there any other way to get the information you need?"

"No."

"Then perhaps we need a new Surgeon General."

Lafferty felt his stomach churning. He reached for an antacid, but his pocket was empty. "What I'm telling you," he replied evenly, "represents the consensus of the medical community, within the strict limits of secrecy that has been imposed on me by the administration. I serve at the President's pleasure. When he feels that the country would be best served by my resignation, I'd be happy to provide it."

"Ed," the President interjected with a wave of his hand, "I've got complete confidence in the conduct of your work. Now, do you really think that studying one of these people against their will can help?"

"I do. And we're losing precious time."

"Can't you use a deceased one?"

"I'd love to. The problem is, none of them have died sir, as far as we know."

Macchio turned to the President. "John, you're in the middle of an election campaign. We can't afford for this crisis to continue into the spring. Let's find a way to get him his volunteer."

"We also can't afford to trample on civil liberties," the President replied. "If it got out, we'd have a major scandal. What other recommendations do you have, Ed?"

Lafferty gritted his teeth. "Sir, I strongly recommend two things. Number one, that you declare a national emergency immediately and shut down every source of environmental carcinogen in the country."

The President slammed his hand onto the table. "My God, man, you're talking about shutting down the economy!"

"We've discovered that human cells have become exquisitely susceptible to carcinogenic agents," Lafferty persisted. "Thousands of times more susceptible than they've been in the past."

"What does that mean?"

"It means that exposure to the slightest additional carcinogen may be enough to induce malignancy. We must minimize the exposure as best we can."

The President shook his head. "That would be political suicide. What's your other recommendation?"

"That we begin immediate prophylactic chemotherapy on the entire population of the United States."

Everyone spoke at once. The President raised his hands for quiet.

"We've got a national crisis on our hands," Lafferty persisted, the desperation audible in his voice. "Decisive and immediate action is required while there's still time to reverse this epidemic."

The President shook his head. "Do you know what you're suggesting? Let's mull this over for twenty-four hours and meet again tomorrow. There've got to be alternatives."

Lafferty shot out of his chair, knocking it backwards onto the floor with a crash. "There's panic out there!" he shouted. "The hospitals are bursting! The medical system's drowning! Everyone knows someone who's sick! People aren't stupid. What do you expect them to think?"

He looked around the table. They were staring at him as if he had gone mad. All except Calvin Hodges, chairman of the Joint Chiefs of the Armed Forces, who wore a frown on his face. Lafferty stomped out of the room. Those morons! Were they blind to everything but the Gallup Poll? He decided to resign his position at tomorrow's meeting.

As he left the White House, he felt a heavy hand on his shoulder. He turned to see Hodges standing beside him. He was a bulldog of a man, six feet two and barrel-chested, his gray hair cropped close to his scalp.

"We need to talk, Ed," Hodges said quietly. "Meet me in my office at the Pentagon in half an hour."

* * *

Ellen heard about the explosion on the morning news. She rushed to Jackson Hall, but the security men would not let her in. Frantic, she tried to call the office, but no one answered. No answer at Lois' home either.

A sense of helplessness overpowered her. For the first time since her mother had died, she felt complete despair. She had hated Bob Newman's arrogance. She had hated his coldness. She had hated the way he had made her cry. Now she hated him for dying. Their lives had been intertwined by some force larger than either of them. The tension between them was just a prelude to the inevitable joining of their paths. But he was dead.

She walked aimlessly, eventually finding herself in front of her apartment. She walked up the steps, unlocked the front door, and began crying inconsolably. She sobbed until the tears would no longer flow. When the hurt became unbearable, a numbness began to envelop her, soothing the raw pain like a narcotic. She flopped onto her bed and stared at the long, dark shadows on the wall. As exhaustion overtook her, a picture formed in her mind of the day she had spent at the beach last summer. She could hear the rhythmic pounding of the waves against the sand. She saw wispy white clouds high in the blue sky. The warm sun felt so good on her shoulders. The breeze blew gently through her loose hair. . . a smile formed on her lips when sleep finally enveloped her.

* * *

Hodges rose to greet Lafferty when he stepped into his Pentagon office.

"Have a seat, Ed. Have you met Leon Stark?"

Lafferty turned to the short, middle-aged man with thinning hair who was seated in the room. "Yes, we've met at some function or other." He extended his hand, wondering what the head of the FBI was doing here.

"I'll get right to the point," Hodges began. "I agree with your assessment of the crisis facing this country, and with your recommendations."

"Why didn't you say something at the meeting?" Lafferty complained. "I could have used some support."

Hodges mashed his teeth. His thick neck and hard jaw line reminded Lafferty of a bull. "I've been arguing with the President about this all week. The effects of this epidemic on military preparedness have been disastrous. I'm watching the armed forces disintegrating in front of my eyes. Desertions are running at ten percent. Communications and logistics are a nightmare. The security of the nuclear arsenal is in jeopardy. The President's never been a bold leader. He rules by consensus."

"What can we do?" Lafferty asked bitterly. "We live in a democracy. We elected the man."

Hodges crossed his arms over his chest. "Fortunately, the armed forces are not a democracy," he replied. "I can initiate mandatory chemotherapy to those under my command with a simple order."

Lafferty eyed Hodges. He was not sure he liked the direction of this conversation. "That would be against the President's wishes."

Hodges blew air loudly out of his nostrils. "The President has entrusted me with maintaining the armed forces of this country at their highest state of readiness. I intend to carry out that assignment. I'd like you to present me with a detailed description of what chemotherapy to administer, how often, and how to monitor it. Something my medical officers can follow."

Lafferty stared at Hodges for a long moment. He was rapidly getting in way over his head. He turned to Stark and swallowed audibly.

"What's your role in this?"

Stark raised his chin and looked at him through his bifocals. "What I'm about to tell you is not to leave this room."

Lafferty's stomach tightened. He nodded slowly.

"My intelligence apparatus doesn't think this epidemic is a result of natural causes. We've been tracking the accidents to industrial plants in the country and the facts are clear. For at least the past three years there's been a determined effort on the part of someone to leak carcinogens into the environment. We don't know who's behind this or what their ultimate motive is. It may just be the workings of a sick mind. But whatever the reason, we're dealing with a sophisticated and intelligent network of individuals who are threatening the security of our country. We haven't cracked it yet, but if it's related to these mental changes you've discussed, we need to know everything we can about them. That's why I'm providing you with your medical volunteer."

Lafferty took a deep breath in an attempt to calm his racing heart.

"You said a dead body would suffice?" Stark asked.

Lafferty nodded. "It would be a start, anyway."

"Okay, you've got it. It's a little toasted on the outside. We've set up a special lab for you in the Pentagon where the data isn't going to disappear like it did with the CAT scans. The body will be there for your team in two hours, if you agree to work with us."

"Where'd you get the body?"

"It's the body found in Robert Newman's lab."

Lafferty's eyes widened. "It's not his?"

"No. It belongs to a man by the name of Peterson. He had the brain findings you described on CAT scan."

"How do you know all this?"

"Let's just say we've been keeping tabs on Newman," the FBI director replied.

"Is Newman still alive?"

"We don't know, but we think so."

"Is he involved in this conspiracy you're talking about?"

"He may be a target," Stark replied. "We're trying to locate him. The same goes for his division chief, who may also be in harm's way. I've got my men searching for both of them. Hopefully, we'll find them before the bad guys do. In the meantime, you, me and Hodges here all agree that decisive action must be taken immediately."

"I agree that decisive action *should* be taken immediately," Lafferty corrected him. "But I never suggested overriding the constitutional authority of the President."

"These are extraordinary times," Hodges responded. "The survival of our society is at stake and that *does* overrides the constitutional authority of the President. You see it coming. The President doesn't, and he's leading us down a path of destruction. You have a patriotic duty to perform. Will you help us?"

Lafferty looked from one man to the other. He was never really one for patriotic acts. And there was a reason the founding fathers had established a hierarchy of authority. However one cloaked it, what they were discussing was subversion against the only elected official among them. He took another deep breath to calm himself.

"How do I transfer my team over here?"

41

Ellen groaned and opened her eyes. The phone was ringing. For a moment she didn't know where she was, but gradually she recognized the familiar outlines of her bedroom in the dim light. She looked at the digital clock by her bed--2:33 a.m. She muttered an obscenity as she groped in the dark for the receiver.

"Uhlo?"

"Ellen, it's Bob Newman. Sorry to bother you at this hour, but you're the only person I could think of to call."

"Bob?" she was awake instantly. "Is that really you?"

"Yes, it's me."

She bolted upright in bed. "Where are you? What happened?"

"I can't explain over the phone, but I need your help." She could hear the tension in his voice. "It might be dangerous," he warned.

Her heart thumped wildly in her chest. "Just tell me what to do."

"I was hoping I could count on you. Listen carefully. Get over to the hospital right away. Go to microbiology. There are two sets of blood cultures there from last night belonging to a patient named George Peterson."

"The guy you did the bone marrow transplant on?"

"Yes, but that's not important. You must find those culture bottles. Slip them into your purse, and don't let anybody see you."

"You want me to steal them?"

"Borrow them, if it makes you feel better. Just find them and then get your ass out of there."

The conversation was moving too rapidly. "Bob, I'm happy to help you, but do you mind if I ask you why you need me for this? I mean after all--"

"Because if I set foot in that hospital, I'm a dead man."

He said it so matter-of-factly that it took a moment for the words to register. "What do you mean you're a dead man? Are you hurt?"

"Not badly."

"Then someone *is* trying to kill you! I knew it wasn't an accident. And neither was the airplane explosion, right?"

"Right. Peterson tried to cut me to shreds with a hunting knife last night."

"Why?"

"The answer's in those blood cultures. So is the answer to the cancer epidemic. There's a lot more at stake than just my own life."

Ellen felt her neck and shoulder muscles tightening.

"Why would Peterson try--"

"Ellen," Bob interrupted. "Time is very precious right now. By the morning those cultures will probably be at the bottom of Lake Michigan."

"Okay, I'm going. What do you want me to do with them?"

"Bring them back to your apartment. I'll be waiting for you."

She felt a sudden flush. "How are you gonna get in without a key?"

"Leave it under the door mat. And don't go anywhere near the Genetics building. It's probably under observation. Make sure you're not followed when you leave."

"You're scaring the hell out of me, you know."

"I know this is a lot to ask, but I need you, Ellen."

"I've been waiting a long time to hear you say that," she murmured.

"What?"

"Never mind. Help yourself to some coffee. I'll be back as soon as I can."

"Thanks, Ellen. Be careful. Very careful."

She hung up the phone. Bob was alive! He was in danger, but she believed in him. She knew there was danger in this for her too, but she wasn't afraid. Just incredibly tense. She dressed quickly, grabbed her coat, and shoved her key under the doormat.

The street was deserted. She glanced at the lone street lamp across from her building. There was no man in an overcoat. She hurried to the hospital.   An ambulance was parked in the semicircle in front of the ER. She walked through a set of double doors and found herself in the waiting room. She continued to the main lobby, took the elevators to the fourth floor, and stepped into the eerily-quiet corridor. She headed towards Microbiology, past an elderly guard seated behind a counter, watching a miniature TV.

"Hey, Miss!"

She turned, her heart thumping.

"Can I help you?"

She approached the counter.   "I'm on my way to Microbiology."

"This is a restricted area."

"I'm a med student here."

"Where's your ID?"

She looked down and realized she was wearing her street clothes. She smiled at the guard, using all the charm she could muster. "Pleeeese, I left it at home. It's an emergency."

The guard shook his head. "Sorry. Not without an ID."

She wasn't going to go all the way back home now. She headed up one floor to the OR and cracked open a door marked STAFF ONLY. The locker room was deserted. Against the back wall, she found a metal rack, its shelves filled with blue hospital scrubs. They were all men's sizes. The smallest one she could find was huge on her. It would have to do. She put on the shirt and pants, tied the draw string around her waist, and stuffed her own clothes in an empty locker.

She slipped through the door and began heading back towards the elevator. She had taken only two steps when she heard a voice behind her.

"Ellen!"

Her heart leaped into her throat. She froze for a moment, then continued walking.

"Ellen! Wait up a sec!"

She heard running footsteps behind her and felt a heavy hand on her shoulder. She stopped and turned around. David stood over her, dressed in street clothes. Her knees began to tremble.

"What are you doing here, Ellen?"

"I'm working, David."

"At three o'clock in the morning?"

How was she going to get rid of him? "I'm on call for surgery tonight. You should be in bed."

"I couldn't sleep. You know, it's dangerous to be wandering through these halls alone this time of night." There was a threatening tone to his voice and he had a wild glare in his eyes.

She'd feel a lot safer once she was out of his sight. "I'll be fine, David."

"I'll walk with you."

"That's not necessary. Go back to your room."

"I don't mind," David persisted.

"David, I'd rather you didn't."

"Come on," he took her by the arm. "We can talk."

She tore her arm away violently, too violently.

He stood glowering down at her. "Is something wrong, Ellen?"

She backed away from him. "Nothing's wrong, David. I just don't want company right now. I'll see you later."

She turned and walked deliberately down the hall, feeling his eyes on her back. After turning the corner, she ran to the stairwell by the elevator. The stairs were covered with metal plates and she could hear the tap tap tap of her footsteps as she headed down. When she reached the third floor, she headed back to the clinical laboratories. The old guard was still behind the counter watching TV. This time he didn't stop her.

She passed chemistry and hematology before reaching microbiology. An Indian woman wearing a turban and a red dot on her forehead stood by a sink, running water over some glass slides. Across from her was a counter with dozens of blood culture bottles, each with a label across the front. She casually began turning the bottles, looking for Peterson's name.

"Can I help you find something?"

Ellen looked up. The Indian woman was peering at her.

"I'm from genetics," Ellen said. "We sent some samples down here yesterday and they may have been mislabeled. Do you mind if I check?"

"Sure, but they're probably in the incubator. Let me finish staining these."

Ellen waited while the woman completed her work and approached her.

"Okay, what were the samples?"

"Blood cultures."

"Do you have the date?"

Ellen nodded. "Last night."

She led Ellen to a large incubator where she could see a few dozen bottles through the glass door.

"What's the patient's name?"

"George Peterson."

The woman began searching through the bottles. After a few moments she pulled two out.

"Here they are. She took a marker from her coat pocket. "What is the mistake?"

"His last name is spelled with an 'A' here," she said, pointing at the label. "I'm sure you're busy. I can take care of it."

"It will just take a second," the woman replied, already correcting the first bottle.

A bell rang on the other side of the room.

"I have to destain the slides."

"Here, let me put these back," Ellen said, taking the two bottles.

"Make sure the incubator door is closed," the woman called out as she headed back to the sink. "There's a problem with the latch. I'll check it in a minute."

Ellen opened the incubator door, keeping her back to the sink. Her scrubs had no pockets and the bottles were too large to hide completely in her closed hand. She slid one under her bra and wrapped her fingers around the other, hiding most of it from view.

"Thanks," she called out as she left the room.

She hurried to the stairwell and began descending towards the first floor. That had been easy. She'd have these bottles to Bob in fifteen minutes. Someone really ought to do something about security in the hospital.

She heard footsteps on the metal stairs above her. There were dozens of people in the hospital on any given night, but she picked up her pace, frightened. The tapping grew louder and faster. Whoever was above her was running! As she passed the second floor a shape bounded over the handrail, landing in front of her and making the stairs shudder. David stood barring her way, a menacing look on his face.

"I'll take those bottles, Ellen."

She turned and sprinted back up the stairs. The second floor landing was right above her. If she could reach it and get out of the stairwell, there might be someone in the hall. At least her screams might be heard. As her foot reached the top stair, a hand closed around her ankle and she fell onto the landing, still clutching the bottle. David began pulling her towards him. She flipped on her back, kicking at him wildly.

Her bottom smacked against the top step as he dragged her down the staircase. With her free hand, she grabbed the top of the handrail, shrieking at the top of her lungs. She felt tugging at her waist and realized that David had a stronger grip on her pant leg than her ankle. She let go of the bottle and pulled on the drawstring of her pants. The baggy scrubs slid off her legs and David went crashing down the stairs. She saw him on the floor of the landing below, his back against the wall, his legs splayed out in front of him. One fist held Ellen's pants. He looked dazed.

Naked from the thighs down, she picked up the bottle and scrambled back up the stairs. She put her hand on the door knob and pulled. It was locked! She heard motion below her. David was on his knees, looking up at her with a fiendish grin. In a frenzy, she rushed up the stairs towards the third floor.

David was right behind her as she reached the landing. Just as her hand touched the doorknob, he grabbed her arm. She screamed and clawed at his fingers. He lifted her off the floor and shoved her against the wall. The back of her head smacked against the concrete wall and the stairwell began to spin. He began prying open the fingers of her right hand, which still clutched the culture bottle. With her free left hand, she swiped him across the face, her nails leaving deep red gouges across the white birthmark on his cheek. He shrieked, grabbing his wounded face. Ellen hit him as hard as she could. The bottle smashed against his cheekbone and shattered. David roared in pain and stumbled backwards, his hand covering his left eye. His foot went over the top stair. Ellen shoved and he crashed down the steps, landing at the bottom of the staircase in a distorted jumble of limbs.

She stood there for a moment wondering whether David was dead or merely unconscious. Then he began to stir and pulled himself into a kneeling position. Snapping out of her trance, she grabbed the door knob. The door wouldn't budge! She pulled again with all her strength. On the third tug, it flung open and she darted out into the corridor.

She reached under the gown and pulled the second culture bottle from her bra. A door close behind her. She looked back and saw David leaving the stairwell. She caught a glimpse of his bloody face. He was limping on one leg, but nonetheless moving quickly. She had no particular plan in mind. All she knew was that if David laid hands on her again, he'd kill her. She took a familiar path and found herself in the skyway connecting the hospital with Jackson Hall. She knew this area. She might be able to use it to her advantage. If she could get out of his line of sight, maybe she could slip into one of the labs and get to a telephone.

David's heavy footsteps were close behind her as she left the skyway. She ran past the genetics office and tried the next door. It was locked. She passed Bob's burnt out lab and tried the door down the hall. It too, was locked. The hallway dead-ended at a closed door. She looked back. David grinned maniacally and slowed to a walk, knowing he had her trapped. Ellen grabbed the door knob, slipped inside, slammed the door shut behind her, and turned the lock.

There was no way out of this room, other than the way she'd come. But there was a place to hide, a hidden room that David might not find. She stepped into the black, revolving door of the darkroom, swiveled the mechanism around a hundred and eighty degrees, and was plunged into darkness. The back of the door now faced the room behind her. There was no way to know it concealed another room, unless one had familiarity with research labs.

She heard a loud crash. David had broken into the outer room! She held her breath. She could hear David moving about behind the darkroom door. Then it grew quiet. A few minutes went by. She began to think that David had given up. Suddenly, she heard tapping on the wall of the revolving door. Then it began to turn! She groped for the red lamp she knew was on the counter and yanked on the string, bathing the room in an eerie red glow. David appeared in front of her, his body framed in the black semicircle of the door. Blood covered his face. His left eye socket was empty, a thick fluid draining from it onto his cheek. The other eye glowered at her. She rammed the lamp, bulb first, towards the eye socket. David howled and fell forward onto her as the room was plunged into darkness. She struggled to push his body off of hers, hearing it fall to her feet with a thud. In panic, she stepped forward in the direction of the revolving door, tripping over David's body. She groped in the darkness for the hand holds. She found one and began to swivel the door. It was stuck! She pushed as hard as she could, but the door only rotated part way and wouldn't budge further. She groped around on the floor and felt an object in the door's path. It was David's foot. She managed to get his foot clear and rushed out of the darkroom and into the light.

She had lost a shoe in the struggle. She flung off her remaining one and began to run. Then she realized that she no longer had the culture bottle. She must have lost it during the struggle. She stopped and looked back at the darkroom door.

Trying to suppress her terror, she stepped back through, bent down on her hands and knees, and groped on the floor for the bottle. Her hand touched the side of it, but it rolled out of her reach. She felt around blindly, touching David's legs and trunk, following the sound of the rolling glass. She touched the bottle again and grabbed it. At the same time, David's body moved underneath her. A hand grabbed her wrist. Overtaken with panic, she bit into it. He shrieked and let go. She stumbled into the revolving door and clawed hysterically for the handles. The door turned and she fell through onto the other side. She looked behind her. The door was turning again! She got to her feet and ran barefoot into the hallway, flinging herself through the first door she reached and shutting it behind her.

She was in the animal room, with row upon row of long racks, each holding dozens of cages. A thousand beady, red eyes stared at her. She threw the light switch, plunging the room into darkness, and slid between the farthest rack and the back wall.

The sound of rats scratching at their bedding accosted her from all directions.

"I know you're in here. Just give me the bottle and I won't hurt you."

Ellen crouched down further as David flipped the light switch. He started down the rows, looking behind each rack, then rolling it to the other side of the room. Ellen had one chance now, and if she blew it, she was dead. David started down the row in front of her. She could see his back between the cages. She reached up, grabbed the top of the rack and pushed her feet off the wall with all her strength. The rack slammed into David's back, teetered momentarily, then crashed down on top of him, taking Ellen with it.

She found herself on top of a pile of cages and animal bedding. Something hard was stuck against her rib cage and it hurt to breathe. David's hand and face were underneath her. His one eye glared at her, but he wasn't moving. The culture bottle lay shattered on the floor beside her in a red puddle.

She lifted her head and came face to face with a rat, it's pink nostrils an inch from hers, sniffing at her face. She realized with horror that rats were crawling all over her. She slid off the pile of cages, her body convulsing. The rats scurried off her and scattered across the floor. She trembled uncontrollably. Trying not to step on them, she darted out of the room and ran down the hall. She heard a crash behind her. She didn't look back, but rushed headlong down the marble stairs of Jackson Hall and flung herself against the exit door leading out of the building. It was still dark outside and cold. In bare feet, and half-naked, she ran back to her apartment.

She banged on the door until she heard Bob's voice. "Who is it?"

"Ellen."

The bolt clicked and the door opened. Bob's hair was disheveled, he had a two day stubble on his face, and his shirt was half-unbuttoned, revealing a chest of thick curly hair. But he still had his shoes on. He was a man ready to move in an instant.

"What the hell happened to you?" he whispered.

She fell against his chest, sobbing.

He pulled her into the apartment and shut the door.

"Shhh. You're okay," he whispered, stroking her hair. "Tell me what happened."

"I don't have the bottles," she cried. "I had them, but there was a fight. . .and they broke."

"A fight with who?"

"A guy I know from school."

"I figured I'd be safe here for a while, but I see that I've put you in as much danger as I'm in."

She stepped away from him, a look of terror in her eyes. "We've got to get out of here! David's after me and he knows where I live!"

Bob glanced at the door. He began gathering together a pile of papers on the coffee table.

"I'm going to change," Ellen yelled, rushing into her bedroom. She was back in a moment, dressed in a dark sweater and pants.

He took her by the arm and led her towards the door. "Let's get the hell out of here," he whispered.

42

Bob paid the cab driver and Ellen and he stepped out onto the dark suburban street and hurried up to the house. They had to ring three times before the door opened. Joe stood in front of them in a half-open robe and bare feet. His jaw dropped.

"Bob! You're alive!"

"Of course I'm alive. Let us in, would you? I want to get off the street."

Joe stepped aside and they brushed past him. He shut the door and turned to see Bob drawing the window blinds in the living room.

"What happened to you? I thought you were killed by the explosion in your lab."

"Ellen's cracked a rib. Do you have an ace bandage?"

"I think so." Joe disappeared for a few moments and returned with a first-aid kit.

"Where's Nina?" Bob asked as he searched the contents of the kit.

"She's visiting her sister in Boston."

"Good. Anyone who knows where I am is at risk."

Joe led them to the couch. "The two of you look like you've just been through a war zone. Are you going to tell me what the hell happened to you?"

"Sit down," Bob said. "I'll explain everything from the beginning." He pulled a bandage out of the first-aid kit and unrolled it. "Ellen, stand over here. Pull up your sweater."

She did so and he wrapped the bandage tightly around her ribcage.

"Does that feel better?"

She nodded. "It doesn't hurt so much to breathe."

"Good."

"All right," Joe said. "Start talking."

Bob sat across from Joe and began sifting through his pile of papers. "Get a look at this."

He lay some X-ray films on the coffee table and went over them in detail with Joe. Ellen watched in silence, trying to absorb what they were discussing. She had not yet had the opportunity to ask Bob anything.

"Now what do you conclude from all this?" Bob asked.

Joe stood up and paced the floor, then returned and looked at the bands on the films again. He studied them for five minutes while Ellen and Bob sat silently. Ellen glanced over at Bob. A strand of black hair lay across his brow. His open collar exposed a lean, muscular neck and a strong jaw. And his steel-blue eyes showed no signs of fatigue, just their usual piercing intensity.

Joe put down the films and looked at Bob. "Have you repeated this?"

"Yes."

Bob tossed another set of films towards Joe. Joe studied them for a full ten minutes. The silence in the room was interrupted only by Joe's occasional deep sighs of concentration. Ellen noted beads of sweat forming around his temples. Finally, he looked up.

"Christ Almighty, there's a dormant set of genes in our chromosomes!"

"Triggered by carcinogens," Bob added.

"Yes. Those carcinogens in your experiments are activating all our junk DNA!"

"What we thought was junk DNA," Bob corrected him. "That eighty percent of DNA that doesn't code for anything we know of, it's actually the genome of another organism."

Joe began pacing the room again. "How the hell is that possible?"

"There's precedent," Bob replied. "Every living animal cell contains mitochondria, which carry their own set of genes, and which once existed as independent microorganisms until they fused with the cells of our early ancestors millennia ago. I'm saying it happened a second time in our history and that this second time it was not a primitive microorganism, but a higher organism, an organism as complex as ourselves, perhaps more complex. All this time we've thought that cancer is caused by a defect in our immune system. We should have known better. Reptiles and fish and insects don't even have immune systems to speak of, and they don't have trouble with malignant cells. Cancer is the growing tissue of another organism encoded in our own chromosomes. Once I saw the data, it didn't seem so strange, and I wondered why no one had suggested the possibility before."

As the two men fell into an abstract scientific discussion, Ellen tried to imagine another organism growing and differentiating inside her own body. The thought made her hair stand on end. Was it possible that the term 'invasive tumor' was more than just a metaphor?

"Let's put aside for a moment the origins of this genetic material," Joe said. "If you incubated the cells with the carcinogens for only twenty four hours, then one must conclude that those cancer genes have become exquisitely sensitive to activation. Do you realize the significance of this data? You've hit on the etiology of the cancer epidemic!"

"Precisely," Bob responded. "The cancer genes are activated when the concentration of carcinogens reaches a threshold level. We've reached that concentration in our environment and those genes are snapping on. I wanted to put the rest of the puzzle together before I said anything, but this is more than just a cancer epidemic. It's a conspiracy, Joe."

Joe squinted. "A conspiracy?"

"Yes, a conspiracy to raise the concentrations of carcinogens in order to achieve the malignant transformation of as many people as possible, as quickly as possible."

"What do you base that on?"

"First, the vinyl chloride attacks. Second, the Edison plant in New Jersey is going to be blown up, spewing radiation all across the east coast. Delany's aide told me they were plotting to destroy that plant."

"What?" Joe exclaimed. "When?"

"Soon," said Bob. "And there'll be more of the same, I'm sure."

"Why? If there's a conspiracy, there's got to be a motive."

"There is. But you're not going to believe it."

"Try me."

Bob stood up and rubbed the back of his neck. "Okay, here goes. Cancer is an intelligent, parasitic organism that we've been harboring for millions of years and that has declared war on us."

Joe stared at Bob as if he had gone mad. "Oh come on, give me a break."

"Joe, whatever we doctors throw at cancer, it adapts, it defends itself, and it counterattacks. These are the attributes of a rational entity with an agenda. Let me tell you what happened last night. You can reach your own conclusion. I was sitting at my desk in the lab, trying to figure out who was behind this conspiracy to induce malignancies. At the same time, I was marveling at how fascinating this discovery was. The genes from another species in our own DNA! I knew that somehow, the two were connected, the conspiracy and the cancer genes. It was after midnight. All of a sudden, a patient of mine who had had a bone marrow transplant last week, opens the door. I had sent him down earlier that night for a CAT scan because he was complaining of visual hallucinations. I ask him what he wants and he yells 'Sartan', and lunges at me with a knife."

"This sounds like a repeat of the story with the old lady," said Joe.

Bob nodded. "I had to kill the guy, Joe. I had no choice. Then I smashed his skull open. The frontal lobe of his brain was gone, just gone, and in its place was a mass of snake-like tendrils. It had a skeleton and it was organized."

Ellen felt a shiver go down her spine.

"Bob, the man had a brain tumor," Joe said.

Bob sat down next to Joe and looked him in the eye. "Don't you think I know what the hell a tumor looks like, Joe? Whatever was in that man's skull was not human tissue."

Joe frowned."

"There's also the CAT scans. I talked to Ron Glass. The woman who attacked me, and another cancer patient named Blaire, had extremely odd formations in their frontal lobes on head scan. Those scans have disappeared from the file room."

Ellen shuddered. "David Blaire is the man who attacked me!"

"Are you sure?"

"Of course I'm sure. I dated him for two years. Ever since he got his melanoma, he's been acting strange. I don't know what's in his head, but he's not the man I used to know."

Joe rubbed his chin. "Bob, even if that tissue you observed was the body of this cancer organism, that still doesn't prove it's intelligent. The growth of such an organism adjacent to neurologic tissues could be affecting the human brain in such a way as to cause violent, antisocial behavior."

"That wouldn't explain the deliberate efforts to induce malignant transformations with vinyl chloride. And if you saw that man's brain for yourself, you'd be convinced in a moment. It wasn't just a mass of unorganized tissue. It had lobes and nerve roots, and those god-awful tendrils."

Joe frowned. "You certainly know that tumors can develop bone, hair, even nerves."

"Have you ever asked yourself why? Now we know."

Ellen was becoming panicky. David had one of those organisms in his skull. He had been within a hairsbreadth of her. What if one of those things was growing inside her own body?

"People were getting cancer for thousands of years before we had high concentrations of carcinogens in the environment," she said.

Bob turned to her. "Not in the epidemic proportions of today."

"How long do you think this has been going on?"

"Who knows? A few years? A few hundred years?"

"But people die of their cancers," she persisted. "If what you're saying is true, the cancer organism would be destroying itself along with its human hosts."

"People are living much longer today with malignancies that used to be rapidly fatal, and many patients are being cured. We like to think it's because we have better treatments today. But maybe we doctors have nothing to do with it. Maybe this other organism is learning to adapt to its host, to control the human bodies it invades without destroying them."

"You know, there's something else," Joe said. "This could explain something that came up in that division-chief meeting we just had. There's a group of cancer patients who appear to recover completely, without any therapy."

"Do they still have malignant cells in their bodies?" Bob asked.

"They've all refused further evaluation," Joe replied. "They just check themselves out of the hospital."

Ellen thought about David and how his personality had changed so drastically. He had recovered from his melanoma without any therapy at all. She shuddered again at the memory of his gouged cheek and his one, gory eye glaring at her in the darkroom. She looked down at her left hand. Pieces of David's skin were still embedded under her nails. Her entire body convulsed. She suppressed a scream, and began frantically looking through her purse for a nail file.

Joe stood up. "And you think you're a target of this intelligent organism because your gene vaccine could splice out the cancer genes from our chromosomes?"

"Exactly," Bob replied. "That's why they're trying to kill me."

Joe leaned against the wall and closed his eyes in concentration. After a moment, he said, "Bob, you and any other intelligent organism, must realize that you can't possibly remove thousands of genes with your technique. So what makes you such a threat?"

"You're right, if it was necessary to remove all the genes of the cancer organism in order to kill it. But the data from my experiments suggest that Gp-78 is activated by environmental carcinogens, and it then turns on all the other cancer genes. Splicing it out might be the cure. We need a sample of the Gp-78 gene in order to complete its sequence. That's why I sent Ellen to get Peterson's blood samples. Now we need another source of cells."

"How are you going to prove that Gp-78 controls the cancer genome?"

"There's no time for that. Unless you can come up with a better suggestion, we need to take a leap of faith and manufacture a vaccine to splice it out before we all succumb to this assault."

Joe rubbed his temples. "Perhaps we should notify the authorities. If you're right, we'll need help."

Bob walked over to the window and peeked through the blinds. "Which authorities? If Delany is involved, anyone else could be."

Joe frowned. "I've got some contacts in the Surgeon General's office. Listen Bob, I find this whole thing a bit hard to swallow. Are you absolutely convinced of this?"

Bob stepped away from the window. "Joe," he said evenly, "go have a look at the brain of that old lady, Stone. That woman had a non-human brain in her skull. I'll bet my life on it. As a matter of fact, I *am* betting my life on it. Look at it and reach your own conclusions."

"I'll check the autopsy report in the morning."

"That's a waste of time. Becker's the one who's been bringing the vinyl chloride into the hospital. I suspect he's been transformed and is doctoring all the reports. Have the body exhumed and look at the goddamned thing yourself."

"She's been dead for a week."

"The ground's been frozen," Bob replied. "The body won't have decomposed yet. Joe, listen you're my best friend. Do this one thing for me. If she has a normal brain, I'll admit I'm wrong and I'll let you come up with another reason they're trying to kill me, okay?"

"I'm sorry, Bob. I know how tough the past few weeks have been. I do think you're wrong about this, but you've got me spooked enough to want to be sure." He looked at his watch. "It's a quarter to seven. I'll go talk to Becker now."

"You'll exhume the body?"

"I'll exhume the body."

"Thanks. We'll wait for you here."

Joe placed his hands on Bob's shoulders. "You know, I had a feeling you were alive all along."

"Oh? How so?"

"You're a man of your word, Bob. You told me that if anything happened to you, you'd seen to it that the story would get out and you'd nail Delany."

Bob's eyes narrowed. "The story should have hit the press. I don't know why it didn't."

Joe dropped his arms. "Which reminds me, I forgot all about the explosion in the lab. What caused it?"

"I did. Peterson had some kind of plastic explosive with him. He obviously was planning to blow up the lab after he killed me, and make it look like an accident. I left the explosives in the lab, turned on the gas vents and lit it up. I figured they'd find Peterson's body, burnt beyond recognition, and mistake it for my own, at least for a while. Thought it would give me some breathing room."

Joe jabbed at Bob's chest with his finger. "You think of everything, don't you? I'll be back as soon as I have an answer. I hope, for everyone's sake, that you're wrong, Bob."

"Believe me, so do I," Bob replied, accompanying Joe to the door. "Remember Joe, if I'm right, there's a ticking bomb in every one of us. We all carry the genes. You can't tell anyone I'm alive."

"How do you know I can be trusted?"

"I don't have a choice. You're the only person who can help me neutralize the cancer genes."

"Hang tight. I'll be back as soon as I can."

Bob closed the door behind Joe and turned back into the living room. Ellen was sitting at the coffee table, holding a nail file and concentrating intently on her hands.

"Ellen what are you doing?"

Ellen grimaced. "I got some of David's skin under my nails when I scratched him. Just the thought of it is making me ill."

Bob stared at her hands for a moment, then grabbed her wrist. She looked up. "What?"

"Ellen, you've just brought me my cell sample."

43

Delany leaned his head down towards that of his shorter companion, the mass of tendrils on his forehead glistened in the late afternoon sun, quivering expectantly. Their tendrils touched, hesitantly at first, then earnestly, swarming over each other in rhapsodic motion. When Delany's DNA sequences had been updated with the events since their last encounter, the tendrils retracted back beneath each man's forehead, showing no evidence of what lay beneath.

Delany raised his head and looked out over the Potomac. Two boats on the river's opposite bank bobbed along the surface of the water.

"Couldn't Peterson follow simple orders?" Delany asked. "I'd hardly call blowing up half the building discreet."

His companion laughed heartily. "Perhaps not discreet, but audacious, you'd have to agree. It would have accomplished the job, but something went wrong."

"Peterson must have been killed in the explosion along with Newman."

"You're forgetting that there was only one body found," his companion replied.

"Well then, whose is it?"

"Since we haven't heard from Peterson, I can only assume that it's his and that Newman is still alive."

Delany's eyes narrowed. "Then who blew up the lab?"

"Newman must have blown it up himself to get us off his scent. He's a crafty devil."

A cold breeze blew across the river. Delany raised his coat collar. "I warned you that Newman was less of a threat if we just left him alone."

"You warned me that Newman might figure out what we are, and that's impossible," the shorter man rasped. "But, the gene deletion vector *is* a threat, however unlikely it is that he'd know how to use it effectively. Do you still believe it's safe to leave that in his possession?"

Delany sighed. "No, it would be too risky. I think he suspects something."

"You think he *knows*?"

"Not the whole truth. But he knows I tried to have him killed. And he suspects some sort of conspiracy."

"Well, one man can't hide from thousands for very long. We'll find him."

Delany's hands were cold and he slid them into his coat pockets. "I hope you're right. They've got Peterson's body. What do we do about that?"

The companion laughed again, a deep, belly laugh. "You worry too much, do you know that? They'll never get anything out of that charred hunk of meat."

Delany watched the boats bob in the gentle waves. "I wouldn't underestimate these people. They don't think like we do. Their history isn't stored in their DNA. To compensate, they appear to have developed an uncanny intuitiveness. The logic of their thought processes eludes me, but give them enough hints and they'll reach the correct conclusions, even without the benefit of DNA memory."

"Enough of your doubts! the shorter man growled. "You're tiring me. Everything's proceeding according to schedule. The Edison and Susquehanna plants were destroyed within the past hour. According to our calculations, the carcinogenic load will induce an additional twelve percent malignant transformation in the surrounding population centers."

Delany nodded. "That's good, very good."

"Yes, but they've still got some fight left in them. The military's begun prophylactic chemotherapy on all its personnel. We were unprepared for this counterattack. If it's initiated for the civilian population nationally, it'll dramatically slow our growth. You must prevent that."

Delany nodded. "I'll see to it. Now, about the girl, Newman's sister-in-law. Why? It seems pointless."

"She's completely recovered from her illness and I'm almost certain that Newman used the vaccine on her. We'll know for sure soon. If he did treat her, and if they are allowed to examine her, they may be able to figure out how to use Newman's technology. We can't allow that. You needn't bother yourself with this. I'll see to it personally."

Delany stared at him for a long moment. "At least you should find out whether the vaccine works."

His companion hesitated. "Yes, perhaps you're right. We'll kill her afterwards."

Delany turned and looked back across the river. He could see the Jefferson Memorial in the distance, seemingly floating on the tranquil water. He remembered standing in this place in a different time, a different life. Remarkable that those memories still existed in some corner of his mind. Suddenly, they were gone, as unexpectedly as they had appeared. Delany sighed. And sighed again.

44

By the time Joe reached the University, he had convinced himself that Bob's theory about an intelligent cancer organism was ridiculous. Bob's ideas were infectious, and while listening to him, it had all begun to make a strange kind of sense. But away from his presence, it seemed preposterous. There had to be a saner explanation. Since he'd promised to check out the old lady's body, he figured that was as good a place as any to begin searching for clues.

He entered the main office of the pathology department and asked the secretary if Becker was in.

"Yes, Doctor Malcolm, he's in his office."

Becker was sitting behind his desk, a small, wiry man in his fifties with a balding head.

"Joe, good to see you. So sorry to hear about Bob."

"Thanks, Alex. It's a terrible loss. We're all going to miss him."

Becker motioned Joe to a chair. "Any idea how it happened?"

"Probably an accident in the lab. One of the gas outlets was left on."

Becker shook his head. "Terribly unfortunate, a man in his prime, with so much yet to accomplish. And after making that tremendous discovery." Becker peered over the rim of his glasses and cleared his throat. "Are you going to be able to recover his work?"

"Hopefully we can piece it together, but it'll take time. I'm afraid Bob didn't keep his notes in order."

"I see. Unfortunately we're all guilty of that. What can I do for you, Joe?"

"I wanted to speak to you about a woman by the name of Mildred Stone who died last week from metastatic lymphoma. You performed an autopsy on her."

Becker furrowed his brow. "The name doesn't ring a bell."

"I'd like to see the pathology report."

"Is there a problem?"

"No. It's more for the sake of a friend, actually."

"Oh? A relative of the deceased?"

"More or less. I promised I'd find out the cause of death."

"Well, I'm sure the pathology report was sent to her doctor, but I'll see if I can dig it up. I'll have my secretary call you."

"Actually, Alex, I need to see it today. I hate to be a bother."

"Oh, no bother, Joe. It's probably still in the temporary bin. Some of the bacteriology and virology cultures will still be pending."

He got up and began to search through a pile on a cabinet behind his desk.

"Here it is, Mildred H. Stone."

Becker opened the folder and Joe approached him, looking over his shoulder at the report.

"Let's see. . . Gross external findings normal. Internal organs showed tumor nodules present in liver, spleen and small intestine. Heart was normal. Microscopic findings showed extensive metastases in liver, spleen, intestinal lamina propria and bone. Diagnosis, metastatic lymphoma. Cause of death, massive organ failure secondary to tumor infiltration."

He looked up and smiled. "Satisfied?"

"What about the brain?"

Becker hesitated. "The brain?"

"Yes. You must have examined the brain."

The smile faded from Becker's lips, replaced by a nervous frown. "Yes, of course." He looked down at the folder and began leafing through the papers. "Here it is. . . Brain anatomy normal."

"Can I see the slides?"

Becker's lower lip began to tremble. "Of course." He went to the slide file and began searching through the drawers. "Funny, I don't seem to be able to locate the slides of the brain. . . I'm sure they're here somewhere. . . This is most disconcerting. I'm going to have to speak to the resident who performed this autopsy. The entire report should be kept in one place until the file is complete. That's standard procedure here."

"Alex, your name's at the bottom of the report. You performed this autopsy."

Becker studied the document. "So I did. Funny, I don't remember the case. It must have been pretty routine. One of the secretaries must have misplaced the report. We'll find it."

Joe recalled Bob telling him that that the pathology report would be a waste of time. Could the son-of-a-gun be correct about the cancer organism, too? The first theories that viruses were encoded in the human genome were also ridiculed, as was the notion that cells had receptors with which they could take up pieces of foreign DNA. Both of these were ultimately proven to be true. But a higher, rational organism?

"Alex, I'm going to have Mrs. Stone's body exhumed."

"What?"

"I want to see that brain myself."

Becker slammed the folder on his desk. "This is outrageous! Are you questioning my professional competence?"

"I want to see that brain and you don't seem to be able to locate it."

Becker's lips twitched. "I told you, the slides will turn up. Haven't you ever misplaced anything?"

"Nevertheless, I'm going to have the body exhumed."

Becker's nostrils flared. "On what grounds?"

"On the grounds that the brain was never examined."

"Of course the brain was examined. This is ridiculous!"

Becker looked at Joe intently, tiny beads of perspiration on his upper lip. Joe turned to leave.

"You have no grounds to exhume that body, Joe. I won't allow it! I'll take this to the University ethics committee."

"That's your prerogative, Alex, but the police will make the decision regarding exhumation."

"Are you suggesting negligence on my part?   I resent the accusation."

Joe put his hand on the door knob. "I'm not suggesting anything. I simply want to see the body."

Becker's arms began flailing. "The woman was not even your patient. If you think the police are going to dig up a body just on the basis of your personal curiosity, you're crazy! I happen to know the chief of police. We've worked together on many cases and he doesn't act on a whim."

Joe opened the door. "I happen to know him, too. I saved his son's life. Have a nice day, Alex."

* * *

The air was getting distinctly colder as the sun drew close to the horizon. It would be dusk in an hour. Joe stood over the grave and waited while two men dug out the dirt covering the coffin. Tom O'Malley was at his side.

"Thanks again for digging up this body for me on such short notice, Tom. I'm sure your busy."

"Not as busy as my colleagues in New Jersey at this moment, the poor bastards."

Joe paled. "What are you talking about?"

O'Malley turned to him. "Haven't you heard?"

"No, what?"

"The Edison power plant in New Jersey was blown up an hour ago. They're expecting massive radiation exposure from Boston down the coast to Philadelphia."

There was a tremor in Joe's voice when he responded. "What happened?"

"Too early to say. Either a gross systems failure, or sabotage."

"Sabotage?"

O'Malley shrugged. "You know, terrorists." He nodded his head in the direction of the grave. "Now how about telling me the truth, Doc. What are we doing here? And don't give me any more baloney about misplaced organs."

Joe shifted his feet. "Sorry about that, Tom. I should have leveled with you. About a month ago, right after Bob made his discovery, he was attacked in one of the hospital rooms by a patient. At the time we chalked it up to a delirious state of mind."

"And the patient's name?"

Joe hesitated. "Mildred Stone."

O'Malley exhaled loudly. "Joe, you're gonna have to come clean with me if I'm gonna get to the bottom of this. You can't be undertaking your own investigation under my nose."

"You're right, and I apologize."

"So why are we digging up this body?"

"I told you the truth about that. There's no record of the condition of the woman's brain at autopsy."

"And what's so important about her brain?"

Joe wasn't about to tell Tom anything as crazy as a parasitic organism in the human genome. "The woman exhibited extremely bizarre behavior when she attacked Bob. It's crucial to know if her behavior could be attributed to any brain pathology."

"What are you expecting to find?" O'Malley asked.

"I don't know what to expect."

"But you believe Becker purposely falsified the report."

"All I know is that the guy was sweating bricks when I confronted him this morning."

"I've worked with Becker on a number of cases and he's always struck me as a 'play it by the books' kind of guy," O'Malley responded.

"We'll see." Joe was certain that Becker was guilty of something, at the very least, incompetence.

The diggers reached the casket and they lowered two burlap straps into the hole. Joe glanced at O'Malley. "There's one more thing, Tom."

"Yes?"

"There were two men in my office yesterday claiming to be police officers, who turned the place upside down. They said they were working on your orders. Did you give your men orders to search my office?"

"Absolutely not. The men were to seal off the laboratory only. I would have told you if we needed to search your office. Did you get their names?"

"Anderson, badge number three oh one and Paul, badge number two sixteen."

O'Malley's eyes narrowed. "Those aren't the men I sent out there. Believe me, I'll get to the bottom of this, and when I do there'll be hell to pay. Did they cause damage?"

"It'll take some time to re-file everything, but no. I'm certain they were looking for Bob's notes on the gene vaccine."

"Think so?"

"I do."

"Funny you should say that. I was thinking the same thing. This case is getting more and more bizarre."

"I bet you'll never see those two cops again."

"Those men aren't on the force," O'Malley snapped. "And we don't take impersonation of police officers lightly. We'll find them. This police department isn't inept, despite what the papers report."

"Look," Joe said. "They're pulling up the coffin."

The burlap straps had been wrapped under the wooden coffin, which was being hoisted up by a pulley. When the casket cleared the ground, it swung away from the hole and was lowered onto the snow-covered lawn. One of the workers pried open the casket lid. Joe and O'Malley peered inside.

"Whew!" O'Malley pulled his face away. "It sure as hell stinks."

The old woman's wrinkled face had a waxy look. She wore a blue dress and one gnarled hand rested on her chest.

"We're going to have to turn it over," Joe said. "The skull would have been entered from the back."

They put on gloves and flipped the tiny corpse over. It was frozen and stiff. Joe felt under the hairline.

"They generally make the cut back here. . . ah, here are the sutures."

O'Malley handed Joe a pair of scissors and he cut the stitches holding together the edges of the scalp. He pulled the upper part of the scalp over the back of the head, exposing the skull bones.

"Here's where the skull was sawed open," Joe said, pointing. "So Becker did examine the brain. Let's see what he found."

He lifted off the top of the cranium. He stared for a moment, looked up at O'Malley, then back at the cranial cavity.

It was empty.

"Damn."

The sun touched the horizon. Joe stuck his head into the casket and peered into the cranial cavity. He squinted. Was it just his imagination?

"You got a flashlight?"

"Sure." O'Malley handed him a light.

Joe pointed it into the cavity and bent over again. He stared at the backside of the frontal bone, behind the forehead. There they were, just as Bob had predicted. He ran his forefinger over the dozens of tiny holes on the backside of the frontal bone where no holes had any business being. He felt a shiver go down his finger and up his arm. He withdrew his hand quickly.

"Tom, this has been very helpful. I've got to go now."

"Are you all right, doc? You look kind of pale."

"Yeah, I'm fine. Thanks for your help."

"I'm going to have to have a chat with Becker about the missing brain. This is a violation of state law. You sure you're okay? I can have one of my men drive you back."

"No, I'm fine. I've got my car here. So long, Tom."

"Take care, Doc."

Joe hurried to his car.

45

Joe returned to Jackson Hall after leaving the cemetery. There was still one more thing that needed checking. It was after eight in the evening and the department was deserted. The office was still a mess, but to his relief, his computer was functioning. He tried to access GenBank, the national data base for the human genome, but the internet connection was dead, probably damaged by the explosion. He walked around the corner to the department library.

The library computer was online. After connecting to GenBank, he entered 'Gp 78' and waited. After a moment, to Joe's pleasant surprise, the computer announced that Gp 78 was in the database. The gene was located on chromosome nine, towards the upstream end. As he marched up and down the chromosome, he grew alarmed. He picked up the telephone and dialed home. Ellen answered on the second ring. After inquiring if they were all right, he asked to speak to Bob.

"We were getting worried about you," Bob said. "What did you find out?"

"Becker was evasive as hell. Bottom line, the old woman's brain has disappeared. No records. As I promised you, I had the body dug up."

"And?"

"The brain was missing. But the holes in the frontal bone were there, dozens of them, just as you described them. I'm in the library on Genbank right now. Listen to this. Gp 78 is encoded on chromosome nine, near the upstream end. It may very well control the expression of the other genes on the chromosome. I selected half a dozen other tumor antigens at random, and they're all encoded on chromosome nine, downstream from Gp 78. Most of these genes are normally expressed in the early stages of fetal development, but are subsequently shut down by some unknown mechanism."

"I've already done the same exercise," Bob said. "I could have saved you the trouble."

"Can we make a vaccine to cut out Gp 78?"

"Yes, but we first have to complete its sequence and manufacture the right restriction enzyme."

At that moment, Joe was startled by a strangely familiar voice coming from the hallway. He pulled the telephone receiver away from his ear and strained to listen.

". . . He's not here. Can you believe we had him yesterday morning and just let him go?"

"Somebody was here recently," said a second voice. "The door's open and the lights are on. Check the bathroom."

Joe replaced the telephone receiver on the hook, shut off the lights, and crouched down behind the door, leaving it open a crack so he could see down the hallway. He heard footsteps approaching the library. Then he saw a figure pass by, heading towards the restroom. It was one of the 'police officers' who had ransacked the office the day before.

Presently the man returned. His partner, who Joe recognized as the other 'officer', met him in the hall.

"Well?"

"Nobody there."

"First Newman, and now we've lost Malcolm. Stark's gonna be pissed."

"Yeah, the chief will be shitting bricks. Let's stake out the house. He's got to show up there sooner or later--if he's not already dead."

Joe listened to the two men's footsteps fading down the hall. He was stunned. Stark was the head of the FBI! When the stairwell door slammed shut, he rushed to the phone.

"What happened to you?" Bob asked. "The line went dead."

Joe was breathing heavily. "You two have got to get out of there, now!"

"What's going on?"

"Two guys posing as cops, they're headed for my house as we speak. But they're not cops, and they're after me--and you, too."

"Who are they?"

"They're with the FBI and Stark's been transformed. We can forget about contacting someone in the government. It's lucky I didn't make the call yet."

"Shit. Who the hell do we trust?"

"No one," Joe replied. "Get the minivan out of the garage. The keys are in the kitchen cabinet. You and Ellen meet me in the Immunology Building garage in fifteen minutes."

"Good. Be careful, Joe."

"Same to you two."

* * *

It was dark and silent in the parking garage D level. Joe watched a set of headlights approach down the ramp. The van came to a stop and he slid in through the side door. Bob was in the driver's seat, with Ellen at his side.

"Any trouble," Joe asked.

"No," Bob replied. "What next?"

"The first thing is to find you two a place to work," Ellen said. "The University labs are out of the question."

Joe reached behind to the back seat and folded it down flat. "I was thinking about my cabin in Wisconsin. It's in the middle of nowhere. I only wish we still had some of your virus. It's going to take us weeks to make more, weeks we can't afford."

Bob reached into his pocket and pulled out a vial of turquoise fluid.

Joe looked at the vial, then at Bob. "Where'd you get that? Your lab was blown to pieces."

"After Peterson tried to kill me, I pulled some out of the incubator. I figured I might need it."

"I shouldn't be surprised at anything you come up with, Bob. Okay, let's stop wasting time and get to work."

"We're going to need to take some of the heavy equipment and the police may still have our labs under guard," Bob said.

Joe locked the rear seat into place. "It's too dangerous to go back to Jackson Hall. I've got the master key that will get us into the immunology labs upstairs. They've got what we need. We should be able to fit an incubator and centrifuge back here, along with the smaller stuff."

"How long will it take to get it all down here?" Ellen asked.

"A couple hours," Joe responded.

"Okay, I'll take the van and meet the two of you back here at eleven."

"Where are you going?" Joe asked.

"To get a supply of food."

The two men looked at her, then at each other. "We're going to need to eat, you know."

"Right," Joe said.

"What do you mean, 'we'?" Bob said. "You can't come with us, Ellen. It's too dangerous."

"I'm going," she said, defiantly. "We have to keep an eye on each other. If one of us stays behind and develops cancer, our cover's blown."

"She's right again, Bob," Joe said.

"Yes, of course, I wasn't thinking. No one, and I mean no one, can know where we are."

"Except Nina" said Joe.

"Including Nina," Bob replied.

"Now wait a minute. I can't just disappear without telling Nina. She'll die from worry. Obviously, she can be trusted."

"Bob's right, Joe," Ellen announced. "I'm sorry. If your wife, or anyone for that matter, has a cancer organism growing inside of them, it's only a matter of time before they're transformed. It's not a question of who can be trusted. No one can be trusted."

Joe was stunned for a moment, then said, "Then we'll bring Nina along."

"We can't do that either," Ellen replied. "If the transformation rate is really twenty five percent, we're stacking the odds against us by bringing even one more along. The best thing we can do for our loved ones is to come back with a vaccine as fast as possible. Nothing can be allowed to get in the way of that."

"Joe, Ellen's right. You've got to leave her here. She may even be safer than with us."

Joe was silent for a moment, then he sighed. "I need to tell Nina something. Let me call and tell her that I need to go away for a while on important business. She won't want to be alone if I'm gone for any length of time, so she'll stay with her sister until I come home."

"Agreed," Bob said. "But don't tell her I'm with you. Don't even tell her I'm alive."

"Of course not. The best thing we've got going for us is that everyone thinks you're dead. And there's a body to prove it."

"Okay then, let's go," Bob urged. "Ellen, can you pick up some clothes for us when you get the groceries?"

"I'll try to find something."

"We'll have the equipment by the elevators when you return."

46

The van's headlights faded as dawn approached, revealing a narrow country road winding through open fields, and the dim silhouette of hills ahead and to the west. Ellen watched from the back of the van as the growing light of day revealed a smooth blanket of snow covering the landscape. They could have been moving through the barren terrain of a lifeless planet, so still was it outside. They passed a sign reading, 'Bear Creek 13 miles'. She marveled at how peaceful the passing scenery appeared, giving no expression to the tension she felt inside.

She glanced at the two men sitting up front. Joe was behind the wheel, with Bob beside him. The fate of humanity was now in their hands. Could they stop this invader whose attack was so insidious as to almost defy recognition? Even if they succeeded in producing a vaccine, how could they possibly deliver it to every man, woman, and child on the planet?

Since their departure from Chicago, the two men had been heavily engrossed in the technical plans of how to insert this amino acid into that enzyme and that nucleotide into such-and-such nucleic acid sequence. She had quickly found the discussion far beyond the molecular biology experience of a second year student. After listening for a few moments to their discussion, their voices faded once again into the sounds of the rumbling engine and the wind blowing past the van.

Her thoughts drifted back to the cancer organism. If it really was an evolutionary question of survival of the fittest, which of the two species was more fit to survive? How long might it be before humanity's last breath was squeezed from its lungs? She wondered whether her body was, at this moment, a breeding ground for a growing cancer organism, and she shuddered. What would happen if they took over her body and mind? Would she turn on Bob and Joe?

The flat plains gave way to forested hills. Joe turned off onto a narrow, winding road and soon they were in a heavily-wooded forest. The snow had been plowed from the center of the road, leaving a path just wide enough for the van to pass. After a half hour, Joe slowed and turned onto a path where the snow had not been cleared. They passed occasional forks in the road, but they were few and far between. They took another turn and, after a few minutes, stopped in front of an iron gate. Joe got out to unlock the chain. Ellen could not see a cabin, but she figured it must be just up ahead.

"It's beautiful here," she whispered.

Bob looked back at her from the front seat. "It is," he replied. "Too bad we can't enjoy it."

"Do you think this cancer organism really means to kill us all?"

His gaze hardened. "It's either us or them. Understand that there is no coexistence possible. Two genomes can't both be active in the same cell."

"But haven't we coexisted for millions of years?"

"They've been hibernating," Bob replied. "Now that their genes are awakening, they're shutting ours down. Our race is dying."

"Maybe they fear us as much as we fear them," she wondered aloud.

Bob rolled his eyes. "Ellen, you're too sentim--"

Suddenly, he ducked his head behind the seat.

"Is something wrong?"

He put a finger to his lips and a pistol appeared in his hand.

"Where'd you get that?" she breathed, frightened at the site of the weapon.

She heard a noise behind her, and turned to see an elderly man getting out of a pick-up truck. The man looked at her through the window, his wrinkled face peering out from under a red, knit cap. He wore a heavy, brown coat, gray pants and rubber boots. Too late to hide, she smiled at him. The old man smiled back and waved, then approached the gate.

"What's going on out there?" Bob demanded from his crouched position.

Ellen glanced nervously at the gun in Bob's hand. "Be careful with that thing, would you?"

She cracked open the window and listened.

"Joe, this is a surprise," the stranger said. "I was stopping by to check on your pipes. Didn't expect to see you for a couple of months."

Joe had just unfastened the chain and was pushing the gate open. He looked up with a start.

"Bill! Good to see you." The two men shook hands.

"The electricity's off, and there ain't much firewood, neither."

"Don't worry, this was a spur of the moment trip. I'll take care of all that."

"How long you plan on staying?"

"A couple of weeks."

"Well, after you get settled in, drop on by for a drink. The old lady will be glad to see you. I'll bring over some firewood to keep you and your friend warm."

"Thanks, Bill. We're gonna keep a low profile. So don't mention to anyone that we're here, okay?"

Bill flashed a knowing smile. "I never saw you, or the pretty lady with you. We'll have that drink in February with you and your *wife*."

"Looking forward to it, Bill. And thanks."

"Enjoy." He turned back down the path, waving goodbye to Joe. As he passed the van he gave a wink to Ellen, who smiled and waved through the window. Then he backed the truck into a clearing, turned, and drove off.

Joe swung the gate open and got back behind the wheel. "You can sit up now," he said as he pulled forward. "Thanks to you, he thinks I'm cheating on my wife."

"Sorry, I couldn't take a chance of him seeing me," Bob replied.

Joe noticed the gun in Bob's hand. "Where'd you get that?"

"I picked it up after I returned from Washington," Bob replied. He put the gun away. "So who was that guy?"

"Bill and his wife are the only people around for miles. He keeps an eye on the place for us. Nice folks, but loners."

"Do we need to worry about him?"

Joe drove through the gate and put the van into neutral. "I hope not. Anyway, he didn't see you."

"But he saw *you*," Bob replied, with a note of urgency. "I'll shut the gate."

As they waited for Bob to return, Ellen said, "Joe, I've been meaning to ask you what happened to that little girl in the screening clinic."

"That sweet thing? We admitted her for a lymph node biopsy. She vanished before we could do the procedure. In retrospect, she probably was transformed."

Ellen felt a sudden crush of sadness. The poor thing. She was just a little girl in pig tails. "Joe, how can we tell if one of us becomes transformed? It seems pretty obvious that the transformed people retain their human memories. If I didn't know David as well as I do, I never would have realized there was anything unusual about him."

"I'll tell you one thing, I know Bob like a brother. I'll know when he responds out of character."

"And what about me?"

Joe grinned, then realized from her expression that she wasn't joking.

"Do you think you'd be able to tell?" she persisted.

"Tell what?" asked Bob, who had just returned.

"Tell if I became transformed," she answered.

"There's no point in worrying about that," Joe said. "It's not going to happen to you."

"I'm not a child, Joe," Ellen shot back. "We all know that it might happen, probably will eventually if you two don't come up with a vaccine very soon. Yes, I'm scared. I can't help it."

Bob leaned towards her and looked directly into her eyes. "I'll know," he said.

"Really? How?"

"I'll know from your eyes. Eyes never lie."

She returned his gaze. "I believe you would," she whispered.

"I'm scared too," Joe said in a low voice. "But we're going to stick together and get through this. We have to keep believing that."

"He's right," Bob said. "Ellen with a little luck, we'll have a vaccine in a couple of weeks. All the transformed individuals we know about had known cancers. It takes months for even the most malignant cancers to spread throughout the body." He didn't add that, with the frequency of malignancies increasing dramatically, nothing precluded many cells in a single body from becoming cancerous at once.

"Well, maybe you're right," Ellen replied. "But if it does happen to me, I wish to die a human being. You do know what I mean, don't you?"

There was a moment of silence, then Bob replied, "I know what you mean, Ellen. You have my word that I'll honor that wish."

"Mine too," Joe said.

Joe put the van into gear and drove past a bend in the path. Then he stopped, turned off the motor and said, "We're here. Anybody hungry?"

"Well I'd certainly know if Joe was transformed," Bob said. "For starters he'd probably stop thinking about food. Let's unpack first, then we'll eat."

Ellen stepped out of the van and looked around. The cabin was nestled in a lovely, snow-covered clearing, surrounded on all sides by dense woods. It was a wood and brick ranch with blue curtains in the windows. The roof was covered with a heavy layer of white snow, a brick chimney poking out from the roof. She could see a range of gentle, old hills in the distance. It would have been so romantic, were not the circumstances so grim.

"Ellen," Joe said, "Bob and I will start unloading. Why don't you unlock the cabin door and clear out a space in the living room where we can set up shop."

"Okay," she said, taking the keys. She unlocked the door and stepped into the cabin. Opposite her was a fireplace containing a couple of half-burnt logs. A mantle held some simple pieces of pottery. Directly in front of the fireplace was an oval rug, a sofa, a rocking chair, and a small, wooden coffee table. A door on the far side of the room led into the kitchen. There she found a wood-burning stove, a small kitchen table with four chairs, and some blackened pots hanging on the wall. The kitchen door led out to a porch. The forest reached up to within ten feet of the cabin. There was a small pile of firewood a few feet away, not enough to last more than a couple of days. The bathroom, across from the kitchen, contained a cast-iron tub on short legs. She giggled as she tried to picture Joe squeezing himself into that tub.

On the opposite side of the cabin were two bedrooms. From the window of one, she could see the men unpacking the van. She walked out to rejoin them.

"I've decided we should use the larger bedroom for a lab. I need help moving the bed."

"The living room has more room," Bob objected.

"The living room is going to be our social area where we can unwind and maintain a little sanity," she replied firmly. "That should more than make up for a slightly smaller work space."

"But--"

Ellen didn't let him finish. "Since I can't help with the vaccine, I'm going to be responsible for keeping house. You two will share the second bedroom. I'll sleep in the living room on the couch. Now I don't want to hear another word about it."

Bob opened his mouth to respond, then shut it.

"Well I guess that takes care of that," Joe said with a laugh. "Ellen, don't let that man push you around when you're right. Bob, let's go move that bed."

Once the bed was moved, the three of them began transferring the equipment into the cabin.

"Joe, is your electric supply going to be able to handle all this output?" Bob asked as they set the centrifuge on the bedroom floor.

"I think we'll be okay. There's no outside electricity source. I've got a generator behind the kitchen, connected to a fuse box. The incubator and refrigerator are the only large power consumers. The rest of the stuff won't be going constantly."

"All right. Where do I plug this in?"

"We're going to have to plug everything into the extension cord. Give me the other end of it and I'll run it over to the generator." He took the cable and disappeared out of the room. A moment later, there was a rumble, then a purring sound.

"Give it a try now!" Joe yelled.

Bob plugged in the centrifuge and saw the red light go on.

"Looks good!" he called back.

Joe came out from behind the kitchen. "We'd better get the rest of the van unpacked. Why don't you two finish that up while I try to get some heat going. I hope I've got some firewood left over from last season."

"I saw some outside the kitchen door," Ellen said.

"Great." Joe disappeared into the kitchen.

In a couple of trips they had the van emptied. Joe had started a fire in the fireplace and in the wood-burning stove.

"It's going to get a lot colder," he said. "Around here, its bitter cold at night."

"Fortunately, we have this archaic technology to keep us warm," Bob said, setting up one of the carbon dioxide tanks beside the incubator, which Ellen had agreed could be placed in the corner of the living room since they couldn't maneuver the bulky object into the bedroom. "What I wouldn't give for a gas furnace."

"Actually," said Joe, "these wood-burning stoves are very efficient generators of heat."

"It's warming up already," Ellen agreed, shivering with pleasure as the warm air reach her.

"Anybody hungry?" Joe asked.

Bob looked up and frowned. "Already?"

"It's been a long day and we've got a long night ahead of us. I can't work on an empty stomach."

"You'll never fill that stomach."

"Listen," Ellen said. "Why don't you two stop bickering and finish setting up your equipment. I'll fix up something to eat."

47

The site that greeted Lois, as she stepped through the University hospital's main entrance, brought a thin smile to her lips. The hot, sweaty mass of humanity overflowed from the emergency room all the way through the main lobby and down the opposite hall. Hospital security guards and city police were trying, with minimal success, to maintain a semblance of order. The sounds of misery were deafening. She passed a woman sobbing in grief as she held her listless child to her chest. Farther up the hall, a man pleaded with a nurse for his wife to be seen. She lay moaning on the floor beside him, her head resting on the lap of an elderly woman who stroked her hair and wailed. She saw a man shove a pregnant woman aside in an attempt to get ahead in line. A sign inside the lobby read, UNLESS YOU

HAVE A LIFE-THREATENING ILLNESS, YOU WILL NOT BE SEEN TODAY. Her smile broadened into a joyous grin. In the week since Newman had disappeared, the tide of battle had turned decisively in Sartan's favor.

She squeezed past the crowd and made her way to the elevators. When she exited on the fifth floor, it was immediately apparent that the chaos had spread throughout the hospital. The hallways had been converted into patient care areas, with the sick lying in beds lined up along the walls. Debbie was standing in front of the nurses station, busily handing out orders to her staff. She saw Lois approach and drew away from the commotion.

"I'm glad you could come. Excuse the mayhem here."

"I've never seen anything like this," Lois whispered.

Debbie blew a strand of hair off her face. "Let's walk down the hall for a moment." She led Lois down the corridor and past the elevators.

"This hospital looks like a scene out of World War Two." Lois said. "How are you holding up?"

"We're not," Debbie replied. "We're working triple shifts, giving high dose chemotherapy in the outpatient clinics, if you can believe that. We've got no choice. All beds are being reserved for the terminally ill. In the meantime, people are literally trampling over each other to get into the clinics. It's complete pandemonium."

Lois drew a long, satisfying breath of air into her lungs. "Does anybody know what's causing this?"

"Everyone's got a pet theory. It could be some toxic or infectious agent, or the power plant explosions, or the depletion of the ozone. Who the hell knows? We're treating everyone who has any abnormality, even a high white cell count, with high-dose chemotherapy. Some of the doctors are even talking about starting prophylactic chemo. How about you? Have you been screened?"

"I'm an old lady," Lois responded. "I'm not going to worry about cancer now. Besides, the sign downstairs says, terminally ill only."

Debbie smiled sympathetically.   "Well, you should have yourself checked. Any news on Joe?"

Lois shook her head.   "Nothing, and it's been a week already."

"How's his wife handling it?"

"So far, better than I expected. He called her the day he disappeared and told her not to worry, that he'd be gone for a few days."

"Well, I sure wish he was here," Debbie replied. "We could use his calming presence." She stopped in front of a room at the end of the corridor. "Thanks for coming for Janie. It's very thoughtful of you to take her."

"Nonsense. She's Bob's niece. Of course I'll take her. Is she really well enough to leave?"

"She's remarkably better," Debbie replied. "And we just don't have the room for her. I've kept her here as long as I could."

"How's she taking the news?"

"I haven't told her yet. I was waiting for you. Poor child. With Bob gone, she has no family. You ready?"

Lois nodded. Debbie opened the door and Lois followed her in. The young girl was sitting in the chair beside the bed, reading a book. She appeared quite a bit healthier than the last time Lois had seen her. Too healthy.

Debbie put a smile on her face. "Hi, sweetheart."

"Hi, Debbie," Janie smiled back. "I haven't seen you in a couple of days."

"I've been trying to hold down the fort. What are you reading?"

"A book of Hemingway's stories. Bobby gave it to me for my birthday."

"I love Hemingway, too. You remember Lois Baines, don't you?"

"Of course she does," Lois said, smiling. "Hello, Janie."

"Hello," the girl replied, the smile fading.

Debbie sat down at the edge of the bed.   "Guess what, honey? I've got some good news. Doctor Smith says you're ready to leave the hospital. You can be discharged today."

"I knew this was coming," Janie said flatly.

"You don't need to worry, you're going to stay with Lois."

Janie stared at the floor. "I don't want to burden anyone. I can stay with a friend's family. I've already checked into it."

"Nonsense," Lois replied. "I insist that you stay with me."

"That's very kind, but I don't want to impose."

"It's no imposition. I want you to come live with me, if it's all right with you that is. My own children are all grown up and gone and I miss having a young girl in the house."

"I'll be okay on my own," Janie said, her eyes still riveted to the floor tiles.

"Janie," Lois said, "I promised Bobby that if anything happened to him, I would take care of you. I'm not about to break that promise."

Janie lifted her eyes and looked at Lois.   Then her face wrinkled up and she broke into tears. Lois knelt beside the girl and pulled her to her chest. "It's okay, dear," she said, stroking her hair. "Everything's going to be all right. You'll see. We're going to get along famously. Now why don't you pack up your things, okay?"

Janie nodded, her head still nestled against Lois's chest.

"I've fixed up my daughter's old bedroom for you. I think you'll really like it."

Janie wiped the tears from her eyes. "Please let me know if I become a nuisance."

"Honey, you'll never be a nuisance. Now let's pack up your things."

"I've got to get back to the station," Debbie said. "Janie, I want you to come visit, okay?"

Janie nodded. "Thanks for everything. You're the most wonderful nurse anyone could ever ask for."

Debbie put her arms around Janie's thin body. Janie clung to her for a long while. Then Debbie left the room, her eyes overflowing with tears.

48

Ellen poured a cup of tea and sat down at the kitchen table. Bob and Joe were in the lab, where they had been working for ten days with almost no sleep. Things were not going well and the two men were frustrated, Joe more than Bob. At least Joe showed it more. He had lost his appetite, which was a pretty worrisome sign. To keep from feeling useless, she cooked, cleaned, kept the fire burning, worried about her 'boys', listened to the radio reports, and watched through the window for strangers. She laughed out loud, realizing that she had become a neurotic housewife. At least she got to chop wood.

She had begun keeping a journal to pass the time, and she opened it to make her daily entry, as she sipped from her teacup.

"What are you constantly writing in that journal of yours, anyway?"

Ellen looked up to see Bob standing over her. She instinctively covered the notebook with her forearm.

"I wasn't reading it. I can respect your privacy."

"I didn't mean to suggest you couldn't," she responded, closing the notebook. "How are things going?"

Bob frowned. "We're still having trouble isolating the sequence in front of the Gp 78 gene. Without that sequence we can't tailor a restriction enzyme to splice out the gene from the chromosome. But we'll figure it out. I'd be worried if things were going too smoothly."

Ellen shook her head. "You know, you have an amazing sense of optimism. It's contagious. I find it hard to be negative around you."

He went to the window and gazed outside. "Have you checked yourself yet today?" he asked, his back to her.

"No lumps or bumps. You?"

"The same."

"I'm in constant fear that I'll wake up tomorrow with a tumor somewhere. I keep imagining cancer genes inside the cells of my body becoming activated. I hope I'd be aware of it, because I'd kill myself to prevent me from sabotaging the vaccine production."

He turned towards her. "Don't worry. This is far from over. The human race is too damned selfish to go down without a hell of a fight. What's the radio saying today?"

"It's pretty alarming. The epidemic is running wild through the country. The AMA is calling on the government to respond with large-scale distribution of chemotherapeutic drugs.

"Shit, we're running out of time. Any rioting?"

"There've been some incidents at the screening centers. The Council of Mayors has petitioned the President to deploy the national guard to help the police forces maintain order."

Bob opened the refrigerator door and removed a can of Diet Coke. He pulled the tab and took a long gulp, then returned to the window. Ellen looked at his tall figure. In Chicago, Bob had been so intense and serious, while Joe was the calm, reasoned one. Here the roles seemed reversed. Bob often tried to joke with Joe, and she frequently heard him laughing. Was he attempting to raise his friend's spirits, or was this all some kind of a game to him? It wasn't as if he didn't take it seriously. He was dead serious. But she'd be damned if he wasn't on a high. She couldn't fathom how he could be cheerful when facing the probable destruction of mankind. Did he care about humanity's future or was all this just another mountain to climb, another medal to pin on his chest?

"Bob, can I ask you something?"

He turned from the window. "Sure."

"You seem really happy since we came up here to this cabin. Are you?"

He was quiet for a moment. "I suppose maybe I am."

"Why? We could be living the last few days of our lives."

He looked at her for a while, chewing his lower lip. "Maybe it's because, for the first time in five years, I don't feel alone."

That was not the response she had expected.

"You know, you can be the biggest ogre in the world, and then you'll say something like that and make me want to cry."

"I've got to get back to work, Ellen." He started out of the kitchen.

"Bob . . ."

He turned back.

"You don't have to always play the superhuman hero. It's okay to let your feelings show, you know."

He rested his hands on her shoulders. "What I'm feeling, Ellen, is that time is short and the work is great." He smiled at her. "If you'll excuse me."

He turned again and retreated back to the lab. Ellen continued to stare at the doorway, long after his figure disappeared. Finally, she opened her journal and picked up her pen.

49

Janie sat on the sofa reading her Hemmingway. It was late, but she wanted to finish one more chapter before going to bed. Lois stepped up to her and gave her a hug.

"You look happy today. It makes me feel happy, too."

Janie was happy. In the two weeks she had spent with Lois, she had developed an affection for the older woman.

Janie smiled. "I feel happy."

"You know dear, I'm so pleased at how healthy you look. Your recovery from Pompe's disease is remarkable. Bob's treatment was very effective."

The smile vanished from Janie's face. "Bobby was a very good doctor."

"He certainly was. But I'm referring to the vaccine."

"The vaccine?"

"Honey, I know Bobby didn't want you to tell anyone, but he meant outsiders. It's okay for me to know."

The girl averted her eyes and began fidgeting with her hair.

"It's okay, dear. You don't have to say anything. I'm just happy that it worked. It means that others can also be helped with the vaccine. It's good to help other people, if you can."

Janie thought for a moment. "Would it help other people if the doctors knew that it worked for me?"

"Of course, dear. It would tell them that the treatment can be used successfully. But you don't have to say anything, if you promised Bob."

Janie hesitated. "Well, if it would help someone else, I suppose it would be all right."

Lois raised her eyes expectantly. "Then he did give you the vaccine?"

Janie nodded slowly.

"I'm glad to hear that, dear." She approached the girl. "You really are a wonderful dear." She reached her hand out towards Janie's neck. "So sweet, so--".

Lois halted suddenly in her tracks, grimaced, and raised her hands to her temples.

"Lois, is everything all right?"

The older woman shrieked and began clawing at her head. She swayed, then fell to the floor with a thud. Janie rushed over to her. Lois's face was ashen and there were beads of perspiration on her brow. She lay motionless on the floor.

"Lois, are you okay? Can you hear me?"

Lois's body began to convulse, and saliva foamed at her mouth.

Janie rushed to the telephone and called for an ambulance. Then she called ward Five East and asked for Debbie.

"It's Janie. There's an emergency! Something's happened to Lois! I think she's having a seizure. I don't know what to do!"

"I'll send an ambulance over right away to pick her up."

"I've called for an ambulance already."

"Good. You're right by the hospital. They should be there in a moment. Is Lois breathing?"

Janie looked over at the woman. The convulsions had stopped and she lay still on the floor. Janie could see the shallow rise and fall of her chest. "Yes. She's breathing."

"Okay, that's a good sign. Put a blanket over her and wait for the paramedics."

"I hear the ambulance coming," Janie said.

"Good. You'll be at the hospital in a few minutes. I'll meet you in the emergency room."

"Thanks, Debbie. They're knocking at the door."

She put down the phone and rushed to the door.   Two paramedics entered with a stretcher.   They examined Lois and attached some wires to her chest.

"It's not a heart attack," said one of the paramedics, observing the monitor.   "But her blood pressure's off the wall." He spoke to Lois.   "Ma'am, I'm going to insert an I.V. in your arm and then we'll take you straight to the hospital.   Can you understand me?"

Lois did not respond.   The men worked quickly and had her in the stretcher and at the front door in minutes.

"Do you want to go with her?"   one of the paramedics asked Janie.

She nodded and followed them down the stairs to the ambulance.   She got into the back of the vehicle with Lois.   She held her hand until the ambulance arrived at the emergency room.   Lois was whisked off the ambulance and into an exam room.   Debbie grabbed Janie and led her away.   Neither of them saw the tall, young man with the white mark on his cheek, and the patch over his eye, who watched them as they passed through the packed waiting room.

Debbie took Janie into the staff conference room and sat the girl down.

"I'm going to wait with you here, honey.   The doctors will tell us as soon as they know something."

Janie nestled her head on Debbie's shoulder.

"Everything's going to be fine, Janie.   Just you wait and see."

After almost an hour, a man in a white coat approached. Debbie stood up and Janie quickly got to her feet.

"Well, what is it, Mark?" Debbie asked.   "A stroke?"

"No.   She's had a massive brain hemorrhage.   I'm afraid she didn't make it."

Janie let out a sob, and Debbie cradled the girl's head against her chest.   Then, two men in white uniforms came into the room. They put Lois's body on a stretcher.

"Where are they taking her?" Janie asked.

"Pathology."

"Why?"

"Her hemorrhage was due to a tumor in her brain which ruptured an artery. Dr. Becker is studying all patients with brain abnormalities, looking for clues to the cancer epidemic. He'll perform an autopsy prior to burial."

Janie stared at the figure on the stretcher. "She was such a nice lady," she said. "She took me in for no reason." She began to sob again.

Debbie put her arm around Janie's shoulders. "Come on, honey. There's nothing else we can do for her here. You'll stay with me. I'm going to take you home, then I'm needed back here. Don't worry, I'll be home tonight."

She led the girl to the parking lot.

"Debbie, I need to go to Lois's apartment to get my things."

"Of course, dear, we'll stop there on the way."

50

"Damn, the film's overexposed again!"

Ellen rushed to the kitchen, where Joe was holding the ruined negative up to the window. It was completely black, obscuring the marks that would have indicated whether the radioactive probe had bound to the DNA. She looked with alarm from Joe to Bob. They had been yelling at each other all day.

Bob kicked the door post. "We've wasted three fucking days because of overexposed film!"

"Well," Joe replied evenly, "we keep trying until we get it right. That's science."

Bob turned on Joe. "You're living in another world, you know that?" he shouted. "It's not just science. Time's running out. Has Ellen told you the news today?"

Joe turned to Ellen. "What news?"

She hesitated, not wanting to make things worse. "Why don't you guys take a break for a couple of hours. You've been working non-stop for days. Let's take a walk in the woods."

"A walk in the woods?" Joe groaned. "This hardly seems like the time. What's the news?"

Ellen blew a deep breath. "A couple more nuclear plants were blown up this morning, one in New York, the other on the California coast. The atmosphere is contaminated for hundreds of miles. The army is being deployed to help maintain order in the cities. Physicians and nurses have been ordered to report their whereabouts to local officials."

Joe chewed his lip. "It sounds like we're heading for martial law. Oh man, even if we get the vaccine made, how are we possibly going to deliver it to the entire country under these circumstances? And we don't know whether it will do any good for people who already have cancer."

"I told you yesterday," Bob replied, working hard to keep his voice level, "one thing at a time. Right now, we focus on making the vaccine. We'll deal with delivering it later. And I'm tired of your pessimism. If you want to give up, fine. I'll see you back in Chicago."

"You're right," Joe grumbled. "Sorry to sound so downbeat. Now let's think this through again. There's got to be some external source of radioactivity, either in the freezer, where we develop the film, or in the kitchen somewhere."

"Maybe the atmosphere's become radioactive from the nuclear plants," Ellen suggested.

Joe shook his head. "Atmospheric radiation high enough to cause this kind of background? We'd all three be dead. I'm going to get the Geiger counter and run another survey."

He went into the bedroom and returned with a rod-shaped sensor, attached by a black cord to a hand-held box. Beginning with the freezer, he started to survey the kitchen.

"I've done that a dozen times," Bob muttered. He motioned Ellen out of the kitchen. "Leave him alone in there if he wants to screw around wasting his time."

"I just don't get it," Joe said when he joined them in the living room. "It's got to be coming from somewhere."

As he approached them, the noise from the Geiger counter increased suddenly in intensity.

"What the--?" He moved the rod back and forth, trying to find the source of whatever the counter was sensing. The noise became a staccato when he pointed the rod directly at Ellen. She took two steps back as Joe approached her.

"Why is it doing that?" she asked, her voice trembling.

"Relax, dear," Joe said cautiously. "Hold still for a moment."

It took all her will power to remain motionless as Joe scanned her, beginning with her shoes and working upwards. When he reached her neck, the noise from the counter sounded like a hundred submachine guns firing at once.

"It's that necklace," Joe said. "It's hot as a devil's ass."

Ellen tore the necklace from her neck and flung it to the floor. She stepped away, her eyes wide.

"What the hell is it?" Joe muttered. "Bob, get me a Plexiglas shield."

Bob brought one from the bedroom. Joe placed it over the necklace and the Geiger counter quieted. He knelt down to get a closer look.

"Where did you get this, Ellen?"

Ellen tried to control her trembling. "From David Blaire. . ."

"How long ago?"

"A few weeks."

"You've been wearing it since then?"

Her voice broke. "He was dying of melanoma. He told me not to take it off until he recovered. How was I to know that. . . that . . ."

Joe reached over and put his arm around her. She melted into him, sobbing uncontrollably against his chest.

"It's okay, dear. It's not as bad as you think."

She pulled away from him. "I'm going to be the first of us to get cancer," she said, her voice controlled.

"I don't think the exposure you had places you at much greater risk than the rest of us," Joe reassured her. "The stone is not that radioactive."

"It sounded pretty radioactive to me."

"Ellen," Bob said, "the gamma counter is very sensitive. Relative to the rest of the environment, that necklace is giving off a lot of radioactivity. But it would probably take months of exposure to do you harm."

"He's right," Joe agreed. "Besides, in a few days it won't matter. We'll give you the first vaccination. Now let's get rid of this thing."

He picked up the necklace and dropped it into the Plexiglas box. I'm going to take this outside and bury it. Bob, load another film into the cartridge."

He put on his jacket, grabbed a shovel from the closet, and stepped out the back door.

51

"There's no place to park here," Janie said as Debbie pulled up in front of Lois's apartment. "I'll run up and get my things. I'll only be five minutes."

She got out of the car and went into the building. It was strange, only two weeks and this place already seemed so familiar to her. Almost like home. Well, not anymore. Home was wherever someone was willing to give her a bed for a few nights.

She reached Lois's apartment and put the key in the lock. The door was unbolted. She must have forgotten to lock it in the panic of a few hours before. She stepped inside, turned into the living room, and stopped dead in her tracks. A man was sitting on the couch, dressed in a brown coat, with a white mark on his left cheek and a patch over his right eye.

He smiled at her. "Hello, Janie."

Janie took a step back. "Who are you?"

"Don't you recognize me?"

"No. I've never seen you before in my life. What are you doing in this apartment?"

"I was waiting for you."

Janie retreated until her back was against the wall. Her voice trembled. "Waiting for me? What do you want? Who are you?"

"Sartan," he hissed at her like a snake as he rose from the sofa.

When Debbie finally left the car double parked and went up to Lois's apartment, the door was wide open. Janie's body lay in the middle of the floor in a pool of blood, her throat slashed. Debbie put her hands to her face and screamed and screamed and screamed . . .

52

Bob and Ellen leaned over Joe's shoulders as he transferred the negative into the developing solution. They were crowded into the kitchen pantry, the only light coming from a dim, red bulb.

"So?" asked Bob impatiently. "Do you see anything?"

"Give it a minute," Joe responded. He swirled the film around a few moments more, then pulled it out and held it over the pan, letting the liquid drip off the edge. "All right. Let's take a look."

They clamored out of the pantry. Joe stepped over to the window and placed the film up against the pane. "There it is!"

"Let me see that," Bob said impatiently. He took the film and held it up to the light. "Yes!" he exclaimed. "Right where it should be. We've got our vector!"

The two men grabbed each other in a bear hug.

"Congratulations!" Ellen exclaimed with delight.

Bob turned towards her, grinning. He grabbed her around the waist and squeezed, lifting her off the floor. They looked into each other's eyes, both of them beaming with happiness.

"Let's cut the restriction enzyme gene out of the gel right now," Joe said. "We'll anneal it with the viral DNA, run another gel tonight, and we should have the results tomorrow morning."

Bob lowered Ellen to the floor. "If all goes well, we'll have our first batch of vaccine in three days."

Joe turned to Ellen. "This will take us about three hours to set up. Then we'll have the whole evening free. There won't be anything else to do until the morning."

"Great, I'll prepare a celebration dinner."

"You read my mind," Joe replied, smiling. "Come on Bob. Let's get cracking."

As Bob followed Joe out of the kitchen, he brushed past Ellen, his arm grazing her breast.

"Excuse me," he muttered, avoiding her gaze.

Ellen touched her nipple as she watched Bob leave, feeling her desire for him like a wave of heat.

* * *

Ellen had covered the kitchen table with a cream, knit tablecloth she had found in one of the drawers. Each place setting had a wine glass and a salad bowl in which she had cut the cucumbers in the shape of virus capsids. There was a vase containing a few evergreen twigs in the center of the table. It was the best she could do under the circumstances. Still, there was an air of festivity in the cabin.

"A toast," said Joe, raising his wine glass. The other two followed suit. "To the rapid completion of the vaccine and its successful delivery." He took a sip and swirled it around in his mouth before swallowing. "Not bad. Ellen, how about a news update?"

"Do you really want to spoil the moment?"

"Just the headlines."

She put down her glass. "Okay, the headlines. The power grid is out across twelve western states. There are reports of people freezing to death in Colorado and Wyoming. And an aircraft carrier was commandeered and run aground while trying to ram the dock in the port of Baltimore. Oh, and someone drove a truck loaded with jet fuel into the passenger terminal at the Atlanta airport. Casualties are estimated in the thousands."

"My God!" Joe whispered.

"Eat your salads," Ellen ordered.

They finished their salads in silence. Ellen stood up and began collecting the bowls. "Now that the first vaccine is three days away, have you guys figured out how to deliver it?"

"We've got a game plan," Joe replied. "We figure we'll drive back to Chicago, contact the police, and get their help producing and distributing the vaccine in mass quantities."

"How do you know the police aren't transformed?" Ellen asked.

"We don't. But we have no alternative. We may have to play it by ear."

Ellen sat back down in her chair, still holding the empty bowls. "I think we should try to get to Washington."

"Washington?"

She nodded. "I've been thinking about it. This is going to require a national effort and only the federal government will have the infrastructure to do it properly."

"But who would we contact there?" Joe asked. "We know the FBI chief is transformed. His men almost nabbed me."

"Someone else, then," Ellen replied. "Maybe the military brass at the Pentagon."

Joe drummed his fingers on the table. "How would we make that kind of contact?"

"I don't know, but that's our only chance to get this vaccine delivered."

Bob, who had been listening quietly, said, "She's right, Joe. The local authorities won't be able to deal with this. Maybe we should drive straight to O'Hare airport and get a flight to D.C."

"Fine by me," said Joe. "Let's just make sure Delany isn't making the flight arrangements."

Ellen went into the kitchen and returned with the main course, a beef stew.

"That smells great," Joe said as she began to serve. "You're an incredible cook, has anyone ever told you that?"

Ellen laughed. "Never. You're too easy."

She sat down and they began to eat.

"There's something I've been wondering," Ellen said. "If all the junk DNA in our chromosomes belong to the cancer organism, how come it's got five times as much DNA as we do?"

"I've been wondering the same thing," Joe said, chewing on a piece of meat. "It's a hell of a lot more DNA than any organism should need. Bob?"

Bob shrugged. "Beats me. It's got to be serving some purpose. As long as it's responsive to gp-78, it doesn't matter."

"How sure are you that the vaccine's going to cut out the gp-78 gene?" Ellen asked.

"A hundred percent sure," Bob replied. "It works on fundamental biologic principles. I don't know for sure if it will shut down the rest of the cancer genes, but it *will* splice out gp-78. If we had time, we'd test it, out of the one chance in a million that something might go wrong. But we don't have time. We'll test the completed vaccine on one of us."

Ellen took a sip of her wine. "I guess that means me. You have so much faith in technology. It's like a religion to you."

"Sure I have faith in technology," Bob retorted. "It beats sleeping naked in a damp cave."

She couldn't help responding to the challenge, despite her desire to make the evening a pleasant one. "You know, technology isn't the solution to everything. There's a place for old-fashioned natural methods, too. What kind of society will we have when everything can be had with the push of a button? If you have your way, it won't be long before women don't get pregnant. They'll just have their babies in test tubes."

Bob put down his fork. "What's wrong with that?"

She looked at him, incredulous. "Are you serious? It would take away a woman's pleasure at feeling a life growing inside her womb."

"It would also take away the nausea, the constipation and the indigestion of pregnancy, not to mention the pain of childbirth. And it would allow the fetus to be monitored for defects."

"The pain of childbirth binds a mother to her infant," Ellen countered.

"My mother gave birth under sedation," Bob replied. "Yours probably did, too. My mother still loved her children. If you ask me, it would be more binding for a mother to watch her fetus develop in a bottle over nine months. She could actually see her baby growing in front of her eyes."

"Sounds kind of gruesome to me," Ellen replied with less than full conviction, as she became intrigued by the idea.

"I bet if you spent a week in any other century you'd reevaluate your love affair with the past," Bob continued. "Things weren't as pretty back then as they've been painted."

Ellen pushed her plate away. "I don't have illusions about the past," she said. "I just happen to think it's foolish to abandon everything we've learned over thousands of years. Just promise me you won't cry, Bob, when you wake up one day and all those wonderful, old, familiar things you love are gone."

His face turned white. She looked at him with alarm. What had she said?

Bob gazed at Ellen, but he kept seeing Diane. "Excuse me, I'm going out for a walk." He grabbed his coat and headed out the back door, leaving Joe and Ellen staring anxiously at each other.

It was cold out and the wind was gusting, but it felt good against his skin. He hurried, half-running, up the path that followed the brook behind the house. He reached into his coat pocket, pulled out his gloves, and slid his hands into them. The wind bit into his exposed neck and he tightened his coat collar. In a few minutes he reached the stream, which was now a frozen ribbon of ice, covered with snow. The moon was almost full. He stumbled over a branch, but caught himself and continued his quick pace. He climbed up onto a bluff and suddenly he was standing over an open valley, looking across at the outline of hills on the other side. The wind howled at him, bit at his skin, numbed his cheeks. Still, he didn't move off the ledge. The wind grew fiercer, the howling deafening him as it blew past his stinging ears. *Promise me you won't cry for me, Bobby*, Diane had pleaded as she rested her head on his chest the day she died. *I promise, sweetheart, I won't cry*, he had answered, drawing her frail body against his.

Suddenly he drew the icy air into his lungs and let out a long and agonized howl, the cry of a wounded animal. It pierced the clear, night air, reverberating across the valley and echoing off the opposite hills. His body shook like a leaf, unaccustomed to the uncontrolled rush of air in and out of his lungs. Then the wind became a whisper and the night grew quiet, but for the anguished sobs of a lonely man.

53

Lafferty entered a laboratory in a closely guarded section of the Pentagon and approached his chief medical officer, David Brown, who stood over a bench, dressed in a white coat.

"Anything yet, David?"

Brown shook his head. "We're not gonna recover any DNA from this body, after the heat it's been exposed to. The tissue's too cooked."

"How many attempts have you made?"

"This is the sixth. It's hopeless."

"Well, keep trying. We need a breakthrough."

"We need another volunteer, Ed. That's what we need."

"I'm working on it," Lafferty grumbled.

"I've been hearing that for weeks now."

Lafferty hesitated for a moment. "We might get a body from Pensacola."

"Yeah?" Brown replied eagerly.

"A navy flier with melanoma, who's been AWOL for the past month, died unexpectedly of a stroke about an hour ago."

"Fantastic! . . I mean, for us, not for the poor SOB."

"Don't get too excited. He had the stroke at ten thousand feet, after commandeering a Tomcat. Burned two acres of Florida Everglades when it crashed. Hodges gave orders to ship the body up here--if they find anything to ship."

54

Bob awoke to the aroma of fried bacon. He lay on the cot, feeling the chilly morning air which had seeped into the cabin during the night. Joe was still asleep in the adjacent bed, snoring loudly.

He got out of bed, dressed, and walked next door to the lab. After satisfying himself that the viral cultures were growing well, he went into the living room. The fire had been rekindled and the room was beginning to warm up. He threw on another log, scattering a few embers onto the floor which he swept into the hearth. He walked to the window. The sky was clear-blue, and the sunlight reflected brilliantly against the white snow.

"Nice day."

He turned to see Ellen standing at the doorway to the kitchen, her body silhouetted against the door frame.

"Beautiful," he answered, gazing at her lush curves.

There was an awkward moment of silence.

"You came back late last night," Ellen said.

"Sorry if I woke you."

"You didn't wake me. I was up. You know, sometimes I like to take a long walk alone, just to think. Solitude can refresh the mind."

"You do a lot of thinking, don't you?"

She frowned and lowered her eyes. "Sometimes too much."

"I don't think so. You think well. I didn't realize that about you at first, but you've got a good head on your shoulders."

She smiled. "Thanks. Ready for breakfast?"

"It smells wonderful."

"Why don't you wake up Joe."

He walked back into the bedroom where Joe was still asleep. Bob shook him. "Hey! Joseph, wake up. Ellen's got breakfast ready."

Joe joined them shortly, and Ellen served bacon with scrambled eggs, toast with jam, and coffee.

"Where do things stand with the vaccine?" Ellen asked as she spread jam on her toast.

"The virus is growing in the monkey cells as we speak," Bob answered.

"And you really think we'll have the first vaccine in three days?"

He nodded. "Now we just wait for enough virus."

"So I guess you two can relax."

"I don't know how relaxed we can be," Joe said, sipping from his coffee, "but we've really got nothing to do for the next forty-eight hours. In fact, why don't we go for a hike along the creek? It's a beautiful day."

"That sounds wonderful," Ellen chimed in enthusiastically.

"You two go," Bob said. "I'll keep an eye on things here."

"Come on, it'll do you good," Ellen insisted. "We've all been cooped up in here too long."

"Someone ought to keep an eye on the cultures," Bob insisted.

"Come on, Bob," Joe said. "Nothing's going to happen to the cultures. We'll only be gone a few hours."

Bob frowned. "I suppose a short walk would be okay," he said reluctantly.

Ellen cleared the table. They put on coats and boots and prepared to go out. As they stood by the back door, Joe said, "Let me just check on the cells before we leave."

He disappeared into the makeshift lab and pulled a flask out of the incubator. The media was a healthy, orange color which told him that the cells were receiving the proper amount of carbon dioxide. He smiled. They would be ready for harvesting in two days. Nothing could go wrong. It was all so straightforward.

His face turned suddenly grim. He glanced behind him. He could hear Bob and Ellen talking in the kitchen. He reached over to the carbon dioxide tank supplying the incubator and shut it off. He glanced behind him again as he replaced the flask and closed the incubator door. Then he returned to the kitchen.

"Everything looks fine," he said. Those viruses are reproducing happily."

They left the cabin, and headed through the clearing towards the forest. As they entered the woods, a gust of wind shook some snow off the trees above them.

"You know, it's colder than I thought," Joe said. "Mind if I run back and get my wool sweater?"

"Sure, we'll wait for you here," Ellen replied.

"I won't be but a minute," Joe called out as he headed back towards the cabin.

Joe stomped the snow off his feet on the back porch and swung open the door. He went to the closet adjacent to the kitchen, opened the fuse box and, after evaluating its contents for a moment, pulled out one of the fuses. He tried the light switch on the wall. It was dead. He smiled, snapped the wire, and replaced the fuse. Then he went back to the kitchen, opened the freezer door, and removed a small vial.

He hurried to the front door, then remembered his sweater. He returned to the bedroom and put it on, then left the cabin through the front entrance. He stooped down a few feet away from the parked minivan, glanced both ways, and buried the vial in the snow. He placed a stone over the spot and went around back to join the others.

"Everything okay?" Bob asked, as Joe approached them.

"Fine, my sweater was buried under a pile of clothes. Sorry to keep you waiting."

* * *

It was dusk when Ellen stepped onto the back porch, with Bob and Joe behind her. They had spent the day exploring the stream until they had reached a frozen lake a few miles away. There, they had eaten the sandwiches Ellen had brought along, and enjoyed the sunny winter afternoon, before heading back. They had been gone a lot longer than planned, but she was glad she had talked Bob into the excursion. He seemed to relax as the day wore on, although Joe seemed tense.

She opened the door, reached for the light switch, and flicked it up. Nothing happened.

"The light's out," she said.

Bob stepped in behind her and started removing his coat and boots. "Check the other lights," he told her.

She disappeared from the kitchen and returned a moment later. "The electricity's out in the whole house."

Bob looked at her with a panicked expression. She turned to Joe, who looked calm. "Let's not fear the worst," he said. "Let's check the cells."

Then she understood. The incubator! She followed behind the two men, who had already rushed into the bedroom.

"The power's out," she heard Bob say.

"It's cold in here," Joe said. "If the CO_2 was flowing, the cells might still be alive." He took a flask from the incubator and put it under the microscope.

"Damn. We don't have any electricity. The scope light's out, too. Let me see if I can get the juice back on."

He headed for the kitchen and opened the fuse box. Bob and Ellen followed him.

"One of these fuses must have blown," Joe said, pulling one out. "This one looks okay." He returned it to its place and examined two more before removing the sabotaged fuse. "This one's shot. We should have a spare in this box here." He found the right fuse and replaced it. The cabin lights went on. "Now let's see about those cells."

They hurried back into the bedroom. Joe picked up one of the flasks. The media in it was bright-red.

"It looks really alkalotic," he said as he turned on the microscope. He lay the flask under the lens and examined the contents.

"Well?" Bob shouted.

Joe didn't answer immediately. He scanned the flask for a full minute. Then he took his eyes away from the microscope. "Let me see another one."

Bob grabbed another flask from the incubator and shoved it into Joe's hand. Joe examined it under the microscope, then looked up solemnly. "They're all dead," he whispered.

"Let me see," Bob said, pushing Joe off the chair. He examined all of the flasks, one by one. Then he stood up, his face white. "Maybe the cell stock is still viable."

They all rushed into the kitchen. Bob opened the freezer door. Everything inside had melted. He grabbed a stock vial and held it up. It's contents were liquid.

"Fuck."

They stood around dejectedly. Finally, Bob broke the silence.

"Listen, it's not the end of the world. The virus should still be viable. All we need is some more cells. This will only set us back a couple of days."

"Where are we going to get more cells?" Ellen asked.

"One of us will have to drive back to the University," Bob said.

"No," Ellen replied, "it's too dangerous."

"There's no choice. I'll be back by morning."

"It'll have to be me," Joe said.

Bob turned towards Joe. "Why you?"

"You obviously can't go. Every transformed person in the country probably knows what you look like. And Ellen wouldn't know where to look. So that leaves me."

Bob hesitated. "I guess you're right. You'll have to be very careful."

"I'll leave right away," Joe said. "Don't worry. I'll be back in no time."

"I wonder why the fuse blew," Ellen muttered.

"We might have overloaded the system," Joe answered. "Or it could have just been bad timing. We blow fuses every few months here."

"Now you tell us?" Bob asked with annoyance.

"Listen," Ellen said. "There's no use second guessing things now. We know what we need to do. Joe, I'll make you a sandwich and a thermos of coffee for the road."

55

"I hear you found something."

"Yup," Brown responded. "Hot off the press."

He led Lafferty to a lab bench and held two X-ray films up to a viewing box.

"Frankly, I didn't think we'd recover any DNA from the pilot's body, but by God, we did. These are two protein analyses. The normal cells are on the right, and the malignant cells from the pilot are on the left."

Lafferty examined the films closely. "There's no overlap," he said.

"Exactly."

"How do you interpret these findings?"

"This data, together with the autopsy findings, leave only one conclusion possible, however incredible. That's why I called you down to see this immediately."

"What autopsy findings are you talking about?"

"Haven't you seen the brain, man?"

Lafferty shook his head.

"Jesus! Come with me."

He led Lafferty into the autopsy room. Drainage holes were scattered about The concrete floor to collect the run-off from the autopsy tables. A single body lay on a narrow table, draped by a white sheet. Brown drew the sheet down to reveal a burnt carcass. The eye sockets seemed to stare at Lafferty. Lafferty glanced away. He's dead, he's not really looking at you, he thought.

"Over here."

Lafferty went around to the head of the body.

"The skull's fractured," Brown said, "but the cranial contents were preserved." He removed a suture holding the top of the skull in place.

"Brace yourself," he said as he lifted the bone off the back of the head.

Lafferty's face went white. He looked at Brown, then back at the open cranial cavity. "This isn't possible," he whispered.

"I wish."

Lafferty backed away from the body.

"You're to keep this under the strictest secrecy," he said in a hushed voice as he fought back a wave of nausea. He rushed out of the room, leaving Brown holding the top of the man's skull in his hands.

56

After Joe departed, Bob and Ellen sat on the sofa, drinking coffee and watching the fire.

"I'm glad you didn't go straight to bed," Ellen said. "I didn't want to be alone."

"I don't think I could sleep just now," Bob replied.

He knew he wouldn't sleep all night. He couldn't get the idea out of his head that there had been too many coincidences. First, Ellen's necklace, which had delayed their efforts and exposed them all to ionizing radiation. Now, a fuse had blown, just as they were approaching the final stage in preparation of the vaccine. He was convinced that Ellen was innocent. Her response to the discovery of the radiation in the necklace was too convincing to have been faked. Nobody was that good an actor. Which left Joe.

"Do you think Joe's going to be all right?" Ellen asked.

"He'll be okay," Bob said. "He can handle himself."

But how could Joe be the saboteur? Joe had had numerous opportunities to simply kill him, if he really wanted him out of the way. And besides, Joe had played an essential role in getting this far with the vaccine construction. Bob had misgivings about letting Joe go, and he wasn't comforted by the fact that he had taken the van, leaving him and Ellen stranded hundreds of miles from civilization. But there really had been no alternative.

"I never should have left the cabin today," Bob muttered.

Ellen looked at him. "It wasn't your fault, Bob. I won't let you blame yourself for this."

He didn't answer her.

"Do you really think we'll get through this?" she asked.

"Yes," he replied, with more optimism than he felt.

"I wish I had your confidence."

They stared at the fire in silence. The flickering flames cast long, dancing shadows across the room. Ellen spoke again.

"It's odd. Here we are in such a peaceful setting, sitting by a warm fire. It's hard to believe that a war for the future of humanity is being waged around us."

"You look at everything from such a historical perspective," he replied.

"History is the crux of all human endeavors," Ellen responded, still staring into the fire.   "It anchors us in the universe."

"You're searching for yourself," Bob said.   "You want to belong somewhere.   You won't find your place by searching the past."

They fell silent, eyes transfixed on the flames in front of them.   Ellen felt the heat from the fire on her feet and she curled them up onto the sofa.   Bob looked over at her.   She was staring at the fire, the flickering flames dancing in her eyes, her skin glowing with its warmth.   Her silky, brown hair lay across her rosy cheeks.   She had a dreamy expression on her face and there was a faint smile on her lips.   She had never looked so beautiful.

She must have felt his gaze, for she turned and looked at him.   She smiled, her eyes locked on his.   They were bright and alive, soft eyes that spoke the truth.   He wanted to reach out and take her into his arms.

"I never should have let you talk me into taking that walk," he muttered.

Her eyes narrowed.   "Are you going to blame me for this?"

"I'm not blaming anybody.   I'm just saying this was not the time to go out frolicking in the snow."

An angry expression flashed across her face.   "Jesus Christ, let it go!   It happened.   None of us could have foreseen it.   Now shut up!"

"You're telling me to shut up?"

"Yes!   Shut up right now!"   She grabbed him by the shirt collar and kissed him hard on the lips.   "That's for the kiss you gave me in your lab.   I only wish I could have returned it earlier."

He stared at her, stunned, then seized her by the arms and drew her to him.   She struggled for a moment, then her lips parted and she sank them into his.   All the emotions that had lain under the surface for weeks exploded in an irresistible burst of passion.   Ellen felt the same helplessness she had experienced the first time he had kissed her.   She wrapped her arms around his chest, trembling with desire. Bob grabbed her up in his arms and laid her down on the rug in front of the fire, his hard body on top of hers. He was kissing her everywhere and she kissed him back with abandon.

He reached down between her breasts and unbuttoned her blouse. Then he ran his tongue along the side of her neck and under her jaw while she fumbled at his shirt buttons. She couldn't wait and she tore open his shirt and palmed his naked chest while he unfastened her bra clasp. He closed his mouth around her nipple. A shudder went through her body.

He stroked her face and neck. Her skin was so soft, so smooth, so--. His hand froze. A moment later, Ellen's body froze, too.

"Bob, what is it?"

He didn't respond.

"What's wrong?" she pleaded.

He hesitated, unsure what to say, unsure if his fingers had even felt what he thought they had. He moved them back towards the spot. Ellen grasped the implication and her hand flew to her neck, pushing his away. She bolted upright, her eyes wide with terror.

"Bob, there's a lump here on my neck! I have it don't I?" Her voice rose in pitch, and Bob saw a crazed look in her eyes.

"Ellen, relax!" he shouted, grabbing her shoulders. "Let me take a closer look. It may be nothing."

He felt her neck again. The mass was barely palpable, but it was there. He could see it, slightly raised above the line of her skin. His fingers explored it. It was hard and slightly matted in texture. He tried to move it but it was firmly attached to the surrounding tissues.

"Tell me what it is, Bob," she whispered.

"Does it hurt?"

"No."

He felt the rest of her neck and found three more lumps on the upper border of her clavicle. There was no doubt. He looked at her solemnly.

"I'm scared," she whispered.

"Joe will be back soon. We'll have the vaccine ready long before you have to worry about anything."

"Joe's not coming back."

Did she share his suspicions? "Why shouldn't he come back?"

"Maybe they've killed him, maybe he couldn't find any cells. Maybe he has cancer, too."

"Ellen, Joe is a very resourceful person. He'll be okay, and so will you in a few days."

She straightened up. Her cheeks were wet, but her eyes were defiant.

"Bob, you don't know how long it'll take before I'm transformed."

"Cancer doesn't spread that fast, Ellen. You have at least a few weeks."

"You don't know that," she insisted.

He looked at her calmly. "Ellen, I'm going to make sure nothing happens to you."

"But what if I do something to you?" She gazed at him with a hard expression. "Bob, if I'm transformed, I'll kill you. I won't be able to help myself. I can't take a chance of that happening."

"It's not going to happen."

"Stop saying that. It might happen. From this moment on you can't trust me."

"Ellen--"

"Let me finish. Now, listen to me. None of us knows how long it takes to be transformed. I can't leave here, because I could give away your location. So you either have to kill me or tie me down until the vaccine is ready."

"Don't be ridiculous."

"Bob, either you do it or I'm going to slit my wrists. I told you before that I want to die before I become a traitor to the human race.   And you promised me you wouldn't let that happen."

"I won't."

"Then start thinking rationally, and do what must be done." She put her hand to his cheek. "Please, Bob, I'm begging you. Do it for me. It'll just be until Joe gets back. You've got to do it to save all of our lives."

He knew she was right. He nodded and dropped his eyes. She smiled and kissed him briefly on the lips, then disappeared into the kitchen. She returned, her clothes back on, carrying a bundle of rope.

"Here."

The rope dangled from his hand. "Ellen. . ."

"You have to."

He began to tie her hands behind her back.

"Tighter."

He bound her tighter. When he was done, he looked at her and said, "Ellen what can I do for you?   You look so uncomfortable."

"Just sit here with me."

"I'm not going to leave you alone for a minute." He kissed her on the forehead, and he saw a tear roll down her cheek. She rested her head on his chest and he held her as best he could in her bound position.

"It's all right, it's all right. Everything's going to be all right," he said, hoping to convince her--and himself--that it was true.

57

Lafferty squeezed his stomach. "You got an antacid?"

Hodges shook his head. Lafferty turned to Stark, who shrugged. "Sorry."

Lafferty winced. "Okay. What I've just shown you is the biochemical analysis from the pilot's body."

"And?" Hodges said. "What does it all mean?"

"It means we have the answer to the epidemic, and to the cause of the mental changes occurring in affected individuals."

They both leaned forward. "Let's hear it," Hodges almost shouted.

"We've gone over the data half a dozen times," Lafferty began. "There's only one way to interpret it. All those thousands of new genes I just showed you are the genetic code of another species of life, and Gp78 is the most abundantly-expressed gene of them all. Somehow, don't ask me how it happened, the genes for another organism ended up in our chromosomes. I suspect those genes have been there for millions of years, lying dormant. They're activated by high levels of carcinogenic agents." He paused. "Do you get what I'm saying?"

Stark looked at him carefully. "If I understand you correctly, you're suggesting that certain chemicals can turn on these dormant genes and that they grow into an organism which we have known as cancer."

"Exactly. Only they're no longer just a mass of undifferentiated cells. They're differentiating into complex organisms."

"And what about the mental changes?"

Lafferty opened his briefcase and pulled out a set of glossy prints. "This is what we found in the guy's skull."

They stared at the photos in silence.

"What the hell is it?" Hodges finally muttered.

"You're looking at the body--or the brain, I don't know which--of this other organism."

"It fills the entire skull," Hodges whispered. "Where's the human brain?"

"Gone," Lafferty replied. "At least the frontal lobes are gone. The brain stem is still intact." He showed them another photo with the organism's tendrils wrapped around the brainstem.

"Holy shit," Hodges muttered. "How do we kill that thing? We've started chemotherapy for the entire armed services. Is that going to work?"

"It'll buy us some time, perhaps a few weeks," Lafferty replied. "But eventually the treatments will be lethal to our own bodies. Besides, chemo kills dividing cells. I don't know if it will work on people in whom these creatures have already differentiated."

"Has your team come up with anything else?" Hodges asked.

Lafferty nodded excitedly. "You said Newman was still alive."

"*May* be alive," Stark interrupted.

Lafferty jabbed at the photo. "Now I know why they tried to kill him."

"The gene vaccine," Stark said.

Lafferty nodded. "Yes. A gene deletion vector could cut out the cancer genes. That's the ultimate weapon against this thing. We've got to find Newman."

"He's disappeared without a trace," Stark said."

"What about his notes? We might be able to reconstruct the vaccine from them."

Stark shook his head. "They're not in his lab, or his home."

"Shit!" Lafferty muttered. Without the gene vaccine, the situation was hopeless. If it were he, what would he do with a discovery like that? He looked up, suddenly.

"Colleagues, then," he shouted. "We must find out who his colleagues were. Newman might have told them how to construct the vector."

Stark shook his head again. "His closest colleague was his division chief, Joe Malcolm. He's also disappeared."

Hodges stood up. "Well, keep looking for them. In the meantime, we'll just have to make do without them." He grabbed the photograph and shook it at Lafferty. "Now, how do we know who's harboring one of these creatures in their skulls?"

"The simplest would be a CAT scan," Lafferty replied.

Hodges shook his head. "No one of those things is going to submit to a CAT scan. There's got to be another way."

Lafferty thought for a moment. "Yes. A blood test could serve as a screening. A high level GP-78 would indicate the presence of one of these creatures."

Hodges nodded, already considering the logistics. "I like that better. We'll screen the entire military, and detain any affected people until we have a way to treat this. Everyone else will continue receiving chemotherapy."

He glanced from one man to the other. "The military will be an easier operation. The President, the government and the civilian population present a much more difficult dilemma."

"Anyone could have one of these things in their heads, including the President," said Lafferty.

Hodges nodded. "Understood. The first order of business is to clean up the army, or at least enough of the army so that we have a reliable force and have neutralized any armed resistance. Then we tackle the government, starting from the top and working our way down the levels of authority. Then we can direct ourselves to the civilian population."

"Are you suggesting we keep the government in the dark for now?" Stark asked.

"We have no choice."

"And how do we clean up the army?"

Hodges leaned forward, his eyes glinting. "It'll have to be done in complete secrecy, and simultaneously at all bases. If any of these creatures get wind of it, and manages to get control of some of our offensive weapons, we'll have a civil war on our hands. God help us if they get a hold of some nukes."

He walked to the door. The sound of the deadbolt, banging into place, reverberated through the room. Hodges spun around and faced the two men.

"We start testing right here, right now. The three of us. Any objections?"

Lafferty's mouth dropped. He shook his head slowly and Stark did the same.

"Fine. What do you need?" Hodges demanded, glaring at Lafferty.

"Uh. . . I guess three syringes, some needles and some red-top test tubes. . . That's to draw the blood. Then the chemistry lab will need to run the samples."

Hodges picked up the phone. "I want a blood drawing tray and some red-top tubes delivered to my office, immediately."

A few moments later there was a knock on the door. Without taking his eyes off the other two, Hodges unlocked the door, grabbed the tray and the box of test tubes, and slammed the bolt shut again. He handed the tray to Lafferty.

"Okay, Doc. Do your thing."

Lafferty struggled to control his shaking hands as he inserted a needle on the end of a plastic syringe. Hodges rolled up his sleeve and Lafferty tightened the tourniquet around his thick arm. The veins bulged out like water pipes. He drew the blood, then placed the syringe on the table.

Hodges, pressing a bandage to his arm, turned to Stark. "Label the first tube "A" and transfer the blood into it."

Stark nodded, took a felt pen and removed one of the test tubes from the box. He picked up the blood-filled syringe and pushed the needle through the red rubber stopper. A stream of blood shot into the tube. When it was full, Stark yanked the needle out. "Looks like you drew extra," he said, placing the syringe, still containing a good bit of Hodges blood, on the table.

Hodges took the tube of blood from Stark and closed his fist around it. "Okay, now it's his turn," he said, pointing to Stark.

Lafferty repeated the procedure on Stark. Hodges took the syringe, labeled a second tube "B", and injected Stark's blood into it. He lay the syringe down beside the first one.

Lafferty put a third needle on a syringe. Then he hesitated. "I'm not sure I can draw my own."

Hodges grabbed the tourniquet. "Here, hold these," he said, handing Stark the two blood-filled tubes. "It's been twenty years since I took that medic course, but I'll be damned if I can't hit one of your veins."

He turned his back on Stark, tightened the tourniquet around Lafferty's arm, and uncapped the syringe.

Lafferty's face grew pale. "Twenty years? . . ." he muttered as Hodges's burly fingers ran down his forearm. "I better sit down."

Hodges hit the vein on the first jab and Lafferty watched as his bright red blood filled the syringe. Hodges removed the needle and filled another tube, which he labeled "C". Then he grabbed the phone. "Send a tech from the lab up here, pronto."

When the tech appeared, Hodges unbolted the door and handed him the tubes. "I want these tested for GP-78. I think Stat is the word you use, isn't it?"

"Yes, sir," the man replied.

"Report the results to me personally."

"Yes, sir. It'll take about an hour, sir."

"Make it forty minutes." He rebolted the door and sat down behind his desk. He pulled a pistol from the drawer, cocked it deliberately, and lay it on the desk, within easy reach. Then he reached back into the drawer, removed a deck of playing cards, and began to shuffle them.

"We've got forty minutes, gentlemen. Anyone for a game of poker?"

58

It snowed almost constantly for four days after Joe left the cabin. Bob and Ellen watched the snow pile up in mounds against the window sills. Ellen became increasingly panicky and Bob found himself unable to relax. It was not just Joe and the vaccine. Something else was bothering him, an unfocused feeling of dread.

On the afternoon of the fourth day, he developed a splitting headache and went into the kitchen to find some aspirin. Suddenly, he heard a scream. He rushed out and found Ellen lying on the floor in front of the couch, her hands and feet still bound, a crazed look in her eyes. He rushed to her side.

"I'm killing him!" she screamed.

Bob knelt down beside her and grabbed her shoulders. "Ellen, snap out of it!"

She looked right through him, her eyes wide with terror. He took her in his arms and lifted her off the floor. Her body was rigid as a board. He laid her on the couch and slapped her across the face.

"Ellen!"

The terror faded from her eyes and her body relaxed.

"Oh Bob, I just had the most terrible vision!"

"What vision?"

"I had a kitchen knife in my hands and I was stabbing you with it. God, I was killing you!" She began to sob.

Bob shook her. "Ellen, you've got to fight this. You've got to hold on! Joe will be back soon."

The terror in her eyes was replaced by a gaze of defiance. "I want you to kill me *now*. They can't transform a dead body."

"Don't be ridiculous,"

"Kill me!" she insisted. "That way I can't harm you."

"You're not going to harm me," Bob replied.

Ellen began to tremble again. "Oh God, I can feel it! My head! It's in my head!" She shrieked. "Help me, Bob! Help me!"

He took her in his arms and held her tightly. "I'm here," he whispered. "Look at me."

She fixed her eyes on his. "I am Ellen Rhodes. I am Ellen Rhodes! I . . . am . . . Ellen . . . Rhodes . . . NO! GET OUT!"

She struggled violently against her bonds, tearing the flesh of her wrists and ankles. Bob held onto her as she writhed against him. "Hold on!" he cried. "Hold on!"

Suddenly, her body went limp. Bob relaxed his hold. Her face was wet with perspiration and her eyes were shut. He checked her pulse. It was rapid, but steady. She had exhausted herself. He covered her with a blanket and watched her for a while, but she did not wake up. He began pacing the floor, the tension inside him becoming unbearable. He glanced back at Ellen. Something had to be done. Where the hell was Joe?

59

Five thousand top-ranking military officers filed into the auditorium of the D.C. convention center. Hodges stood up and went to the podium. He cleared his throat and the room became hushed.

His deep voice echoed through the large chambers. "I've ordered you here today because of the gravest crisis to our country, and to civilization, that humanity has ever faced!"

He gave a signal and an elite group of heavily-armed, carefully-screened men slipped into the room and quietly sealed off all exits. Then the huge screen in the front of the room filled with the image of the contents of the navy pilot's skull.

"One out of four of you has one of these in your skulls!" Hodges bellowed. "A simple blood test will tell. No one is leaving this room until he is found to be free of this. Anyone trying to escape will be shot on the spot!"

The room erupted, as dozens of men scrambled for the exits. Shots were fired from all directions. Eventually, Hodges's men got the situation under control, but not until scores of bloody bodies lay on the ground. Hodges grabbed the microphone again.

"Everyone is to stand at attention!"

After some scuffles, and some more shooting, the crowd obeyed. "Everyone remove their dog tags!" Hodges barked. "A medic is going to pass in front of you and draw a sample of blood. You will cooperate with him! If you see anyone refusing to cooperate, you are to help in apprehending him! You're all going to stay where you are until we have the results!"

When the day was out, twelve hundred and seventeen dead bodies were removed from the premises. Another six hundred and forty eight, with high levels of GP 78, were taken away for further evaluation. The remaining officers were sent out, each with an armed brigade, with orders to repeat the exercise in their own bases at seven a.m. Eastern Standard Time.

60

Bob awoke to find Ellen's head on his shoulder. Her slow, regular breathing told him she was asleep. He carefully lifted her head and rested it on the couch. She grunted, but did not awaken. The lump on her neck was now a clearly-visible bulge. He stood up and stretched, trying to get the cramps out of his muscles.

He went into the kitchen and began to prepare breakfast, lobbing a piece of butter onto the pan and watched it sizzle and spatter. What to do? He had the virus. He only needed the monkey cells in which to grow them. It had been almost five days, plenty of time to get to Chicago and back half a dozen times. He had to assume that Joe had either betrayed them or been caught. Either way, it was time to act. He couldn't sit around here any longer doing nothing, waiting for the world to come to an end.

He cracked some eggs and stirred them into the pan. Ellen's tumor was obviously growing very rapidly. At this rate, assuming she already had metastases in her brain, she would lose her mind very soon. That left him with a terrible dilemma. If he tried to set off on foot for the main road, he would have to leave her behind. If he left her alone, she would die of hunger. He knew he couldn't leave her. He had to give Joe more time, at least another day or two. But this doing nothing was driving him crazy.

He dumped the scrambled eggs onto two plates and returned to the living room. Ellen was awake and sitting up on the couch.

"How are you feeling?" he asked.

"A lot better," she responded, smiling. "I think what I needed was a good night's sleep."

He sat down beside her. "You really scared me last night."

She leaned forward and kissed him. "Thank you for taking such good care of me." She looked down at the plates in his hands. "That smells great. But how am I going to eat it?"

He held out a forkful of eggs. "I'll feed you."

Ellen smiled again. "Then yours will get cold. Untie me until I finish breakfast."

Bob hesitated. "You made me promise not to untie you, no matter what."

Ellen laughed. "You're right. I wouldn't want to make a liar out of you. Tell you what, how about just my right hand, so I can lift the fork?"

"That sounds reasonable," Bob replied. He put the plates down on the coffee table and reached behind her back. Then, in a sudden move, his hand shot up to her neck. She tried to speak, but his grip on her throat prevented any sound from escaping.

Fighting a growing nausea, Bob brought his face to within an inch of hers and whispered, "Where's Ellen Rhodes?"

He released his grip slightly, just enough for the air to flow. "Bob, what are you doing?" she rasped. "Have you gone mad?"

"Don't try that crap on me," Bob whispered. "Ellen would never let me untie her. Now you tell me, is her consciousness still in her body?"

Ellen stared at Bob for a moment, then a fiendish grin spread across her lips. "It's too late, Doctor Newman," she hissed. "You've lost the struggle. This is humanity's fate."

"That's better," Bob replied. He let go of her and stepped back. "Now, I want some answers. How do you know my name?"

"I have all of the memories stored in the brain cells of the person you knew as Ellen Rhodes. Her genes have been shut down while mine have become dominant, as you have correctly surmised. Ellen, as you knew her, no longer exists."

"Can her genes be reactivated?"

"She's gone, Doctor Newman."

He clenched his fists, fighting the urge to strangle the figure in front of him. But Ellen's face stared at him from under the hideous smile.

"What is it you want?" he asked Ellen's form.

"Only to allow the natural course of events to unfold. Our turn has come to rule this planet."

"Who are you? How did your genes get into our cells?"

She snorted. "It's your genes that are in *our* cells."

"Who, in the government, is transformed?"

Ellen's face went blank for a moment. Suddenly, the skin on her forehead began to move. Flesh-colored bumps appeared. Bob fell back in horror as dozens of worm-like tendrils wriggled out towards him.

"I don't have those memories," she said. "I haven't been updated."

Bob stared in revulsion at the tendrils writhing over her face. "What. . .what are those things?" he gasped.

"It's how we communicate new memories," she replied. "They join the DNA memory."

"DNA memory?"

She smiled maliciously at him. "You'll have the answers to all your questions soon enough, Doctor Newman."

He forced himself to approach her once again, fighting the sense of dread that grew almost unbearable as he brought his face in front of hers. "I want the answers NOW," he whispered. "I'll kill you if you don't answer me."

"Patience. Just look at your arm," she hissed. "Your other arm."

Bob looked down at his left forearm. There was a lump on it. He felt it with the fingers of his right hand. It was firm and fixed.

"You see," she said. "Your fate is sealed. Your discovery of the gene vaccine was a fluke, not meant to occur in twentieth century human science. It's futile to resist the inevitable."

"No," he whispered through clenched teeth. He went into the kitchen, found the sharpest knife in the cabinet, and sterilized it over a flame on the stove.

"Doctor," Ellen called from the living room. "I can see what you're trying to do. It's useless. Your tumor has already metastasized to your brain. We mean you no personal harm. It's merely the natural course of things, a question of survival of the fittest."

He gritted his teeth and cut into his skin, fighting the pain and the sudden dizziness. When he had removed the mass, he stitched his flesh back together with his right hand, using a needle and thread from the sewing kit, and bandaged his forearm. Then he threw on his coat and stumbled out into the snow.

61

Hodges dialed Stark's private number on a secure line. "The President's had a massive stroke," he said in a staccato. "He's at Bethesda Naval Hospital. He's not going to make it."

"Christ!" Stark muttered. "He couldn't have picked a worse time. Where's the Vice-President?"

"He's in conference with the defense secretary and the Speaker of the House."

"Can you secure the White House?"

"A force is en route as we speak. I'll meet you there in twenty minutes."

* * *

Hodges and Stark sat huddled in the Oval Office with a third, bespectacled man with thinning hair and a narrow face.

"That's how things stand at the moment, Mr. Vice President," Hodges said. I apologize for the manner in which we forced ourselves on you and your staff, but I hope you understand, under the circumstances."

"I understand completely," Jason Stuart replied. "I thank you and the country thanks you."

Hodges scanned Stuart's face. The vice president was young and inexperienced, placed on the ticket to carry the Southern states. Now, he suddenly found himself the leader of a country in deep crisis. Hodges searched for a sign that the man was up to the task ahead. He saw nothing to reassure himself.

"There will be armed forces around you at all times from now on. This situation is beyond anything the country has ever had to deal with. It'll require extraordinary actions. You must take broad powers. Grave invasions of civil liberties will be necessary. Freedom from arbitrary search and seizure must be suspended, because anyone might be the enemy."

The Vice-President looked at Hodges intently. "I understand," he said.

Hodges nodded with satisfaction. Stuart would do, as long as he let Hodges call the shots. "We urge you to declare a state of emergency at once and send out the army to restore order and enforce mandatory public screening and chemotherapy," Hodges continued. "In the meantime, we recommend you keep the President's condition secret, or the country might fall into anarchy."

The Vice-President looked at each of them separately. Then he spoke in an authoritative voice that completely surprised Hodges.

"I accept all your recommendations, except one. I'll inform the public of the President's condition on national TV tonight. They must know that the government is still functioning and that I'm carrying out my constitutional duties. I want you to draw up a plan to reestablish control in the Congress. There's no constitutional provision for martial law in this country, and I want legitimate authority restored as soon as possible. In the meantime, the true nature of the threat must be kept secret from all but a select few, so as not to tip off the enemy."

Hodges felt a surge of blood course through his veins. "Yes, sir. You'll have the plan in the next few hours. One last thing, sir. Will you submit to a blood test and a CAT scan?"

The Vice-President rolled up his sleeve. "Who wants to do the honors?"

62

It was dark along the riverside and so cold that even the bums had sought shelter elsewhere. Delany lit his pipe, took a long drag, and exhaled slowly. The pale-blue smoke formed a halo around his head.

"Why do you insist on smoking that thing?" his companion hissed.

Delany took another drag from the pipe. "I find it soothing. The human enjoyed it immensely."

"You worry me with your predilection for human frivolities."

Delany sighed and extinguished the pipe. "What's the condition of the President?"

His companion grunted. "Unfortunately, severe hemorrhage has been an annoyingly common occurrence during the final stages of transformation."

"Is there hope?"

The shorter man shook his head. "He died two hours ago."

"And the vice president?"

"He's begun taking chemo. And he's surrounded twenty four hours a day by an armed contingent. It'll be almost impossible to get to him. What's the situation on the Hill?"

"Eighty two members of Congress, myself included, have completed transformation. But the entire Congress is submitting to blood tests and prophylactic chemotherapy. Any day they're likely to discover us."

"Not as long as the payola keeps flowing," his companion rasped. "Double the bribe, triple it, whatever it takes to keep the lab tech satisfied."

He looked up into Delany's face. "Is it the moonlight, or are you unusually pale?"

Delany sighed. "It's the chemo. I'm constantly nauseous. My hair's begun falling out. And I have persistent vertigo."

"There's no choice. If we don't suffer from the symptoms, it would raise suspicion. Have you found a way to continue transformation during treatment with these chemotherapeutic agents?"

"It's never been tried. I'm certain they could find a way, but I doubt we could."

His companion flashed him an angry look. "You talk as if they're superior to us."

"Not superior," Delany responded, "but they don't think like we do. They have an astounding ability to improvise. Perhaps they're forced to develop such skills because they're born with no DNA memories. Each newborn must learn the world anew."

"It's obscene! How do they know from whom to follow orders?"

"They willingly follow those they have chosen to lead them, as opposed to our genetic hierarchy of command."

"I find it perverse."

"You are underestimating these people's resourcefulness," Delany replied. "Only a quarter of the population has undergone transformation. Now that mandatory chemotherapy has been initiated we're being prevented from increasing our numbers, and they've swept us out of their military."

His companion spat. "We'll disrupt the public treatment centers. And they may think they have complete control of their military, but we have a few surprises.

"All right then," Delany replied. "I admit I was against open confrontation unless absolutely necessary, but now that they've discovered our presence in their chromosomes, there's no other way. We must transform as many humans as possible by preventing them from reaching the treatment centers. We must destroy their communication and transportation links and isolate their population centers. We must continue the infusion of carcinogens into the environment by sabotaging their industrial complexes."

His companion laughed eagerly. "You're advocating open warfare. Yes, I like that. I like it very much."

"Time is on our side," Delany continued. "They're killing themselves with the chemotherapy. There's only so much of it they can administer before the toxic side-effects become lethal. They must begin to decrease the dosage very soon, and that's when we can overwhelm them. We have only one weakness."

"And that is?"

"We must find Newman. Your concern in that regard was correct. If they obtain the gene deletion vector, they may prevail."

His companion shook his head contemptuously. "It's too late for that. We'll deliver our crushing blow very soon."

"I'd feel better if Newman was in our hands."

"We'll find him. He must surface eventually, if he's not already dead."

"We have thousands searching for him."

"Millions. He's one man against millions."

Delany had no reply.

63

Bob sat on the rocking chair, watching Ellen. He had returned to the cabin, realizing that there was nowhere to go. He might as well keep an eye on her until Joe returned. She stared at him from the sofa, her menacing eyes sending a chill into his bones. She had finally stopped jabbering at him when he refused to answer her.

The visions were coming every hour now, terrible, hideous visions. He felt the presence inside of him. He knew the cells in his brain were rapidly being transformed. He sensed the other presence in his mind, the other consciousness. He felt the awesome sense of awakening, of being alive again after so many eons.

To live! To breathe again! Yes, to feel the blood coursing through our veins!

Bob turned towards Ellen. She had not spoken for hours.

Where are we? Ah, here are the memories, millions of years of memories neatly stored. Yes, we remember. The humans, they have the bodies we want. We shall deceive them cheat them take them. SARTAN! . . . SARTAN! . . . SARTAN is coming for you!

Bob felt the terror, imprinted on his race for eons, the terror of Sartan. And he felt something else, the joyous miracle of escape, the salvation from destruction. The triumph over the evil.

Do not jail us. We want to live. We want to live! . . . We are tired, we will sleep now. But we will be back! We will awaken. We will crush the humans!

NO! I am Robert Newman. This is MY body! This is MY mind!

Who is this presence, this other? Yes, I see you. I know you. You fear us, yes. The war has begun, the war of liberation. But you know not Sartan's fate. You know not my mission. I must seek out and contact the flesh.

Wait. You are hiding something. GIVE me those memories!

Bob's eyes narrowed. His head snapped back suddenly as if from a blow. "NO!"

Gene vaccine? Yes, it is a weapon. A weapon against us. Joe, he has the weapon. Is he of Sartan? I will await his return. If he is Sartan, we will contact the flesh. If not, I will destroy him.

Bob rose from the sofa and stood in the center of the room, fists clenched. He felt an unbearable pain in his head, as if a vise was clamping down on his brain. Then he shrunk back in horror and shielded his face with his hands.

Sartan has returned! Flee! The terror is imprinted in your brain! Run! Run! Run or die!

Bob struck at the empty air in front of him. "I won't run, you fiend!" He fell to the floor, his entire body convulsing. He felt a horror so hideous that he cringed in utter terror. "You won't take me!" he whispered through clenched teeth.

You can stop resisting now. It will do you no good, anyway.

He tried to move, but he had no control over his limbs. "I will not fear. I will not fear. I laugh at you!" He forced a grotesque chuckle from his lips.

It is time, Doctor.

He felt a blow to his head more explosive than any physical force could deliver. Then memories began to flash through his mind. A fog enveloped his consciousness. He fought with all his might to keep his mind clear, but he was losing the struggle. He was helpless to do anything. Was this all there was to it? Was this how the human race was about to end, in a blurry fog? Would there be no struggle, no memorial, nothing to remember that a human species had existed for millennia on this planet?

He felt a sudden dizziness and then the room grew dark around him. What the hell had happened to Joe? Was he still

human, or had he, too, succumbed to the cancer genes? His last
thought as he lost consciousness was that the survival of humanity
depended now on one lone, fat man.

64

Alex Becker looked up from behind his desk when he heard
the knock at his office door. "Come in!"

The large figure of the police commissioner, a loose tie
around his heavy neck, filled the doorway.

"Hello, Doctor Becker," O'Malley said.

"Commissioner," Becker replied, surprised.   "I wasn't
expecting you. Do we have an appointment?"

"No, this is an unscheduled visit. Sorry to interrupt, but I'd
like to speak to you about an important matter."

Becker put down his pen. "Of course. Come in." He
motioned to a chair.

O'Malley closed the door behind him and sat down. He
leaned forward and said in a low voice, "Can I confide in you,
doctor?"

"Of course you can, commissioner. You have my word that
nothing you say will leave my office."

"I came to get your advice on a medical matter, seeing as
you're an authority. Actually, I'm a bit embarrassed coming to
you about this."

"Not at all," Becker responded, beaming. "I'm happy to give
advice."

"Very well.   I'm sure you've heard about the Surgeon
General's announcement yesterday regarding cancers spreading
to the brain."

Becker rolled his eyes. "Certainly I have. What utter nonsense."

"That was my feeling, too. Turns out the announcement was made to raise public awareness. What isn't public knowledge is that the FBI thinks that these cancers can cause some individuals to become violent."

Becker hesitated before responding. When he did his voice had increased in pitch. "Since when does the FBI involve itself in medical matters?"

"My sentiments exactly. But they think there's a connection between the cancer epidemic and the sabotage of the power plants."

Becker drummed the desk with his fingers and averted his gaze. "I thought those were accidents."

"Did you really?"

Becker fidgeted in his chair. "That's what I heard, but I'm no expert on sabotage. I have a hard time making a connection with the so-called epidemic of malignancies."

"So-called?"

"Yes. This whole thing's been vastly overblown."

O'Malley nodded. "I see. That's encouraging to hear, coming from a man of your stature. That's why I wanted to get your view on this matter. I've been ordered to round up some suspects, based on this crazy theory."

Becker pushed his glasses up the bridge of his nose and leaned towards O'Malley. "Commissioner, I consider myself an expert on the pathology of cancer. I can assure you, this whole epidemic is a hoax. Between you and me, it sounds like someone's trying to cover his ass for his own carelessness."

"I'm sure you're right," O'Malley agreed. "You know, I heard it was actually Joe Malcolm who first raised the idea of an epidemic. Now he seems to have disappeared and the FBI has a warrant out for him. You wouldn't have any knowledge of his whereabouts, would you?"

Becker shook his head violently. "None whatsoever, but if Malcolm is involved in a conspiracy, he deserves to be shot!"

"Have you heard anything at all about where he may be? There could be a reward for information leading to his apprehension."

"I know nothing," Becker replied.

"How about Robert Newman?"

Becker clenched his jaw. "Newman is dead."

"That's not what the FBI thinks. In fact, they're looking for both of them."

"Well I hope they find them and hang them!" Becker sputtered.

"You're not very fond of Malcolm or Newman, are you?"

"They're a couple of opportunists," Becker responded, slamming his fist on the desk. "They got to the top by stepping on everyone else! They can't possibly compete with my intellect, so they try to make me look incompetent!"

"Are you referring to the matter of the autopsy on Mrs. Stone?"

Becker's face turned red with rage. "I told you two weeks ago, the specimens were misplaced. These things happen. Malcolm had no right to attack my professional integrity."

"I certainly sympathize with you, Doctor," O'Malley replied. "By the way, have you tracked down her brain?"

"Not yet, but I would have remembered anything unusual. I pride myself on my memory."

"You know, it's a funny thing," O'Malley replied, chuckling. "That brain, or rather the lack thereof, just keeps coming up again and again. It's like a thorn in my side. I sure would appreciate if you could help me out."

Becker's eyes narrowed. "What do you mean?"

"Well, the FBI just can't seem to shake this idea that there's a conspiracy to subvert the government, and that the conspirators' minds have been affected by these cancers."

"I told you, that's preposterous!" Becker shouted. "I'm an expert pathologist. Such a thing is not possible!"

"Somehow, I don't think the FBI is going to take the word of someone who's misplaced the brain of a cancer patient."

Becker glared at O'Malley.

"Don't get me wrong, Doctor. I'm not accusing you of anything. I believe a person is innocent until proven guilty."

"I'm glad to hear it. I resent even the suggestion of wrongdoing."

"Good, then you wouldn't mind submitting to a CAT scan."

Becker jumped out of his chair. "Are you mad? What for?"

"You know how the government can be such sticklers on these matters. They have this crazy idea that losing the brain of a cancer patient is suspicious, under the circumstances."

Becker became rigid. "And what do you think, Commissioner?"

"I think you'd better come with me, Doctor."

"I won't submit to this abuse!" Becker screamed, waving his arms. "There are laws against this!"

"As of today, I am the law in Chicago," O'Malley responded in an utterly calm voice. "I have two police officers outside your office. I hope I won't require their services to restrain you."

"I won't hear any more of this!" Becker shrieked. "I won't be stopped by inferior people like yourself or Malcolm who don't realize my genius!" He raised both fists in the air. "I won't! Do you hear me?"

"Doctor, my men are ready to escort you now."

O'Malley opened the door and two uniformed police officers entered.

"Please take Doctor Becker to the diagnostic clinic at police headquarters. He has agreed to be evaluated by our doctors. Stay with him at all times."

Becker did not resist as the two officers took him by the arms. "You fools!" he shouted as they led him away, "How dare you question me! You're all jealous, that's what you are! But I won't let you get away with it! You'll see! I have friends. I won't let you get away with it!"

O'Malley shook his head from side to side as Becker was taken away.

65

Joe swung open the cabin door and stepped inside. Bob was standing near the kitchen.

"Joe! You're back!" He started to move towards him.

"That's far enough," Joe said, raising the shotgun in his hands. "Where's Ellen?"

"She's in the bedroom, asleep. She's had a rough time since you've been gone. Why are you pointing that gun at me?"

"Bill from down the road gave me this shotgun. It's an antique, but it still shoots."

"You've been transformed, haven't you?" Bob asked, glancing at the mantle over the fireplace where his pistol lay.

Joe smiled. "No, my friend. Not I."

"Did you get the cells?"

"I've got something better than the cells. I've got the vaccine."

"That's impossible. There wasn't enough time."

"Actually there was," Joe responded. "You see, I had enough cells when I left you and Ellen to grow the virus all by myself."

Bob's eyes narrowed. "Where did you get them?"

"I cut the power in the cabin in order to get away from here and finish the vaccine myself. I buried a vial of infected cells in the snow before we went for our hike. When I left the cabin, I just dug it up and took it with me. It was child's play to thaw it out and grow up the virus."

"Then it was *you* who sabotaged the incubator!"

"I did," Joe replied. "You see, when we were having breakfast, I noticed the lump on Ellen's neck, while she was putting on her sweater. It looked awfully suspicious for malignancy. I was about to tell you, when I noticed a similar lump on your arm. Since I was the only one who was lumpless, I figured three was a crowd. I went up the road to Bill's place. I've spent the last few days there finishing the vaccine. Fortunately, the final process didn't require any fancy equipment."

"Listen, Joe," Bob said, taking a step towards him. "Your mind's been affected by the cancer genes. I can still help you, if you give me a chance. Just hand me the gun."

Joe cocked the rifle. "That's the last step you take, buddy."

Bob halted.

"You see," Joe said. "I have this feeling about that lump on your arm--a bad feeling. I think it's *you* who's been transformed."

"Joe, I'm okay. I cut the mass out of my arm myself. See?" He showed Joe the sutures in his forearm.

"Why doesn't that reassure me?"

"What can I do to prove it to you?"

Joe reached into his pocket and removed his wallet. He took out a bill, unfolded it, and glanced at the serial number.

"Shoot."

Bob looked at him in amazement. "You've got to be kidding."

"Either you shoot or I will," Joe said, raising the shotgun.

"Joe, this is crazy. You're going to decide my life on a game of chance?"

"I believe in Robert Newman's intuition. If you're still him, you've still got it. Now shoot."

"Joe--"

"Last chance, my friend."

Bob hesitated. "Three."

Joe looked down at the serial number on the bill, then back up at Bob. He shook his head.

"There's a seven, a nine, and a two. But no three." He smiled. "I can't believe it. I finally won one."

Bob took two steps backwards. Suddenly, a scream pierced the air. Joe turned towards the bedroom and ducked just in time to prevent a heavy object from splitting his skull. Ellen rushed at him in a mad frenzy. He fired, turned and emptied the other barrel of the shotgun. Ellen and Bob both fell to the floor.

Joe reloaded the gun. The two bodies squirmed and then became still. Cautiously, he moved towards them. He reached Ellen first. He knelt down and felt her pulse. Then he did the same for Bob.

"Bill was right," Joe muttered. "This stuff could put an elephant to sleep."

He removed the darts from their bodies. Then he pulled a syringe and a small glass bottle, filled with a blue-green liquid, out of his pocket. He filled the syringe, knelt down beside Ellen's body, and injected the substance into her arm. He placed a new needle on the syringe, refilled it, and injected Bob's arm. He figured it would be at least an hour before the sedative wore off. God knew how long it would take for the vaccine to work--if it worked at all. It might be too late to reverse the transformation. He bound their arms and legs, sat down on the rocking chair, and waited.

PART III

REMISSION

The Sartan cannot live but in the deep, yet I have escaped from the deep.

PESIKTA RABATI
6th century A.D.

66

An occasional corn stalk poked through the snow like an ancient, dismembered scarecrow.   Otherwise, the only thing disrupting the monotonous landscape of barren, winter fields was the black ribbon of interstate 94. Joe listened to the high-pitched whine of the van as it barreled through the frigid air. He had not seen another vehicle since leaving the cabin that morning.

For two anxious days after administering the vaccine, he had watched Bob and Ellen lying in a deathly stupor, their vital signs barely detectable, the horrible tendrils dangling limply from their foreheads. He had carried them to the bedroom and hovered over their bodies like a faithful nurse. On the third day, when they had still shown no signs of awakening, he had screened their blood. The Gp 78 protein was undetectable. The vaccine had worked, but he feared that he had gotten to them too late. Then, on the fourth day, the tendrils shriveled up and fell off. The next morning, Bob had awakened, weak but otherwise apparently fine. 'It just feels like the worst hangover I've ever had,' he had said in response to Joe's anxious queries.   Ellen awoke later that afternoon. As far as any of them could tell, they had recovered, with no ill effects. But Joe could not completely rule out the possibility that their minds had been subtly altered.

By evening, Bob had felt well enough to help him finish packing. They had carefully packed the vials of vaccine, enough for fifty doses, into the cooler. Ellen, after getting up long enough to down a bowl of hot soup, had gone back to bed and slept through the night. They both had felt stronger by morning. It was overcast and cold outside, but Joe had barely noticed the weather in his impatience to get on. Five precious days had already been lost.

He passed a sign for Chicago. Another hundred and fifty miles. The moment of reckoning was two hours away. He glanced through the rear-view mirror and saw Ellen staring out her window.

Ellen watched the scenery flash by in shades of gray, like a black and white movie. The overcast sky choked out the rays of the sun, leaving only a pale illumination on the dreary landscape. She struggled to remember what it had been like under control of Sartan, but it was like a dream that faded from the mind with morning. The one reality that stayed with her was the terror, the likes of which she had never known. And she remembered something else, the overwhelming urge to contact the flesh of another member of Sartan, tendrils to tendrils, to exchange information not stored in DNA memory.

She had heard something recently about computer scientists using DNA to generate tiny supercomputers, based on the fact that the four bases of the genetic code represented an ideal media for storing and processing data. Nature had apparently done it first. She understood now why human cells contained so much junk DNA. It was used, not to encode genes, but for storing memories, inherited memories. While transformed, she had millions of years, the entire racial history of Sartan, accessible to her.

The DNA memories were gone now. Still, she was left with an uneasy fear that her mind was not completely her own. She sensed that Sartan was still there, had always been there, lurking in the dark shadows of her consciousness. She knew that her fear was irrational, since the vaccine had removed the crucial Gp 78 gene. Still, the cancer genome remained in her cells and she could not ease the feeling of foreboding.

She looked at Bob, sitting beside Joe, staring intensely at the horizon. His unblinking eyes, and the subtle tension on his brow, revealed that he too was struggling. Two creatures fought within him, a sensitive, vulnerable man against a man unwilling to bow his head even to God Himself. Was it the future or the past that he saw in the distance?

Bob was not thinking about the past. The terror of the last few days remained with him, but he had pushed it to the back of his mind, to be dealt with later. For now he needed to concentrate on the immediate future of the next few critical hours. The radio reports indicated that the country was close to a state of anarchy. Communication and transportation links had evidently become extremely unreliable. They had no idea who was friend and who was foe. If they fell into the wrong hands it was over, and if a quarter or more of the population had undergone malignant transformation, how could they avoid it? Joe and he were both fugitives and would probably be recognized by anyone transformed.

They had decided on a plan fraught with danger, but offering at least a chance of success. Unfortunately, it depended on having to trust someone. And the need to depend on someone else filled Bob with unease. They would drive directly to O'Hare airport, northwest of the city. From there, Joe would contact police commissioner O'Malley and try to make a decision on the telephone as to whether or not he was transformed. If possible, they would enlist his assistance in contacting federal authorities. If Joe did not trust O'Malley, they would board a plane for the capital. Once there, they would make contact with the authorities, deliver the vaccine, and help with mass production. It was admittedly a half-baked plan, but it was the best they could come up with.

They reached the outskirts of Milwaukee and passed a burnt out hulk of a truck on the side of the road. A mile later they saw another, and then two more. Before long, the shoulders were littered with overturned and burnt vehicles.

"It looks like a war zone," Bob whispered in amazement.

"I don't like the looks of this," Joe said. "Maybe we should try an alternate route."

At that moment an explosion rocked the van, and they were encircled in a cloud of dust and asphalt. The van swerved up on two wheels and came perilously close to overturning before righting itself with a thud that rammed them down against the seat cushions. As they cleared the dust cloud, they saw a barricade on the road just ahead. Joe slammed on the brakes and the van came to a halt two feet behind a steel gate. In moments, they were surrounded by twelve wild-looking men and women armed with guns. Bob crouched under the front seat and threw a blanket over himself.

The doors to the van flung open. A tall man with blue eyes, and a thick head of curly brown hair, pointed the barrel of an M16 at Joe from the driver's side, while a woman with long black hair and three grenades on her belt threw open the passenger door. The man looked at Joe, then at Ellen and a perplexed expression appeared on his face.

"Where to?"

"Chicago," Joe replied.

The man stared at them again, confused. He turned to Ellen. "You. Come and contact the flesh."

Ellen leaned forward and whispered into Joe's ear, "They're transformed! Let me do the talking."

She turned to the curly-headed man. "There's no time. We have orders to proceed to Chicago. Newman was sighted this morning, heading in this direction."

"That is why you are using the main road. We almost killed you. Why were we not radioed that Newman was in our sphere?"

"The vehicle is not equipped with a radio," she said. "We must continue on our way now."

The man looked at Ellen for a long moment, then turned towards the gate and bellowed, "Open it!" He tossed a two-way radio into the front seat beside Joe and said, "Use this to update us."

The radio bounced off the seat cushion, landed on top of the blanket Newman was under, and bounced again. The curly-haired man stared at the blanket for a moment, then motioned to the black-haired woman. She took a piece of the blanket in her fist and began to draw it up. Ellen looked nervously at the gate. She thought it might just have opened wide enough for the van to get through.

"Joe," she whispered. "The gate!"

Three things happened at once. The blanket came off of Bob. The sharp snap of breaking bone was heard. And the curly-haired man's eyes widened as he recognized the man holding the woman's grossly-deformed neck in his hands.

"Close the gate!" he bellowed as he raised his gun.

Bob dropped the dead woman and she fell beside the van. The curly-haired man pulled the trigger on the submachine gun, but at that moment, Joe's foot slammed down on the accelerator and the van leapt forward. Bob ripped open the glove compartment, grabbed his pistol, and pointed it at the curly-haired man, who was holding onto the door frame as the van careened forward. The van swerved sharply to the left, causing Bob's pistol to fall out of his hand and onto the road. The van grazed the rapidly-closing gate, slamming the driver's door against the curly-haired man's torso. The door flew off its hinges and the van cleared the gate and accelerated down the open highway. The ping of bullets ricocheted around them. Ellen could see eight white fingers clutching the back of the door frame. The curly-haired man pulled himself forward and grabbed the steering wheel with one hand, the rest of his body still hanging outside. The van swerved and Joe struggled to keep it on the road.

Bob grabbed the knife under the driver's seat, unsheathed it, and swept his arm down in a movement so quick that Ellen could not follow it. All she saw was four digits, severed at the knuckles, clutching the steering wheel momentarily before they fell, one by one, to the floor. A single, grotesque finger remained grasping the steering wheel. It's severed end reddened as the vessels began to dilate. A drop of blood fell to the floor, and then the finger finally let go and disappeared under the front seat.

Ellen struggled not to scream. She looked back and saw two jeeps swerve onto the road from the shoulder.

"They're following us!" she shouted.

Bob looked back. "Floor it, Joe."

"I am flooring it!"

As the jeeps closed the distance, Bob grabbed the shotgun. "You got any real bullets for this thing?"

"No," Joe replied. "Just the darts."

Bob swore under his breath as he loaded two darts into the barrels.

"There's Chicago!" Joe announced.

Ellen peered ahead. She could see the twin radio towers of the John Hancock building dominating the skyline as the city rose above the horizon. Joe veered onto the Eden's Expressway, heading south towards the city. Ellen looked back. The two jeeps were right on their tail now. One of them pulled up on their right. Ellen could see the driver's crooked teeth behind his hideous smile. Bob rolled down the window and fired the shotgun. The dart slammed against the jeep's window, startling the driver, but doing no other damage. The jeep's rear window rolled down and a rifle was pointed in their direction. Two shots were fired, and the van swerved and began to bounce and shudder.

"They've hit the tires!" Joe yelled.

The second jeep overtook them from the left side and forced them off the highway. The van came to a jarring stop in the high grass below the shoulder. Bob reloaded the shotgun, handed it to Joe, and grabbed the hunting knife.

"They want to capture us alive," he said. "I'll die first."

Ellen scrambled into the back, grabbed the bag of kitchen gear, and searched through it until she found a meat knife. She had no intention of being captured by those hideous creatures either.

She heard a rumbling noise above her. Two helicopters were closing in on them. Suddenly, there was a loud explosion and one of the jeeps burst into flames. A moment later, the second jeep exploded.

A loudspeaker blared at them from the helicopter, "Drive to the checkpoint up ahead! Do not attempt to leave your vehicle!"

There was no choice but to obey. They were sitting ducks. Joe drove the van slowly forward. Another barricade appeared ahead of them, manned by men in police uniforms. Spikes had been placed on either side of the road, with enough space between them for a single vehicle at a time to carefully maneuver through.

Are these the good guys or the bad guys, Ellen wondered.

An officer approached the driver's side of the van. He was tall and extremely thin, his uniform hanging loosely to his body. His skin was pale and his lips were covered with ulcerations. He was not merely bald. He had no hair whatsoever on his head.

"Close call. Let's see your papers."

Joe pulled his driver's license out of his wallet and handed it through the window.

The officer did not even touch the extended license.

"Your chemo papers!" he barked.

"My what?"

The officer peered into the van, looking at Bob, then at Ellen in the back seat. He directed himself at Bob.

"Sir, please remove your wig."

"I'm not wearing a wig. What seems to be the problem, officer?"

A pistol appeared in the officer's hand.

"All right. The three of you, out of the vehicle. Now!"

"We're not going anywhere," Bob said. "Let me speak to your supervisor."

The officer motioned and two other armed men in uniforms appeared, both as bald and emaciated as the first.

"Sir, I *am* the supervisor here. If you don't comply I'll have you incarcerated."

"On what grounds?" Joe asked.

"You have no medical papers. Obviously, none of you has received any chemo, and you have no certificate of GP status. You're in violation of the laws of the state of Illinois and the federal government."

"What's GP status?" Joe asked.

"Are you for real? Your cancer levels."

"GP-78," Bob whispered.

"Oh. Our GP levels are within the normal limits," Joe said.

"That's impossible since you've obviously not received any chemo."

"They're normal. Have them checked."

"We don't have the facilities to check them here. Now out of the car!"

"Then let us go. You can't arrest us without due cause."

The officer glared at Joe. His glazed eyes were sunken into their sockets and the skin around them was dark blue. He pointed the pistol between Joe's eyes and said evenly, "I should have shot you five minutes ago. Now I'm giving you one last chance to get out of the vehicle or I'm going to blow your face off."

Joe stared down the barrel of the gun. "Well, if you put it that way, we'd be happy to get out of the van."

He stepped out and Ellen and Bob followed suit. They were grabbed, frisked, and handcuffed.

"You'll be taken to a detention center where you'll be screened and receive chemotherapy," said the officer. "Assuming you cooperate. Those who don't cooperate don't get a second chance."

"This van contains items vital to the commissioner of police," Joe said. "I won't leave it, and I demand that you notify Commissioner O'Malley that Doctor Joe Malcolm needs to see him urgently."

The officer squinted at him. "Joe Malcolm?"

He glanced at Bob, then walked over and scrutinized his face. He smiled. "You're Robert Newman."

Bob stared into the officer's eyes, but did not respond.

"And to think that this day started out so rotten. Do you know there's a hell of a bounty on your two heads?"

He turned to Ellen. "And who are you?"

She did not answer.

"Doesn't matter." He turned to one of his colleagues. "Get a car. We're taking them downtown."

67

Ellen sat in a bare wooden chair, tapping her shoes against the gray linoleum floor to the rhythm of *I will survive*. There were no windows in the room and the furniture consisted of four old chairs and a metal-top desk. Joe sat beside her, while Bob stood alone, leaning against the wall. Their handcuffs had been removed a half hour earlier, but an armed guard stood at the door, preventing them from leaving.

The ride to police headquarters had been harrowing. They had been unceremoniously stuffed into the filthy back seat of a police cruiser and driven at break-neck speed through the city, escorted by one police car in front and one behind them. Heavy metal bars had separated them from the two officers in the front seat, one of whom had kept his pistol pointed at them. The city was a ghost town, the streets deserted. When they had reached State Street, the officer in the passenger seat had suddenly dropped his pistol, grabbed a shotgun, and stuck the barrel out the window, glancing nervously up and down the street as they sped along. Their car had been shot at three times before they had come to a screeching halt, were removed from the car, and shoved past an armed guard into the building. They had had their blood drawn and went through a CAT scanner before being locked into this room for the past two hours.

The door opened and a stocky man entered. Like everyone else they had seen, he was bald except for a few wisps of hair on the top of his head. He was muscular, yet like the others, his clothes were too large for him. He sat down in one of the chairs, facing Joe.

"Hello, doc," O'Malley said.

"Good to see you, Tom."

"You're lucky you weren't killed out there, driving through enemy territory like that. You've got some explaining to do."

"Yes, we do," Joe replied, nodding.

"Well then, why don't you start by telling me where the hell you and your friend, here--" he pointed his thumb at Bob, "--have been for the past few weeks. You've got the FBI, the CIA and half the army looking for you. And while you're at it, tell me why all three of you test negative for GP in your blood and have perfectly normal scans. You obviously haven't been receiving any chemo." He rubbed his bald head as if to emphasize the point.

"Tom," Joe replied, "first, you're going to have to prove to me that I can trust you."

"You mean, am I clean? Here."

He pulled a small, black booklet out of his breast pocket and tossed it to Joe. Joe picked it up and opened it. Inside was a record of daily serum GP-78 levels, weekly CAT scans, and doses of chemotherapy.

"I'm clean doc. It's killing me, but I'm clean."

Joe glanced at Bob, who shrugged and responded, "It's your call."

"Tom," Joe said. "Can we speak in private?"

Tom made a motion and the officer standing at the door departed.

"You've got to keep this in strict confidence. We've been in hiding, working on a cure for the cancer epidemic."

"And you've found it?"

"I think the answer to that is obvious."

O'Malley studied Joe for a long moment, then did the same for Bob and Ellen. He pulled out a toothpick from his shirt pocket, stuck it in his mouth briefly, then flicked it into the corner of the room.

"I can't even chew on these anymore," he said with disgust. "My gums are one big bleeding sore." He was silent for a while longer, then leaned forward towards Joe. "Okay, let's just say what you're telling me is true. Now what?"

"How bad is the situation?"

O'Malley blew out of his nostrils. "Until two days ago, we had most of the population of Chicago coming in for daily chemo. But seven centers have been sabotaged in the past forty eight hours. There are gangs roaming the streets attacking anyone foolish or desperate enough to venture out. New supplies aren't getting through and fighting is breaking out over the available chemo at the remaining centers. We're stretched to the limit, past the limit, and we're losing. Now, if you're bullshitting me, doc. . ."

"Are you aware of what's causing this, Tom?

O'Malley locked eyes with Joe. "There's an alien organism in our DNA, but that's not for public consumption. You don't want to see what this thing does to those poor bastards whose brains it invades."

"We know all about that."

O'Malley shuddered. "And your treatment deals with this thing?"

"Permanently."

"If what you're saying is true, doc, I'm gonna give you one big, wet kiss on the lips."

"I'm not bullshitting," Joe said. "We've created a vaccine that splices the critical cancer genes out of our cells. But we're going to need to make a ton of it, and only the federal government can handle that. What I've told you can't go past this room,

Tom. We can't tip off the enemy. Can you get us to Washington in secret?"

"Listen doc," O'Malley replied, "the federal authorities have been scavenging the country for the two of you. As soon as I heard you'd been found, I contacted the Pentagon. You're being transported to Washington immediately. We're preparing a convoy to the airport."

"So the airport's secure?"

"We control Midway. O'Hare is in enemy hands. You'll find that Washington is a secure city. No one gets in or out, under any circumstances, without authorization."

"What about Becker? He's undergone malignant transformation, you know."

O'Malley shook his head. "We examined him from the top of his oversized head to the bottom of his puny little asshole. Would you believe the son-of-a-bitch was clean and cooperating willingly with the enemy? He was doctoring the pathology reports and smuggling vinyl chloride into the hospital. They promised they'd make him famous."

Joe shook his head. "It's despicable. There are always some like that, willing to betray their own people."

O'Malley lowered his eyes. Any chance you've got enough of that vaccine to treat my men before you leave? Some of them are really sick from the chemo. I don't know how long I can keep the force together."

"How many men are you talking about?"

"We've got five thousand people in one capacity or another."

Joe looked at Bob, who hesitated. It was risky. Bob looked at the desperate expression on O'Malley's face, then held up his hands to Joe and opened and closed them once.

Joe nodded grimly and turned to O'Malley. "Tom, we can treat twenty of your men. Once we set up a lab for mass production, we'll have thousands of vaccines in a matter of days."

"I understand. Whatever you can spare."

"Bring in the twenty. I'll need access to the coolers from our van. The vaccines are stored there. And your men can't know what they've received."

"Understood. I'll send over your gear. I just knew someone was going to make a breakthrough. But I'd given you up for dead." O'Malley walked to the door. "We'll be ready to move you out in an hour."

"Hold on a sec," Bob said, speaking for the first time since O'Malley had entered the room, "I want to know the whereabouts of my sister-in-law, Janie Patton. She was a patient at Chicago University Hospital."

"Let me see what I can find out."

"How about my wife?" Joe asked.

"She's fine. She's being housed in a secure compound along with the officers' families. With you being such a hot commodity, we didn't want to take any chances on your family falling into the wrong hands."

"Thanks. I'd like to call her."

"Sorry, we can't trust the phone lines. I'll let her know you're okay."

O'Malley left the room.

"I hope we're not being set up," Bob muttered.

"We don't have any choice but to trust him," Ellen replied.

Two police officers entered the room with the coolers from the van. Joe indicated a spot on the floor where they could set them. He began checking the contents to make sure they had not suffered any damage. He removed one of the vials of blue-green liquid and held it up to the light.

"It's a beautiful color," Ellen said.

Joe smiled. "Everything about this stuff is beautiful. It's a real work of art."

Ten minutes later, O'Malley opened the door and approached Bob. "I'm afraid I've got some bad news. Janie Patton checked out of the hospital two weeks ago to the care of a

Lois Baines. Mrs. Baines died of a brain hemorrhage and your sister-in-law was found murdered in her apartment."

Bob's face turned chalky-white. He was silent for a moment, then he said evenly, "Who killed her?"

"We don't know that."

A look of fury appeared in Bob's eyes. "Aren't you the commissioner of police? Isn't it your duty to defend innocent citizens from murderers? She was a fifteen year old kid, you son-of-a-bitch."

O'Malley looked up into the face of the taller man glaring down at him. "I've got a whole city to take care of," he growled. Then he added in a softer tone, "I am sorry."

"Yeah. Everyone's always sorry."

Bob turned his face to the wall. O'Malley shot a glance at Joe and left the room. Ellen approached Bob. His jaw was clenched, his eyes closed. She placed her hands around his locked fists.

"Bob, I know it hurts, I know. But don't do this to yourself."

Bob lowered his head and his shoulders sagged. "What am I supposed to do? Lois was like my mother, Janie like my own daughter. Everyone I loved is dead." The pain and despair shook his body. "What have I done to deserve this?"

"Don't place this on your shoulders, Bob. Please. . ."

He did not answer her. He just stood against the wall with his eyes closed. Then he whispered, "Ellen, I want to be alone for a few minutes."

"It's okay to cry for them," she insisted. "It's human. You *are* a human being."

For a moment, his lips trembled. Then he straightened his shoulders. "I can't."

"Then I feel sorry for you."

"Don't you understand?" he pleaded. "I need the pain. I need the anger. I need the hatred. They give me the strength to fight this menace."

Ellen shook her head. "No," she whispered. "They're killing whatever humanity is left in you."

"He just needs a little time," Joe whispered as Ellen sat down beside him.

"I wish that was all he needed."

She helped Joe draw up the twenty doses of vaccine into plastic syringes. As they were finishing, O'Malley returned.

"Your flight leaves in an hour. I'm going to escort you to the airport personally."

"Thanks, Tom," Joe said.

"Don't thank me. It's you all who deserve the thanks. I've got twenty men lined up outside, if now's a good time."

"Perfect. We've got the vaccines prepared. I'll give you the first honors."

"Not me," O'Malley said. "I've chosen the twenty who need it worst. It wasn't easy deciding."

"Tom, don't be a hero. You're essential to the functioning of this police force. The entire city is dependent on you."

O'Malley shook his head. "Joe, I can't take the treatment while I've got men who will have to get by without it. I can wait until you've got a larger supply. These men need it more."

He opened the door and called the men in. Twenty walking skeletons shuffled into the room. They were pitiful. The last one was carried in on a stretcher. Joe began administering the vaccines. O'Malley leaned against the wall and closed his eyes, trying to gather his strength. He felt a sharp pinch on his left shoulder and pulled back with a start.

"Commissioner," Bob said, withdrawing the needle, "Joe's right. You're essential to this city's survival. Can't let you deteriorate any further."

"But you said you only had twenty shots to spare."

"That poor guy on the stretcher isn't gonna make it. The vaccine would just kill him a few hours earlier than the chemotherapy will. I'm sorry."

O'Malley looked at Bob without speaking.

"I apologize for what I said earlier," Bob continued. "I don't blame you for Janie's death. You're doing a hell of a job under impossible circumstances." He held out his hand.

O'Malley observed Bob's steely eyes and squared shoulders.

"Good luck in Washington," he said quietly, as he grasped the extended hand.

68

A convoy of four police cars accompanied them towards Midway airport. Theirs was the third in line. The streets were deserted as they turned down Cicero Avenue, heading south. Suddenly, the lead car slowed. Ellen heard shots up ahead.

O'Malley, who was sitting in the front seat, yelled, "Keep driving!" He grabbed the radio. "This is O'Malley. We need back-up now! Code blue skies!"

Ellen peered ahead and saw what was slowing the convoy. Thousands of people were pouring into the street, blocking their path. Most of them had hair on their heads, and some were carrying guns. The crowd fell on the lead car with their bare hands. Many were run over, but the wall of human flesh stopped the car dead in its tracks. A moment later, it had been overturned and its occupants were being dragged out of the windows. Then the crowd fell on the car in front of them.

O'Malley turned to the driver. "Get us out of here!"

The driver shifted into reverse and hit the gas pedal. The car skidded backwards up the street, its wheels screeching. The last vehicle in the convoy was also backing up. Ellen could not count how many bodies they bowled over, but the crowd was less dense towards the rear and they were able to get clear. At the first intersection, the driver slammed the gears into forward and turned sharply right, followed by the rear car. They sped through the side streets of the South Side.

"I thought we had these streets cleaned up," O'Malley shouted.

"It's me they're after," Bob replied. "The gang on the highway must have reported in. They're going all out to prevent me from getting to the airport."

"We'll get you there," O'Malley reassured them. He spoke into the radio again. "This is O'Malley. Is blue skies active?"

"Affirmative," came the voice over the static.

They screeched around another corner and were back on Cicero Avenue, the airport directly ahead. Dozens of blue and white police cars were lined up along both sides of the road, holding the crowd back and leaving a clear path down the middle. They sped down the center of the street at ninety miles and hour and through a gate that led directly onto the airport tarmac. Tanks lined the runway, firing at the mass of bodies attempting to break through the perimeter fence.

The airplane waiting on the runway was a military twin-engine jet. The pilot stood at the rear of the plane, in front of the steps. Their car pulled up and they scrambled out.

"This way!" the pilot yelled, motioning them up the stairs.

They shoved Ellen up first. She hardly noticed the pilot's bald head, it was beginning to look so normal. He was young and wiry. He flashed a smile at her and she could see the bleeding gums in his mouth.

"Watch your step, Miss!"

She had to stoop to get in. There were eight seats in the tiny plane. She threw herself into one of them and Bob and Joe entered behind her, carrying the cooler with its precious contents. The pilot was already latching the door shut. He made his way forward to the cockpit and, still standing, rammed the joystick. The plane jerked forward.

"Hope you don't mind if we dispense with the cocktails," he shouted as he fell into his seat and began flipping switches.

As the plane taxied down the runway, he yelled, "Yow! Company."

Ellen looked out the window. A crowd of about a hundred people had broken through the fence and had reached the runway ahead.

"Sorry folks, this flight's full," the pilot said as he turned the plane and headed down a connecting road towards another runway to their left. "I guess we'll try a western take-off. Ladies and gentlemen, please fasten your seatbelts and extinguish all cigarettes."

The pilots brash attitude reassured Ellen. She did fasten her seatbelt. As the plane sped down the runway she could feel the vibrations down to her bones. Then the wheels left the ground with a sudden upwards thrust and they were airborne. She was shoved against the back of her seat as the pilot pulled the nose of the plane into a steep incline. Ellen looked through the window. The figures scurrying along the runway began to look like ants on a driveway. As they passed through the cloud cover she realized that every muscle in her body was tense. What she wouldn't give for a long, hot bath.

69

"We're entering D.C. airspace," the pilot announced.

The plane descended rapidly over the Potomac River, escorted by two F16 fighters. Ellen could see the Lincoln Memorial on their left and the Pentagon to the right. Then the landing strip came up to meet them and they hit the ground with a shudder. The runway was lined with tanks, jeeps, and armed soldiers. They taxied into a hangar and the pilot squeezed himself to the back of the plane.

"Welcome to the nation's capital," he said as he opened the door. "I hope you enjoyed the flight. And, oh yes, have a nice day."

Two guards in uniform, machine guns slung over their shoulders, stood at the bottom of the steps. They motioned Ellen, Bob, and Joe to a black Cadillac on the tarmac. As soon as they were seated, the driver sped out of the hangar. They left the airport grounds and turned onto the George Washington Memorial Parkway. It was a sunny day in Washington and the crisp outline of the Jefferson Memorial was visible across the Tidal Basin.

"Where's all the traffic?" Joe asked.

"All non-government vehicles have been outlawed within a ten mile radius of the Capitol," the driver responded.

They were waved through half a dozen road blocks before reaching the Pentagon, where they drove through an entrance leading underneath the building. They were escorted to a medical facility where they again had their blood drawn and were made to pass through a brain scanner. Then they waited, presumably for the results of the tests to be read, and after half an hour were escorted by the now familiar bald-headed, emaciated armed guards, through a series of hallways, and finally into a conference room.

"The secretary will be with you in a moment," one of the guards said before departing.

As soon as they were alone, Bob motioned Joe and Ellen to his side. "Keep your guards up," he whispered. "The enemy could be anyone."

Three middle-aged men stepped into the room. One wore a military uniform, the other two were in civilian suits. They too, had the ill-appearing look of chemotherapy recipients.

The man in uniform said, "I'm Calvin Hodges, Chairman of the Joint Chiefs, and this is Surgeon General, Ed Lafferty and FBI director, Leon Stark. We've been trying to track you guys down for weeks. We'd practically given you up for dead."

"It's a set up!" Joe shouted. Stark's transformed!"

Ellen's heart raced. Her eyes darted around the room, searching for an escape. Bob stepped in front of her, shielding her. It was a touching act, but meaningless. They'd never make it out of the building, even if they could get past the three men.

"Relax," Hodges said. "Everyone here has been thoroughly screened."

Joe jabbed a finger towards Stark. "His men tried to nab me in my office a few weeks ago!"

"You're damn right, they did," Stark replied calmly. "They were trying to protect your sorry ass before the enemy got to you. If you weren't so damned paranoid, you would have saved us all a lot of trouble."

Joe hesitated. "You were trying to protect me?"

Stark nodded. "What did you think? We knew you'd be a target once Newman here was presumed dead. We wanted to bring you in for your own safety."

"Then why'd your men trash my office?"

"We were trying to find your friend's notes on the gene vaccine before they fell into the wrong hands."

Bob stepped forward. He stood eye to eye with Stark, studying him. "Ellen, come here," he said, eyes still glued to Stark.

She approached and Bob grabbed her by the shoulders and shoved her in front of Stark. "What do you think?"

Ellen scanned Stark's features, his eyes, his face, his forehead. She sensed nothing to indicate Sartan's presence.

"I don't know," she said.

"Me neither," Bob replied, looking intently at Stark. "We need more than just your word on this."

Stark pulled a black booklet out of his pocket and offered it to Bob. "We're all getting high dose chemo and daily screening.

Each scanner is manned by a team of three. You couldn't get a fly into this building without the security team knowing about it."

Bob handed the book to Joe, who scrutinized it carefully before looking up. "Sorry, I guess I jumped to the wrong conclusion."

"Forget it," Stark replied. "You're here now, that's what counts."

Bob turned to Hodges and Lafferty. "How about you two?" he asked warily.

The two men handed their booklets to Joe, who studied them for a few minutes. "Everything seems to check out."

"Can we proceed now?" Hodges asked impatiently.

Joe nodded.

"All three of you have undetectable GP levels. Am I right to assume you've produced one of your gene vaccines to remove the cancer genes?"

Bob nodded. "Yes, and we've treated ourselves. The vaccine works."

"God, that's fantastic!" Hodges shouted. He turned to Lafferty and thumped his fist in the air. "We've got a weapon against those Cancer bastards!"

Lafferty grinned widely.

"How desperate is the situation?" Joe asked.

"Here, sit down," Hodges replied, motioning them to the conference table. "It's bad. By the time we recognized the nature of the threat, the Cancers had infiltrated everywhere. We've flushed them out of the government and military, but at great cost. Congress is still in session, but they haven't been told the full story. They only know what the public's been told, that certain malignancies are affecting personality and that there's a conspiracy by people so affected to destroy the country."

"Why don't you tell people the truth?" Joe asked. "We heard the rumors in Chicago. You can't keep this secret when so many people are affected."

"The full truth is on a needs to know basis. The President feels that public disclosure would touch off complete panic and anarchy."

"What do you call what we have now?" Bob asked.

"Incomplete panic and anarchy," Lafferty interjected with a grim smile.

"What about the rest of the country?"

"In the cities we control, all facilities producing carcinogens have been cut to essential services. But our communications and transportation networks have been disrupted, making it difficult to supply chemotherapy, or even food, in adequate quantities."

"Can't the army keep the supply lines open?" Joe asked.

"We're trying, but the Cancers are getting more daring by the day. They're vicious. The few we've captured alive are held in detention centers, but no one can get near them."

"What about Delany?" Bob asked. "Have you captured him?"

"The Senator? He's clean. He's getting daily chemo like the rest of the members of the government."

"If Delany is clean, I'm the King of Siam," Bob said. "He's the one who tried to kill me."

"We'll check out Delany again," Stark said. "The screening should be adequate, but we'll bring him to the Pentagon, where we have even stricter controls. Gentlemen, I suggest we adjourn. The President and his cabinet are waiting for us."

The were driven by armed convoy to the White House and led to a room on the second floor where ten bald, emaciated individuals were seated around a long, oval table. They looked to Ellen like a family of egg-heads. After a moment, she recognized the Vice-President, now the President, at the far end of the table. She was shocked at how different he looked in person. His appearance was that of an old man. His face was thin and pale, and what little hair he had had in the past was gone. Some of the others at the table looked familiar, but in their altered physical appearance, she could not definitively identify any of them.

"Mr. President, members of the cabinet," Hodges said, "I'd like to introduce Doctors Robert Newman and Joe Malcolm, and Ms. Ellen Rhodes."

There was a commotion around the room. The President pulled himself out of his seat. He appeared sick and weak, but as he began to speak Ellen could sense a powerful force in the decrepit body.

"I can't begin to tell you how pleased we are to see you three. I just hope it's not too late. Please, have a seat."

They were offered chairs directly across from the President.

"Doctor Newman," the President said, turning to Bob. "If you-all have the means to stop the Cancers, I need to know it now. We're desperate."

Bob nodded. "Sir, we've got the answer. We've produced a gene vaccine to cut out Gp78, which controls all the genes of the cancer organism. The three of us have been treated with it and we are now completely cancer-free and protected."

The room buzzed. One of the members raised a hand for attention. Ellen could not tell if it was a man or a woman, as their bald heads made them all look androgynous. But it was a woman's voice that spoke.

"I don't like the looks of these folks, with their rosy cheeks and heads full of hair. How do we know these three are not a plant to divert us from our efforts?"

Before anyone could reply, Bob rolled up his sleeve, revealing an angry, red scar on his forearm. He leaned forward and looked the President directly in the eye.

"Mr. President, this is where I used a kitchen knife, heated over a stove, to cut out a tumor in my arm. That's how much I hate this enemy. I would not betray this country or the human race. I'll submit to any test you'd like. I have one goal, and that's to rid humanity of this parasitic organism that threatens our existence."

The President looked for a long moment at the scar on Bob's arm, then turned to Hodges. "Can you verify any of this, Cal?"

"Yes," said Hodges. They have undetectable Gp in their blood and their CAT scans show no evidence of tumor infiltration. I personally witnessed the scans. I'm satisfied that they're telling the truth."

The President looked at the woman who had spoken. "Linda, can we continue?"

She gave a slight nod of her head.

"Very well." He stopped suddenly, removed a handkerchief from his pocket, and pressed it to his front teeth. When he withdrew it, it was blood-tinged. "Excuse me. This damn chemo is doing a number on my mouth."

He stuffed the handkerchief into his pocket and returned his gaze to Bob. "Can you make enough of this gene vaccine of yours to treat all two hundred and eighty million Americans?"

"That depends on what resources we have at our disposal."

The President folded his arms across his chest. "You have all the resources of the United States Government at your disposal."

Bob glanced at Joe. "With unlimited resources, I'd say we could produce a few hundred million vaccines in a couple of weeks. Joe, would you agree?"

Joe nodded. "The virus replicates exponentially every twenty minutes. We're limited only by the space and materials needed to keep expanding the cultures."

"That's *very* encouraging," the President said, his voice rising with enthusiasm. He turned to Lafferty. "Ed, can you supply everything these men need to produce an unlimited supply of virus?"

The Surgeon General nodded. "Yes. We have most of the necessary resources at the National Institutes of Health, up in Rockville. The rest can be shipped in."

"Cal, can the military keep the enemy at bay for two more weeks?"

"We can hold on for two weeks, sir," Hodges replied firmly.

At that moment, an explosion rocked the room. The walls shuddered and plaster fell from the ceiling onto the table. Someone yelled for everyone to get under the table. Hodges jumped out of his seat and began shouting into his two-way radio. He turned to the President.

"We're under artillery assault. Sir, I suggest we adjourn to the Pentagon bunker until the situation becomes clear."

The President nodded and they were all ushered to the basement and through a tunnel leading out of the building. As they exited, Ellen saw two large helicopters on the ground, their blades spinning. The sound of the rotors was deafening. As they rushed to the nearer one, the wind from the blades caught her hair, whipping it across her face

They scrambled in and the chopper left the ground. Five minutes later, they landed on a helicopter pad on the Pentagon grounds. They were led deep into the bowels of the building and ushered into a glass-walled room overlooking a large control center filled with busy military personnel. A huge electronic map of the United States covered the wall, dotted with red and blue lights.

Ellen leaned over to Lafferty, who was standing beside her, and asked, "What do the colors stand for?"

"Blue is for the areas under our control, red for the Cancers."

She looked back at the map. The District was solid blue, as was a large section of the Midwest and west. But red lights were everywhere, especially surrounding the major metropolitan areas.

Hodges entered the room.

"What's the situation, Cal?" the President asked.

"The enemy set up an artillery outpost twenty miles from here during the night. It's been neutralized. Sir, I think they were aiming for Newman. He's their Achilles heel and they must know he's here."

The President slammed his fist into his palm. "Well then, we've just got to get cracking, don't we? Everyone take a seat, please. We've got a meeting to wrap up."

When everyone was seated, the President continued. "Ed, you, Doctor Newman, and Doctor Malcolm will begin vaccine production immediately. I'll meet with you daily for a full progress report. Don't let anything get in your way. This is our number one priority. I want all production to take place within the Pentagon perimeters under the tightest security."

He looked around the table. "Now, how do we deliver the vaccine to every man, woman, and child in the country?"

One of the cabinet members spoke up. "I'm not a scientist, but can't we seed the virus into the nation's water sources?"

Joe shook his head. "Won't work. The chlorine would kill the virus, and besides, we'd never get a high enough concentration. It must be injected individually."

"Then we'll use brute force," Hodges said. "We've got the best damn military in the world. We're up to the mission. I'll prepare a plan to deliver the vaccine, district by district, as well as an identification system that can't be tampered with, to allow us to distinguish who has, and who has not, been treated." He blew a long breath. "It's not going to be an easy operation. It'll be a house to house guerilla war and we've got to keep the operation secret. If the enemy suspects, we'll lose the element of surprise."

Joe cleared his throat. "We've already administered the vaccine to twenty police officers in Chicago. It may have been a mistake."

The President turned to Hodges. "Who's in charge in Chicago?"

"Tom O'Malley. He's a good man."

"Fine, you tell O'Malley that those treatments are to be kept under the strictest secrecy. Those men are to shave their heads daily and pretend they're still getting chemotherapy. They're not to breathe a word of this. Any leaks are to be considered treason, punishable by death.   Now, tell me, Doctor Newman, what happens if this vaccine of yours is administered to the Cancers?"

Bob considered the question for a moment.   "Depends on how long they've been transformed.   Ellen and I had large tumor loads in our bodies prior to receiving the vaccine, and our conscious minds had been possessed by the cancer organism, in my case for two days, and five days for Ellen.   We haven't suffered any noticeable ill effects."

Ellen felt a roomful of eyes fall on her.   She tried to blot out the horrid memory of Sartan in her mind.

"Many of our citizens have been transformed for a hell of a lot longer than that," the President said.   "What about them?"

"As long as the human brain tissue hasn't been absorbed, the chances of recovery should be good," Bob replied.

"And afterwards?"

"Brain cells can't regenerate.   Those individuals will likely die as the cancer genes are shut down."

"And how long does it take for the human brain tissue to be absorbed?"

"I don't know the answer to that."

"I do," Lafferty said.   "We've got the data from the specimens we've analyzed.   It becomes significant ten days after the cancer genes become dominant in the brain cells."

The President was silent for a moment.   "So you're saying that millions of American citizens might be condemned to death by this treatment."

"Sir, those people are dead already," Bob replied.

The President ran his hands over his bald head.   "Would anybody like to voice any reservations on this course of action?"

No one spoke.

"Fine," said the President.   "We have a game plan.   One more thing.   I want all those held in detention to receive the first vaccines."

There was a commotion.   Another of the cabinet members spoke up.   "Don't you think we should concentrate first on saving those who haven't yet succumbed? After all, they're our first line of defense. We don't want to lose any more people."

"I want to save every citizen in whom the process might still be reversible," the President answered firmly. "Are there any further comments?"

He scanned the faces around the table. Ellen looked at his confident expression, so alive and radiant in the decrepit body. The President impressed her greatly. She had never thought much of him during the presidential campaign, but he was clearly a courageous and thoughtful leader.

"Mr. President," Joe said. "We have with us thirty vaccines. We can administer them to everyone in this room at this time, if you agree."

"We'll get our treatment when the rest of the country does, no sooner," the President responded. "I'll not put our welfare above that of any other American. Remember who we represent."

Hodges cleared his throat. "Sir, I would strongly suggest that we treat the cabinet and a contingent of the special ops so that--"

The President shook his head. "We can't risk the enemy discovering our secret weapon. Any questions?"

There were none.

70

"Psst! Jimmy! I'm coming through!"

The armed guard turned his head in the direction of the whisper. He slung his rifle over his shoulder, placed his hand on the panel controlling the Pentagon's, high-security gate, and punched in a code. The heavy steel door swung open and the shadow of a man slipped through.

"Don't forget," Jimmy called softly, "Jack Daniels whiskey."

"You got it," Sergeant Theodore Kredich whispered back as the door closed behind him and he melted into the darkness.

71

Ellen strode alone down the building's western corridor, heading for a window she had found a few days ago with a perfect view of the sun set.   She had been confined to the Pentagon grounds for two weeks now and was getting cabin fever.   She wasn't really part of the action and she saw Bob and Joe only at dinner, when they updated her on the situation.   The first phase of vaccine production was nearing completion.   Weapons had been adapted to rapidly fire vaccine-loaded darts, and the military was preparing to launch a simultaneous surprise attack on all major metropolitan areas.   They would first vaccinate those coming into the treatment centers and then go after the Cancers.

It hadn't been quiet.   The enemy had launched repeated attacks on the Pentagon complex, all of which had been rebuffed. And the search for Senator Delany continued, so far without success.   He had somehow got wind that Stark was after him, and had disappeared without a trace.

As she rounded the corner, she saw a familiar, lone figure standing at her window.   His hands rested on the window sill, his head drooping between his broad shoulders as if held down by some invisible weight.   She slowed her pace and then stopped, wondering whether to approach him.   She understood the man now.   He was a human being, a hardened human being, but he had his own frailties just like everyone else.   The hardness was a callus he had built up to protect a wound that had never healed, and maybe never would.   She wondered whether he would have accomplished as much without his wound to drive him forward. If she could take away his pain, would she also take away his drive, his life's breath?

As for the two of them, she really don't know what, if anything, the future had in store. He had been so busy since their arrival in Washington that she hadn't been alone with him once. Whatever passion might have existed between them seemed to have been extinguished, or at least greatly subdued. One couldn't keep a fire burning forever without feeding the flames.

She decide to approach him, after all.

"Hi Bob."

He jerked his head up with a start. "Hi, Ellen."

"Pretty view from here, huh?"

"It's quiet."

"Mind if I share it with you?"

He moved to make room for her. They both stood silently for a while, watching the setting sun.

"They're moving us out next week," he said after a while.

"I know. I heard this afternoon. You'll be going to New York?"

"Yeah. As soon as the east coast population has been vaccinated, they want me to oversee production at the new plant to be set up in Brooklyn."

"That's going to handle distribution overseas, right?"

"Yes."

"What about Joe?"

"He'll be returning to Chicago to coordinate medical support for the Midwest. He's got the tougher job. There are a lot of sick people who'll need urgent attention."

The sun touched the horizon. Ellen moved closer to him until she felt her body brush up against his. "I don't want to jinx anything, but it really looks as though we're going to beat this thing. You did it, Doctor Newman."

He shook his head. "There are millions of affected people around the world. We've still got a fight ahead of us."

"Yes, but if everything works as planned, it'll be over in a matter of days."

He clenched his jaw. "I won't rest until every last one of their genes is ripped out of every single human being on this planet."

She looked at his face, filled with hatred.

"Why do you despise Sartan with such vengeance?"

He stared out the window. "Because they beat me."

"What do you mean? You beat *them*."

He shook his head. "No. They beat me. They had me. They had control of my mind. If it hadn't been for Joe I would have been finished. I can never forget that."

"You're only human, for God's sake. You don't always have to act like some superman. When are you going to acknowledge that you're mortal?"

He inhaled deeply. "I know I'm mortal."

"Than why do you fight it?"

"*Because* I'm mortal."

"I don't understand you. Do you want to be a god?"

"Ellen, God never asked my permission before he brought me into this world. Therefore I don't feel any obligation to live by his rules. No, I don't want to be a god. I don't fear my own mortality, because there's nothing braver than mortals reaching beyond their own limitations. Do you realize that mankind is on the verge of discovering the secret of life itself? God, if he exists, must be having a fit watching us lowly humans, of such limited potential, on the verge of discovering His most sacred secrets. I can just see him laughing to himself while listening to man's first theories about the universe. Then slowly, the smile begins to fade, finally becoming a worried frown, as mankind, in total disregard for the miniscule amount of intelligence instilled in him, proceeds to unravel the mysteries of the universe."

"You do have a chip on your shoulders, don't you?" Ellen said. "You know, I think you really are angry with God for bringing you into this world without your permission. What would you have answered if he had asked you? Probably no, just out of stubbornness."

He burst out laughing and she found herself laughing along with him. When they stopped, they looked at each other and both convulsed with laughter again. Finally, they got control of themselves.

"I don't think I've ever seen you laugh like that before," she said.

"I don't think I've ever heard anything so funny before," he replied, wiping away his tears.

They smiled at each other. Bob draped his arm over her shoulder.

"What are your plans?" he asked.

"I'm going to return to Chicago. I've been away too long. Maybe I can help out somehow. I feel like I haven't done enough during this crisis."

"You've done more than you give yourself credit for. I'm not sure we would have gotten this far without you."

She shrugged.

"Why don't you come to New York with me?"

She felt a wave of heat wash over her. "What would I do in New York?"

"You promised me once that if we lived through this we'd spend some time getting to know each other. Remember?"

She nodded and smiled. "You'll be busy in New York. And I've got to finish med school."

"New York's got great med schools. Vaccine production will be simple, now that we've done all the hard work, and having you near will make it so much easier."

She hesitated. "I really should be getting back home."

"Home is where the heart is."

She smiled. "I like to hear you say that."

"Good. It's settled."

"I'll think about it", she said. "We better be heading for the dining room. They'll be serving dinner soon."

As they strolled down the hall, hand in hand, Ellen was surprised by the wetness between her thighs. Was it that easy to rekindle a fire?

72

"I'm giving you one last chance to answer," the heavyset man hissed as he leaned over Sergeant Kredich.

Kredich lay spread-eagled on a bare, wooden floor, held down firmly by four brutish men. He had ceased his futile struggles to move his limbs. He stared in horror at the gruesome tendrils protruding from the man's forehead.

"I've told you everything I know," he whimpered.

"What are you doing outside the Pentagon?"

"I told you, I . . . I was just going for some whiskey for my buddies."

Delany tapped his companion's shoulder. "We might as well just kill him. We already know their attack plan, down to the smallest detail, and this guy is just a low-level soldier."

The heavyset man turned towards Delany. "It certainly appears so. But it's a basic rule of war to interrogate prisoners. You never know what intelligence you might stumble on."

Delany shrugged. "What do you expect to get out of this small fry that you don't already have? We've got their planned entry points into the cities and our forces are waiting for them. They'll never get within firing range of their own people. They'll have to blow their darts on our body shields. Then we counterattack."

The heavyset man grinned fiercely. "Their bodies are so weakened by chemotherapy that they can't offer resistance. Our forces will massacre them."

Delany grinned back. Sartan was invincible. Three more days, then the humans would die, die, die. And Sartan would rule. He stared down at the pitiful, chemo-weakened human lying on the floor, crying miserably, the mucous pouring out of his nose. Then he frowned.

"Funny, this fellow doesn't look weakened."

"Huh?"

"Look at his mouth. Where are the sores? Where's the bloody discharge?"

The heavyset man turned his attention back to Kredich. His eyes narrowed. "Has there been any reduction in your chemo dose?" he demanded.

Kredich stared in terror at the hideous face above him. "I . . . I'm not sure."

"Not sure? What makes you not sure?"

"My hair's growing back," Kredich sputtered.

"The tide has turned!" Delany cried. "They've had to reduce the dose because of the side effects! They won't be able to suppress our genes any longer!"

The heavyset man frowned. "Either that, or. . ." He addressed himself to Kredich. "I don't see your hair growing back."

"I . . . I've been shaving my head."

"Shaving you head? Why?"

"Those are my orders."

The man brought his terrifying face to within an inch of Kredich's. Kredich cringed. "Why are you shaving your head?" he growled.

"I told you," Kredich pleaded, "I don't know. We were ordered to do it after we got the shot."

"Shot?"

The sweat was dripping off Kredich's face. "We got it a week ago, and then we were ordered to shave our heads twice a day."

The heavy-set man stood up and turned towards Delany. "That son-of-a-fucking bitch, Hodges! He's vaccinating his troops!"

A look of confusion flashed across Delany's face. "You told me the President gave orders that no one was to be vaccinated until the day of the operation."

"I should have known!" his companion rasped. "That fucker never could follow orders. We must get into the building and shut down the vaccine production."

He turned menacingly towards Kredich. Kredich tried to shrink into the floor.

"Please don't hurt me again."

The heavyset man leaned towards Kredich. The slippery tendrils touched his face. Kredich pissed himself.

"We're not going to hurt you anymore, as long as you cooperate," he hissed, his breath hot on Kredich's skin. "You're going to take two of us back in there with you. If you fail, well your pain will be far greater than before."

Kredich squeezed his eyes shut and screamed.

73

"Now remember, one false move and we detonate the explosives on your back!"

Kredich nodded and approached the gate. He knocked twice, waited briefly, and knocked four more times. He looked at the camera above the gate and forced a nervous smile onto his lips. The gate began to swing open and Kredich slipped inside.

"Well?" asked Jimmy, as Kredich appeared. "Did you get the whiskey?"

Kredich did not answer. He merely looked back, shaking with fear.

"What's wrong with you, Teddy? Seen a ghost or something?" Then Jimmy noticed the two figures entering through the still open gate. "Hey. Who are you?"

The reply came in the form of a bullet through the heart.

* * *

"We're in great shape," Bob said to Lafferty, as he and Joe sat with him in a small office outside the virus production facility. "We're actually ahead of schedule."

"We'll be ready to go in three days," Joe agreed.

"I'll inform the President," Lafferty said. "He should be pleased to--"

He was interrupted by the sound of gunfire. "--What the hell?"

Bob was already on his feet and dashing out the door. Lafferty and Joe rushed out after him. Two guards lay dead in a pool of blood at the entrance to the production facility. Armed soldiers were rushing in through the open doorway.

"What's going on?" Bob asked, out of breath.

"We've got an intruder," a soldier replied.

Bob pushed past him into the production facility. The room was the size of a football field, dominated by two dozen cylindrical, stainless-steel vats connected by tubes to a forest of pipes running just below the ceiling. The vats, the size of school buses, were supported off the floor by heavy steel girders. The floor was covered with an inch of orange culture fluid, and more was gushing down from all directions. Bob scanned the vats. Three were riddled with bullet holes, through which the fluid was spraying out in torrents.

Suddenly Hodges appeared beside him.

"We're going to lose the entire virus supply!" Bob yelled above the din. "We've got to shut off the intake valve!"

"We can't get to it!" Hodges shouted back. "He's firing from behind that vat over there!"

"Just one guy?"

"We're not sure yet!"

Hodges began directing soldiers to fan out along the flooded floor. Bob heard more gunfire and saw two soldiers shot dead as they tried to edge in along the wall. Bob's eyes darted around the room, watching in anguish as the culture fluid, containing his precious virus, poured onto the floor. He looked up at the intake valve near the ceiling. He clenched his jaw and dashed into the center of the room, leaping onto a metal ladder whose bottom rung was a few feet off the floor. As he started climbing, a hail of bullets ricocheted around him. He felt warm fluid drenching him. Whether it was the culture fluid spraying down on him from above, or his own blood, he did not know.

"We got him!" came a yell from below. Bob looked down to see a body, dressed in black, being dragged across the floor by two soldiers. He kept climbing towards the ceiling. He reached the top of the ladder and began crawling along the steel pipes towards the intake valve. He reached the wheel-shaped spigot controlling the fluid flow, grabbed it with both hands, and turned the wheel clockwise until it would not turn any further. He looked below. The vats were still leaking, but the torrent had stopped. He sighed with relief and spread himself out along the pipes, exhausted.

"Bob, you okay?" Hodges shouted from below.

Bob looked down at him and nodded. Then he froze. A figure, dressed in black tights, was kneeling behind the vat at the far end of the room, strapping something to the outlet pipe. The bastard was going to blow the entire facility! Bob pointed towards the intruder, but he was concealed from the people on the ground.

Bob crawled forward until he was directly overhead. The intruder looked up and their eyes met. He raised his submachine gun. Bob swung his body over the pipe, hanging on by his hands.

The intruder fired. Bob let go as a hail of bullets whizzed around him. He landed on the huge vat, almost sliding off the slippery surface. He peeked over the edge. A bullet just missed his head and he ducked back, but not before he saw the intruder finish strapping the explosives to the bottom of the vat.

Bob slid on his belly to the large cap covering the hole used to clean the vats from inside. He unscrewed it and yanked it off. Then he dove, head first, into the warm, viscous liquid. He swam down towards the floor, forcing himself to open his eyes, but he could not see a thing in the murky darkness. After what seemed like an eternity, he banged against the bottom and groped frantically around for the drain plug. Just when he felt his lungs ready to burst, his left hand touched something against the smoothness of the metal floor. He grabbed it with both hands and pulled with all his might. The plug popped off and he was swept through the drain, along with hundreds of gallons of culture fluid.

The intruder did not know what hit him. The force of the fluid bowled him over onto the floor. Bob landed on top of him, grabbed him with both arms, and just held on as the torrent nearly drowned them both. He felt himself being pulled away, and saw the intruder pinned to the ground by soldiers, struggling futilely. Bob lay on his back, coughing and sputtering.

"You okay?"

He opened his eyes to see Hodges standing over him.

Bob nodded. "Help me up."

Hodges reached down and pulled Bob to his feet. Bob looked around the room. Four vats, including the one he had been inside of, were still draining the remnants of their contents. The rest were undamaged.

"We've got to go now with vaccine delivery!" Bob shouted to Hodges.

"We're still three days from optimal supply," Hodges objected.

"We've got to chance it. They know we've got the vaccine. If we don't move now, they'll strike again."

An explosion rocked the room. Sirens began blasting, then a voice came over the intercom. "Battle stations! Battle stations! We're under aerial attack! All personnel to battle stations!"

"Come on!" Hodges yelled, grabbing Bob by the shirt and dashing with him towards the door.

74

Ellen and Joe entered the room housing the CAT scanner, in the basement of the Pentagon. Bob was already there, along with Hodges. The technicians who usually manned the facility were not present.

"Lock the door behind you," Bob said.

"Now will you tell me what the hell we're doing down here?" Hodges asked impatiently.

Bob motioned Ellen and Joe to his side, then turned to Hodges. "I've called you down here to inform you that the government's not secure. We've got a mole in the building."

Ellen watched Hodges for his response. He spent a moment digesting the statement, then narrowed his eyes.

"Impossible. The screening's too tight."

"I disagree," Bob replied. "It's been all too convenient. They knew I was in the Pentagon an hour after we arrived two weeks ago. Remember the artillery barrage? And they knew how to get past the security gate and exactly where our production facility was housed. Someone's been passing them information, someone on the inside."

"Christ, we've been through this already," Hodges replied irritably. "I've got a war to fight." He turned to go.

"Not so fast, Cal."

Hodges looked down at the pistol in Bob's hand. He eyed Bob, warily.

"We're gonna screen again," Bob said. "Starting with you."

"Me? Why you son-of-a-bitch. What about them?" Hodges nodded his head in the direction of Ellen and Joe.

"Right now, they're the only two people on this planet that I do trust," Bob replied, cocking the gun.

"Okay, okay, easy with that thing." Hodges removed his black booklet from his breast pocket. "Have another look at my records."

"Screw your records," Bob said. "I want to see your CAT scan. Live. Now get in the scanner."

"Whatever you say," Hodges replied. "Just be careful with the gun."

He lay down on the scanner bed and Bob secured the strap across him.

"Comfortable?"

"Let's just get this over with," Hodges grumbled.

Bob joined Ellen and Joe at the computer station. She put a hand on his shoulder. "Are you sure? He's the last person I would have suspected."

"We're about to find out," Bob replied. He turned to Joe. "You know how to work this thing?"

"I think so."

Ellen watched the computer monitor as Joe began the scan. She could make out certain anatomic structures, but she did not have enough training to interpret the images.

"The brain looks fine," Joe said.

"Satisfied?" Hodges snapped, getting up from the bed.

Bob studied the images on the screen. "Come have a look," he called to Hodges.

Hodges approached the computer station. "I'm not a doctor. I can't read these things."

Bob pointed the pistol at Hodges's chest. "I'm sure you could identify a pencil."

"What are you talking about?"

"Where's the image of the pencil I put by her head?"

Hodges glanced over at the scanner bed. A yellow lead pencil lay adjacent to the head rest. He looked back at the image on the monitor and paled.

"Hey, this isn't what it seems, I swear."

"You're right, it isn't what it seems. I bet, if you check the wiring to this room, you'll find that someone has tapped into the video feed. That's not your brain on the screen."

"Shit," Hodges murmured. "Who the hell's behind this?"

"I hope, for your sake, it's not you. Joe, can you reboot the system?"

"I think so." Joe pressed a button on the control panel. "There we go. Give it a few minutes."

Hodges went under the scanner again. This time, Ellen immediately recognized the small, dark circle, the diameter of a pencil, to the right of his head.

"The brain's normal," Joe said.

"God, that's a relief," Bob breathed. He turned to Hodges. "I would really have hated to have to kill you." He handed him the pistol. "Get the President down here," he whispered.

* * *

"All right," the President said. "So we've got a traitor amongst us." He looked at each of them in turn. "The five of us sitting around this table are the only ones we're absolutely sure about. We'll have to rescreen the entire cabinet."

Ellen watched Joe, Bob, and Hodges for their reaction.

"Perhaps we ought to let the Benedict Arnold go," Hodges said.

"Cal?"

"It may just play to our advantage. Let the enemy continue to think it knows what we're up to."

"Yes," the President responded, smiling. "I like that. It may be useful. Give me a status report, Cal."

"We're under heavy attack," Hodges replied. "They're throwing everything they've got at us. We're holding our own, but the building has sustained damage."

"And our options?"

"We've got to go now," Hodges said, jabbing his finger on the table. "The attack destroyed twenty percent of the vaccine supply. If we wait, we may lose the rest of it. They're going to try everything they can to shut down production."

Ellen could see the tension on the President's face. "They're waiting for our attack. They'll massacre our boys."

Hodges nodded grimly. "Yes, now that we've lost the element of surprise, we're guaranteed huge losses, but we've got no choice. The longer we wait, the stronger they get and the weaker we become. I say we vaccinate our men now and take the fight to the street."

"The vaccine will make the soldiers sick as hell for at least three days," Joe said. "They'll be in no condition to fight."

Hodges averted his gaze. "Sir, I vaccinated a contingent of two hundred troops ten days ago. I know it was against your orders, but I needed a reliable force, even a small one."

"Forget it," the President replied with a wave of his hand. "We should have taken a chance and vaccinated all the troops."

Hodges shook his head. "The Cancers would have discovered it, just as you worried they would."

"What difference would it make now? Cal, how well can our men fight, in their present condition?"

"They can fight, sir."

"How many will we lose? Give me an honest opinion."

"Up to eighty percent," Hodges replied.

Ellen shuddered. They were about to send thousands of young men to certain death.

"There may be another option," Bob said. "Joe and I have been testing the possibility of infection through the water supply."

The President turned to him. "I thought you said that wouldn't work."

"We've done some calculations. If we stop chlorinating the water and we instill the virus at the downstream pumping stations--along with a high dose of steroids--we think we might achieve sufficient infection."

The President put his hand on Bob's arm and looked him in the eye. "Might isn't good enough. We've got to be sure. If we blow our vaccine supply and this fails, we've got nothing left to fight with."

"I realize that," Bob replied. "But it's the only chance we have to reach a majority of the population. If it fails, and I don't think it will, we can get the facility back up to full production in a day or two."

"Plus another two weeks to produce a new supply of vaccine. Cal?"

Hodges shook his head. "We can't hold out another two weeks, sir."

The President blew a deep breath. "Joe, what's your opinion?"

Joe frowned. "This isn't a game of poker. If we bet wrong, the game's over. All I know is, if infection through the drinking water is successful, we'll have reached a significant portion of the population. Not all, mind you. It will still take months to get to everybody. But we'll have a civilian population supporting our efforts. The other option means a guerilla war with the odds increasing against us every day."

"Ellen?"

She wasn't expecting to be asked her opinion. She looked at the President, choosing her words carefully. "If you want to win in battle, you don't fight the enemy's war, you force the enemy to fight yours. They're expecting a frontal assault. It seems to me that we ought to give them that which they're not expecting."

The President looked at each of them in turn. "You people insist on making my job a difficult one. You're supposed to do all the hard work and present me with a foolproof plan, for which I get the credit." He smiled. "I'm joking, of course."

He rose from his chair and leaned over the table. "Well, I've made my decision, and I hope posterity looks favorably on it. God bless us and God bless this great country."

Under cover of night, hundreds of helicopters departed from the Pentagon perimeters towards the nation's water pumping stations, carrying their precious cargo. The radio transmissions indicated that the helicopters were delivering antibiotic additives to try and control the raging infections caused by the chemotherapy. As an additional diversion, twenty battalions were airlifted to the major cities, carrying guns loaded with dummy darts. U.S. forces sustained over twelve hundred casualties, all of whom were awarded the medal of honor, among them Sergeant James Kredich.

75

Outside a detention center near Chicago, an army officer leaned towards his partner. "Are we really supposed to gas all these people?"

"That's the order," the other said. "The medical corps is arriving to administer vaccines to everyone in detention."

"The same vaccines we got yesterday?"

"Yup."

"I ain't feeling too good already. How are these fellows gonna handle it?"

"Are you kidding? They're stronger than us. They haven't been puking their guts out from daily chemo. Now fire the mortars."

"All hell's gonna break loose when they see this stuff coming down on them. There's eight thousand prisoners in there."

"They ain't gonna see nothing. It's invisible and odorless."

The other officer shrugged and pushed the button.

As soon as the gas had done its job, the medical corps began theirs, fanning out in pairs over the compound. One pair of medics, wearing gas masks, headed towards their assignment in the northwest section. The taller man held a clipboard while his partner carried a pouch of syringes filled with a blue-green liquid. They began their work in silence. It was not a pleasant assignment. Bodies lay strewn across the ground at odd angles. When they reached the first of them, the man with the clipboard knelt down and clipped a metal bracelet around the left ankle.

"Zero, zero, one oh one," he said out loud as he wrote the number on the clipboard.

His partner pulled out the first syringe and injected its contents into the unconscious man's arm. Then they proceeded on to the next body. After a time, they came upon a man with an empty eye socket and a white birthmark on his right cheek.

"Look!" cried the man with the clipboard, his eyes bulging behind his mask. "This one's got tendrils hanging out of his head! I've heard about this, but this is the first time I've ever seen it. God, it's disgusting."

The two men stared with a mixture of fascination and horror.

"He's a goner," said the other medic as he prepared to inject the contents of the syringe. "If they've got those things hanging out like that, their whole brain's been eaten away. But the orders are that everyone gets a shot."

He administered the vaccine. "Come on. We ain't got time to gawk."

The other man tore his eyes away from the figure's face and they moved on to the next unconscious body.

76

The limousine sped out of the White House grounds, carrying Bob, Joe, and Ellen down Constitution Avenue. Bob looked out the window as they passed the memorials to Washington and Lincoln, two great presidents, but no less great than the one they had just left. His task ahead was massive, the rebuilding of a nation whose infrastructure had been ripped apart. But if anyone was up to the job, that man was.

The military action had been a huge success. Seventy percent of the nation's drinking water had been seeded with virus, and the concentration had been high enough to infect anyone ingesting it. For two days, the siege of the Pentagon had continued. Then, resistance had melted away. Thousands of dead bodies were found littering the streets, many with tendrils hanging from their foreheads. From the intelligence reports coming in, the majority of the country was already free of cancer.

The army had begun a district by district program to vaccinate the entire population of the United States. Each person vaccinated was to be given a laser-imprinted card, impervious to forgery, which would have to be carried at all times and surrendered to authorities on demand. In addition, virus would continue to be added to the water supply, and to certain food products, for an indefinite period of time. The hope was that, with this multi-pronged approach, the last of the transformed would be weeded out.

The administration had also been in close contact with governments overseas, whose populations have been suffering from the same epidemic of malignancies. While they had not yet been informed of the vaccine, for fear that their governments were not under secure control, most of the developed countries had set up chemotherapy centers similar to the ones in the U.S. The President planned to inform the international community soon, and to ship the vaccines overseas as fast as they could be produced.

As the car neared the Jefferson Memorial, Bob leaned forward and asked the driver to stop.

"Jefferson has always been a hero of mine. If you don't mind, I want to go up there for a minute alone."

"We'll wait for you here," Ellen replied.

Bob got out of the car and walked up the marble steps towards the dome-covered structure. The cold, winter wind blew at his exposed face, but it felt refreshing to be outside for the first time in weeks. When he reached the top of the stairs, he looked out over the river, towards the city. He was acutely aware of the absence of people. The bustle would be returning soon enough. As Ellen had said, in a few weeks things would begin to return to normal. Except that Janie and Lois were dead, along with countless others.

He walked into the structure and looked up at the bronze statue of Thomas Jefferson, proud and erect, his eyes gazing out towards the horizon. Here stood the memorial for one of the great men of history, a man who understood, as few ever had, the price that must be paid at times to defend freedom of the mind. Bob scanned the words etched on the marble wall describing universal human aspirations which had never been articulated in quite that way before or since.

He stood for a while, surrounded by the solitude. Finally, he turned to leave. As he traced his steps back towards the stairs, a figure emerged from the shadows of one of the marble pillars.

"Hello, Doctor Newman."

It took Bob a moment to recognize Delany. The thick white hair was gone and his eyes had lost their brightness. He was so much thinner than when he had last seen him, almost withered away like a dried up weed. But something still remained of his former self.

"I've been waiting for you," Delany rasped. "I wanted to see you one last time. I didn't expect it would be like this, but then, nothing has turned out as I expected."

Bob took a step towards him. A pistol appeared in Delany's hand. Delany was breathing heavily and the pistol shook in his trembling fingers.

"That's close enough. I still have the strength to fire this."

Bob halted. "How did you know I'd be here?"

"Your every move has been monitored, Doctor, and I've always been close at hand."

"I hardly recognize you."

"Really? As a doctor, you should have no trouble recognizing someone moments away from death. Your vaccine, which you so cleverly seeded into my drinking water, has seen to that. My cells are being shut down one by one, as your virus does its work. I congratulate you on your victory."

"Did you expect us to just give up without a fight?"

"No, every species fights for survival. We expected a fight, but not your surprise. We are not like you. We don't share your ability to improvise. We are born with all our memories, with the knowledge of our language, history, physics, and mathematics. It has evolved in us over millions of years. It's in our genes. We are the products of nature, Doctor, while your species rebels against nature's order."

Delany leaned his trembling body against the wall and shut his eyes. Bob could have grabbed the gun, but he was more interested in answers.

"Who are you?" he demanded. "How did your genes come to inhabit our cells?"

Delany's eyes fluttered open. "They are our cells, too. We have traveled together down the evolutionary path."

"But you must have once lived independently of us," Bob insisted.

"Yes, but that was a long time ago, so long that even my DNA memory is fragmentary.   You won the battle, you suppressed our genome. We fused our genes with yours, knowing that someday the struggle could continue on our terms."

"Why now?"

Delany struggled to speak. His voice was weak and labored. "We knew that some day you would create a technologic society, and then we would awaken and exploit it for ourselves. We've been planning a long time for this day. We linked our genetic code to an activation gene constructed to respond to products of technology, the gene you call Gp 78.   When these products reached a   critical   concentration   in   the   environment,   we awakened, ready to use your bodies as vehicles for our minds."

"So you've been dormant in human cells for millions of years."

"Not completely dormant. Your suppression of our genome was never absolute. But until now, the levels of carcinogens could not sustain continued function of our genes, and your tissues often died along with ours."

What is Sartan?" Bob asked.

Delany's body shook like a leaf and he grabbed the pillar to steady himself. When he spoke, his voice was trembling.

"Sartan is a sound, a stimulant."

"But how would our ancestors have known that?"

"Suffice it to say," Delany replied, his voice growing stronger, "that you humans are not entirely devoid of collective memories.   Where do you think your ancestors developed the myth of Satan? They bastardized the sound they heard so long ago, but they never forgot the reality of Sartan. You turned the battle with Sartan into a myth, a symbolic struggle between man's good and evil inclinations. Your ancestors knew better. It is neither a myth nor a struggle for possession of the human spirit. It was, and always will be, a struggle between Human and Sartan for possession of the bodies you claim as your own, but which we both share. You yourself saw the tendrils of our minds. Do you think it coincidence that your ancestors depicted the corrupter of Adam as the snake, or that Satan is depicted with horns growing from his head? You see, we have met before, Doctor. And, I might add, the encounter was not a pleasant one. The trauma left its mark on your species' psyche."

Bob felt an overwhelming loathing for the creature in front of him. He wanted to grab Delany by the neck and choke the life out of him. He could spend the rest of his days killing each and every one of them!

Delany doubled over coughing, as blood poured out of his mouth. He straightened himself up when Bob took a step forward.

"I see the hate in you, Doctor," he rasped. "You want to kill me don't you? Well, I have a surprise for you. Do you know where that hate comes from? That's Sartan within you.

Bob's eyes narrowed, then a look of horrified shock appeared on his face as he finally understood.

"Ah, you see it now, don't you? Yes, you need us. You, of all people, must realize that, Doctor. Don't all your religions speak of the good inclination and the evil inclination in every person? Evil is a bit harsh, but we *do* give you your anger, your drive, your passion. Would you really be human without them? I remember what you were like millions of years ago, before we became a part of you. Trust me doctor, you would not like to be that passive kind of human being again. You have won this battle, but the struggle isn't over. Don't be too sure of yourselves or of your intuition. We have the vast power of nature behind us, while you stand alone. We will see who, in the end, will be the fittest to survive."

Delany doubled over again, then slumped to a sitting position, his back against the pillar. He still held the gun pointed at Bob.

"Why don't you kill me now? You could."

"It would be a meaningless act," Delany rasped. "I don't kill for vengeance or pleasure."

"But I *do* kill for vengeance, Doctor," another voice hissed.

Bob turned to see a heavyset figure step out from behind the shadows, a gun held steady in his hand.

"Stark!"

"Yes, it's me," Stark growled.

Bob looked in confusion from Stark to Delany. "How? Hodges and Lafferty swore you were all tested in the very beginning."

"Well actually, we tested Hodges's blood twice. He'd be happy to know he came clean both times. Too bad you won't be able to inform him."

Bob forced a smile to his face. "You don't look so good, Stark. How do you feel?"

Stark cocked the gun. "Sick. I feel deathly sick. Watching you die will be my final pleasure. My only regret is that I won't be able to store the moment in my DNA memory, to share with my descendents."

"Our bodies belong to us," Bob shouted. "You had no right to them."

"Nature recognizes no rights," Stark responded. "Only realities. Today the reality belongs to you. But don't presume to own what is not yours. We both claim those bodies. You think you can take your destiny into your own hands, but we'll meet again someday. Not you and I, but your species and mine. Remember, we still exist in your chromosomes. You have only removed the Gp 78 gene."

"We'll excise the rest of your genes soon enough!"

"I think you'll find that impossible," Stark replied with a hideous grin. "Delany is correct. Without Sartan, you are only half a man."

He straightened his arm, aiming the gun at Bob's heart. "Goodbye, Doctor Newman."

The shot rang out, the sound echoing off the marble walls. Stark slumped to the ground as Bob let out an involuntary yelp.

He turned towards Delany. The smoke was still exiting from the barrel of his pistol. Delany held it out to Bob.

"Finish him."

Bob took the pistol from Delany's hand and turned to Stark, who lay gasping against the pillar, his coat stained with dark blood. The tendrils began to exit his forehead, squirming out from the skin until they covered his face. Bob took the gun and emptied it into the swarming tendrils.

He took a few deep breaths to calm himself, then turned to Delany.

"Why?"

"I suppose," Delany whispered, "that it's the last shred of humanity still within me as Sartan fades. Please kill me now and finish the job you began."

Bob looked at the withered creature lying against the marble pillar.

"Is there anything left of Senator Delany? Can you be saved?"

"Senator Delany exists no more. This chapter is over for us. Goodbye, Doctor Newman."

Delany closed his eyes. The tendrils began to extrude from his forehead, covering his face. Then he was still. Bob looked down at the two dead bodies lying on the floor.

"Goodbye then, Sartan. Until we meet again."

He turned and walked back to the limousine, not looking back.

77

Bob leaned back against the head board, his bare legs partly covered by the rumpled sheets. Ellen lay her head on his chest and pulled the sheets over her naked torso. He draped an arm around her shoulder.

"You're a very passionate lover," she said.

He smiled at her with a warmth she had never seen from him before.

"It takes two to make great love," he answered.

"I knew you would be," she teased.

"Oh? How did you know that?"

"Because you're incapable of doing anything without passion," she answered. "Can I ask you something?"

"Sure."

"What is it that you want out of life?"

He was silent for a moment. "I really don't know," he whispered.

"I wonder if you'll ever find real contentment. I don't mean you won't find momentary pleasures, like tonight. But will you ever let yourself be happy again? Will you ever belong to the world? A human being has to find pleasure and beauty and purpose in simple things. We're not gods. We can't build universes. We can only inhabit them."

"Say something," she whispered after he remained silent.

"Ellen, you're right," Bob replied. "We are only simple creatures. Occasionally, we outdo ourselves and accomplish something that outlasts us. But our greatness and our immortality lies in our ability to dream, to fantasize about impossible things. It's this quality that has enabled us to reach beyond our abilities, beyond our potential, to accomplish the impossible."

He looked down into her eyes and whispered, "I can't help the stubborn feeling I get inside when someone tells me it can't be done."

"Are you going to spend the rest of your life fighting with God?"

"Not if he gives in," he replied.

She looked up at his gentle smile, deceptive in its seeming serenity. She drew him to her. "You're an impossible man. Just put your arms around me and love me."

Much later, he awakened when he felt her enter the bed and snuggle up to him. He put his arm around her warm, soft body. When he could tell that she was sleeping contentedly, he crawled quietly out of bed. Ellen's journal lay open on the desk. The light of the setting sun filtered into the room from the balcony, enabling him to just make out the words inscribed on the page. He hesitated guiltily for a moment before looking down at the words.

I think I finally understand Robert Newman, the man. One can never be fully aware of oneself until one has made love with another. Only then can one know one's capacity to love and be loved, to give and to receive. One cannot be a full human being until one has touched another soul, and become aware of the dignity that the human race possesses. There is no other way for a human being to achieve this self-awareness.

If Man is part of that universe, then he must have the ability to create beauty; and a man and a woman striving to unite body with soul have created the ultimate beauty of which mortal beings are capable. That beauty is carried in the words, actions, thoughts, and feelings of the two. Yet it stands eternally, a pillar of achievement in space and time, a tribute to Man.

He stood for a while over the open journal, running his fingers across the page. Then he approached the bed. Ellen was sleeping contentedly. He bent down and kissed her cheek, and she smiled without awakening. Naked, he walked out onto the balcony. The sun had just set, leaving a fiery glow on the horizon. A cool breeze swept across his body, sated with love-making. One by one, the lights of the city came on, tiny stars twinkling dimly against the night. How insignificant they seemed in the company of the stars appearing in the sky.

And yet, those tiny lights below seemed to him to shine a little brighter tonight. He watched as they came to life, streaming along the roads, sparkling on the faces of the buildings which were Man's creations. It was lonely on this balcony, so high above the city, yet so far from the distant stars above. But the city below was too great a descent. And the heavens would be forever beyond his grasp.

After a few moments, he returned to where he had found a measure of happiness, to the woman who was its source. He slipped back into bed and Ellen's arms, sure now that it was where he belonged.

TO READ OTHER BOOKS BY THE AUTHOR OR TO SEND A COMMENT, VISIT:

www.raphaelhirsch.com